# HIGH PRAISE FOR KAREN ROBARDS
## AND
## THE SENATOR'S WIFE

"AN EXCITING AND SOMETIMES HUMOROUS PLOT, interesting characters, and a hot romance combine to make this a delightful story."
—*Library Journal*

"Ms. Robards continues to cement her position as one of the genre's premier authors. *The Senator's Wife* is filled with juicy scandals, passionate affairs and deadly motives."
—*Romantic Times*

"KAREN ROBARDS REACHES NEW HEIGHTS WITH THIS SIZZLING NEW NOVEL!"
—*Argus Leader* (Sioux Falls, S. Dak.)

"It is Robards's singular skill of combining intrigue with ecstasy that gives [her novels] their edge."
—*Lexington Herald-Leader*

"Karen Robards' characters catch you from the start and hold you until the end . . . you will hate to say good-bye to them."
—*Book Rack*

*Dell Books by Karen Robards*

# Karen Robards

## The Senator's Wife

A Dell Book

Published by
Dell Publishing,
a division of
Random House, Inc.
1540 Broadway
New York, New York 10036

This novel is a work of fiction. Names, characters, places, and incidents either are the product of the author's imagination or are used fictitiously. Any resemblance to actual persons, living or dead, events, or locales is entirely coincidental.

If you purchased this book without a cover you should be aware that this book is stolen property. It was reported as "unsold and destroyed" to the publisher and neither the author nor the publisher has received any payment for this "stripped book."

"You Take My Breath Away" Music by Stephen Lawrence, lyrics by Bruce Hart. Copyright © 1978 The Laughing Willow Company, Inc. Used by permission. All rights reserved.

ISBN: 0-440-21599-4

Reprinted by arrangement with Delacorte Press

Printed in the United States of America

Published simultaneously in Canada

March 1999

10 9 8 7 6 5 4 3 2 1

OPM

*This book is dedicated, as always and with much love, to my husband, Doug, and our sons, Peter, Christopher, and Jack. It also commemorates the births of my nephews, Michael Chase Johnson, on September 23, 1996, and Trevor James Johnson, on February 24, 1997, as well as that of my honorary nephew, Justin Read Colepaugh, on July 7, 1996.*

## AUTHOR'S NOTE

In this book, the date of the Neshoba County Fair has been moved up, simply because I attended the fair, loved it, and wanted to include it.

# Chapter

## 1

"*H*ONEY, THAT SURE AIN'T NO HOT DOG. Looks more like one of them Vienna-sausage things to me."

The girl was drunk. Crazy drunk. And high as a kite on coke and God knew what else. She was so far out in la-la land she didn't know what she was saying. He reminded himself of that even as he unwillingly followed her gaze to the object of her amusement. He'd just told her that he was going to stick his hot dog between her buns.

What they were both looking at was small and shriveled. Vienna sausage. Not hot dog.

"Pee-wee, pee-wee." She giggled, peering over her shoulder at him as he stood at the foot of the bed. "If that's not your nickname, it oughta be. Pee-wee."

It was a party, and this was a gang-bang for pay. The girl tied to the bed had been worked over twice already and seemed to be loving it. The faint light from the Biloxi casinos on the not-so-distant shore drifted through the porthole to gild her body from the base of her spine to her feet. Her eyes gleamed at him through the curtain of her black hair. Her teeth were very white. Like him, she was buck naked. She was lying on her stomach, spread out in an X shape, her hands and feet secured to the bed frame with the silk scarves she had brought with her. Her round white buttocks, marked with the love-bites one of the others had given her, wiggled at him encouragingly. From all indications, she was one of those rare whores who really liked sex. Strangely enough, the idea that she was eager for what he was about to do to her was unappealing. It seemed to shift the balance of power from him to her. How she had squealed when Clay had put it to her! He'd heard her through the closed door of the cabin as he'd impatiently waited his turn. Her shrill cries of seemingly authentic pleasure as flesh smacked against flesh had made him hard as a rock.

He wasn't hard now.

"You just plannin' on lookin', lover?" she asked. "Or are you gonna do somethin' about it?"

"Shut up." Leaning over, he slapped her ass with his hand, hard.

"Ow!"

She writhed, acting like the slap hurt a lot more than it did. He slapped her ass again, watched her wriggle, and felt himself start to get hard.

Then she spoiled it all by giggling.

"Shut up," he said again, climbing onto the bed between her spread legs and trying to mount her.

"Honey, I sure hope you *can* get your jollies by just lookin', because that thing ain't gonna work tonight. It ain't no harder than a marshmallow."

She was giggling like a lunatic. He found himself suddenly conscious of who might be listening on the other side of the door, just as he had listened with lascivious attention to the two who had gone before him. *Anybody out there in the hallway who wanted to could hear.*

One thing he hadn't heard was giggles.

"Quit laughing," he growled, pushing her face down into the pillows and pulling another pillow over her head to muffle the sound. It helped, a little, though he could still hear her faint gurgles. But at least now the sounds she made should not be audible beyond the cabin.

Ignore it, he told himself. Concentrate.

Taking himself tenderly in hand, he worked at it. Nothing.

It wasn't him, he told himself. It was her. It was her *giggling.*

"I said quit laughing!" He laid on top of her, his big body covering her much smaller one, pressing down hard on the pillow covering her head. It worked. She wasn't giggling anymore, or if she was, he couldn't hear it, which amounted to the same thing.

Good. He maneuvered around until he found a position in which he could both keep her quiet and get his business done. It took some effort with her squirming as she was, but at last he managed.

He liked going in the back door.

As he did it to her, she bucked beneath him as if he was giving her the ride of her life.

"Stupid broad," he muttered, but her frantic squirming did the trick. Praying a stray giggle wouldn't erupt from beneath the pillow to destroy his concentration, he pumped. A couple of minutes, and his business was done. He collapsed, lying on top of her while he regained his breath and his dignity.

It was over, and he'd managed to acquit himself respectably one more time.

Maybe, he thought, in the interests of getting it up more easily, he ought to quit the booze. Or the coke. Or both. Or neither. Hell, they were more fun than riding a woman anyway.

If he took away the pillow, would she start giggling again? He would kill her if she did. Out in the hallway they could hear.

Finally he got to his feet. She didn't move. He put his clothes on, his movements unsteady from some combination of the substances he had consumed and the sex he'd just had and the pitching of the boat.

Someone banged on the door. "Hey, stud-muffin, you 'bout done in there?"

"Keep your pants on," he called back with restored good humor. He had done the thing, done it right, she was still lying there limp as a spaghetti noodle, he had worn her out.

He could go back out there with his head held high, a man among men. Thrusting bare feet into deck shoes, he flicked the pillow away from the girl's head, pinched her ass, and turned away to open the door.

"Next," he said with a grin, exiting into the narrow passage that was darker than the cabin. Ralph staggered past, so zonked out he could hardly stand up.

"She any good?" Ralph asked over his shoulder from the cabin doorway. He was already unzipping his pants, a frat-boy's leer on his face.

He shrugged, feeling on top of the world again. The rest of them were partying up on deck, and that's where he was headed. The music was festive, the girls naked, the booze chilled, the drugs free.

Who could ask for anything more?

Behind him, muffled by the now-closed door but still audible in the close confines of the interior of the boat, he heard Ralph say, *"Sweet Jesus."*

Then, "Shit. Shit! *Shit!*"

# Chapter
## 2

"Hey, I've got it! How's about we get her pregnant?"

Leaning back in his chair, Tom Quinlan didn't immediately reply to his partner's semiserious suggestion. Instead he watched the slender red-haired woman on the TV screen in front of him with frowning concentration. It was a scouting tape, of the sort sports coaches used to prepare for a contest, of a speech she had given the previous week to a dinner audience of car dealers and their wives.

When it was possible, Tom always liked to assess his clients in action prior to actually meeting them. He felt it helped keep his judgments impartial.

The woman was not what he had expected. The Senator's choice of a second wife had clearly been influenced by parts of his anatomy far removed from his brain. She was a little taller than medium height, slim, young, beautiful. Which should have been an asset in the age of television, but in this case almost certainly was not. There would be the jealousy factor from the female constituents to contend with, for one thing.

Tom's frown intensified as he watched her give her cut-and-dried stump speech. She wasn't a good speaker; her delivery was wooden, and her hands clasped the sides of the lectern as though it would run off if she let go. Tom saw the hand of a previous consultant at work there: Someone had obviously drummed that stance into her.

Speech, canned; delivery, canned, was his judgment. Message, dry as dust. Nothing he couldn't work with, though. Appearance—for his money, she got ten out of ten, but that was not a plus under the circumstances. For optimum results she needed to be brought down to a six or seven, just a little above average. And maybe made to look a little older.

Tom pondered, his hands templing under his chin as he watched her performance. Her shoulder-length hair was a deep wine-streaked auburn, not carroty in the least, but indubitably red. A color *du jour,* he wondered, or natural? Whatever, it needed to be toned down. Red was forever associated in the public's mind with Jezebels, which she in particular did not need. Her clothes were all wrong too. Her suit was black, the neckline scooped in front but not indecently so, with silver trim and large rhinestone buttons down the front. Worn with black hose and heels, it should have been an appropriate choice for an evening appearance by a politician's wife. The problem was it showed too much of a body that, admittedly, deserved to be flaunted. The material was some kind of clingy knit, and the skirt, at four inches or so above the knee, was way too short. To add insult to injury, the suit looked real expensive, like it had cost the equivalent of maybe a couple of months' salary for the average voter.

Plus her heels were too high, he saw as the camera moved to a side view; the shoes themselves, strappy and pointy-toed, were too sexy. And her jewelry, which he had no doubt went perfectly with the outfit, could only be a negative in the view of the audience she needed to win over. The dime-sized baubles in her ears and the glittery necklace around her throat not only looked like real diamonds, they almost certainly *were* real. More to the point, the audience would *assume* they were real. No costume jewelry for the second Mrs. Lewis R. Honneker IV, wife of His Honor the multimillionaire senator, no sirree.

Or so the voters would say to themselves.

There, basically, was the problem, summed up in a nutshell. She looked like what she was: a trophy wife, bent on enjoying all the perks that came with her marriage to a rich man twice her age. Tom's job was to soften up her image, tone down her looks, and get her to talk about the kinds of things dear to the hearts of the ladies whose votes her husband needed: kids, jobs, husbands, getting supper on the table. *Think working women,* he told himself. Soccer moms. Make her over until she came across like one of *them.*

That was the key to getting the Senator's poll ratings up.

Initial assessment completed, Tom relaxed a little.

"Getting her pregnant's an idea," he said. "Women love that kind of stuff. They'd surefire warm up to her if she waddled like a duck and her tummy stuck out so far she couldn't see her feet, wouldn't they? Get to work on it, why don't you, Kenny?"

His partner snorted. "*You* get to work on it. I'm a married man, remember? Besides, she looks like the type that wouldn't give you a sideways smile if you didn't have at least a million big ones in the bank."

"Yeah, well, that lets both of us out, doesn't it?" Tom said with a wry smile. His bank account at the moment ran into the low three figures, and Kenny's was in similar shape. It was a lucky thing this job had come along when it had. Everything else they had in the oven—low-profile, behind-the-scenes stuff, all of it—paid peanuts compared with this, and offered zero exposure. "The lady's image needs some work, no doubt about it. The red hair's definitely got to go. And the jewelry. And the clothes."

Kenny grinned. "See there, you've got her naked already."

This attempt at humor made Tom shake his head with a rueful grin. "Okay, let's can that right now. *R-E-S-P-E-C-T* is the key word here. The lady's our client, don't forget."

"Yeah, I know. And no client, no money. And I like to eat."

"Don't we all." Tom glanced at the screen again. "Any cute kids to trot out?"

Kenny shook his head. "Just stepkids. From his first marriage. All older than she is. And the word is they don't much like her."

Tom grimaced. Knowing the players as he did, he wasn't surprised to hear that. Though a lot of things could have changed, in eighteen years.

"Dog?" he asked, then as Kenny shook his head, he continued on a note of declining hope: "Cat? Bird? Hamster?"

Kenny shook his head again. "Nope."

"So basically we got nothing to work with, right?"

"Basically," Kenny agreed. "Except the lady."

"Life ain't ever easy, is it?" Tom sighed.

"Which brings us back to getting her pregnant."

"Getting her a dog would be easier," Tom said. "A mutt, from the pound, that she saves from being put to death by the kindness of her heart. Big, clumsy, and adorable. Or little, scruffy, and adorable. Adorable's the key."

"Now you're talking," Kenny said.

"So get on it. Check around, find us an adorable pound mutt she can save."

"Me? Why me?"

"Because I'm the senior partner. Because I'm going to deal with the lady while you're out finding the dog. Because it was your idea."

"*My* idea was to get her pregnant. The dog's *your* idea."

Tom ignored this. "We'll do some ads with her and His Honor and the dog. Walking through fields, throwing sticks, that type of thing. Warm and fuzzy stuff."

"You're serious about the dog."

"Yup."

"Think the Senator will agree?"

"The way he's dropping in the polls? Sure."

"The dog can always go back to the pound after the election, right?" Kenny's voice was dry.

"Now *that's* cynical. Methinks you've been in this business too long, my friend." Tom smiled, linking his hands behind his head and leaning back in the cushioned comfort of his leather desk chair. Like the rest of the furnishings of his new office, the chair was rented. He was on the comeback trail, and the trappings of success were important. Appearances were everything in this business. In politics, as in life, winning was the name of the game. Nobody wanted to know a loser.

He might be climbing out of the loser pit by his fingernails, but he was climbing.

"Hey, I know the way it happens. So do you. If Honneker drops much farther in the polls, he'd *let* you get his wife pregnant. Beg you to on bended knee, in fact. Whatever works."

Tom laughed shortly. "Whatever works. Maybe we should have that put on our business cards: Quinlan, Goodman and Associates, Political Consultants: Whatever works."

"Not a bad slogan." Kenny straightened away from the desk, reaching for a doughnut. He'd brought a dozen in with him that morning, and now, at ten-thirty, five were missing from the box on the desk. Tom had eaten exactly none.

"Thought you were watching your diet," Tom said. "Wasn't that a heart attack you had last year?"

"A *mild* heart attack," Kenny said defensively. "More of a warning, really. And it wasn't brought on by doughnuts. It was stress."

"Yeah, right." If stress alone brought on heart attacks, he'd be dead by now, Tom thought. Instead he was hale and hearty at thirty-seven, despite the events of the last four years. Kenny was only a few years older, but he was pale and pudgy, and sweated easily. Tom didn't have that many good friends, and he worried about Kenny. Especially since he'd been responsible for the stress that Kenny mentioned. Not that Kenny had ever blamed him for his heart attack. But

Tom blamed himself. He'd screwed up, and it had cost them both nearly everything they had.

"When do we get to meet the lady?" Kenny asked, reaching for another doughnut.

Tom swatted his hand away and grabbed the box, which he sheltered protectively on his lap. Kenny scowled at him.

"At lunch. She's speaking to a group at the Neshoba County Fair. I want to see her in action in real life before we start in on her."

"The voters hate her, don't they?"

"She's his biggest negative. Like him, hate her, is what the polls said. Voters loved Eleanor, the first wife. Women were outraged when His Honor married the GSW here."

"GSW?" Kenny's brows lifted.

"Gorgeous second wife. A hated breed among women, apparently."

"I can see why," Kenny said, glancing at the monitor where the tape still played. "That lady's got homewrecker written all over her."

"It's up to us to change her into a *mom.*" Tom deftly fended off a snatch at the doughnut box. "If not literally, then figuratively. By the time Election Day rolls around, the good voters of Mississippi are going to perceive Mrs. Honneker to be a sweet southern lady who's one of them. They'll want to vote for him *because* of her."

"What do you think you are, a genie? I think we should just settle for them not hating her."

"Not good enough," Tom said, stuffing the box of doughnuts into the trash and squashing it with his foot. He grinned as Kenny howled, and punched the

TV's power button. The screen went dark. "We're on the comeback trail, remember? We need to razzle-dazzle 'em. So we bust our fannies, and we make the voters love her. *She's* the key to this election. Come on, Kenny, time to go meet the boss."

"Happy, happy, joy, joy," Kenny said, but allowed Tom to drag him from the apartment with no more than a single longing look in the direction of the squashed doughnuts.

# Chapter
## 3

*M*ISSISSIPPI IN JULY had to be the hottest place on earth, Veronica Honneker thought despairingly. The temperature had already reached 94, and was still climbing. If the atmosphere got any more stifling, she wouldn't be able to breathe. The big white canvas tent she stood beneath sheltered her from the sun, but that was about all that could be said for it. Though her purple linen shift was short and sleeveless, it was still too much to be wearing on so hot a day. Her pantyhose could have been made of lead for all the air they let reach her legs. Her bra pinched. She could feel her antiperspirant giving up the ghost even as she swung into the closing lines of her luncheon speech. Moisture trickled down her back; her armpits felt wet. The small electric fan whirring on the floor of the platform beside her, ostensibly provided for her comfort, barely stirred the air.

"Remember, a vote for my husband is a vote for education. And education is the bridge that will take the state of Mississippi into the twenty-first century," Ronnie concluded her standard speech, trying to ignore a fly that had buzzed around her head for at least the last three minutes. Swatting at flies looked ridiculous, as she had learned from watching other speakers do it on videotapes provided by one of Lewis's many flunkies. Don't swat flies, do smile, hang on to the sides of the podium if you can't think of anything else to do with your hands. . . . She'd had so much advice drummed into her head since marrying Lewis that she was sick of it.

Her smile was genuinely warm with relief as she finished talking. Ronnie unfolded her cramped fingers from the edge of the podium and acknowledged the polite applause with a wave. Almost before she had left the dais, her audience had turned its attention to their desserts. If not forgotten, she was certainly dismissed.

They didn't like her, she knew. She had never been, and never would be, one of *them*. She was a northerner, a *carpetbagger* as the locals called her behind her back, a young, beautiful woman of no particular pedigree married to a rich, distinguished older native son whose roots went deeper than those of the state icon, the five-hundred-year-old Friendship Oak.

The hostess—Mary something, Ronnie hadn't quite caught the last name—touched her elbow, steering her to the table closest to the speaker's platform. As always, this was where the biggest contributors would sit. And she always, always had to make nice to big contributors.

"Mrs. Honneker, this is Elizabeth Chauncey. . . ."

Ronnie smiled and offered her hand to the elderly woman just introduced.

"I know your mother-in-law," the woman informed her, and proceeded to tell her in excruciating detail just exactly how that was. Ronnie listened, smiled, and responded as intelligently as she could before being drawn on. It took over an hour to greet everyone in the tent. By the time she had clasped hands and exchanged a few words with the last potential donor/voter, Ronnie's head ached, her hand throbbed, and she felt limp from the inside out.

This was another thing about being married to a senator that she hated. Meet and greet, be nice to the voters. Always on. Smile, no matter how she felt. Well, today she felt lousy. All she wanted was to go home, take a shower and a couple of Tylenol, and lie down.

Fat chance of that.

"That went well," Thea, her press secretary, said cheerfully as fair officials hustled them toward the back of the tent, where a state trooper was holding open a canvas flap for their exit. Thea Cambridge was thirty, only a year older than Ronnie herself. She was attractive, with short dark hair, a slim figure, and a nice sense of style. She had worked for Ronnie for two years now, and Ronnie considered her a friend.

Passing through the triangular opening, Ronnie walked into a wall of blazing heat, blinding light, swirling dust, and nauseating smells: hot dogs, cotton candy, livestock droppings, vehicle exhaust. For a moment, as her eyes adjusted, she could see nothing. She paused, blinking, her retinue milling around her as they all took a minute to get their bearings.

Mississippi in July was her idea of hell on earth. If it was not for the thrice-damned polls, she would be summering in Lewis's cottage in Maine, as she had since they'd been married. Just the thought of that cool green shoreline made her feel hotter now. Lewis's summer house was almost the best thing about being married to him.

Mississippi in July was, arguably, the worst.

"Miz Honneker?" The voice was male, deep, and thick as honey with a down-home southern drawl. Though Ronnie still could not see clearly, she suspected a reporter, simply because they always came after her when she least felt like dealing with them. She stretched her mouth into one more smile.

"Yes?" she said into the glare.

"I'm Tom Quinlan. This is Kenny Goodman. Quinlan, Goodman, Associates."

"Oh, yes?" Vision slowly adjusting, Ronnie saw two men dressed in white shirts and lightweight summer suits standing in front of her. One was plump and sweating, light blue coat open and yellow tie askew, with pale skin and a thick crop of curling black hair. The other, the man who had spoken, was taller, leaner, with blond hair that was just beginning to recede around the temples and the tan complexion of someone who spent a great deal of time outdoors. His gray suit coat was buttoned over a broad-shouldered, athletic-looking frame, his navy tie was in place, and he looked altogether cooler and more collected than his companion.

"How nice to meet you," she said, offering first the blond man and then his companion her hand while Thea and the state troopers looked on with varying degrees of caution. It was necessary for the Senator's wife to be accessible to attract votes, of course, but there was also a slight degree of risk anytime a stranger approached her. Nuts were everywhere these days—and she was a favorite target.

However, these men seemed harmless enough, even
if they did appear to expect her to know their names.
Were they perhaps contributors? Big contributors?
*Should* she know their names? Lewis's office sent a list,
periodically updated, of people for her to memorize.

She was almost sure that the names she had just
heard were not on it.

Her smile widened, just in case. Money was the life-
blood of politics, as Lewis had drummed into her head
from the time of their marriage. For Lewis, as well as
all the other politicians she knew, *show me the money*
was not just a popular catchphrase. It was a way of
life. A way of staying alive. For she was convinced that
politicians only lived while they held office. Lewis's
senate seat and all that went with it were as necessary
to him as the air he breathed, Ronnie thought. He
needed the attention, the limelight, the power, the way
other men needed food and drink.

If only she had understood that before she married
him.

"We're political strategists, Miz Honneker. We're
working for you now," the blond man said dryly as
she shook the other man's hand. His tone made it clear
that she had been unsuccessful at concealing her ignorance of their identities. Not that it mattered. Consultants' opinions were more important than their votes.
And since their marriage, Lewis had inflicted so many
of them on her that by now they were about as welcome as a pair of buzzing flies.

"Oh." Ronnie's hand dropped to her side, and she
stopped smiling. Her cheeks ached so from her mara-
thon effort in the tent that it was a relief to let them
relax, if only for a few minutes. Her headache, forgot-

ten for a moment, returned in full force. Flexing her
sore fingers, she glanced at Thea.

"We got a fax from the Washington office this
morning," Thea said apologetically in response to that
glance. "I was going to show it to you later today. I—
didn't realize that they would be joining us this soon."

Thea knew how Ronnie felt about consultants. After the last one advised her to gain twenty pounds—
"Look how much more popular Oprah was when she
was heavy!" he had said—she had vowed not to listen
to any more.

"Mrs. Honneker, you're supposed to judge the Little Miss Neshoba County Pageant in five minutes," a
plump woman in a gaudy floral dress called as she
hurried up to them. The dress struck a chord in Ronnie's memory: Rose. The woman's name was Rose,
and her dress was bedecked with enormous cabbage
roses.

It was the kind of memory exercise that she usually
did rather well. One of her few assets as a political wife
was her ability to remember names, she thought.

"Thank you, Rose," Ronnie said with a smile. Rose
beamed. It was clear that she was flattered to have the
Senator's wife remember her when they had only met
for a moment several hours earlier. Things like that,
Ronnie had learned, made people feel important. And
making people feel important was a way to win votes.
And winning votes was the name of the game.

"Mind if we tag along?" the blond man asked.
Quinlan—that was his name, she would remember it
by associating the name with a quiver full of arrows,
and he seemed to be tightly strung, like a bow.

Ronnie shrugged her assent. Nodding politely as

Rose chattered away, she was escorted toward the tent where the pageant would be held. Thea, a fair official, a state trooper, and the two newcomers to her retinue followed close behind as they navigated through the eddy and swirl of activity that made up the fair. Young couples walking hand in hand, women in casual clothes pushing babies in strollers, teenagers in baggy shorts calling to each other, groups of older women in floral dresses: Ronnie smiled at all impartially as they wove through the crowd. A few smiled back.

A very few.

Sometimes she felt like the most hated woman in Mississippi.

They were almost at their destination when it happened. Ronnie had just spotted the white canvas peaks of the large tent on the other side of the busy cotton-candy machine. A steady stream of people were filing in through the front of the tent, past a large, balloon-bedecked placard that said *Little Miss Neshoba County Pageant, 2 P.M.* As usual, Ronnie was being led toward the back. A trio of officials already awaited her at the tent flap, which was being held open. They were looking her way, their expressions expectant.

The woman exploded out of nowhere. She came running in from the left, from somewhere beyond the cotton-candy machine, screaming words that seemed to make no sense. She was a big woman, tall and heavy, dressed in too-tight green shorts and a striped blouse, her hair dyed blond and her face florid and sweaty from the heat.

"Whore!" she screamed, darting toward Ronnie.

Ronnie stepped back, alarmed, and instinctively threw up her hand as something that glinted silver in the sunlight came hurtling through the air at her. A smell, sharp and distinctive. A blow, as something hard struck her upraised arm and bounced off. The sensation of liquid splashing everywhere, pouring over her, thick and heavy and cool.

*Ohmigod,* she thought.

# Chapter
## 4

*T*HE LIQUID SPLASHED onto Ronnie's head, covered her face, rained down the front of her dress. She heard screams, felt people rushing past, sensed a struggle. Eyes closed, gasping, dashing the substance from her face with frantic hands, she staggered backward, stumbled, lost her balance. *Her worst nightmare was coming true.*

She was caught from behind before she could hit the ground and steadied against a man's hard body. Seconds later an arm went around her shoulders, another slid beneath her knees, and she was lifted clean off her feet. Blinded, dazed, she felt as incapable as an infant of doing anything to save herself. If she was being abducted, she was helpless to ward it off.

Still, she tried, fighting frantically to be free.

"It's all right, I've got you safe," a man said into her ear. Reassured by something in his voice, she quit struggling. Then, much louder, he barked, "Where's a rest room?"

There must have been a reply, because as she clawed, terror-stricken, at the ooze coating her eyes she felt herself being borne away in strong arms through the heat that meant sunlight. Moments later he turned sideways, shouldering them both through a door into a darker, cooler environment.

"Can you stand up?" Even as the question was asked Ronnie found herself on her feet. Afraid to open her eyes lest more of the liquid should get into them, she stood swaying unsteadily in her self-imposed darkness, unsure of anything, even the identity of her rescuer. She felt dizzy, sick, terrified. Something hard pressed into her stomach, and she grasped it instinctively. It was cold and slick and rounded, and the accompanying sound of running water helped to identify it: a sink. Her rescuer's arm was around her waist. She let it support her, leaning back gratefully against the warm, solid strength of the man behind her. If he had not been there, she would have collapsed.

"I'm going to put your head under the faucet. Rinse out your eyes."

Ronnie felt a hand on her head gently pushing it down, and she obediently bent, leaning forward under his direction, supporting herself with her arms on either side of the sink. Her hair was pulled back and held from her face by one of his hands. Tepid water rushed over her forehead, over her eyes, over her cheeks and nose. It felt good against her eyelids, good against her skin.

Oh, God, was the liquid acid? Would she be blinded, or scarred for life?

Fresh terror curled in the pit of her stomach at the thought.

"Open your eyes. You want to let the water run into them."

Ronnie opened her eyes, cringing at first, but the water felt good in them, too, and after a moment she could actually see, a blur of shapes and light. Good. She was not blind.

"Here." The roughness of a wet paper towel moved down her face from forehead to chin. He wiped her face twice, three times. "Okay, stand up. Let's check the damage."

Ronnie straightened. Her knees felt weak, and she was glad of the sink's support behind her as she half sat on it, clutching it with both hands for balance. She blinked furiously; her vision was still blurry. Her chin was lifted by fingers beneath it, and another paper towel passed over her streaming eyes and across her cheeks and chin. He pushed her hair back behind her ears, and tilted her face first one way, then another, wiping judiciously. Throwing one paper towel away, he wet another, and ran it down her right arm.

"Oh, God, was it acid?" Ronnie asked in a croaky voice even as her vision cleared. Her rescuer, she saw now, was the blond man she had just met, the political consultant, Quinlan. He stood in front of her, frowning as he scrubbed at her arms.

"No, not acid. Paint. How do your eyes feel?"

*Red* paint. Ronnie saw it on his suit, smeared all down the arms and front of his jacket. His clothes had been ruined, too, as he'd carried her into the rest room.

For she was in a rest room—a gray-tiled one with three stalls and a urinal, a pair of dingy white sinks, one of which she was partly sitting on, and a large chipped mirror affixed to the wall. A men's room. With an overflowing waste can near the door and a faint unpleasant smell.

When she didn't answer right away, he repeated the question patiently.

Ronnie blinked once, twice, as his words penetrated. "They burn a little, but I can see. I think they're all right." At the thought of how easily she could have been blinded, a wave of nausea hit her. "Oh, God, I'm going to be sick."

She stumbled into the nearest stall, dropped to her knees, and emptied her stomach into the bowl. When she was done, she managed to get shakily to her feet and turned to find Quinlan watching her from the stall's doorway.

"Sit," he directed when she swayed. Ronnie sank down on the open seat, leaning forward, crossing her arms on her knees and cradling her head there.

"Stay put." He left her for a moment, then returned, hunkering down in front of her.

"Here."

The paper towel he handed her was wet and cold. Ronnie wiped her face. The nausea receded, leaving her with a hideous taste in her mouth. She needed a drink of water badly.

"Better?" Quinlan asked when she lifted her head. With him crouching on the floor in front of her, their eyes were on a level. His were blue, she saw as their gazes met, a deep grayed blue with a darker ring around the iris and the beginnings of crow's feet at the corners. His brows and lashes were thick, dark brown tipped with gold. His nose was straight, his lips a little thin but well cut and firm. The lean angularity of his face gave him an austere look. No sins of the flesh for him, she thought. He looked like the type who ate, drank, and did everything else in moderation, and scorned those who were less disciplined.

"I'm okay," she said, not quite certain it was the truth, and stood up, one hand on the wall of the stall for support. He stood, too, directly in front of her, frowning when she seemed less than steady on her feet.

"If I were you, I'd give it a minute."

"I need a drink of water."

He moved back out of her way to allow her to exit the stall. As long as she had the wall for support, she managed, but when she let go to traverse the few steps to the sink, she tottered sideways. She couldn't believe she was so unsteady on her feet. That, the nausea, and the icy cold feeling that was snaking along her limbs, combined to put her in a state that, despite her brave words, was still very far from being "okay."

He caught her elbow before she completely lost her balance, then wrapped his arm around her waist. Supporting her over to the sink, he turned on the cold tap. She bent to cup her hand under the flow and rinse out her mouth, then take a drink. After a moment she felt strong enough to sluice her face with both hands.

"I'm sorry," she managed as he passed her a dry paper towel. Straightening, she met his gaze in the mirror. He stood behind her, one arm around her waist, obviously on guard in case she should start to lose her balance again. As she dried her face, he watched with a frown. Seen as a backdrop for her own slenderness, he looked unexpectedly big and broad-shouldered. Though she was wearing three-inch heels, he still topped her by several inches. His arm encircled her waist from behind. His hand looked large and brown and masculine as it lay flat against the purple linen covering her stomach.

With a brief flicker of feminine awareness, she registered that he was a very attractive man.

"For what? Getting paint thrown on you? It sure as fire wasn't your fault." Through the mirror, his gaze ran over her. His voice dripped of the South like a hot biscuit overloaded with honey.

"I don't think playing nursemaid ordinarily falls under a political consultant's job description." Her voice was rueful.

"We're an adaptable bunch." His eyes crinkled at the corners, and he smiled at her through the mirror. "Whatever it takes to get the job done."

"I can't believe I threw up."

"It's the shock. I don't think you're hurt much, though. Not physically."

That was what she thought herself. Ronnie took a deep breath, willed herself to get a grip, and leaned forward to examine her face in the mirror. As he felt her weight shift solidly onto her own two feet, his arm fell away from her waist and he took a step backward.

Though her eyelids were slightly swollen, the eyes themselves weren't injured, Ronnie decided, noting the normal size of her pupils and the rapidly returning clarity of her vision. But if she wasn't hurt, she certainly was a mess. The front third of her hair was soaking wet, tucked behind her ears and dripping onto her shoulders, and her bangs stood up around her forehead like a cockatoo's crest. Bright red paint still streaked her hair, smeared her ears and neck, speckled her arms, spotted her dress. Her face was utterly white except where her mascara had smudged. Her brown

eyes were bloodshot and watery, her full mouth
blurry-looking and unsteady. Blush, powder, lipstick,
eye pencil—all had vanished. Her dress, a lovely Anna
Sui original in delicate Irish linen, was ruined. Red
splotches that looked like obscene giant poppies dotted
the purple cloth; fine splatters of paint, drying now,
ran clear down the length of her legs and across the
toes of her high-heeled beige sandals.

Nothing she had on, with the exception of her un-
derwear, had escaped the paint.

"Oh, my pearls!" Horrified as her gaze touched on
them, Ronnie lifted a hand to the expensive choker
that Lewis had given her shortly after they had married. "They have paint all over them! They'll be
ruined!"

She found the clasp, but could not release it. Her
arms felt heavy as lead when she raised them. Her fingers were clumsy.

"Hold still." Moving close behind her, he pushed
her hair aside and dealt with the clasp himself, his fingers warm as they brushed the nape of her neck. As the
pearls slid free, she reached for them, meaning to hold
the choker under the gushing water. He shook his head
at her and did it himself.

"You'd better check your earrings," he said.

Thus prompted, Ronnie saw that the pearls in her
ears were striped with red. She tried to remove them,
but her fingers could not seem to grasp the tiny clasps.

"Could you help me, please?" she asked. He
glanced at her through the mirror, saw her difficulty,
and set the pearl necklace on the sink ledge. This time
his fingers were cold from running water as he deftly
freed the pearls from her ears.

"Don't drop them down the sink," she cautioned. "They're real."

"I don't doubt it." His voice was dry. Holding her earrings in his fist so that they could not fall into the sink but water could pass through his fingers, he looked at her through the mirror. "You've got paint in your ear."

Ronnie turned her head, examining the ear he indicated. He was right. Wetting a paper towel, she wiped out that ear and then the other, determined not to give in to the weakness that made her knees feel like jelly. She then went to work on the streaks in her hair.

The red smears on the paper towel looked like blood, she thought as she exchanged one paper towel for another. Thank God it wasn't. She'd been lucky, she thought: the woman had only come after her with paint, not a gun.

Not for the first time, Ronnie wondered if the cost of getting everything she had ever wanted was too high.

She'd aimed to marry well, and she had. She'd aimed to be rich, and she was. She'd aimed to be well known, in the public eye, a personage rather than a nonentity. All those girlhood dreams had come true.

But none of it was as wonderful in reality as it had been in her fantasies, in her *plans*. She'd gotten what she wanted, all right—but it didn't feel as good as she had imagined it would.

Today it didn't feel good at all.

At the center of her charmed life, there was a gnawing emptiness. The realization made Ronnie feel sick all over again. "I can't go back out there," Ronnie said, staring at herself in the mirror, her fingers curling around the rim of the sink. The used paper towel fell from her nerveless fingers. "I can't."

"I'd say your engagements were just effectively canceled for the rest of the day." Quinlan removed the earrings from the stream of water and wrapped them and the necklace in a paper towel. "We need to get you checked out by a doctor, for one thing."

"Oh, God, it's going to be in all the papers," Ronnie said, shivering as she thought of the headlines that were sure to result. It wasn't her fault, none of it was her fault, but nevertheless she was going to be made to look bad, she knew. They always made her look bad: newspapers, TV, magazines, whatever. The *second* Mrs. Honneker, they called her. There was always the hint of a sneer.

Quinlan started to reply, but whatever he had been going to say was lost as the door to the rest room burst open.

"Ronnie!" Thea stood poised on the threshold for an instant, backlighted by the brilliant sunshine outside. Her gaze found Ronnie, and she darted into the small rest room, followed by what seemed like a veritable army of people: Rose, a trio of state troopers, fair officials with their orange badges, and five or six others.

Turning to face them, Ronnie felt her heart start to pound. They were crowding around her; who were all these people?

"Oh, God, we didn't know where you'd gotten to! Are you okay?" Thea clutched her arm, anxiously looking her up and down. Ronnie took a deep, calming breath and started to answer in the affirmative.

A camera flash went off in Ronnie's face before she

could get out so much as a word. Reporters. Of course. They were like buzzards, drawn by instinct to the scene of carnage. Where the scavenger birds scented death and decay, the scavenger press scented the possibility of lurid headlines.

"Oh, no!" She threw up an arm to shield herself from the flashing lights in an almost exact reenactment of the gesture she had used to block the paint thrower's aim. The irony of that was not lost on her.

In both cases she was defending herself from assault.

"Mrs. Honneker, can you tell us . . ."

The rest of the question was lost to Ronnie as they all crowded closer, pushing her back against the sink. The hard enamel dug into her spine. Her stomach churned anew; her knees threatened to give way. Flashbulbs exploded around her like bottle rockets on the Fourth of July. Words bombarded her from all sides, so many she could hardly make sense of them. She felt like an animal at bay.

"Ronnie, oh my God, I can't believe what happened, should I call an ambulance?" Thea touched Ronnie's dress just above her hipbone, then drew her hand back and stared at the red paint on her fingertip, her expression horrified.

"No," Ronnie said, dry-mouthed. "I'm all right."

Cameras continued to flash. The questions being hurled at her were growing louder.

"Mrs. Honneker, we're so sorry. . . ." A fair official pressed close to apologize. Behind him, a strobe light was being set up and turned on. Blinking, Ronnie threw up a hand, temporarily blinded by its brilliance. "Oh, please. . . ."

"Leave her alone," Thea said, turning protectively to face the cameras.

"Mrs. Honneker, about the incident . . ." Another reporter. Another camera. Ronnie shook her head. All she wanted to do was escape, but there was no place for her to go. She was backed against the sink, surrounded, trapped.

"I can't—"

"Please leave her alone," Thea repeated, louder this time in an effort to be heard over the din, turning with Ronnie to face this new attack.

"Was it paint?"

"What do you think was the significance of the color? Do you think the fact that your assailant used red paint means anything?"

"Did you know her?"

Questions pelted Ronnie from all sides. She felt as if she were being publicly stripped. They all knew what had happened, or would soon find out, and they would print sensational stories punched up by the word *whore*.

She couldn't bear it. Her mouth trembled. It took every bit of willpower she could summon to make it stop.

The hideous thing was, none of it was her fault. None.

"All right, that's it." The words crackled with authority. The slurred southern voice was suddenly hard and crisp. "Mrs. Honneker has nothing to say right now. All your questions will be answered at the appropriate time."

Quinlan, who had been jostled to one side of the rest room by the arrival of the throng, was now taking charge. He shouldered in front of her, dislodging the circle of importunate questioners with hard words, looks, and a couple of shoves. With relief, Ronnie realized that the reporters were backing off some. Where they had ignored Thea's protests, and her own, they seemed to respect Quinlan's. Because he was a man? Ronnie neither knew nor cared. All that mattered was that he was getting the job done.

Of course, she reminded herself, he worked for her now, for the campaign. Instead of being annoyed at his advent, as she had been less than half an hour before, she felt a wave of thankfulness.

"No TV!" Quinlan's back tensed. His voice was sharp.

Sneaking a peek over his shoulder, Ronnie saw local TV newswoman Christine Gwen barreling through the door with a cameraman on her heels. Blond, thirty-something Christine was the barracuda of Jackson TV news. Whenever possible, she liked to draw blood.

"Who the hell are you?" Christine asked, glaring at him even as she directed her cameraman where to set up. Then she paused, her tone and expression changing in an instant. "You're Tom Quinlan, aren't you? Are you working for Senator Honneker now?"

There was an immediate buzz from the other reporters, and more flashing cameras. Quinlan shook his head, refusing to answer. Ronnie made herself very small behind his sheltering back.

"Clear this place out, will you?" Quinlan addressed this crisp request to one of the state troopers, who nodded.

"It's a public rest room," Christine protested even as the troopers started trying to shoo people outside.

"I know that, ma'am, but we're going to have to ask you to leave," one of the officers said, moving toward her. *"All* of you."

"You ever hear of freedom of the press?" a reporter demanded as he dodged around the officer to take another picture. Ronnie didn't think he got what he was after; Quinlan's body effectively blocked her from view.

Another reporter chimed in: "You can't make us leave! The public has a right to know!"

"Are you getting this on camera, Bill?" Christine sounded shrill. Her cameraman apparently made some gesture to answer the question in the affirmative, because Quinlan gave an ugly-sounding mutter under his breath and turned to Ronnie.

"This isn't working. Our best bet is to make a run for it." The words were meant for her ears only. As he spoke, Quinlan slid out of his suit coat and draped it over Ronnie's head. Knowing that it was meant to shield her from the cameras, she hugged it close, huddling inside it.

She could picture her face, white and shocked and streaked with paint, on every evening newscast in the state.

"Mrs. Honneker, can you tell us what the woman shouted as she threw the paint?" a reporter yelled from somewhere near the door.

" 'Whore,' " another reporter answered the first. There was a sudden, almost embarrassed silence. Ronnie died a little inside. The stories were going to be ugly; they would hurt the campaign.

Lewis would blame her.

"We don't know for certain that's what she said,"

Thea protested, but her voice sounded lame, and no one appeared to take much notice.

"I heard," Rose volunteered. "That's what she said, all right: *whore*."

"You were an eyewitness?" The print reporters wrote furiously while Christine turned to the camera, scorning the policeman who was trying to get her to leave.

"Are you up to running?" Quinlan asked, his head bent close to Ronnie's. He had turned to face her while the crowd's attention was distracted. Ronnie glanced up at him from beneath the sheltering folds of his coat. Her knees were weak, her chest felt tight, and she wanted to throw up again. Under normal conditions she would have looked for the nearest place to lie down. But these conditions were far from normal, and there was nothing she wouldn't do to get away from the press. If running was what it took, she would run.

She nodded.

"Come on, then," he said. Wrapping an arm around her shoulders, he pulled her through the crowd as she huddled under his coat, out of reach of the cameras. Sheer surprise and a few strategic straight-arm shoves got them out the rest-room door unmolested.

When the wall of light and heat that was the day hit them, they ran. Moments later the pack was in full cry on their heels.

# Chapter
## 5

"MR. QUINLAN. Thank you."

"Miz Honneker, you're welcome."

He turned his head and smiled at her, the skin around his eyes crinkling. Ronnie smiled back.

They were in Quinlan's car, a late-model Buick Regal with a cream exterior and tan velour upholstery, speeding away from the fairgrounds. The road they were on was picturesque, with verdant farmland stretching to meet shimmering blue sky on either side, but they were speeding east, not west, as they should have been to reach Jackson.

"There's something you should know, though: If you're taking me home, you're headed in the wrong direction."

"I'm not taking you home."

"You're not?" At this, Ronnie lifted her head from where it had been resting wearily against the seatback to look at him with raised eyebrows. A small pile of discarded red-streaked wet-wipes rested in the open storage area of the console between them. Quinlan traveled with a box of wet-wipes in his glove compartment, and Ronnie had used the first few minutes of the ride to scrub away as much of the paint remaining on her as she could.

"Nope."

"Why not?" Sudden visions of kidnapping and worse danced lightning-quick through her head, only to be dismissed. Though in real-world time she had only been acquainted with him for little more than an hour, and she knew nothing about him except for his name and what he did for a living, she discovered that she trusted him completely. He had rescued her, cared for her, protected her when she was vulnerable. The experience had forged a bond between them that Ronnie imagined was probably much like that felt by soldiers who had gone through a battle together.

"For a minute there you were looking at me like I just turned into Ted Bundy." A sideways glance and a quick grin accompanied this accurate reading of her thoughts.

"The thought occurred." She settled back against the headrest again, glad of the cool blast from the air conditioner. Ditches on either side of the road boasted weeds, not water, and the ponds in the fields they passed looked brackish and stale in the bright sunlight. It had been so hot for so long that even the trees looked wilted. "So why aren't you taking me home? At the very least I need to take a shower and change."

The skin on her legs tingled from the alcohol in the wet-wipes. She had scrubbed at them through the nylon of her pantyhose, but scattered red-paint freckles still marred them.

"Where do you think that pack of jackals we just escaped from is going to head?"

"Oh." Ronnie drew in a breath. She hadn't thought of that. Sedgely, the Honneker family estate just outside Jackson that was their Mississippi home, would be surrounded. Her last glimpse of the reporters, caught from over her shoulder as she and Quinlan jumped into his Buick, had found them scattering in all directions as they ran for their cars. They would be hot on her heels already. If they couldn't find her, and she devoutly hoped they could not, they would head for Sedgely. Beautiful Sedgely, with its antebellum mansion, driveway lined with oaks bearded with Spanish moss, and genteel stone fence that wouldn't keep out an enterprising six-year-old much less a rabid horde of newspeople, was probably even now under siege.

"I'd better warn Dorothy." Ronnie picked up the cell phone on the console with a glance at him. "May I?"

"Help yourself. Dorothy?"

"Lewis's mother. She's at Sedgely." She punched in the number as she spoke.

"Oh, yes. Grandma."

Selma, Sedgely's longtime housekeeper, answered on the second ring. Ronnie held up a hand to shush Quinlan.

"Selma, this is Mrs. Lewis. Is Mrs. Honneker in?"

"No'm, she's not."

Ronnie supposed that Dorothy was at one of her numerous ladies' luncheons, which was just as well. She would rather Selma be the one to break this kind of news to her disapproving mother-in-law.

"Can you get in touch with her? Did she leave a number where she can be reached?"

"She's at Miz Cherry's."

Honoria Cherry was one of Dorothy's oldest friends. Like the Honnekers, the Cherrys were old tobacco money. They owned the neighboring estate of Waveland.

"Selma, listen: Would you call her over there, please, and tell her that a woman threw paint on me at the fair, I'm not hurt, and the press will be descending on Sedgely. I don't want her to be caught by surprise."

"Tell her to say she doesn't know anything about it if she's asked," Quinlan instructed while Selma talked in Ronnie's other ear. "Tell her to tell Grandma that too."

"Selma says that reporters have already started to call, and there's a strange car parked opposite the rear entrance. It's empty, though," Ronnie said to Quinlan, covering the mouthpiece with her hand.

"Probably a reporter sneaking around, hoping to get a quick picture or a quote. Tell her what I said. She don't know nuthin' about nuthin'."

Ronnie repeated his words into the receiver, assured Selma that she was all right, and hung up.

"Now for Lewis," she said with a grimace, and punched in the number of his cell phone. When a disembodied voice said he couldn't be reached, she was relieved. Lewis was going to be less than happy about this latest turn of events.

"The Bell South customer is not available at this time," she said to Quinlan, mimicking the prim tones of the recording, and dialed Lewis's office in Washington. She gave the news to Moira Adams, his administrative assistant, requesting that it be passed on to Lewis when they located him. Duty done, she hung up and replaced the phone on the console. "Now what? I can't go home."

"I thought I'd take you home with me." That deep, too-southern voice was starting to grow on her, though as a general rule Ronnie wasn't a fan of southern accents. Probably because Lewis adopted one whenever he crossed into Mississippi airspace and discarded it the minute he was winging toward Washington again. During the winter months, which they spent in their Georgetown row house, his southern origins were hardly detectable in his voice.

As a consequence, she supposed, that slow, slurring drawl always sounded artificial to her.

"I don't think that's a good idea," Ronnie objected. "Think what the papers could do with that. 'Senator's Wife Hides Out in Home of Political Consultant,' or something. They'd end up making it sound like they'd caught me red-handed in a love nest."

She felt, and sounded, bitter. His expression as he glanced at her remained tranquil.

"I have an apartment in Jackson, and you're right, it wouldn't be a good idea for me to take you there. If for no other reason than that they'll be staking out my place too. I meant my mother's house. She'll be there."

"Your *mother's* house?"

"She lives just outside of De Kalb, which is about thirty miles from here. Nobody will think to look for you there. Give you a place to clean up, and a little breathing space, while we decide how to handle this."

"You're from Mississippi?" Ronnie didn't know why she felt surprised. That down-home accent should have been indication enough. But political consultants always seemed to come from somewhere else. They were constantly on the move, flying from place to place, campaign to campaign, election to election, the ultimate migrant workers. It was hard to imagine one with roots in a place like Mississippi.

"Yup. Lived here most of my life. Actually I went to Ole Miss with Marsden. We roomed together one year."

Marsden was Lewis's oldest son. By his first wife, the sainted Eleanor. Ronnie's stepson, although he was eight years her senior.

"Well, now, *that's* certainly a recommendation," Ronnie said dryly when she recovered from her surprise at the revelation, which gave her sense of trust in him a severe jolt. "Being a friend of Marsden's is all you need to get a job with me anytime."

"Don't get on with Marsden very well, hmm?" He glanced at her again, humor in his eyes.

"I'd call that the understatement of the century. Marsden thinks I broke up his parents' marriage, among other things. He loathes me. And I promise you, the feeling's mutual."

"And did you?"

"Did I what? Oh, break up Lewis's marriage? No." She hesitated. How much should she tell him? The surprising intimacy that had sprung up between them had to be weighed against cold facts: he was a hired political consultant brought in by Lewis's office to "handle" her, and he had been Marsden's college roommate.

As far as inspiring her with confidence, his resume struck out on both counts.

"Most of Mississippi thinks that, you know." His tone was faintly apologetic as he delivered that unpalatable truth.

Ronnie grimaced, glancing down at her ruined dress. "It's pretty obvious."

"That's what we're going to change. Stick with me, lady, and in six months you'll be as popular as corn dogs at a fair, I promise."

In spite of herself Ronnie had to laugh. "Does that come with a money-back guarantee?"

"Absolutely." He was smiling. "It's all a matter of spin, you see. Most voters tend to view everyone in the political arena in terms of a stereotype. It makes it easier for them, doesn't require as much work. The stereotype you fit into right now is 'the other woman,' younger and more attractive, who comes along and steals a basically good man from his faithful, loving wife of many years. If you think about it that way, it's easy to see why they don't like you."

"But it's not true. *Really* not true. I didn't steal Lewis. He was already separated when we started dating." Ronnie couldn't help it. She had to be clear on that point at least.

"Which was?"

"About six years ago. I had been working in his office for a few years before that, but we didn't have a personal relationship until I knew that his marriage to Eleanor was, for all intents and purposes, over."

"How'd you two meet, anyway?"

"I was just nineteen, a sophomore at the American University in Washington, and Lewis came and spoke to a class I was taking. I thought what he had to say was interesting, so I asked him a lot of questions. After class he came up to me in the hall and asked me if I would like to apply for a part-time job that had just become available in his office. I did, and was hired. I started out doing secretarial-type things for him and worked my way up the office food chain."

"So you worked for him."

Ronnie nodded, hesitated, and decided that there was no harm in giving him a bare-bones outline of the rest of it. After all, *she* had done nothing to be ashamed of, whether Marsden—and the voters of Mississippi—chose to believe it or not. What she wouldn't say was how persistently Lewis had pursued her from the start. The truth—that Lewis had asked her out repeatedly, from the time she had joined his staff as a nineteen-year-old part-timer to the moment she had finally said *yes*—did not reflect well on her husband. Loyalty dictated that she keep that part to herself. "When I graduated, he offered me a full-time job as a legislative aide. He and Eleanor were separated by that time, although they kept it quiet for fear it would hurt his chances for reelection. After a while Lewis and I started dating. Eleanor was already involved with someone else. That's the way it was all during Lewis's last campaign, although Lewis and Eleanor appeared together in public when they had to. After the election was over, Eleanor got a quickie divorce, and Lewis and I got married. He thought that would give voters six whole years until the next election to get used to me. Only it's been three years already, and they don't seem to like me any better now than they ever did. What happened today is a prime example."

"That sure wasn't any valentine, I agree." Quinlan slanted a glance at her. "You have any plans to have a baby with the Senator?"

"What?" Shock brought Ronnie upright in her seat.

She could not believe he had asked her something so personal.

"A baby'd warm the voters up to you, you know. Everybody loves a new mom and her sweet little baby. If you're planning on having kids anyway, it's something to think about doing before the next election. Three more years gives you plenty of time."

"If and when I decide to have a baby, it certainly won't be to help win an election!"

"Just a thought," he murmured, unapologetic. His glance at her contained a hint of speculation. Ronnie wondered just exactly how much he really knew about Lewis. If he'd been Marsden's college roommate, presumably quite a bit. But maybe not. Not many people knew the private Lewis. She wasn't even sure if Marsden did.

"Just how close are you and Marsden?" Ronnie asked suspiciously.

"Friends once, more what I'd term acquaintances now. Don't worry, I won't be giving him weekly updates on you and your doings. I work for you, not him." Quinlan smiled at her as he spoke.

"Just so we have that straight."

He slowed at a stop sign, then turned left on a blacktop road that was even narrower than the one they'd left behind. On this one, two cars could pass each other if they both hugged the gravel shoulder, but it would be a tight fit. Sagging wire fences stretching between weathered fence posts bordered the road on both sides. In field after field small herds of black-and-white cows grazed in patches of shade provided by the occasional tree. A quartet of pigs lolled in a muddy stream, only the tops of their heads visible above the brown water. A pair of plump white geese pecked at something in the scrub grass beside the road. A farmer in a straw hat and denim overalls waved from his tractor. Quinlan honked, and waved back.

"Do you know him?" Quinlan in his elegant suit seemed to have no connection to the hardworking farmer.

"I know everyone around here. My family has lived in these parts for generations. Ah, here we are."

He slowed, turning in at a gravel driveway. Ronnie got just a glimpse of a battered metal mailbox on a weathered post before they passed it. Ahead of them was a two-story farmhouse, white clapboard, with narrow windows and a gray-painted porch and shutters, homely rather than grand, and obviously old. A big oak spread its branches over the scraggly front lawn, while a grove of silver maples sheltered a second entrance and a picnic table to the side. A sagging barn, bigger than the house and in dire need of paint, stood on a little rise at the end of the driveway. Not that *driveway* was quite the right word for the gravel trail over which the car bumped. It was more of a farm track, continuing on past the house through a small field with a grove of what looked like apple trees and a vegetable garden on the right, and a chicken coop and some other kind of outbuilding on the left. Quinlan pulled up alongside the house and stopped in a patch of shade provided by the silver maples.

A teenage boy in baggy khaki shorts and a white T-shirt came out through the screen door at the side entrance, then paused on the concrete stoop as he saw the car. The door banged shut behind him.

Quinlan got out of the car. "Hey, Mark! Why aren't you at work?"

Mark shrugged without answering. Another car pulled up behind them, tires crunching on gravel, and a horn tooted as Ronnie got out. In motion once more, the boy headed toward the newly arrived car, whose driver's-side door was opening invitingly.

"See ya," he said to Quinlan with a wave, and slid behind the wheel as the blond girl who had been driving scooted into the passenger seat.

"Ten o'clock," Quinlan warned.

"Midnight," the boy shot back, slamming the door.

"Ten," Quinlan responded, unyielding, but if the boy heard, he gave no indication of it. He was already looking over his shoulder as he backed down the driveway with more speed than care. The car reached the road, pulled out, and was off in a shower of gravel, with a honk and a wave from both occupants.

"Loren invited him to go swimming, so he called in sick." Ronnie looked around to find a sixty-ish woman wearing blue gingham slacks and a white blouse standing on the side porch Mark had just vacated. She had weathered skin and short white hair, and she was frowning distractedly as she addressed Quinlan.

"I figured it was something like that. That little girl is pure bad news." Quinlan sounded grim. He then seemed to recollect his audience and looked around for Ronnie, who stood uncertainly on the other side of the car.

"Mom, this is Mrs. Lewis Honneker, wife of His Honor the Senator. Miz Honneker, this is my mother, Sally McGuire."

"Oh, my," Mrs. McGuire said, stepping down off

the porch, hand outstretched. "This is a pleasure, Mrs. Honneker. I knew your—my goodness, would he be your stepson? That's Marsden, of course. Well, I knew him pretty well at one time, and I know the rest of the family too. At least I did. Anyway, it's good to have you visit."

"Thank you." Ronnie smiled her best senator's-wife's smile and shook hands. The other woman's gaze ran over first her and then Quinlan with growing surprise.

"My goodness, whatever happened?" she asked, eyes wide as she looked at her son. "That's not blood, is it?"

"We got in the way of some paint," Quinlan answered, shepherding Ronnie toward the house. "Miz Honneker here needs a shower and a change of clothes and then maybe something to eat. You got anything good in the kitchen?"

"You know I do." His mother was behind them as Quinlan ushered Ronnie through the screen door and into the cool dimness of what looked like an old-fashioned back parlor. There was even an organ against one wall. "There's turkey, and some ham, unless Mark ate it all, which he probably did. And I have some cake, too, fresh baked. Red Velvet."

"My mom's the best cook in Mississippi," Quinlan informed Ronnie with conviction, putting his arm around his mother as she joined them. "Wait till you taste her Red Velvet cake. But first things first. The shower's up those stairs, second door on the right."

"Those towels on the rack are clean," Mrs. Mc-Guire said. "I just put them out. And there's shampoo in the closet. Anything else you find you need when you get up there, you just holler."

"Thank you." Ronnie hesitated, feeling that it was slightly rude to go off to take a shower just like that, as though she belonged in their house. But from the expressions on the faces of both mother and son, she saw that they expected nothing less. She headed toward the narrow staircase at the far end of the room, all too conscious that they were still watching her. What would Quinlan tell his mother when they were alone? she wondered.

The full story of what had happened, no doubt.

The knowledge made Ronnie squirm inwardly as she climbed the stairs. It was humiliating to be so disliked, and for such a reason.

# Chapter

## 6

TV EVANGELIST's Daughter Found Dead
*The body of the 23-year-old daughter of*
*televangelist Charlie Kay Martin was found at*
*4:00 P.M., Friday, floating in the Gulf of Mexico*
*just off Deer Island. Biloxi police spokesperson*
*Sgt. Connie Lott said that the coroner's findings*
*were not consistent with an accidental drowning*
*in the death of Susan Marie Martin, and foul play*
*is suspected. Long estranged from her family,*
*Martin was thought to be living in Biloxi at the*
*time of her death. A spokesperson for Mr. Martin*
*said that the televangelist would have no immedi-*
*ate comment, but added that he and his wife*
*were "heartbroken." Sgt. Lott said the investiga-*
*tion is continuing.*

The article in the daily newspaper was small. Marla
Becker would have missed it altogether had it not been
positioned right over a travel agency's ad for a two-
night, three-day junket to Las Vegas for the incredible
price of $199, airfare and a daily buffet breakfast in-

cluded. A trip to Vegas was Marla's dream. To her it was the ultimate destination, the one place where her fantasies could actually come true.

It wasn't that she wanted a vacation. She figured that, with her blond, leggy good-looks, Vegas was just the place to hook up with a high-rolling sugar-daddy type who would be interested in introducing her to the kind of life to which she was dying to become accustomed.

But then there was Lissy. Lissy was her daughter, a pony-tailed blond pixie whom she loved with a fierce devotion even though the mere fact of her daughter's existence was enough to explode that daydream like an overfilled balloon. What sugar daddy would want a mistress who came complete with a seven-year-old daughter? And even if he existed, who would watch Lissy while she took off to Vegas to catch him?

Still, Marla liked to imagine her dream might one day come true, so she hungrily read every travel article and ad pertaining to Vegas. And today her obsession had led her to the story about Susan.

Even though it was there in front of her, printed in the newspaper for everyone to see, Marla found it hard to grasp the reality of it: Susan was dead. Marla had been growing increasingly worried about her roommate over the past three days, but she had never expected *this*. Susan shared the two-bedroom apartment with her and Lissy, and she hadn't been home since Thursday night. Susan partied hard, and sometimes she'd stay away over the weekend, or even longer, if she met a hunky guy, but she always called to let Marla know. This time Susan hadn't called.

Marla wet her lips, staring down at the article. She

was surprised to find that she couldn't reread the story because the paper was shaking.

Just like her hands.

Thank God Lissy wouldn't be home until after five. She had been invited to spend the afternoon swimming with a friend, whose mother had promised to drop her off when they were done. Marla didn't want Lissy to see her so upset.

Oh, God, how was she going to tell Lissy about Susan? Lissy really liked Aunt Susan, as she called her, though they weren't related by blood.

Lissy had already experienced so much loss in her life. Now this.

*Susan was dead.* Even though Marla deliberately put the thought into words and then said them aloud, they didn't seem real.

How could such a thing have happened?

She had last seen Susan at about six P.M., Thursday, when she had driven her and Claire Anson to the Biloxi Yacht Club and dropped them off. They had dates, they'd said, with some rich guys on a huge yacht—the *Sun Cloud,* or something. The *Sun Ray?* She couldn't quite remember its name, though she had a feeling that it might be important. *Sun*-something, she was sure. Pretty sure.

Susan had expected to make a lot of money from that date, maybe as much as a thousand dollars. She'd better, Marla had half threatened. Ever irresponsible, Susan was two months behind with her share of the rent, and Marla couldn't afford to carry her forever.

She had Lissy to think of. The money she earned had to support Lissy, not Susan, dear friend though Susan was.

Marla dropped the paper. It fluttered to the floor and lay there in an untidy heap while she got up from the couch and took the three steps needed to carry her to the kitchen phone.

What was Claire's number? Marla was so rattled she couldn't remember. She had to look it up, in Susan's red suede phone book that was kept in a drawer near the phone. Touching Susan's phone book made her sick to her stomach, like she was touching her friend's corpse or something.

Oh, Susan! They'd been roommates for two years, in three different apartments. It was hard to imagine that she would never see her again. She and Lissy and Susan had been—family. There was no other word for it.

Claire's cheery voice answered on the fourth ring. "I'm either out, showering, or sleeping. Whatever, I can't talk now. Leave a message, and I'll get back to you. 'Bye."

Marla left her name and phone number, and added that it was urgent. Then she hung up.

For a long time she simply stood there staring at the phone.

Susan was *dead,* all her zest for living reduced to a corpse that had been found floating in the Gulf of Mexico. The paper said the cops suspected foul play. So she'd probably been murdered.

But who would want to kill Susan?

Marla pondered: What should she do?

Should she call the cops and pass on the information she had? No. She couldn't risk it. She had fled with Lissy years ago, when it started to seem likely that the judge in her divorce case would hand down a custody ruling favoring her right-wing, religious-fanatic husband over the teenage pothead and recreational dope user she had been then. Marla had never learned exactly how the legal issue of Lissy's custody had turned out, but she had little doubt that her husband (ex- by now, surely) had prevailed. Not that it mattered. Lissy was *hers,* just as she was Lissy's. Neither of them was ever going back.

Should she call Susan's family? She didn't know any of them, and from what Susan had said, she didn't particularly want to. She doubted that they even cared that Susan was dead. Certainly Susan had severed all ties with them. Her father, Charlie Kay Martin, was famous, on TV every week with *The Family Prayer Hour*. He was a fist-shaking, fire-breathing, hell-prophesying preacher who reminded Marla of Lissy's dad. Certainly the way Susan had turned out was an object lesson in what happened to girls who were raised in harshly punitive, religious fundamentalist homes.

She couldn't go to Susan's family.

Who, then?

Marla reached for the phone, meaning to call the Beautiful Model Agency for which she, Susan, and Claire worked part-time. Not exactly as models, though that was what they called themselves. Well, they did model sometimes.

The thought of what they occasionally modeled almost made Marla smile despite the circumstances.

Billie, who set up their dates for them, would know what to do. Maybe she had even set up the date for Susan and Claire on that boat Thursday. Marla wouldn't have been included, because she didn't do overnights. Lissy kept her home.

Just as her hand curled around the phone, there was a knock at the door. It was a small apartment—a living-room–dining-room combination, galley kitchen, and two bedrooms, one of which she and Lissy shared. The only door was in the dining-room section. Standing in the kitchen as she was, Marla was maybe five feet away from it.

The knock was soft, polite, not at all alarming. Not one of her friends, who would have banged or done shave-and-a-haircut, six bits, or something equally silly; not the landlady, whose knock was brisk and no-nonsense. Not Lissy, who would have called out to let her mother know it was her.

Who, then, could be knocking on the door in the middle of a Monday afternoon? A salesman maybe? For vacuum cleaners or something?

Marla knew she was spooked by what she had learned about Susan, but still she was surprised by the hesitation with which she approached her own front door. It was as if a little voice inside her head was whispering, "Careful, honey."

Susan's voice?

Marla moved quietly, her bare feet soundless on the stained beige carpeting. Another knock came just as she reached the door. She jumped nearly a foot in the air. She had to draw a deep, steadying breath before she was calm enough to press her eye to the peephole.

There was a man outside, a man in a gray Nike T-shirt and an Ole Miss baseball cap. His face was round, pudgy, pale. His hair on either side of the baseball cap was short and dark. The best word Marla could come up with to describe him was nondescript. He was glancing impatiently up and down the hall.

As Marla watched, he pulled Susan's key ring from his pocket and slid a key into the lock.

# Chapter

## 7

ESPITE A CERTAIN self-consciousness about her appearance, Ronnie eventually came downstairs. The sound of Quinlan's voice as he talked to his mother guided her to the kitchen. She hesitated outside the entrance for a moment, feeling awkward about intruding. But she would feel equally awkward hanging out in the hallway, or the living room, or upstairs. Sooner or later she knew she would have to join them, or else one or both of them would come looking for her. Might as well assume an air of confidence and sail right in.

She would not feel so ill at ease if she'd had access to a lipstick or a powder compact, or even a curling iron. Having left her purse behind, she had no cosmetics with her. Consequently, there was nothing on her face except for what remained of her faithful mascara and a touch of the hand lotion she'd found on a shelf in the bathroom. Without mousse, gel, hairspray, or curling iron, she had been able to do nothing with her still-damp hair besides blow it dry and tuck it behind her ears.

But there was no help for it, she told herself, and walked into the kitchen.

Quinlan and his mother were seated at a round oak table at the far end of the kitchen, where a large, multi-paned window overlooked the backyard. Like the rest of the house, the kitchen was old-fashioned. Squares of white and gold linoleum, worn in places, covered the floor. The cabinets were painted a mustard color, pre-sumably to match the harvest-gold appliances. The counters were white laminate and held such items as a wooden bread box and spice racks. Yellow gingham cafe curtains hung from simple brass rods at the win-dows. Near the stainless steel sink, an automatic cof-feemaker dripped, filling the air with the bracing scent of fresh coffee. A red-striped dish towel hung from the handle on the front of the stove. That clue, plus the unidentifiable but savory aroma that mingled with the smell of coffee, led Ronnie to conclude that supper was in the oven.

It was an unexpectedly homey scene, Ronnie thought.

Both Quinlan and his mother looked up as she en-tered. Quinlan had exchanged his stained suit for a navy polo shirt and jeans, and his hair was slightly damp, leading Ronnie to assume that, like herself, he'd had a shower.

"Feeling better?" Mrs. McGuire asked. Quinlan merely grinned, slowly, adding about two dozen creases to his cheeks and the lines around his eyes as he looked her over. In blue-and-yellow plaid slacks and a yellow T-shirt with matching plaid trim, both at least a size fourteen where she wore a size six, Ronnie felt like a clown. If the pants had not had a drawstring waist, she wouldn't have been able to keep them up.

"Nice outfit," he said, meeting her gaze at last.

"Thanks," she replied with a saccharine smile. His knit shirt revealed broad shoulders and surprisingly muscular arms, and his jeans fit him. Obviously the clothes were his own, kept at his mother's house. Lucky him.

"Don't tease," Sally McGuire told her son, shaking her head at him reprovingly and standing up. To Ronnie she said, "Would you like a piece of cake? And a glass of milk? Or a cup of coffee?"

"I'd love some cake. With milk, please. They just seem to go together, don't they?" Ronnie gave Quinlan one more quelling look as she sat down.

"They do," Mrs. McGuire agreed over her shoulder, lifting a glass cover from a cake stand on the counter and cutting into a scrumptious-looking red layer cake lavished with creamy white icing.

"Thanks for loaning me some clothes," Ronnie said as Mrs. McGuire slid a huge wedge onto a plate and placed it before her.

"Oh, you're welcome. I just wish I had something more your size." Pouring milk into a glass, Mrs. McGuire chuckled suddenly. "In more ways than one. Too bad we can't have our cake and be slim, too, isn't it?"

"It is," Ronnie agreed as the glass of milk joined the cake in front of her. Sliding her fork through soft cake and buttery icing, Ronnie inhaled the heady scent. Her mouth suddenly watered. She didn't often permit herself sweets, but today she just couldn't summon the willpower to resist the treat. "It looks wonderful. I don't eat a lot of desserts."

"I can tell," Quinlan said. There was something in his expression that told Ronnie he admired her figure. Well, there was nothing surprising in that, she thought. Keeping an admirable figure was the reason she watched what she ate, swam whenever she could, and worked out with Nautilus equipment three times a week.

The cake melted on her tongue in a burst of creamy sweetness. Ronnie's eyes almost closed at the gustatory pleasure of it.

"This is scrumptious," she said, and took another bite.

"Mom's Red Velvet cake is famous. Everybody who's ever eaten any remembers it." Quinlan was half-way through his own piece of cake. His hunk had easily been twice as big as hers, and he seemed to be putting it away with no trouble at all.

If this was the way he ate ordinarily, she was surprised he managed to stay so lean.

She put another small bite of cake into her mouth, savoring it. It was so good, such an unexpected treat for her chicken, fish, and salad-accustomed palate, that she wanted to make it last as long as she could. Only the knowledge that Quinlan was watching her with amusement kept her eating steadily.

"This is really delicious," she said with careful understatement to Mrs. McGuire, and took a sip of milk. Whole milk, of course, where she never drank anything but skim.

If she ate like this often, she soon would weigh two hundred pounds, she thought.

"It was my grandmother's recipe. I can still taste her cream cheese frosting. It was out of this world." Mrs. McGuire settled into her place at the table with her own cake and milk.

"It couldn't have been better than this," Ronnie said, taking another bite.

"Oh, before I forget, here are your pearls." Quinlan pulled a paper-towel-wrapped bundle from his jeans pocket and pushed it across the table.

"Thanks." Ronnie said. Unwrapping the paper towel, she slipped the necklace into her own pocket and put the earrings back on her ears. With her fingers once again steady, it was the work of only a moment.

"They're lovely." Mrs. McGuire admired the jewelry with her eyes. Quinlan's gaze followed the same path as his mother's, but he didn't say anything.

"Thank you."

Mrs. McGuire smiled at her. "Are you from Mississippi originally?" she asked, cutting into her own slice of cake.

Ronnie shook her head. "Massachusetts. I grew up in Boston."

"Is your family still there?"

"My father and one of my sisters are. My other sister lives in Delaware with her family. My mother is in California now with her new husband. So we're kind of scattered."

"You're one of three sisters? So am I. The oldest, as a matter of fact."

"I'm the youngest." Ronnie put the last bite of cake into her mouth with regret. It would be months before she would allow herself something so fattening again.

"How old are you?" Quinlan asked suddenly. His

brows met over his nose in a slight frown as he looked at her.

"Twenty-nine," Ronnie answered as Mrs. McGuire *tch-ed* at her son in disapproval.

"You look younger," Quinlan said as his mother good-humoredly took him to task for asking a lady her age.

"You must be—thirty-seven," Ronnie guessed, refusing to be put on the defensive because of her youth. She knew what he—and his mother—were probably thinking: that Lewis, at sixty, was more than twice her age. She reminded herself that Quinlan, at least, worked for her. She did not have to explain herself to *him*.

"Good guess. You ought to try working one of those age-and-weight booths at the fair." His frown relaxed, and she no longer felt as if she were being judged. "How'd you know?"

"Easy," she said. "Marsden's thirty-seven. If you were college roommates, it stands to reason you'd be about the same age."

"Oh, dear, don't you like Marsden?" Mrs. McGuire shook her head, alerted by something in Ronnie's tone. "I always thought he was such a polite boy."

"He used to call my mother *ma'am* whenever they met," Quinlan explained. "And tell her how nice she looked."

"Marsden didn't approve of his father marrying me," Ronnie said to Mrs. McGuire. "I don't think I've seen his polite side yet."

"What about Joanie? And Laura?" Quinlan asked. He had finished his cake and was sipping a cup of coffee.

"I'm afraid they're in Marsden's camp." For the first year or so of the marriage, Lewis's two daughters had in fact been as close to rude as they dared to be in their father's presence. Apparently having resigned themselves to it somewhat by this time, they were simply cool whenever they had to be in the company of their younger stepmother. Not that they were in Ronnie's company very often. Though both lived near Sedgely, the only time Ronnie saw them and their families were occasions such as Easter, Thanksgiving, and Christmas. And Lewis's birthday, of course, which was coming up next month and for which they had a huge party every year.

"I always thought Joanie in particular was such a nice girl," Mrs. McGuire said. "There was a time . . ."

She broke off, looking self-consciously at her son.

"Go on, Mom, spill all the family beans," Quinlan said dryly. To Ronnie he added, "I used to date Joanie. Mom hoped we'd make a match of it."

"Really?" Ronnie smiled at him with exaggerated sweetness. The more she learned about his connections with Lewis's children, the less inclined she felt to rely on her earlier feeling that she could trust him. "Too bad you didn't. Then you'd be my . . . stepson-in-law."

"Sounds incestuous, doesn't it?" Quinlan chuckled, dispelling the tension. "All that's water under the bridge. I married somebody else, Joanie married somebody else, and I haven't thought about her in seventeen years. Does she have any children?"

"Two," Ronnie said. "A boy and a girl."

"I know Marsden has a couple. What about Laura?" Mrs. McGuire asked.

"One. A girl, Jilly. She's six."

"That makes you a step-grandmother," Quinlan said, as if he had just discovered the fact and found it in equal parts appalling and amusing. "Do the kids call you Grandma?"

"They call me Ronnie, when they speak to me at all," Ronnie said coolly. "Believe me, we aren't the Brady Bunch."

There was a silence as everyone digested this.

"I don't think we're going to be able to do family pictures." Quinlan was frowning, his thoughts having clearly turned to business while mulling over Ronnie's words. "You know, doting Grandma and Grandpa surrounded by the kids. When Grandma is younger than the children, the imagery just doesn't work." His gaze fastened on Ronnie. "What we need to do is make you look more mature. Less glamorous. Grandma to His Honor's Grandpa is too much to hope for, but you should at least be able to look like somebody's mom."

"But the fact is I'm *not* somebody's mom. I don't think I ought to try to look like something I'm not." Ronnie's chin came up, and she returned his thoughtful regard unflinchingly. She'd been down this road before, with other consultants. They all wanted to change her, to improve her. She was tired of it; what was so wrong with her the way she was?

Both Quinlan and his mother seemed to be studying her. Their eyes were the same, Ronnie discovered, glancing from one to the other. Like Tom, his mother had been blessed with deep gray-blue irises surrounded by a ring of smoky charcoal, set beneath thick, dark-brown brows and lashes. Beautiful eyes, she thought. Then, weighing eyes.

"Projecting an image is what politics is all about. All I'm asking is that you try to project the kind of image that will help your husband get reelected." Quinlan's voice was patient. He leaned forward, his arms folding on the tabletop. His plate had been pushed to one side.

"What exactly do you have in mind?" Ronnie asked warily.

Quinlan looked her over again, slowly. Ronnie got the impression that every aspect of her appearance was being analyzed, with much found wanting.

"Do you dye your hair?"

"What?" Surprise at the question made Ronnie's voice go up an octave.

"Do you dye your hair?" He repeated it as though it were the most reasonable question in the world.

"That's not something you should ask a lady," his mother protested mildly, while Ronnie responded with an indignant "No!"

"I can't believe that dark red color is natural," Quinlan said, staring at it intently. "It's too—red."

"Well, I do beg your pardon, believe me," Ronnie replied, affronted. "Not that the color of my hair is any of your business. You work for me, not the other way around."

"Tommy . . . ," his mother began, only to be silenced by a shake of her son's head. He focused on Ronnie, his gaze intent.

"Listen up, Miz Honneker: I was hired to make the good citizens of Mississippi want to vote for your husband come the next election. He's well liked in the state, well thought of, highly electable. His biggest negative is—you. *You* are what we've got to make more acceptable to the voters. You know they don't like you. You had ample proof of it today. You think they don't like you because they believe you stole the Senator from his first wife. That's a fair enough assessment. But the way you look is not helping. It's like rubbing salt in the wound. You look like the kind of woman who could—and would—steal another woman's husband. You just look too damned young, and too damned—sexy, for a politician's wife. At least a winning, sixty-year-old politician."

"Oh, dear," Mrs. McGuire murmured, glancing from Ronnie's angrily flushing face to her son's determined one as they locked glances across the table. "I think I better leave you two to hash this out alone. Tommy, dear, mind your manners. Please."

Mrs. McGuire rose, picked up her plate and glass, and left the table. Depositing her dishes in the sink, she walked out of the room.

When she was gone, Ronnie held Quinlan's unyielding gaze for a moment longer, the light of battle in her eyes.

"This isn't going to work," she said with precision. "It's obvious that you have a problem with my being so much younger than Lewis. Well, *I* have a problem with your having a problem with that and with the fact that you have such close connections to Lewis's children. I just don't feel comfortable working with you. Although I'm very grateful for all your assistance today, I'm afraid I'm going to have to terminate our association. I'm sorry." She pushed back her chair and stood up, reaching for her dishes.

Quinlan remained seated, watching her. "Are you

trying to tell me I'm fired?" He didn't sound, or look, particularly perturbed by the idea.

"My, you do catch on quickly, don't you?" Ronnie gave him a quick, glittering smile, and turned away to carry her dishes to the sink.

His voice followed her, faintly amused and dripping honey. "Miz Honneker, darlin', I was hired by the Committee to Reelect the Senator. Not by you. They're the only ones who can terminate my employment."

Ronnie turned back from the sink, rigid with temper. "I won't work with you. I don't trust you. And if I say you're fired, you're fired. Believe me, Lewis will back me up."

Quinlan's brows snapped together and his lips parted as he started to reply. Obviously thinking better of what he had been about to say, he grimaced and stood up, leaving his dishes behind. His gaze met hers as his brow cleared.

"No need to go off half-cocked," he said with wry humor, walking toward her. "I guess that red hair must be natural, because you do have the temper to match. Politics is a game, and to win the game sometimes we have to do things we don't want to do. I know you don't want His Honor to lose the election because of you. I can help you become an asset to him instead of a liability. That's what you want, isn't it?"

Ignoring her fierce frown, he took her elbow and steered her toward the back door, which opened off a closet-sized mud room piled with boots, backpacks, and miscellaneous jackets.

"You want to help him win the election, don't you?" he coaxed, opening the back door. He ushered her across a small concrete stoop, down two shallow steps, and over a too-crisp patch of dandelion-infested lawn.

"Yes," she said unwillingly, allowing him to steer her toward an old-fashioned wooden porch swing hanging in the shadow of a tall oak. "But . . ."

"Then let's talk this out."

They reached shade and swing and Ronnie sat, not entirely of her own accord. The swing swayed beneath her. A sudden breeze was pleasantly cool as it touched her face. A huge bumblebee buzzed past. Tobacco growing in a nearby field rustled as the breeze turned into a gust of wind. The swing swayed again, and Ronnie looked up to discover Quinlan's hand wrapped around the chain.

"I'm on your side," he told her, standing over her, his expression serious. "Just because I know Marsden and Joanie and Laura doesn't mean a thing. I'm here to help *you*. Everything that passes between you and me is confidential. I won't go bearing tales on you to anyone. Any suggestion of mine that you don't like, all you have to do is say no. But I get paid to make the suggestions. Now, you think about that, and you decide if you still want to fire me. If you do, I'll quit. On the other hand, if you think we can work together despite the fact that I know your in-laws and I think your hair's too red and you're sexy, I'll do my best for you. And my best is pretty damned good, if I do say so myself." He paused. "It's your call."

# Chapter

## 8

ONNIE'S TEMPER, always quick to ignite and just as quick to burn itself out, had already cooled. The old saw about someone being able to charm the birds from the trees flitted through her mind as she looked up at him. He smiled at her beguilingly.

"Will you really quit if I want you to?" Unwilling to be won over so easily, Ronnie decided to make him work for it.

"Absolutely."

"Anytime?"

"All you have to do is say the word."

"And you won't get mad if I don't want to follow your advice? You won't go running to Lewis or Marsden or any of the campaign people to complain?"

"Nope."

"If you do, I will fire you." It was a warning, delivered with appropriate sternness.

"Understood."

Ronnie surrendered, though with a frown and a glinting look up at him. "Then I guess we can give it a try."

"Thank you." He looked down at her for a moment, then asked gravely, "So the pregnancy thing is definitely out?"

Ronnie stiffened. Her eyes narrowed.

"Just kidding," he said, and grinned. "Okay, that's out. No pregnancy. And I take it you don't want to tone down your hair. To mouse brown, or something."

"No!" The truth was, although her hair was naturally dark auburn, she had her hairdresser enhance the color monthly. But that was something she preferred to keep to herself. Certainly it was not anything he needed to know.

"How about your clothes?"

"What's wrong with my clothes?" she asked defensively.

"Too . . ." He hesitated. A humorous gleam appeared in his eyes as he met her gaze.

"Too what?"

Expressive eyebrows said what he did not.

"Go on. Say it," she dared him.

"Sexy," he said. "I can't help it. It's God's honest truth."

"Today I was wearing a dress. A simple shift," Ronnie protested, outraged. "It was *linen,* for goodness' sake! I bought it at Saks in Washington."

"Then I'd say that's the problem. It looks like Washington, not Mississippi."

"That's ridiculous!"

"Did it look like what the women you met today were wearing?"

Ronnie hesitated. An inescapable vision of Rose in her gaudy dress popped into her mind. "No-o."

"That's the point I'm trying to make. In order to

vote for you, they have to like you. Voters tend to like people they perceive as being like themselves. The key is for you to dress like the people you meet here in Mississippi. Maybe a little nicer, a little neater, but in the same vein."

"It was a perfectly appropriate summer dress," Ronnie protested again.

"Okay, let's analyze this. What you have to ask yourself is, what kind of reaction will your outfit arouse in voters? What you wore today was a simple summer dress, without a doubt. I'll even take your word for it that it was linen. No problem there. But it was purple, sleeveless, body-hugging. Short skirt. High style. Seeing you in it, young male voters probably thought, *Yo, that's one hot mama*. Older male voters probably thought the same thing—and they might have also thought that their wives don't look and dress like you. Older women might have remembered Eleanor, made a mental comparison, and turned against you in solidarity with her. And younger women, even women your age who can wear that kind of short sleeveless dress and look good, might think that they couldn't afford it and resent their perception that the reason *you* can afford it is because you married a rich older man for his money. So in that outfit you can't win."

"So what you're telling me, basically, is that stylish clothes are out."

"No, that's not what I'm saying. I'm saying short, tight, *sexy* stylish clothes are out. I want you to look real pretty, real feminine, but also real conservative. Knee-length or longer skirts. Not much skin showing. Nothing that is tight, or clings. Think something a mom would wear to a PTA meeting. Think something a Sunday-school teacher would wear."

"In other words, think dowdy." Ronnie's voice was dry.

"Think *winning*," Quinlan corrected. "As in, winning the election."

"Do you actually think what I wear is going to make that much difference?"

"It'll help."

"Fine. I'll keep it in mind. All right?"

"That's all I ask." He glanced down at the watch on his wrist. "We've got to start working on getting you home, you know. It's after five o'clock."

Ronnie was surprised by how much she didn't want to return to Sedgely at the moment. Her chest got tight just thinking about it. The memory of what had happened that afternoon came flooding back. Everyone would blame her for this latest public-relations disaster. And there would be reporters lying in wait.

She just didn't feel up to dealing with it.

"Not yet," she said, casting about for some valid means of delaying the inevitable. She patted the swing beside her. "Sit down and talk to me. No advice," she added with a darkling look up at him, "just conversation."

Quinlan hesitated, then let go of the chain and sat down beside her, keeping the swing in motion with his foot, which was shod in the same dark sock and polished loafer he had worn with his suit.

"About what?"

Ronnie smiled at him, pleased at her success. "About you. If you get to ask me questions, then I get to ask you questions. How long have you been married?"

"I'm not married." He was gazing out over the swaying tobacco field, so that his face was in profile to her. Ronnie's gaze wandered down his high forehead, along his straight nose, over his strong chin. He had a nice profile, ascetic yet very masculine.

"But you said . . ." Ronnie clearly remembered him saying that he and Joanie had each married different people.

"I'm divorced."

"Oh." Ronnie thought that over. A possibility made her eyes brighten. "Are you involved with anyone?"

"Why?" He glanced at her, his expression guarded. She thought she detected a faint speculative gleam in his eyes.

"That's not an answer."

"That's the best I'm prepared to do."

"Thea is single—and looking."

"Who's Thea?" His voice went slightly flat.

"My press secretary. You met her today."

Quinlan thought a moment. "Short black hair, short gray skirt, nice legs?"

"That's Thea." Ronnie frowned. "Did you think *her* skirt was too short?"

"No, not really."

"Our skirts were the same length!" Ronnie pounced on the inconsistency.

Quinlan shook his head. "So? *She's* not the wife of a United States senator running for reelection. The stakes are not the same. It doesn't matter if her skirt is short. Nobody is judging her."

"That's what I hate about politics." Ronnie subsided with a sigh. "Everyone is always judging me."

"You should have thought about that before you married His Honor. Why did you, by the way? Is it a great love match?"

Ronnie started to reply, then shook her head. "Oh, no. We're talking about you now, not me. What about your marriage? Was it a love match?"

"Sure." He smiled easily. As his cheeks creased and his eyes crinkled with amusement, Ronnie found herself relaxing and smiling with him. He had a wonderful ability to put people at ease, she thought. Or at least to put her at ease. "At the time. I was twenty-one, in my senior year of college. So was she. We were crazy about each other. She got pregnant, we got married. But it didn't last."

"How long were you married?"

"Twelve years. Oh, the marriage was really over after about five, but we hung on for the sake of the kid."

"You have a child?" Ronnie didn't know why she was taken aback. It was perfectly reasonable that a man his age would have a child, or children. Marsden had two.

"You met him," Quinlan said, surprised. "Mark."

"Oh." Ronnie suddenly saw the exchange she had witnessed between Quinlan and Mark in a whole new light. "I didn't realize he was your son. How old is he?"

"Almost seventeen. He thinks he's thirty." Quinlan's voice was dry.

"Does he live with you?" Ronnie was frowning. She had gotten the impression that Mark lived here, in the farmhouse, with Mrs. McGuire. Did that mean that Quinlan did, too?

Quinlan shook his head. "Not all the time. Christmas, summers, about every third weekend. It's flexible. He knows I'm always available."

"Do you live with your mother, then?"

He shook his head. "I spend a lot of time out here, particularly when Mark's in town. He and Mom are pretty tight, and I don't like to leave him alone in my apartment. But most of my things are at the apartment, so I suppose I live there. I travel a lot. Being on the road several months out of the year is an occupational hazard of what I do for a living."

"Have you been working as a political consultant for long?" Ronnie was suddenly curious as to how such a career happened. As far as she knew, it wasn't something one could choose to major in at college. He must be well known in the field, because Christine Gwen had recognized him.

He cocked an eyebrow at her. "Wondering if I'm any good? I am. One of the best in fact. I've been working on political campaigns since I was in high school."

Ronnie did not doubt that he was telling the truth, but something was off. Political consultants went to the highest bidder, and the best commanded hefty fees, easily six figures a year. But Quinlan struck her as having had to scramble to get this job, as being hard up for work, as hurting for money in fact.

Before she could pursue that line of inquiry further, the screen door opened and Mrs. McGuire stepped out onto the back stoop.

"Tommy?" she called.

"Here," he answered. Her head turned and she found them on the swing.

"Telephone," she said. "Kenny."

Quinlan frowned. "Excuse me." He stood up and headed for the house. Mrs. McGuire came toward Ronnie as he left. They passed each other on the driveway.

"I believe we're going to get a storm." Mrs. McGuire reached the swing and stood beside it for a moment, staring out over the tobacco field. Gathering clouds darkened the northern horizon. The afternoon was still stiflingly hot, but there was an intermittent, cooler breeze that ruffled leaves and hair and whispered of an impending change in the weather.

"I hope so," Ronnie said. "Anything would be a relief from this heat."

"I sort of like the heat." Mrs. McGuire smiled at her. "I guess because it says *summer* to me. Some of my happiest memories are of this farm in the summer. Tommy's daddy and I moved here in the summer. He was born the following summer. His brother was born three summers later. And always, when the boys were growing up, in the summer there were ballgames and cookouts and swimming and happy times."

"It sounds like you have an idyllic life here," Ronnie said.

"Not idyllic, but good. Until Tommy's daddy died anyway. After that, things changed." She sighed. "But that's the way life is, isn't it? The one thing you can count on is change."

The screen door banged, interrupting. Ronnie glanced around to discover Quinlan returning. His ex-

pression was grim. Ronnie felt a twinge of anxiety.
What had occurred to make him look like that?

"Is something wrong?" she asked when he reached
them.

He glanced down at her, then over at his mother,
who was watching him with a gathering frown. It was
obvious that she, too, realized something was amiss.

"Could you excuse us a minute, Mom?" he said.

Mrs. McGuire's eyebrows went up, but she nodded.
"Of course."

"What is it?" Ronnie asked sharply even as the
other woman was crunching her way across the gravel.

Quinlan looked down at her for a second without
replying. His expression told her he was uncomfortable with what he had to say.

"What is it?" she asked again, her hands clasping of
their own accord in preparation for what she felt in her
bones would be bad news.

"My partner, Kenny Goodman, just got off the
phone with a reporter from the *Globe*. It's a weekly
tabloid, in case you haven't ever run across it."

"I know what it is," Ronnie said, her hands twisting
in her lap. It was obvious he was reluctant to continue.
"Go on."

"They want a comment from you on a story they're
getting ready to run." He hesitated, rubbing the side of
his jaw as if uncomfortable. Ronnie simply looked at
him without speaking. Her stomach started tying itself
in knots again. His gaze met hers. "They say they have
a woman who claims to have had a long-standing, intimate relationship with your husband. A prostitute.
She's telling all in the issue that hits the stands next
week."

# Chapter

## 9

"IT MAY NOT BE TRUE," Quinlan offered when Ronnie didn't say anything. She could feel her face whitening, could feel the blood draining from her skin to pool in some deep subterranean place inside her body. She felt dizzy suddenly.

"Are you all right?" Quinlan sat down beside her, his weight making the swing lurch. Ronnie didn't answer. She couldn't. Instead she concentrated on breathing: in, out, in, out.

He repeated the question. This time she managed to nod.

"It's a tabloid, remember. They pay people for stories. This woman's getting a nice chunk of change to smear your husband. Like I said, it may not be true."

Ronnie knew it was true. She knew it without a doubt, in the same deep place inside her body where her blood had pooled. Her gut, she supposed. Wasn't that where gut instinct was supposed to originate? At the idea, she felt a near hysterical bubble of amusement.

She must have looked as terrible as she felt, because

he took her hand. His skin was warm, his fingers long
and strong. With his other hand, he rubbed the back of
her hand gently.

"Miz Honneker?"

"Ronnie." She managed a glance at him, and a faint
if wavering smile. "After everything we've been
through together today, I think we should be on a first-
name basis."

"Ronnie." His hand tightened on hers, the fingers
closing around her palm. His other hand joined the
first, so both hands were clasping one of hers. His expression was both grim and compassionate as he
looked at her. "I know this is a bad thing to dump on
you, and I wish I didn't have to be the one to do it. But
as soon as this breaks, you're going to have reporters
all over you like fleas on a dog. You need to be prepared. You need to be strong, and you need to know
what to say."

Ronnie was having trouble drawing breath. Was it
possible to suffocate from emotional distress alone?
she wondered. His hands holding hers seemed like the
only source of heat in a suddenly icy world. "Oh, God,
reporters. I don't think I can do this. I really don't
think I can."

Quinlan shifted sideways on the swing so that he
faced her. His knees brushed hers. His eyes were intent. "I know this is a shock. I know how you feel."

She made an inarticulate sound of skepticism.

"Oh, I do," he continued. "My marriage ended
when I found out my wife had screwed half the guys in
the county while I was on the road. I know it hurts,
and I know you feel like you've been kicked in the
stomach by a mule. But there's more in the balance

here than just your relationship with your husband."
He gently chafed her hand.

"The election." Ronnie's voice was wooden.

He regarded her steadily. "That's right, the election.
If your husband has any hope of riding this thing out,
you have to stand by him. You have to stand at his side
with your head held high and tell everyone that you
support him no matter what. Your reaction is the key
to how the voters will perceive what's happened: tabloid trash or career-ending scandal. Again, remember,
it may not even be true."

*It is true,* Ronnie thought, but did not say it. "What
if she has proof? What if the woman the *Globe* is talking to can prove that she has been—seeing—Lewis?
She must have some sort of proof, or they wouldn't
dare print it." Her voice was not quite steady, though
her head was clearing. Why the knowledge that a prostitute was claiming a relationship with her husband
shook her so she couldn't imagine. She had known for
some time that he would bed anything female that
breathed.

Ronnie started to tell Quinlan that, but bit back the
words. Whatever the state of their marriage, Lewis was
her husband, and he had an important, well-respected
position in the world. No matter how wounded or angry she was, she couldn't reveal the extent of his wom-
anizing to anyone, not even Quinlan, who was suddenly assuming the dimensions of someone who was
almost her best friend. Loyalty forbade it. So did her
own pride.

"No matter what they have, we can ride it out. It all
depends on the spin we put on it. What you have to do
is stand by him. If there's proof, which I don't know

about one way or another at this point, then we can do a Clinton: Say your marriage is strong *now,* and any problems you may have had have been worked through. Heck, if it comes down to it, His Honor can confess to making a mistake with this woman, shed a tear, and promise to go forth and sin no more, and you can say you have forgiven him. This hooker thing doesn't have to be a fatal blow; the campaign can survive."

"And what if I say to hell with the campaign?" Despite all her rationalizing, Ronnie's voice shook. She had thought she had grown accustomed to Lewis's chronic unfaithfulness, but having it shoved in her face in such a way hurt more than she would have believed possible. Had he ever loved her? The pain that accompanied the question was such that Ronnie forced it from her mind. Perhaps it was the prospect of having what had been, until now, a strictly private agony revealed in such a hugely public way that was upsetting her so. To be humiliated in front of the whole world—imagining it made her feel sick. She pulled her hand from Quinlan's and stood up, walking blindly away.

"That's up to you," he said, falling into step beside her as she moved out of the protective shade of the oak into the blazing sunshine. "Strictly your call."

Ronnie walked on, jaw set, stride brisk. She didn't feel the baking sun, didn't hear the crunch of the gravel driveway give way to the noiseless asphalt beneath her feet. Heat rose in shimmering waves around her, blurring the landscape, but she didn't notice. She saw nothing. She felt as if she had been sucked into a vacuum, as if she were in a separate place, alone, and that none of the rest of the world was quite real.

How had this happened?

As a young girl growing up in Boston, she had always been conscious of the vague sense of unhappiness that hung like a cloud over her family. They never talked to each other. They never laughed together, never cried together, never hugged or kissed or shared anything except the most mundane bits of everyday life. Her parents seemed to have no time for anything except earning a living, and they weren't very good at that. She had looked around at their modest ranch house, which was just like all the other modest ranch houses in the working-class neighborhood where they lived. She had looked at her sisters who were eager to get married and out of the house, and at her discontented mother and her drone of a father and seen the poverty of their lives and been frightened. That kind of existence was not for her. She wanted something different, something *more*. She wanted to be *happy*. How to get what she wanted became the question.

What made for happiness? Money was a key factor, she decided, listening to her parents fight endlessly over its lack. And love. She wanted more than anything to be loved. In a nutshell, what she wanted was a life as different from her parents' joyless existence as she could possibly make it.

Hungrily she read about rich people with their big houses and fantastic careers and exotic travels and dazzling romances, and ached. They seemed so happy, so loved. Their lives seemed so much *larger* than her own, or that of anyone else she knew. They had what she wanted: glamour, excitement, romance.

Desire hardened into determination. *She* could have such a life. She would.

In high school she dated very carefully, wary of a too-intense involvement that might distract her from her goal, and she set her sights on college. At American University she studied hard, and made friends sparingly. Though she dated, she did so with care. Marriage and children had deflated the dreams of many a woman before her. She was determined not to settle for less than having it all.

She thought about law school; she thought about medicine; she thought about a career as a television journalist à la Diane Sawyer or Barbara Walters. Nothing seemed beyond her grasp. Anything—*everything*—was possible.

Then Senator Lewis R. Honneker IV walked into her life. Lewis had it all: he was rich, famous, successful. He was good-looking, in a beefy, twinkly-eyed Irish way, and personable, too, with a hail-fellow-well-met style that promised endless good humor. Even his age was, in her eyes, more of an asset than a liability. His maturity seemed to promise stability, something that had been sorely lacking in her life since her parents' divorce.

He had found her attractive; Ronnie had known that from the beginning.

But at first, there had been Eleanor. Ronnie was not foolish enough to become the mistress of a married man. That was not the life she wanted for herself.

When Eleanor left him, and he started to pursue her in earnest, everything suddenly changed. Lewis could charm the birds out of the trees when he wanted something, and he very seriously seemed to want her. It was easy to fall in love with him, easy to be swept off her feet. Easy to marry him.

Easy to become the second Mrs. Lewis R. Honneker IV.

With the simple act of marrying him, she acquired everything she had ever wanted. Or so she thought at the time.

How, three short years later, could it all have gone so wrong? It was unbelievable, as though a glittering diamond had turned to ashes in her hand.

The only answer was that what she had grasped had never really been a diamond at all.

But everything was still in place, she reminded herself. She still had everything—almost everything—she had dreamed of as a teenager in that cookie-cutter house.

She was *somebody* now. Wife of a U.S. senator. Invited to all the best parties in Washington. Welcome at the White House. Rich, famous, photographed. One of the people she had once read about in magazines.

So her prince had turned out to be a toad. So what? That happened to women all the time. That was reality, which could not have been expected to conform itself totally to a young girl's dream. The key was not to ruin her life over it. This was not the time to let her heart rule her head. To do so would be nothing short of self-destruction.

*Hang tough,* she told herself. And count your blessings.

Her head came up and she stopped walking. The world came into focus again. The black asphalt that uncurled before her shone almost silver in the relentless glare of the sun. Ditches on either side of the narrow road were choked with weeds and wildflowers.

Beyond rickety post-and-wire fences, spotted cattle grazed on crisping fields.

A crow cawed as it flapped overhead. The heat of the pavement seeped through her borrowed flip-flops. The smell of hot tar and manure rose to assault her nostrils. Her skin felt as if it were being broiled by the sun.

A shadow ran alongside hers, longer and broader than her own, unmistakably male in shape and form just as hers was unmistakably female: Quinlan's. She glanced up to find that he was watching her, his eyes narrowed against the brightness. Sunlight bronzed his skin, and gilded his blond hair.

*He's handsome,* she thought as she looked at him.

For a moment she held his gaze. She realized that his future, as well as her own, depended on what she chose to do. His paycheck, lots of peoples' paychecks, came from the campaign. It was within her power to blast that campaign to hell.

"I'll stand by him," she said.

"Attagirl." He smiled, clearly pleased with her. Ronnie despised him in that moment. Like Lewis, political victory was his god. Anything was worth sacrificing on the altar of the almighty election.

"We'll get the Sunday supplement out to do a story on you. You talk about your marriage, about how it's had some rough spots but you've stuck it out. We don't have to be real specific, but they'll get the idea. That kind of approach might even kill two birds with one stone: squash the hooker thing and make you seem more sympathetic at the same time."

"That *is* a happy thought." Ronnie's voice was as

brittle as she felt. Quinlan didn't seem to notice. From the expression on his face, he was busy plotting. *Spin.*

Ronnie pivoted and began walking back the way she had come.

# Chapter
# *10*

*A* HAND, GHOSTLY PALE, grasped the edge of the mauve dust ruffle and lifted it. The intruder was wearing rubber gloves to search the apartment; that was why his hand looked so corpselike. As she realized that, Marla felt her heart give one great explosive leap, like a Thoroughbred racehorse bounding over the finish line. Then it seemed to stop beating entirely as an almost upside-down face popped into view, peering from beneath the bed.

Seen at that angle, the quarter-face (black hair, furrowed brow, bushy black eyebrows, basset-hound eyes) should have been comical. Cowering against the wall in the darkest, most remote space under the bed, Marla felt not the smallest desire to smile.

If he found her, she knew she would die.

Thank God Lissy was not home.

She lay motionless, not breathing, her head pillowed on her arms so that the pale oval of her face would not give her away. She peeped at the man through the veil of bleached blond hair that cascaded over her face and arm. Though she feared attracting his notice by the sheer force of her terrified gaze, she could not bring herself not to look at him. Like a bird targeted by a cobra, she was mesmerized, fascinated, unable to take her eyes off her potential killer.

If she so much as blinked, she feared she would miss the instant in which he saw her and launched his strike.

After an agonizing moment that seemed as long as a year, the ruffle dropped back into place. Still Marla lay unmoving, breathing only when she had to.

Terror almost suffocated her. Her lungs shrieked the need for a long, steadying breath, but she was afraid he might hear. Even the ragged little inhalations she could not control might be enough to bring him down on her, muffled by her arms though they were.

A shadow darkened one area of the dust ruffle. He still stood near the bed. Did he know she was there? Could he somehow feel her presence, just as she tracked his whereabouts with terror-heightened senses more fine-tuned than any radar?

Was he toying with her?

The urge to move, to explode screaming from beneath the bed in a frantic run for the door, was almost overpowering. To put a quick end to this torment, this terror, this blood-freezing, horror-movie-esque scene, would be a relief.

It would also be stupid beyond words.

He would catch her. There was no way she could get out from under the bed, run across the bedroom and living room to the door, get it open, and escape. Not in such close quarters.

Her only hope for survival lay in being as still and quiet as a log beneath the shelter of the bed.

There was a creak as the mattress sagged near the center. Marla stopped breathing.

*He was sitting on the bed.*

Something hit the floor with a soft thump. A pillow, denuded of its case. A corner of it nosed under the dust ruffle, its pink-and-white ticking stripes silent testimony to what was happening.

Bedspread, blanket, and sheets hit the carpet in a wadded heap. Marla could see them through the opening created by the pillow.

The bed shook. Something substantial hit the floor. The mattress.

Would the box spring be next?

Of course it would. If he was searching for something, and there didn't seem to be much doubt about that, he would not forget the box spring.

And if he lifted the box spring, he would see her. There was no doubt about that either.

A ripping sound made her eyes widen. Through the gap created by the pillow, she could see the edge of her quilted, gold-colored mattress, which was now standing on end. She could see a foot clad in a black sneaker, the leg of a pair of navy blue trousers from the knee down—and a hand in a pale rubber glove, wielding a knife.

The knife sliced through the heavy mattress cover as easily as if it had been a sheet of paper.

That same knife would slice through her flesh with just as little effort.

Marla heard a faint, unfamiliar clicking sound, and realized that it was her teeth chattering with fright. She clenched her jaw, grinding her teeth together so tightly they ached.

If a miracle didn't happen in just a few moments she was going to die.

Marla didn't believe in God. She hadn't since her mother died when she was ten, despite all her childish prayers to an Almighty that her pain-wracked mother had embraced with her whole heart. She hadn't believed for fourteen years. She didn't believe now.

In this moment of extreme terror, her instinct was to pray. It was a remnant from her childhood, she knew, when her mother would drag her to church twice a week and supervise her prayers every night.

But she was an adult now, not a child, and she knew that prayers were never answered. There was no one to pray to.

He finished with the mattress. Marla knew because it slumped to the floor, its once-slick brocade surface cut to shreds.

The dust ruffle was yanked away. It went sailing, to land in a wad in the corner near the closet.

Marla could now see everything in the bedroom up to a height of about two feet. She could see the bedclothes, the mutilated mattress, the contents of her dresser drawers, which had been dumped in a heap.

She could see two black-sneakered feet attached to two legs in navy pants, standing beside the bed.

She could see her own reflection in the pair of full-length mirrors that covered the closet's sliding doors.

*No!*

Horror numbed her. *All he had to do was turn around and he could see her too.*

The phone in the living room rang. Its shrillness was

so unexpected that Marla started. It rang twice, three times.

Then the answering machine picked up.

Susan had recorded the message. It was both eerie and eerily comforting to hear her familiar voice on the tape. There was a grinding sound, a pair of clicks (their answering machine had never worked smoothly) and then the beep.

The intruder moved into the living room, the better to hear any message.

Marla's heart leaped again. This was her chance. Maybe her only chance. She slithered out from beneath the bed, elbows and heels digging deep into the thin carpet, and scrambled on hands and knees across the few feet that separated the bed from the closet—the only other possible hiding place in the room—as the caller left a message.

"Susan, this is Paul. Where were you Saturday night? I waited till ten. Call me. Bye."

Paul was a guy Susan had been dating. A nice guy, which was probably why she never had been really interested in him. Susan had been like that.

Reviewing her own history with men, Marla wondered if all women were like that. Was there something about assholes that drew women to them?

There was a click as Paul hung up. Marla shut the closet door another few inches. She dared not close it all the way for fear he would remember it had been partly open.

Quick, soft footfalls told her that the intruder was returning to the bedroom.

Marla felt her stomach lurch. Her throat closed, and

her hands clenched into fists at her sides. Stay calm, she warned herself. Stay calm.

Inside, the closet was a mess of clothes that had been yanked from hangers, and shoes, purses, and other miscellaneous items that had been dislodged from the overhead shelf. Marla burrowed down beneath a pile of some of her favorite summer outfits, made herself as small as possible, and closed her eyes.

A sliding sound and a thump from beyond the door made her shiver: She was as sure as it was possible to be without actually looking that he was lifting the box spring.

# Chapter

## 11

"*N*O, I'M NOT PERFECT. But then, I'm asking
... you to elect me to the United States Senate,
not nominate me for sainthood."

A gust of laughter followed that closing line, as it
had countless times over the two-plus weeks since the
Big One, as the campaign staff called the hooker thing,
hit. Ronnie's own public-relations disaster, the paint-
throwing incident, had been totally eclipsed by the Big
One, which had broken in the *Globe* five days later. By
that time Quinlan had her so programmed about what
to say, she could have spewed out her lines in her sleep.

Standing at the podium, his tanned face wreathed in
a broad smile, Lewis waved in response to thunderous
applause and headed toward his seat, shaking hands
on the way with the governor and the other politicians
on the dais.

Ronnie felt as if her face might break from the rigidity of the smile she forced on it. Seated on the platform
beside Lewis's empty seat, she was on full public view.
Her job was to watch worshipfully as he spoke, clap

enthusiastically when he finished, and smile, smile, smile.

What she really wanted to do was puke. It was all so fake. He was fake. *She* was fake.

The embryonic strategy that Quinlan had hatched on that blistering July afternoon had worked perfectly. He and Kenny Goodman and Lewis and Marsden and a gaggle of staff and consultants had honed it to perfection: Admit the fault, and it had no power to hurt.

They called it pulling a Clinton.

The president had shown how it was done, and by God, the technique was successful, they all now agreed. Lewis was having to work for his money for a while, pressing the flesh across the state at a pace he hadn't felt the need to adopt in years, but the challenge suited him. He was at his best in a tough campaign.

The party line was this: So he had slept with a Washington hooker while his lovely second wife was busy tending the homefires in Mississippi. So what? What it all boiled down to was not a question of character, not a matter of morals, not a betrayal of trust. He had simply made a mistake. Hell, it only proved he was human like everybody else. Boys will be boys, and all that. The tale was good for a poke in the ribs and a knowing chuckle from the men, most of whom seemed to harbor a sneaking admiration for his prowess with the opposite sex. His young wife was a babe, and he had women on the side to boot—for a sixty-year-old grandpa, that wasn't too bad. In certain circles it made him seem more vigorous, more manly. Of course the wife was a little mad at first, but she was over it now,

and their marriage was the stronger for having been
tested.

Or so went the spin.

The whole sordid episode was rapidly being reduced
to nothing more than fodder for jokes. Lewis was even
poking fun at himself in his speeches.

To which Ronnie listened with smiling support,
while inside she felt—what? Not even angry any
longer. Just—empty.

Lewis sat down beside her. Ronnie's hand was in
her lap. He reached over, caught it, and raised it to his
lips. His twinkling hazel eyes—the eyes that she had
once thought promised such honesty and integrity—
met hers and he smiled. The kiss he bestowed on her
fingers was a public-relations gesture, Ronnie knew.
Her stomach knotted. But they were on the dais, the
cynosure of all eyes, the Senator and his wronged
wife. . . .

Ronnie smiled back at him. Adoringly. While her
body went as rigid as if it had turned to stone and her
stomach churned.

What she really wanted to do was spit in his face
and walk out. Forever.

Yes, she had the life she had always wanted—but
the price was growing increasingly hard to pay.

By the time the dinner at the private club was over,
and she had worked the room at Lewis's side, it was
ten o'clock. Her face felt frozen into its perpetual
beaming smile. Her head whirled with the inanities she
had uttered. Her fingers ached from being squeezed.

"You're handling this just beautifully," the wife of
one of Lewis's supporters whispered in Ronnie's ear as
she grasped both Ronnie's hands and leaned forward

to kiss her cheek. The woman was the wife of a judge, what was her name? Ah, JoAnn Hill. Easy to remember because she was so buxom. *JoAnn Hill had twin hills.* Once before, when they had met, Mrs. Hill had been cool to the point of coldness.

She was a contemporary, and acquaintance, of Eleanor's.

In the silver-lining department, at least the scandal had served to shift some of the women to Ronnie's side. They seemed to regard her with a degree of sympathy now. The politicians' wives, especially, had been supportive. Ronnie wondered if they dealt with similar hypocrisy in their own lives. Probably on a daily basis, she decided. Politics, as someone wiser than herself had once said, was a dirty business.

At least now, in the words of Quinlan's other, ongoing attempt at spin, she was one of *them.* A woman struggling with problems like all the rest.

Taking leave of their host, John Heyden of the processed chicken fortune family, Lewis shook his hand warmly, while Martha Heyden bestowed the requisite social peck on Ronnie's cheek and gave voice to the expected pleasantries, none of which Ronnie really heard. Their ritual leave-taking from political functions was so familiar to her by that time that she could put herself on autopilot and still manage to make appropriate replies.

"You keep them from gettin' carried away with that inspection crap, you hear, Lewis?" Heyden said, clapping Lewis on the back as the senatorial party turned toward the door.

"That's what I'm headin' down to Arkansas for, John." Lewis was all affable charm, a big, warm, man's man who had never met a stranger. At least that was the impression he gave. And it was true, Ronnie had to admit. What the world didn't know was how shallow the man was behind the charm, and how incapable of sustaining any kind of real relationship.

With Lewis, what you saw was all you got. The man had no emotional depth.

No wonder he had never initiated a divorce from Eleanor. The situation he'd found himself in with her must have suited him down to the ground.

Finally they were walking out the massive oak doors, across the porch, and down the stairs to the waiting cars. Parked at the head of the driveway under the supervision of Lewis's security detail were two big black limousines, the first of which would whisk Lewis to the private jet that would take him to Little Rock for the all-important chicken-business meeting. The second was for Ronnie. She was scheduled to speak in the morning, to a breakfast gathering of university women, and then be interviewed by the local paper and TV station. That meant spending the night in Tupelo. Rooms for her and her entourage were booked at the Hyatt.

"I'll call you tomorrow, honey." At the foot of the steps Lewis stopped to give Ronnie a quick kiss on the cheek. His lips were warm, the arm he slung around her shoulders strong. Yet it was all for show. The public gesture of affection was typical of him. It meant nothing, though Lewis seemed more pleased with her since the scandal hit than he had been for some time. She had subjected him to no ranting, raving, or screaming. No threats of divorce. No scenes. Just silence in private, and in public a smile.

Just as she smiled now, and said a brief, "Have a good flight."

"You boys take care of my wife now, you hear?" Lewis said in friendly fashion to Tom and Kenny, who would be staying the night at the Hyatt, too, along with Thea, to be on hand for the interviews the next day. Lewis turned away with a wave and, accompanied by his own entourage, entered his limousine. The door shut and seconds later the car pulled away from the curb.

The door to the second limo was open and waiting. A uniformed driver stood holding it. Ronnie walked over to it and slid inside, leaning her head tiredly back against the soft leather and closing her eyes as the others joined her.

"Are you all right, Ronnie?" Thea asked softly. Her press secretary had been a source of support over the past weeks, and Ronnie was grateful to her for it. As a woman, and a friend, she had sensed some of Ronnie's discontent, though Ronnie had been careful to show the same stoic face to her staff that she showed to the public. One never knew who might talk to the press, and under what circumstances.

"I'm just tired." Ronnie didn't bother to open her eyes. If she did, she would have to converse with the lot of them, and she didn't feel up to it. She knew it was irrational, but she felt almost more hostile toward Quinlan than she did toward Lewis. It was Quinlan who had come up with the "spin," after all. Quinlan who had sold the lie she was living to the world, and persuaded her to go along with it. Quinlan who had trotted out polls telling her how to dress, what issues to tackle in her speeches, even what pet name the embattled spouses should call each other in public.

(*Honey* was preferred by voters by a substantial margin over *darling*—too elitist—*sweetheart*—too loverly—and *dear*—too old-fashioned; so, thanks to Quinlan, *honey* was what Lewis now called her every chance he got. For her part Ronnie had managed maybe two *honeys* in two weeks. The endearment stuck in her throat every time she tried to utter it; one of these days she was afraid she might choke on it. If she did, that would be Quinlan's fault too.)

Although Ronnie's eyes were closed and she was doing her best to pretend she was alone in the car, Quinlan spoke to her: "Tomorrow, at that university-women thing, when you're taking questions from the floor, if you're asked about Doreen Cooper . . ."

Doreen Cooper was the name of the prostitute Lewis had visited about once a week for the last year whenever he was in Washington. The one who had tape-recorded her conversations with him, had taken pictures of them together, and told the world all about Lewis's preferences in bed.

". . . just say that you view what happened as a test of your marriage, which is now stronger than ever."

"I know what to say." Ronnie's eyes snapped open, and she fixed an unsmiling gaze on Quinlan, who was sitting directly across from her.

He smiled soothingly at her. Handling her was his job, and he was working hard at it. So far it had been rough going, she knew.

"I know you do," he said. "You're doing just great. But this question-and-answer thing tomorrow is the first time you've spoken in public in such an open forum since the story broke. Just keep repeating the same answer in different ways: 'It was a real test, but it is behind us.' 'Marriage is a challenge at best, and this incident has tested ours. But as a couple we're stronger than ever.' 'The problem is now behind us.' The key words are *test, challenge,* and *behind us.*"

"Do you want me to write them on my palm in ink so I won't forget?" Her sarcasm was punctuated by glittering eyes that fixed him through the gloom. She was getting tired of being fed words over and over again like an idiot parrot.

"Just don't let them throw you." He was imperturbable, just as he had been all along. No matter how angry some of his suggestions made her—and a few had made her plenty angry—he kept his cool. Just knowing that he was "handling" her made Ronnie see red.

"Oh, Tom, can't you go over this with her tomorrow? She's tired." Thea intervened before Ronnie could reply. Thea and Tom were good friends now, having spent a great deal of time in each other's company during the past weeks. No doubt they appreciated the crisis that had brought them together. What a cute how-we-met story it would make! *See, there was this cheating senator and his dimwit wife, and . . .*

"Yeah, Tom, give her a break." Kenny nudged his partner with an elbow. Kenny was good-natured and kind, and Ronnie often got the feeling that he felt a little sorry for her. Quinlan, on the other hand, had been relentless. Say this, say that, do this, do that, wear this, wear that. Hold the Senator's hand. Let your eyes tear up. Be dignified. Smile.

In Ronnie's opinion the campaign theme song, played whenever Lewis or she arrived for a speaking engagement, should be changed from the Trumanesque "Happy Days Are Here Again" to "Stand By Your Man." By now Ronnie could almost hear the words of Tammy Wynette's country lament every time Quinlan opened his mouth.

"Fine," Quinlan said, and subsided.

Thea smiled at him. Ronnie closed her eyes again.

A fruit basket awaited her on a table in her hotel suite. Ronnie was glad to see it, because she was hungry. At dinners such as the one she had just attended, she was never able to eat. She was "on," which was not conducive to digestion.

It was a large basket, clearly expensive, crammed with more oranges and grapes and grapefruit than she, alone, could eat in a month. Probably it was from the group she was addressing the next morning. Stepping out of her shoes—sensible pumps with two-inch heels in a style dictated by Quinlan—Ronnie walked over to it and looked for the card. She found it beneath a bunch of grapes, one of which she popped into her mouth as she pulled the card free.

The grape was sour. Ronnie made a face, and mentally passed on a second one.

*Honey, you're doing great. Love, Lewis,* the card read in a stranger's handwriting.

A *fruit basket?* From *Lewis?* Ronnie felt a bubble of hysterical laughter rise in her throat.

Never since she had met him had he sent her such a thing.

As a gift from a penitent husband to a wronged wife, it was ludicrous.

Of course he had instructed someone on his staff to send a gift to her hotel room. Or maybe a diligent staff member had come up with the idea on his or her own. Something to keep the little woman happy. Something to let her know she was appreciated. Something to keep her toeing the party line.

And be sure and call her honey.

It was even possible that *Quinlan* had initiated it. Although he was supposed to be on *her* team, in deed if not words he had proven to be Lewis's flunky rather than her own.

On second thought Ronnie absolved Quinlan of this particular boneheaded gesture. A fruit basket was far too clumsy a gift to have been sent at his instigation. Quinlan would have taken a poll and found that the optimum gift from an erring senator to his ever-loyal spouse was a fabulous piece of jewelry, or something.

Ronnie walked into the bathroom. The floor was dark green marble tile, and it felt cool beneath her stockinged feet. She leaned over to turn on the taps to the bath—sleep had been illusive lately and she'd found that soaking in a hot bath helped—and turned back to the sink. For a moment she stood motionless, staring at her reflection in the mirror.

She didn't look like herself. Oh, her features were the same, as delicate and elegantly cut and lovely as ever. And her hair was the same deep red, and her eyes the same chocolate brown. But there were shadows under her eyes where she had never had shadows before, and a small vertical crease between her brows that stayed put even when she stopped frowning. Lifting a well-manicured hand—her nails were now tipped in pale pink at Quinlan's instigation rather than the deeper shades she preferred—she pressed the cool pad of her forefinger against the crease, hoping to smooth it out. Eyeing herself critically, Ronnie thought that she looked haggard. Was she starting to show her age—surely twenty-nine did not look so old!—or was it stress? Of course it was very possible that her washed-out appearance could be attributed to the pale pinks and soft browns of her makeup, colors she never chose for herself but that had been recommended by the image consultant Quinlan had hired.

Just as the beige dinner suit she was wearing had been recommended by some cohort of Quinlan's. Polls showed that earth tones and pastels had the most appeal for Mississippi voters, he had told her.

Well, hooray for Mississippi voters. Earth tones and pastels did nothing for her.

But here she was, wearing them.

No wonder she didn't look like herself, Ronnie thought. She *wasn't* herself any longer. She was some creature Quinlan and Lewis and the rest of them had conjured, the ultimate political wife, with everything from her clothes to her makeup to her remarks dictated by polls.

They had turned her into a Stepford wife.

No, Ronnie corrected, she had allowed herself to be turned into a Stepford wife.

Bright, beautiful, ambitious Veronica Sibley, as she had been before she married, had been all but erased from existence. In her place was Mrs. Lewis R. Honneker IV, the Senator's wife.

Ronnie suddenly realized just what the price was for her place in the sun: Nothing less than her life.

Mrs. Lewis R. Honneker IV was no more real than a Barbie doll. She was a plastic creation who could be manipulated at will to suit someone else's needs.

How long had it been since she had felt any kind of genuine emotion? Ronnie asked herself. How long since she had really laughed, or hugged someone and meant it, or had sweet, hot sex?

Plastic creations didn't need to feel.

Ronnie realized that she did.

She had had it with being a Barbie doll. She wanted to be real again.

She wanted to *feel*.

Ronnie stared at her reflection for a few seconds longer. Then she turned, bent, shut off the bathwater, and padded across tile and carpet to her suitcase.

In anticipation of possible downtime while traveling, the staff at Sedgely had standing instructions to include a casual outfit or two along with her working clothes.

Ronnie found a T-shirt and a pair of jeans, and pulled them from the suitcase. She laid the clothes on the bed, then hesitated, looking down at them. She didn't feel in the mood to wear jeans. She felt like wearing something—outrageous. For a moment she pondered. As the solution came to her, she searched her suitcase again for the sewing kit the staff invariably included. She located it, extracted a pair of scissors, and turned back to the bed, a small smile curving her lips.

Fifteen minutes later, looking far different from the proper society matron who had entered the suite, she stepped out into the plush-carpeted hall and strode purposefully toward the elevators.

The door to her suite shut behind her with a final-sounding click.

# Chapter

## 12

TOM DIDN'T KNOW what time it was when the phone beside his bed began to ring. All he knew was that it was somewhere deep in the foggy mists of night.

"What the . . . ?" As he was jolted awake, he cursed, grabbing for the source of the shrill sound and nearly knocking over both the lamp and the clock radio on the bedside table in the process. It was pitch-dark in his hotel room; he might as well have been blindfolded for all the help his eyes were as he floundered around for the phone.

With one hand he righted the lamp and pushed the clock back onto the table—2:25 the time blinked at him as his other hand fumbled onto the phone, crawled over it, and at last snatched up the receiver. The blessed cessation of the shrill ringing was his reward.

"Hello?" he growled into the mouthpiece.

"You sleeping?" Kenny asked. Tom scowled at the familiar voice.

"Not now," he said, rolling onto his back and blinking up into the darkness. "What's up?"

"There's a problem."

"Why am I not surprised?" Tom sighed. "What is it? His Honor found himself another cutie?"

"Nope. It's the missus."

"The missus?" For an instant Tom was at a loss. Then his eyes opened wide. "Mrs. Honneker?"

"She's downtown at the Yellow Dog—a bar. Drinking like a fish and dancing with every guy who asks her. I gather she's looking pretty hot too."

"What!?" Tom sat bolt upright in bed, wide awake now. He felt for the lamp, located its switch, and flipped it on. The room was flooded with light. Tom blinked. "How do you know?"

"A reporter thought he spotted her and phoned the hotel here, trying to confirm whether or not it was her. When she didn't answer, the call was put through to my room."

"Jesus!" A thought occurred to Tom. "Maybe it isn't her. Did you check?"

"I checked. She got in a taxi and headed out about half an hour after we arrived. Doorman heard her ask the driver about local nightspots. I'd say it's about a ninety-nine-point-nine-percent chance that the redhead at the Yellow Dog is our gal."

"Jesus H. Christ!" Tom groaned, flinging back the covers and swinging his legs over the side of the bed. "We've got to go get her. What in God's name is she doing? What did you tell that reporter?"

"That Mrs. Honneker is in her hotel room sleeping like a baby."

Tom groaned again, rubbing the bridge of his nose

in an almost certainly futile attempt to ward off the
Excedrin headache that threatened. "That won't hold
'em for long. Give me ten minutes, and meet me in the
lobby."

"Uh—Tom."

"What?" He was impatient now, on his feet, grabbing at the suit he had discarded just a couple of hours
before. Draped over the back of a chair, it wouldn't be
too badly wrinkled, and anyway he didn't care. The
important thing was to get the pesky woman under
lock and key fast, before anyone could prove it was
her. Or worse, take pictures.

The mere idea made him nauseous.

"I—uh—I'm kind of busy."

"You're *busy?* In the friggin' *middle of the night?*
When we're dealing with a crisis? What in Jehosh-
aphat's name are you doing?" Tom balanced the phone
between his shoulder and his ear and shoved one leg
into his pants.

"I've—got company."

"You've got company?" For a millisecond that
didn't compute. Then light dawned. Pants still only
half on, Tom stood stock-still, rigid with shock. "A
*woman?* Are you telling me you've got a woman in
your room? What about friggin' *Ann?*"

Ann was Kenny's wife, and a good friend of Tom's.
This just kept getting better and better. At the rate
things were going, any minute now the Senator would
come bursting into his room, his plane having been
fogged in or something, demanding to know where his
wife was.

"Can we talk about it tomorrow?" Kenny sounded
sheepish, as well he should.

"Damn right we'll talk about it tomorrow." Tom recollected himself and started pulling on his pants again. "I can't believe this. Any of it."

"Anyway, you don't need me. The way I see it, this is a kind of delicate situation. It'd be better if you fetched the lady out of that bar alone. Less embarrassing all around. It'll attract less notice if anybody's watching, and in the morning everybody can pretend not to know what she got up to during the night."

"What do you mean, everybody? Never mind. I don't want to know. Damn it to hell, Kenny, you're a married man. With a bad heart. I'm gonna rip a strip off your hide in the morning."

With that Tom slammed down the receiver. Unbelievable. The whole thing was unbelievable.

And it was happening on his watch, every unbelievable bit of it.

Again.

He was on the road in five minutes flat. Fortunately he didn't have to fiddle around with cabs. In preparation for getting his client to her various appointments the next day, he had rented a car. It was coming in handy now.

Not wanting to alert the hotel staff to his mission, Tom looked for an all-night gas station as he drove, found one on a corner a block away, pulled in, and asked directions to the Yellow Dog. A sleepy attendant had no problem directing him. It was the best-known bar in town.

It was also, he discovered as he cruised past the darkened storefronts that lined Main Street, impossible to miss. A huge yellow neon dog flashing off and on above a square, two-story converted warehouse was a dead giveaway.

He pulled into the crowded parking lot just across the street. Ignoring a couple intertwined on a car hood in the parking lot and another groping each other on the sidewalk, he headed toward the glass double doors at the front of the building.

The bass pulse of the music could be heard as far away as the street. When the doors swung open to admit him, the volume of sound almost made him take a step back.

"Five-dollar cover." The price of admission was shouted at him from a booth just inside the door by the attendant on duty, a beefy kid not long past college age who looked as if he could have made some money as a pro wrestler. A crowd of young women in miniskirts and their equally young-looking, jeans-clad escorts pushed past him on their way out the door as he extracted a five-dollar bill from his wallet and handed it over.

"We close in an hour," the kid mouthed over the music, his expression semiapologetic as he took Tom's money and stamped his hand with a grinning dog in glow-in-the-dark ink. A glance over the kid's head found a large clock. It was two-fifty A.M.

At nine A.M. she was scheduled to speak to a women's group; then there were the press interviews at noon.

Jesus H. Christ.

Tom nodded, and at last was allowed to pass through the narrow doorway into the dark, pulsing cavern beyond.

"One?" A waitress, slim and blond with a bare,

tanned midriff under a clingy little knit top, held up a single forefinger. She, too, had to shout to be heard over the music.

Tom nodded, and followed her miniskirted backside into the snake pit of writhing, strobe-illuminated bodies that was the club. The dance floor, as far as he could tell, was in the middle of the room, and it was full. But that didn't seem to matter a whit to anyone. Patrons were dancing everywhere, in the aisles, in front of the bar, even some on tables. The roving strobes zoomed around the room seemingly at random, as blinding and disorienting as photographers' flashbulbs as they illuminated their victims for a second or two and moved on.

Thank God, the place was so dark and weirdly lit that it was almost impossible to tell male from female at a distance of more than five feet, much less recognize anyone. No wonder the reporter had to call to confirm it was her.

Maybe, Tom thought with a last lingering trace of hope, it wasn't. Maybe he was on a wild-goose chase, or was even the victim of a gag set up by Kenny.

Please God.

The waitress stopped before a tiny round table with a white marble top. For form's sake, Tom sat down in one of the uncomfortable ice-cream-parlor-style chairs and ordered a Heineken, the single word bellowed at the top of his lungs and lost in the cacophony before it had so much as escaped his lips. The waitress, apparently adept at lipreading in the dark, nodded and took herself off.

The sheer volume of sound was mind-blowing.

Cliché or not, the phrase *he couldn't hear himself think* was nothing short of the literal truth. Tom couldn't.

He shook his head to clear it, fought the urge to clap his hands over his ears, and began a methodical visual search of the place. Besides his errant client, he also sought reporters spying on her. Of course that only worked if the reporter was someone he knew; but just as likely it wasn't.

As he had already noted, it was almost impossible to recognize anybody. Tom gave up almost immediately on the reporters. After a couple of minutes spent squinting at first one slim young body and then another, Tom realized that in order to find his primary quarry he was going to have to go from table to table and from dancing couple to dancing couple, leaning close and staring intently into the face of nearly each and every person present. The only ones automatically disqualified were those obviously too heavy, or sporting a buzz cut. Even short haircuts could be misleading; she might have put her hair up. Or be wearing a baseball cap.

Who knew?

The waitress came back with his bottle of beer, placing it on the table in front of him on top of a tiny paper cocktail napkin. With a shouted "Thanks" Tom extracted his wallet and fumbled around for a bill, which he handed over with a wave indicating she should keep the change. She illuminated the money with a quick flash from a tiny flashlight, which dangled from a chain around her wrist. From the wattage of the smile she turned on him, Tom guessed the bill was a ten or twenty instead of the five he'd intended to give her.

Blast it, he didn't have that kind of money to throw away.

But that was the least of his worries, Tom thought, downing half his beer in one gulp preparatory to standing up and starting his search in earnest. Finding out if—

There she was. There was no mistaking that red hair as the light hit it. She was dancing, gyrating really, with a jeans-clad kid who didn't look much older than Mark. Her head was thrown back, and she was laughing as she danced. Her teeth gleamed blindingly white in the blaze of ultraviolet light. She was wearing cut-off jeans, the real short kind with raggedy fringe around the thighs, a tight black T-shirt, and high-heeled sandals that made her legs seem two yards long. As Kenny had warned him, she was looking hot. The kid looked enthralled.

Tom stood up, filled with a surprising degree of reflexive anger, as if she were betraying *him*. Which was stupid. She was his job, not his wife.

Deliberately he gulped the rest of his beer, and considered his options. His first impulse was to go over there, wrap a hand in that too-red hair and drag her out of the club by it, but that had to be discarded. First, it would attract too much attention, and second, he could not manhandle the woman who was his ticket back into the political big time. It wouldn't be good for business.

He was going to have to use all his wile to get her out of there without attracting undue notice. The first thing to do, obviously, was to get rid of the kid whose hands were even now sliding around her waist. A minute or two more, and Tom had little doubt they'd be cupping her butt. And from all appearances, the lady seemed to be loving it.

It didn't require genius to figure out that Mrs. Lewis R. Honneker IV had come out tonight with every intention of getting laid.

*Sorry, darling,* Tom thought with an ironic twist of his lips, and headed toward his quarry.

By the time Tom reached them, she had her arms around the kid's neck and was dancing against him in a way that would make a priest think dirty thoughts. And from the look on his face, the kid wasn't even vaguely considering the priesthood.

Tom tapped him on the shoulder. Not surprisingly, he was ignored. Tom tapped a little harder—more of a shove, really—and at the same time detached one of his client's cool, slender hands from the kid's neck and tugged her toward him.

Over the kid's shoulder she blinked at him in surprise. The kid turned toward him with murder in his eyes.

Tom really couldn't blame him. He'd want to murder anyone who broke in on that too.

"What the—?" the kid began angrily.

"My wife," Tom yelled, flashing the huge square diamond and thin gold band on the lady's left ring finger in the kid's face.

"Oh." The kid's expression altered ludicrously. His arms dropped and he backed away, holding his hands up in front of him in an age-old gesture of surrender. "Sorry, man. She didn't say she was married."

Tom nodded as the kid disappeared. The slim hand he was grasping detached itself and slid around his neck, to be joined by its fellow.

The faint scent of some expensive perfume teased his nostrils as she plastered herself against him. In his arms she felt slender, supple, feminine and very, very sexy. With a sense that he was somehow losing control of the situation, Tom set his hands firmly on either side of her waist and frowned down into a pair of come-hither chocolate-brown eyes.

# Chapter

## 13

"*L*IAR," RONNIE MOUTHED, not missing a beat of the dance. Quinlan's body felt hard and strong and headily masculine against hers as she moved against it; his neck was warm beneath her hands. Having him show up here was a surprise, but not a bad one, she decided. From the first she'd considered her own personal political consultant to be a very attractive man.

"There's a reporter here," he said into her ear. His breath smelled faintly of beer. "We need to leave."

Ronnie took advantage of the dip of his head to press closer to him. His chest felt good against her breasts. He was bigger than she was, wider, taller. His cheek as it brushed hers was rough with stubble. His hands on her waist were strong. He was wearing the same suit he had worn earlier in the evening, a dark navy pinstripe. She'd noted at the time that it emphasized his build, showing off his broad shoulders and flat stomach, his narrow hips and muscular thighs. The only fault she'd been able to find with his appearance at the dinner was that, all buttoned and pressed and unsmiling, he had looked uptight. Now he had five-o'clock stubble, his white shirt was open at the collar, and he wasn't wearing a tie.

Ronnie felt herself begin to tingle.

"Did you hear what I said?" When she didn't reply, his voice in her ear turned impatient.

Ronnie shook her head and clung closer. "I want to dance."

He pulled back to look down into her face. She smiled sensuously up at him, rubbing her body against his as she moved with the music.

His frown deepened into a full-fledged scowl, and he leaned forward to speak into her ear again. "You've been drinking."

It was an accusation, tinged with an undertone of outrage, and it made Ronnie smile.

"You're right," she agreed, and tightened her hold on him. He swung her around, reflexively she thought, to keep from being bumped by the couple on their left. People were dancing all around them, close together, doing everything but making love on the dance floor.

The procession of boys she had danced with earlier hadn't done much to fire up her libido. She hadn't really wanted to sleep with any of them. But Quinlan was something else again.

How would he be in bed? she wondered. Just considering the possibilities was enough to send heat shooting clear down to her toes.

It had been a long time since she'd felt like that about a man.

"Let me take you back to the hotel." His voice in her ear was coaxing now. Ronnie liked that. She snuggled closer.

"Maybe," she said. "After we dance."

"Ronnie . . ."

It was the first time he had called her by her given name since the day she had met him. Usually he didn't call her anything at all, just shot "suggestions" at her. When he had to address her as something, it was as *Miz Honneker,* in an ironic-sounding southern drawl that increasingly made her want to hit him. Ronnie rewarded him now by stroking the nape of his neck with a forefinger. He stiffened.

His hands were still on either side of her waist. They tightened. His fingers dug into her middle. She got the impression that he was trying to work some space between them.

*Not a chance, buster,* she told him silently, and tightened her arms around his neck. Her hips pressed against his. She discovered that he was as affected by her proximity as she was by his.

He'd found her attractive from the beginning. She had experienced the admiration of too many men not to recognize the signs.

"Tom." She purred his name. It felt right on her tongue. Just as he felt right in her arms.

"We have to go." He was talking in her ear again.

"Go if you want. I'll find somebody else to dance with me."

They were barely moving now, just swaying in time to the pulsing beat. The fine tropical wool of his suit felt scratchy against her bare arms and legs. The sensation was erotic, as though she were naked in his arms while he remained fully clothed. Other couples pressed against them on all sides, limiting movement. Not that anyone seemed to care. Ronnie discovered that they had somehow worked their way into a dark corner not too far from a door discreetly marked Exit. Though there were people all around, the sense of being alone with him was intense.

Her arms wrapped tighter around his neck. Her fingers stroked the warm skin of his nape. His broad shoulders were curved protectively around her, and her breasts snuggled against his chest. Her hips brushed his hips, her thighs pressed his thighs. The last holdout against a totally enveloping embrace were his hands on either side of her waist.

If he had asked, she would have told him that resistance was futile.

She pressed closer, until every inch of her body from shoulder to knees was in contact with his. Letting go of his neck, she slowly slid her hands over his shoulders and down his arms to his wrists. Tugging, she removed his hands from her waist and pulled them around her body. He did not fight her, though she got the impression that his capitulation was reluctant. *Too bad*, she thought, luxuriating in the feel of his arms around her as her hands slid back up to lock behind his neck. A faint, satisfied smile curved her lips, and she rested her head on his shoulder.

"Do you realize it's after three a.m.? You have to give a speech at nine in the morning." He was scolding now, but she didn't mind: His breath was warm on her ear. As if to give the lie to his tone, his arms were wrapped securely around her body, holding her close against him.

"Maybe," she said, looking up at him with a tiny smile. The hard angle of his jaw was just about at the

level of her nose. It was dark with stubble, and entic-
ingly male.

"What do you mean, 'maybe'?" He sounded tense
as he spoke in her ear again. His face brushed her
cheek; his unshaven jaw felt abrasive against the softness of her skin.

"Maybe I'm not going back." She tilted her head,
rubbing her cheek against that hard masculine jaw. It
smelled faintly of—what? Some sort of shaving cream
maybe? Something with a hint of menthol. It was also,
she discovered when she tasted it with her tongue, a
tad salty. She turned the taste into a kiss, pressing her
lips against the bristly skin just beneath his jawline.

He made an inarticulate sound, and his head jerked
back, putting the spot she'd kissed out of reach of her
mouth. His hands returned to either side of her waist,
gripping firmly, and this time he succeeded in putting a
little space between them.

It seemed to take him a minute to get beyond that.
Ronnie watched him take one deep breath, then another. Dark and unreadable, his gaze met hers, and
held for an instant. His jaw hardened. Then he leaned
forward to speak in her ear again. There was a kind of
forced jocularity to his tone that tickled her funny
bone. Try though he might, he wasn't fooling her. He
was as turned on by her as she was by him.

"No more of that, now, you hear? Look, you've had
a hard couple of weeks, I know. So you went out tonight to blow off a little steam. I understand. Tomorrow everything will look different. Let me take you
back to the hotel and—"

"And what?" This time she kissed his ear, drew the
lobe into her mouth, and bit down lightly. Where his

jaw had been hard and bristly, his earlobe was soft and tender.

"Damn it, Ronnie, stop it!" He jerked his ear out of reach and pulled his head back to glare down at her. Which simply left his neck exposed. She smiled, and ran her mouth down the warm brown column.

"How much have you had to drink?" His voice was rough, and his body felt taut as a coiled spring against her. His fingers dug into her waist so hard they almost hurt. Ronnie could feel the pounding of his pulse against her lips.

"Not that much," she rose up on tiptoe to whisper in his ear. Tightening her arms around his neck, she explored the delicate whorls with her tongue. He shuddered.

"That's it. We're out of here." There was steely determination in his voice, and in the hands that came up to pull her arms from around his neck.

"I don't want to go," she said, resisting as his hands shackled her wrists and pulled them down. Her arms were imprisoned between them, his hands circling her wrists, hers pressed flat against his chest, creating a small degree of space between their bodies. She met his gaze. "And I'll make the biggest scene in the world if you try to make me. If you don't want to play, fine. I won't have any trouble finding someone who does."

"Is that what you want? To play?" He was standing still now, no longer making any pretense of dancing. His eyes gleamed at her through the darkness. He looked flushed, ruffled, angry.

Ronnie smiled up at him, a small, deliberately seductive smile. And nodded.

His gaze held hers for an instant. His face was hard, his jaw set. Then he muttered something under his breath that sounded like "damn." His hands tightened around her wrists, and his mouth came down on hers.

# Chapter 14

*R*ONNIE HAD FORGOTTEN what it felt like to be kissed like that. His lips were hard and hot and angry—and hungry. She opened her mouth under his and kissed him back and felt her body rev up with all the excited, searing passion of a horny seventeen-year-old.

He pulled his mouth from hers and looked down at her. She smiled up at him with dreamy anticipation. His hands tightened around her wrists. His eyes were hooded, restless, gleaming. His jaw was tight.

"That's it. That's all the playing I'm prepared to do on a public dance floor with a reporter lurking somewhere around. You're coming with me."

"Where to?"

"Where do you think? Back to the hotel." He sounded savage.

"Goody." Ronnie was smiling as she let him pull her toward the exit. "Back to the hotel" was ripe with possibilities.

The exit he chose was the one nearest them, a rear door that opened onto an alley. He kept one hand locked on her wrist as he propelled her around the building, then across the street to the parking lot, which was dark except for the yellow circles of illumination provided by security lights in each corner. As he walked he kept glancing around, obviously on the alert for something. The reporter he kept talking about? Ronnie didn't care.

There were other couples there who were also apparently in the process of leaving the Yellow Dog. Several had paused at various spots between the parking-lot entrance and their cars to embrace. Ronnie eyed them enviously. Her lips still tingled from Tom's kiss.

She wanted him to do it again. In fact she intended to see to it that he did, and a lot more besides.

He pulled her around the rear of a pale-blue subcompact, opened the passenger door, pushed her down into the seat, and reached over her to secure the lap belt. Ronnie took advantage of his proximity to run her hands over his chest beneath his suit coat. The white shirt felt cool and smooth; his body beneath was warm and muscular.

The seat belt clicked into place. His gaze met hers. Then he kissed her mouth, quick and hard. Ronnie didn't even have time to respond before he withdrew and slammed the car door shut.

Ronnie settled into her seat, watching him as he walked around the front of the car.

He got in beside her, shut his door, fastened his lap belt, and sent her a grim glance.

"Tom." She tried out his name again, smiling at him. Her head rested against the seatback, and her face was turned toward him.

"Ronnie," he said in not nearly as loverly a tone as

she had used. Then, "Do you have any idea what that's going to look like if anybody in there was taking pictures and if those pictures hit the papers?" He inserted the key into the ignition and started the car.

"You mean when you kissed me?" His profile was really very handsome, she decided. *He* was very handsome. Especially his mouth, which was sensuous in a way she had hitherto failed to notice.

"That, and the rest of it." He shot her a glance she couldn't read, and reversed out of the parking space.

"If they print a picture of you kissing me, it's going to look like we're having an affair," she said. "The rest of it was only dancing."

"Is that what it was?" Tom's voice was dry. "Luckily I don't think a photographer could take recognizable pictures under those conditions. Damn it, Ronnie, one more scandal will sink this campaign." He shifted the car into drive and headed for the parking-lot entrance.

"I don't care."

He glanced at her again. His face was harder now, his gaze more dispassionate. She had the impression that he was exercising tremendous self-control. "You will in the morning. When the booze wears off."

"I told you I didn't have that much to drink."

He pulled out into the street. His answer was derisive. "That's what you told me."

"Don't you believe me?"

"No."

"You think I'm coming on to you because I'm drunk." Her words were measured.

"Something like that, yes."

"Are you drunk?"

"I had one beer."

"So you're not drunk?"

"No."

"You kissed me. Twice."

The look he sent her way should have made Ronnie cringe in her seat. Instead she crossed her long, bare legs very deliberately at the knee, and smiled at him.

"Look, *Miz Honneker,* here's the situation: This campaign is just coming back from the brink of being derailed by a sex scandal. The voters seem willing to overlook your husband's lapse, they are liking you better because of the way you've handled it, and all in all things are looking pretty good. The key now is not to blow it. Your going barhopping falls under the category of blowing it. There are reporters everywhere, and you can take it as gospel that one of them is going to spot you. In fact you were spotted. The reporter just wasn't one-hundred-percent certain it was you. But you can bet your bottom dollar that the guy who thinks he saw you in the Yellow Dog will be at your nine-o'clock speech to see if you look like you got a good night's sleep or were out partying till four a.m. Unless he's already somehow managed to positively ID you, which means he'll have a nice lead for tomorrow's paper and the campaign is gone to hell."

He turned left at an intersection. Tugging at the hem of her shorts, which had ridden up to nearly the tops of her thighs, Ronnie shifted her legs again. The movement earned them a searing sideways glance.

"Do you have a girlfriend?" Ronnie asked, not the least bit interested in the possible ramifications of her night out at the moment.

"What? Why?"

"I just wondered, that's all."

"Did you hear anything I just said?" He sounded exasperated.

"I heard every word. And I asked you a question: Do you have a girlfriend?"

His eyes narrowed. "Asking for Thea again?"

Ronnie shook her head. "This time I'm asking for me."

His hands tightened around the steering wheel. His lips compressed. Ronnie got the impression that he was weighing several options before replying.

"Yes, I have a girlfriend."

"What's her name?"

He hesitated, shooting her a hooded glance. "Diane."

"Is she local?"

"She lives in De Kalb, near my mother."

"Why haven't I met her? You've practically lived with us for the past three weeks."

"Because I like to keep my private life separate from my professional life, that's why." His reply was short.

"Don't they ever get mixed together? Your private life and your professional life?"

"Not if I can help it."

"What happens if you can't help it?" Her question was soft, with an almost baiting quality to it.

"I can help it." His voice was grim.

There was a pause as he stopped at a four-way light and waited through the changes. A police car on their right cruised past them, and then it was their turn.

"Is she pretty?"

"Who?"

"Your girlfriend. Diane."

"Yes, she's pretty."

"As pretty as me?"

He glanced at her, clearly exasperated again. "No, she's not as pretty as you. Who is? Now, would you please shut up and let me drive? All we need is to get pulled over."

His voice was rough. Ronnie smiled and was obediently silent. This late at night, or early in the morning, really, the streets were practically deserted. The business establishments were dark and empty as well, except for an all-night gas station cum minimart. As they drove past it, Ronnie saw the multistory rectangle that was the Hyatt. It stood on the next corner.

"We're here," she said.

"Thank God."

"You sound like you want to be rid of me."

"I'll be glad to get you safely back to your room." He pulled into the Hyatt's parking lot, found a spot near a side entrance, stopped the car, and got out. Ronnie waited while he came around to open her door. When she didn't move but simply sat looking up at him with a small smile, he gave her a very hard look, leaned in, and undid her seat belt.

No kisses on his part. No touches on hers.

"Let's go," he said, straightening, and catching her hand.

"Don't you kind of feel like a warden escorting a prisoner back to jail?" Ronnie asked wryly as she let him pull her from the car.

"No, I feel like a very lucky political consultant who has just managed to head off one hell of a scandal by the skin of his teeth. I hope." He shut the car door and turned to face her, still holding her hand. Surprised to find that she was slightly unsteady on her feet, Ronnie leaned against the side of the car. The place he had chosen to park was a good distance from the nearest security light and was consequently thick with shadows; overhead a blue-tinged moon floated high in a sea of stars. A warm breeze blew a strand of her hair across her mouth. Ronnie pulled it free. He watched her, his expression suddenly intent. Their gazes met. His fingers tightened around hers at the same time as his lips compressed.

Before Ronnie could say anything, he turned away, pulling her after him as he headed toward a dimly lit side door.

"Why are we going in this way?" It was really very hard to walk fast in three-inch heels, Ronnie discovered.

"In case anybody's had the bright idea of staking out the lobby. To catch you coming in from your night on the town."

"I never thought of that."

"Apparently not."

Tom used the key card to his room to open the side door and ushered her through it. It closed behind them with a soft click. The long corridor in which they found themselves unfurled through a double line of closed doors. Semicircular sconces glowed dimly against beige-and-green wave-patterned wallpaper. The forest-green carpet underfoot muffled their footsteps. A deep hush lay over everything, reminding Ronnie irresistibly of Sleeping Beauty's castle after the Wicked Fairy cast a spell over everyone in it. She and Tom might as well have been the only two people alive.

Tom held her hand as they walked down the hallway. Though there was nothing romantic about his grip—Ronnie got the feeling he was hanging on to her for insurance, just in case she should get it into her head to try to run away—she curled her slender fingers around his larger, broader hand and was content.

She wanted him, and she meant to have him. His mind might temporarily resist, but his body was already hers for the taking. She knew as well as she knew that it was hot in the summer in Mississippi that he burned for her just as she burned for him.

The hotel's main elevators rose in a central core off the lobby. Secondary elevators were positioned near the back of the hotel, one in each of three wings. Tom stopped in front of one of these and pushed the button. Seconds later the door slid open with a *ding*. He stepped inside, pulling Ronnie with him, and pressed the button for the sixth floor.

"My room is on seven," Ronnie protested as the door shut and they started to rise.

"We're going to walk up the last flight. Just in case. It wouldn't be real hard for a good reporter to get your room number. I don't want somebody surprising us as we get off the elevator."

"Careful, aren't we?"

"You better believe it."

The motion of the elevator affected her balance, and she staggered a little. His grip on her hand tightened, steadying her.

"So you didn't have that much to drink, eh?" The question was sarcastic. Ronnie shook her head stubbornly, hanging on to his hand for dear life; her head was starting to swim.

Their clasped hands brushed her bare thigh below

her shorts. That tiny touch sent heat shooting through her body. He felt it too. She could see it in his eyes.

"What in God's name are you wearing?" His gaze found her denim cutoffs, and slid from them on down her legs. Ronnie knew she had nice legs, long and slim and tanned. Her feet, almost bare in strappy, high-heeled sandals, were very pretty too, long and slender with coral painted toes.

"They're called shorts," she said as the elevator reached its destination and stopped.

"They're short, all right." He looked her over, his eyes darkening. "Nice getup for a senator's wife."

"A senator's wife is no different from any other woman."

"Yes, she is. Her husband has to keep getting elected."

They stepped out into the sixth-floor hallway. A quick glance around located a lighted exit sign over a doorway next to the elevator. Tom headed through it and into the stairwell, and Ronnie, having little choice in the matter since he still held her hand, followed him.

As Ronnie looked up at the double flight of stairs facing them, her knees threatened to sag.

"Do you really think all this is necessary?" she asked. "I feel like I went to sleep and woke up in a James Bond movie."

"Better safe than sorry." He let go of her hand and indicated that she should precede him. With a sigh Ronnie started to climb the stairs. She went slowly; each step required increasing effort. The metal hand-rail was cool to the touch, and she clung to it; the concrete steps amplified the sound of their footsteps. As she reached the seventh-floor landing, she glanced back. Tom's attention was riveted on the movement of her backside and bare legs.

He must have felt her watching him, because he looked up. Naked lust glinted in his eye for an instant, as unmistakable as the cold rush of air-conditioning sliding under the stairwell door to curl her toes. Then his brows snapped together and he glanced away. Seconds later he stepped up on the landing beside her.

"Do you have your key?" His voice was gruff.

Ronnie nodded, unzipping the small leather pouch that hung from her belt and extracting the key card.

He took it, motioned to her to be silent, and quietly opened the solid metal door. A quick glance out into the hall obviously revealed something amiss. He froze, then slowly, carefully, eased the door shut. Close as she was, Ronnie heard only the faintest click.

"What?" she asked as he let loose with a string of profanities under his breath.

"They're staking out your room. Two of them, a woman and a man, probably a reporter and photographer. Shit. *Shit.*"

"You're kidding."

"Do I look like I'm kidding?" The grimness of his expression said it all. "What they're doing is smart, I have to give them that. If they'd waited in the lobby, you could have given them the slip. We *would* have given them the slip. But if you're out, you have to go back to your room sooner or later. It's a no-lose situation for them. If you're in there, you have to come out. If you're out, you have to go in. Either way they get what they want. *Shit.*"

"If they don't have any pictures of me at the nightclub, they can't prove where I've been. Maybe I just went for a walk."

"At three a.m.? In beautiful downtown Tupelo? Dressed like *that?*" His gaze ran over her, and he shook his head. Then he grabbed her hand and started back down the stairs. "Come on."

"Where to?" Ronnie was perfectly willing to go with him anywhere. To tell the truth, she didn't find the idea of reporters waiting outside her hotel room door nearly as upsetting as he seemed to. What did it matter? She almost welcomed the idea that the campaign would be over. She was sick of pretending.

"My room. Where else?" Tom sounded grim. Ronnie smiled.

His room was on the fourth floor. They walked down the stairs—Tom didn't want to chance any stray elevator sounds that could possibly attract attention—and along the silent hallway. He let go of her hand to insert his key card into the lock, then stood back to let her precede him into the room.

Unlike her accommodations, his was a run-of-the-mill hotel room: brown carpet, beige walls, two uncomfortable-looking, orange-upholstered chairs flanking a round table in front of a single window with closed, multicolored drapes, an entertainment center with a TV, and a lone, king-sized bed. From the look of the bed—the covers were thrown back to reveal rumpled white sheets, and one pillow was on the floor—Tom had occupied it earlier. One tall bedside lamp was turned on.

"You got out of bed for me," Ronnie said, turning to face him. She stood in the middle of the room, in the narrow corridor between the bed and entertainment center, and he was just a few paces behind her. "I'm sorry."

He stopped, thrusting his hands into his trouser pockets and rocking back on his heels a little as he met her gaze.

"Sit down while I try to figure out how we're going to get you out of this mess." He indicated one of the chairs behind her with a nod.

Ronnie smiled at him. His hair was rumpled, his cheeks and jaw were dark with stubble, and he looked both tired and harassed.

Instead of sitting down, she moved toward him. His eyes narrowed warily at her, and his hands came out of his pockets, but he held his ground.

"We could just—wait them out," she suggested, stopping within touching distance. "They can't stay there forever."

"They don't have to," he said shortly. "You're scheduled to give a speech at nine a.m., remember? If you don't come out of your room, all dressed and ready to go, then I'd say they're pretty safe in assuming you're not in there."

"Is that so scandalous? Maybe I slept somewhere else," Ronnie pointed out with a shrug.

"The question is, where and with whom?" Tom's voice was dry. "If they find out you're not in your room, and decide to go after the story, that's what they'll be asking, believe me."

"Maybe they'll write that I'm sleeping with you."

"Given that little comedy at the Yellow Dog, I'd say that's not beyond the realm of possibility."

"I wouldn't mind." She reached out and hooked a

finger in the open collar of his shirt, her gaze on his as she undid his top button. "Would you?"

"I'd mind a whole hell of a lot," he said, imprisoning her hand with his before it could do any more damage. "Particularly since it wouldn't be true."

"We could make it true." She stepped closer, until their bodies almost touched. Her free hand came up to caress his cheek. The pad of her thumb stroked the corner of his mouth.

"Ronnie . . ." His voice was a warning. "Stop."

"I don't want to," she said. Coming up on tiptoe, she pressed her lips to his mouth.

# Chapter
## 15

OR A MOMENT HE JUST STOOD THERE, unmoving, while her hand slid behind his neck and her mouth coaxed his. She watched his reaction from beneath lowered lids. His eyes were open and fixed on her face. When her tongue slid between his closed lips, he stiffened. She could sense resistance in every hard line of his body; she worked her fingers down inside his shirt collar at the back of his neck, caressing his warm skin. At the same time, she drew his lower lip into her mouth and bit down.

Dark color suffused his face. He made an inarticulate sound. Then his lids shut, his mouth opened, and the hand that held hers prisoner between their bodies released its grip to slide around her waist. He took control of the kiss with a thoroughness that dazzled her. Wrapping his arms around her, he pulled her close and slanted his mouth across hers, kissing her with a raw hunger that made her quiver with pleasure. Locking her own arms around his neck, she kissed him back.

His lips were firm, and dry, and excitingly expert.

The inside of his mouth was hot and wet and tasted of beer. The arms holding her close were strong; his body was bigger than hers, and hard where hers was soft. She slid her fingers through the hair at the back of his head. The strands were short and silky.

When he lifted his head, she smiled up into his eyes. His gaze moved over her face, touching on each individual feature, lingering on her mouth. His arms were taut around her, flattening her breasts against his chest. His hips and thighs molded her own. She could feel the urgency in him, the tension in the arms that held her, the rigidity of his shoulders and back. She could feel the telltale hardness of him pressing against her abdomen. His face was flushed and his eyes were dark with desire.

He wanted her. There was no mistaking that.

"Tom," she whispered.

His eyes darkened still more. His jaw tensed.

"Ronnie." He said her name in echo of the way she said his, almost as if he were mocking her, or himself. But there was passion in his voice and, she thought, a kind of tenderness too.

Her hands slipped beneath the edge of his suit coat, sliding it from his shoulders. He seemed to hesitate for a moment, and again she thought he meant to resist. But he let her go for just long enough to shrug out of it. The coat dropped with a faint rustle to the floor. She went to work on his shirt buttons, then slid her hands inside his shirt, stroking the hair-roughened chest she bared.

"Ronnie." His voice was rougher this time, lower, deeper, with an edge of warning to it. But he did nothing to stop her. He liked the way she was touching him, she could tell.

His skin was scalding hot, and faintly damp with perspiration. The underlying muscles were hard. His eyes glittered restlessly as he watched her. His hands curved on either side of her waist.

His shirt was unbuttoned perhaps three-quarters of the way when she slid her hand down under his belt buckle.

He caught his breath, and caught her hand, too, pulling it out and away from his body. His eyes blazed down at her. For a moment he went so still he could have been a stone statue except for the bright blue flame in his eyes. Then he released her hand. His arms came back around her, and he kissed her again, bending her back over his arm, his mouth hard and demanding. Ronnie clung to him, kissing him back greedily. Her head spun, her knees felt weak, and her body quaked with desire.

His hold shifted, and he swung her clean off her feet. Ronnie's eyes opened in surprise. Then she wrapped her arms around his neck, thrilling to the ease with which he carried her over to the bed. With one hand he pulled the covers out of the way. Then he bent to lay her gently on the mattress. Her arms around his neck pulled him down with her. Sitting beside her, leaning over her, he kissed her mouth, her neck, her ear. Ronnie arched her back as his mouth found her collarbone where it was left bare by the scoop neckline of her T-shirt.

"God, you smell good," he whispered against her skin, and lifted his head. Their eyes met.

Ronnie smiled at him. His hair was ruffled and his

eyes gleamed and he looked handsome and sexy and very male. Her gaze never leaving his, she reached down for the hem of her T-shirt and pulled it up over her head, then tossed it aside. All she wanted in life right at that moment was to be naked in his arms.

"You're beautiful." His breath came faster. His arms were braced on either side of her body as he leaned over her. His gaze slid down to her breasts. Her bra was an everyday, serviceable one of white nylon that covered her better than most of her swimsuit tops. She had nice breasts, full and firm and round without being overly large. Just now they were swelling against the confines of her bra, the nipples erect and clearly visible as they nudged at the thin material.

He looked up again, meeting her gaze. His body radiated heat. His jaw was hard and set, and his eyes gleamed.

Without warning he got to his feet.

"Tom," she protested, reaching for him.

"You don't want to go to bed with your shoes on," he said, his voice slightly hoarse.

Quaking inside, her fingernails digging into the mattress, she lay still as he walked to the foot of the bed and slid his hand around one of her slim ankles. Lifting her foot in its high-heeled sandal, he balanced it against his thigh while his fingers worked at the strap. In just a moment the shoe was off. He bent his head, lifted her foot again, and pressed a kiss to her bare instep that sent lightning bolts of heat shooting up her leg. She shivered, closing her eyes. Then he gently replaced that foot on the mattress and picked up its fellow, repeating the operation. By the time she was barefoot, Ronnie thought her insides would melt.

Carrying her shoes, he returned to the head of the bed. His face was flushed, his hair untidy, his eyes dark. At their backs was some emotion she couldn't quite decipher. Desire was there, hard and hungry, and it was stamped on his face too—but there was something else as well.

Something that she was too turned on by to try to decipher.

He put her shoes on the nightstand, placing the leather confections carefully side by side, then turned and stood looking down at her for a moment. His shirt was unbuttoned all the way now, so that she could see the hard muscles of his chest and the wedge of dark brown hair that covered them. One shirttail hung free of his pants. Ronnie moved a little on the mattress, wordlessly inviting him to join her. Her gaze locked with his.

"You are gorgeous, and sexy, and I want you so damn much it gives the term blue balls a whole new meaning," he said. Passion roughened his voice and hardened his expression, but there was a touch of ruefulness there, too, that did not quite fit the situation.

"Tom. Come to bed." Ronnie reached for his hand to tug him down, not in the frame of mind at the moment to puzzle over nuances.

"I have to take care of some business first," he said, eluding her hand by the simple expedient of grasping the covers and flipping them over her. Ronnie found herself covered to the neck.

"Business!" She sat bolt upright, the covers spilling around her to pool at her waist, indignation in her voice.

"Remember the reporter?" He met her gaze, hesi-

tated, then bent to cup her face with his hands and kiss
her mouth. Easing her back down onto the pillows
with his kiss, he caught her hands when she would
have locked them around his neck.

"Tom!"

"Let me get rid of the vultures, and I'll be back," he
said, straightening.

"You can't just leave me!"

"It'll take fifteen minutes, tops," he promised soothingly. "Then we'll have all the rest of the night."

Ronnie eyed him with a mixture of desire and re-
sentment. That he could think of business when she
was burning with need for him was infuriating. But he
wanted her too. She knew she wasn't mistaken about
that.

"Close your eyes, think pleasant thoughts, and I'll
be right back," he said. "Okay?"

"Fifteen minutes." The look she gave him was militant.

"That's all it'll take, I swear." He kissed each of her
hands, and released them. "I'll be back."

He turned and walked away from the bed, scooping
up his jacket on the way to the door. A moment later
Ronnie heard the faint click that told her he was gone.
She glanced at the bedside clock: 4:20. Fifteen minutes . . .

Her body throbbed with passion. She turned over,
flopping facedown among the pillows, burying her face
in their softness. Her limbs felt curiously heavy; her
head swam.

Fifteen minutes. It wasn't very long. She would
make him pay in the most pleasurable possible way for
doing this to her; she would keep him up all night.

In the meantime as she waited, she would do as he had suggested and close her eyes.

The shrilling of a phone not far from her ear awoke her. The sound went right through her head, making it ache. Blinking, Ronnie rolled onto her back, trying to orient herself as she stared up at the shadowy recesses of an unfamiliar ceiling. As the screeching continued, she groped for a pillow and flung it in the general direction of the offending instrument. Her eyes widened as Quinlan walked into view around the foot of the bed.

"Morning, Sleeping Beauty," he said, meeting her gaze, and picked up the phone. Shirtless, he wore only charcoal-gray dress trousers. A hotel towel was draped around his neck, and one half of his lower face was covered with white foam. The other half was clean shaven.

Memory flooded back.

"Great. Thanks," he said into the phone, and replaced the receiver.

Ronnie glanced at the bedside clock: 7:05.

"Fifteen minutes," she growled, hitching herself up against the headboard and glaring at him as he stood looking down at her.

His mouth quirked into a half smile. "You were asleep." He bent to pick something up from the floor. Her black T-shirt, she saw, as he tossed it at her.

"Get dressed. We need to get you back to your room. That was hotel security. They're on their way now to escort our friends from the press out of the building."

Ronnie glanced at her T-shirt, then realized that all

she was wearing from the waist up was her flimsy bra. Not that she minded Tom seeing her like that; in fact she wished he would do more than just look.

He moved away from the bed, pulled the curtains open to admit bright morning sunlight, then headed back to the bathroom.

Covering her eyes with her hand, Ronnie groaned. The light felt as though it had a billion sharp edges, all of which stabbed through her eyes into her skull. After a moment the worst of the pain subsided, and she lowered her hand, squinting as she fumbled with the T-shirt in her lap. From the bathroom she heard the sound of water running.

Her eyes were still not focusing properly as Ronnie pulled on her T-shirt, then swung her legs over the side of the bed. Her head hurt abominably, and swam as she sat up; her mouth felt as if it were stuffed with cotton.

"Here." He was back, crouching in front of her, offering her two aspirin tablets on one flat palm and holding a glass half filled with water in the other. He was still shirtless, his shoulders broad and surprisingly bronzed for a blond man. His face was now clean shaven.

"Could you please shut the curtains?" She accepted the aspirin and the water with a grimace.

"Head hurt?" Amusement combined with sympathy in his voice as he stood up and obligingly pulled the curtains about halfway closed.

"Yes." She swallowed the tablets and chased them down with a gulp of water.

When she looked up, he was buttoning up a clean white shirt. His gaze slid over her.

Ronnie braced a hand on the mattress and stood up. A virulent attack of light-headedness almost made her sit down again.

"Whoa." He was at her side, holding on to her arm.

"I'm okay." She shook him off when he would have helped her. Walking with great care, she made it to the bathroom.

She used the facilities, washed her face with soap and ice-cold water, found some mouthwash in his shaving kit, and rinsed her mouth, then used his brush on her hair. After that she felt marginally better. Looking at herself in the mirror, she thought she looked like a perfect example of the morning after the night before. Her face was pale, with shadows under her eyes. The ends of her hair straggled limply around her face. Her black T-shirt was badly wrinkled. At least her waist pouch, which she still wore, contained a tiny lipstick and powder compact. Unzipping it, she coated her lips with deep raisin, smoothing and thinning the color until it was barely there. She was sweeping the powder puff over her face when he tapped lightly on the door.

"You alive in there?" he asked.

"I'm coming." Ronnie restored her cosmetics to the waist pouch, zipped it up, and opened the door. He was waiting for her, fully dressed with a red tie looped untied around his neck. From one hand dangled her sandals.

"We need to go. Don't forget you have to give a speech in just about"—he glanced at his watch—"an hour and a half."

"Don't remind me." She walked up to him and took her sandals from his hand. As she did so, a vivid recollection of how they had been removed from her feet brought her gaze up to his. He was remembering too; she could tell by the sudden hot gleam in his eyes.

"Tom . . ."

"Later. Right now we have to get you into your room and ready to go to work."

Before she could reply, he opened the door and stuck his head out, glancing up and down the corridor. Wrapping one hand around her wrist, he pulled her out into the hall, heading at a brisk pace for the stairs. Ronnie's head throbbed, as she had to almost run to keep up. She clutched her sandals in one hand.

Despite an aching head, dry mouth, queasy stomach, and Jell-O knees, Ronnie realized that she felt happier than she had in a long time. As her gaze fixed on the broad back of the man dragging her ruthlessly after him up three flights of stairs, she also knew why:

Tom.

# Chapter

## 16

"*I* SEE YOU FETCHED HER BACK to the hotel all right and tight." Kenny spoke under his breath as he stood beside Tom at the back of the Banning Creek Country Club ballroom, both of them propping themselves up against the cool plaster wall and watching as Ronnie was introduced. The ballroom had been converted for the University Women's breakfast by the addition of dozens of white-clothed tables and a long, blue-draped dais. The breakfast was sold out; the applause that greeted Ronnie was warm. Tom credited himself for that. His efforts on her behalf were paying off.

"It wasn't her." A woman who'd been up nearly all night drinking and carrying on had no business looking as good as Ronnie did this morning, Tom thought as she started to speak.

"What?" Kenny looked at him in surprise. The volume cranked up a notch in his voice.

"I said it wasn't her. And keep your voice down." If his words were abrupt, Tom couldn't help it. Defending the lady's reputation seemed to have become his mission in life. He knew how Kenny's thought processes worked. Hell, his own worked the same way, and so did those of every other man he knew. A married woman dancing and drinking at a bar with men other than her husband was a slut. Especially a beautiful, red-haired woman with a body that could stop traffic. He didn't want Kenny, or anyone else, having those kinds of thoughts about Ronnie. Whether she deserved them or not.

"But . . ." Kenny was bug-eyed with surprise.

"You hauled me out of bed at two in the morning and sent me off on a wild-goose chase, buddy. It took me an hour to check out every redhead in that bar, and then I worried about it until seven this morning, when I knocked on her door. She answered, Kenny. The ringer on her phone was turned off. She'd been sleeping like a baby in her own bed all night."

"Sheez, man, I don't know what to say," Kenny said by way of an apology. "I thought my information was good."

"Well, you thought wrong."

"I am sure sorry."

Tom's only reply was a grunt. Ronnie was well under way by this time, still clutching the sides of the podium with both hands, though he'd told her not to at least fifty times, and rehearsed her through gestures she could use to enliven her words instead. While he had managed to get the content of her speeches changed, her style of delivery had improved only marginally, if at all. She was still as wooden as a cigar-store Indian. Oddly enough, Tom found her ineffectiveness as a speaker endearing. It made her seem kind of—vulnerable.

His balls still ached from not giving her what she had been begging for last night. It had been a near-run thing. Even when he'd gotten himself in hand enough to escape into the hotel corridor, he'd almost had second thoughts and turned around and gone back in. But sleeping with Mrs. Lewis R. Honneker IV was neither safe nor smart. If His Honor found out—if anyone found out—there'd be hell to pay. For her as well as for him.

He'd used the time in the hall to clear his head, ease the ache in his groin, and come up with a plan for getting rid of the reporter and photographer camped out in front of her room. In the end, that had been easily done: He had called hotel security and asked that they be escorted out. Oh, not at four A.M., because how could Mrs. Honneker or any of her entourage know the pair was out there at that time unless one or more of them were out themselves? No, he had waited until nearly seven, and pretended he'd just then spotted them in the hall. One call, and the thing was done.

Easy.

What hadn't been easy was reentering his hotel room after what he judged was a sufficient interval. As he had all but known she would be, Ronnie was dead to the world, all stretched out in his bed, her face buried in his pillow.

No matter how much she chose to protest, the lady had had too much to drink.

She was sleeping on her stomach with the covers kicked off. Given what she was wearing, she had looked almost naked lying there. The only part of her that was decently covered was her rear, and those denim shorts didn't hide much of that. Looking down at her slender, creamy-skinned body, Tom had felt the lust he thought he'd gotten a firm hold on earlier start to slip its leash.

But in the end he'd done the smart thing, the gentlemanly thing, and bedded down on the floor. This morning there'd been just enough time to get her back into her room, push her into the shower, and make sure she was dressed properly and primed with coffee and answers and able to function before they had to leave for her speech.

He had deliberately left no time for a rehash of what had passed between them during the night, although he knew he was only delaying the inevitable. From the melting looks she'd been sending his way all morning, the lady wasn't ready to let bygones be bygones. He had thought that, without the effects of booze to fire her up and with the bright light of day putting things in their proper perspective, she might be glad to pretend the whole thing had never happened. No such luck. She was going to want to continue where they had left off, and, smart, careful individual that he was, he was going to have to turn her down.

However much he might want to take the lady to bed, starting a hot, steamy love affair with Ronnie Honneker would rank right up there as one of the stupidest things he had ever done. It would be like lighting the fuse on a stick of dynamite, holding it in your hand, then wondering why the hell your hand got blown off.

She was getting to the part about Mississippi's children being Mississippi's future when their eyes met. Despite his best intentions, that glowing look from clear across a crowded room was enough to make his blood heat. Though his head knew better, the rest of him wanted to sleep with her so badly that the need to do it was almost a physical pain.

He glanced away.

"So who was your company?" he asked Kenny in a growling tone, to distract himself.

Kenny shot him a sideways, defensive glance, reddened, and shrugged without replying.

"Did you happen to give Ann a thought?" Plump, smiling, wholesome Ann was, as far as Tom was concerned, the kind of woman whom the words *wife and mother* defined.

"It was a one-time thing, okay? It won't hurt Ann because she won't know a thing about it."

"Good reasoning." Tom's reply was sardonic.

"It wasn't anything I planned. She—came on to me, and it just happened."

That sounded so much like Tom's own experience of the night before that his annoyance with his partner evaporated. Except of course, he reminded himself, he wasn't married, and he'd had the good sense to call a halt before he'd boffed somebody who was.

But it could very easily have gone the other way.

Ronnie's speech ended, and Tom applauded with the rest. Next came the question-and-answer session. He tensed, but she handled everything thrown at her with aplomb. When a pushy woman asked her point-blank what she thought about her husband carrying on with a prostitute, Tom got so nervous he almost jumped out of his skin. What would she say?

"I didn't like it," Ronnie said slowly. She wore a summer suit in soft yellow silk, knee-length, conservative. Tom had hauled it out of her closet that morning himself, along with sensible two-inch pumps, which were the very antithesis of the sexy sandals he'd taken off her feet the night before. "I *don't* like it. But very few things in this world are perfect. Our marriage certainly isn't. But we both want it to work, and are committed to making it work. I look on what happened as a challenge that will in the end just make our marriage stronger."

*Brava!* Tom was bowled over. She had taken every word and phrase he had been drumming into her head day after day and used them, by God. While the audience applauded her answer, she looked over their heads at him. He gave her a discreet thumbs-up, and a proud smile.

Considering, he decided he felt kind of like Frankenstein observing the first stirrings of his monster.

After that, there were the interviews, which went well, and then a quick lunch, grabbed on the way to the airport. Ronnie laughed a lot as they ate McDonald's hamburgers in the car, mostly at Kenny's and Thea's quips from the backseat, because Tom wasn't talking much. Ronnie rode in the front seat beside him, not touching him, not addressing so much as a single remark directly to him, but there. If she had been an eight-hundred-pound gorilla, he couldn't have been more aware of her presence. Though he steadfastly kept his attention on the road, his peripheral vision couldn't miss the crossing and uncrossing of her slim legs, the sensuous way she shifted her rear around to get more comfortable in her seat, the quick glances she sent his way.

He turned the air-conditioning up to full-blast, and still he felt as if he were burning up.

"Hey, bud, you're awful quiet today," Kenny said, punching his shoulder in good-humored reproof as they pulled into the airport.

"Probably because I was up all night," Tom growled before he thought. Ronnie's eyes immediately went wide on his face. Before she could say anything, Tom added hastily, with a silencing glance in her direction, "Kenny sent me on a wild-goose chase in the middle of the night, looking for something he thought got misplaced. He turned out to be wrong, though. The object was just where it was supposed to be all along."

"Hey, Ronnie, Kenny thought you'd gone out to some bar dancing," Thea elucidated with an amused gurgle from the backseat. "He sent Tom out after you."

"Kenny was wrong," Tom said coolly, while Ronnie managed an amused smile at the absurdity of such a notion. With a flicker of surprise he realized that Thea must have been the "company" in Kenny's room. How else could she know what had gone on? The funny thing about it was, she had been coming on to Tom like a house afire for the last two weeks. Obviously Thea wasn't too particular about where she bestowed her favors.

The plane ride home was no better than the car. It was a small turboprop, chartered for campaign use, and the noise of its engines limited the need for polite conversation. Still, in self-defense, Tom put his head back on the headrest and pretended to sleep. But Ronnie sat close enough to him so that her arm brushed his every time she moved. He could hear the silken slither of her pantyhose-clad thighs every time she crossed and uncrossed her legs. He could smell her perfume.

The same damn perfume.

By the time the plane landed, he was so hard he was surprised he could stand up. Walking normally was an effort.

Through some snafu, the limo that was supposed to convey Ronnie safely back to Sedgely had not shown up. The other three had left their own cars at the airport so that they could drive themselves home.

"I'll give you a ride, Ronnie," Thea offered as they walked out into the pickup area and it became obvious that Ronnie's car was nowhere to be seen.

Tom was all for whipping out his cell phone and giving the limo company a blistering directive to get that damned car here *now*, but he was hampered by the fact that he was carrying both his and Ronnie's suitcases, and his own briefcase. Kenny was lugging his and Thea's luggage in a division of labor that said volumes about the state of various relationships, Tom thought, if anyone had noticed and thought about it.

He devoutly hoped no one had and did.

"Thanks, Thea, but Tom can take me home. I want to talk to him anyway," Ronnie said sunnily. She spoke as if wanting to talk to *Tom* was the most natural thing in the world, which Tom supposed it was if one didn't have any idea what the subject of the conversation was likely to be.

"Sure," he said, because there was no way to put her off without attracting the kind of notice neither one of them needed. Besides, the conversation had to be held sometime. He was a coward for wishing to delay it as long as possible.

The dark clouds gathering in the sky to the west were emblematic of his mood. Ronnie walked beside him to his car, not speaking but happy, he could tell. Her moods were as easy to read as the weather. Though the sky was overcast, it was stiflingly hot and humid. The air was still in anticipation of the coming storm. Even the windsock at the end of one runway hung straight down.

Ronnie waved to Thea as the woman got into a nearby car. Kenny was still walking, heading off to the right. Tom set the suitcases on the pavement behind the car, unlocked the trunk, then opened the driver's and passenger's door before putting the key in the ignition and turning on the air-conditioning.

When he finished stowing the luggage in the trunk, Ronnie was already in the car with her door shut.

Feeling like a man on the way to his own execution, he walked around to the driver's-side door and got in.

# Chapter

## 17

"I CALLED FROM THE HOTEL in Tupelo and canceled the limousine," Ronnie said as Tom pulled out into the long stream of cars leaving the airport. "So don't you go yelling at them."

Despite the fact that she was battling the effects of a slight hangover and very little sleep, she felt ebullient. No longer was she a Stepford wife. She'd broken out, busted loose, and reclaimed her personhood. And, not incidentally, started an affair with Tom.

Tom glanced at her. The lines that surrounded his eyes and bracketed his mouth were more pronounced than usual, she thought, and his face was set in stern lines. With a slight inward smile, she attributed his grim look to lack of sleep.

"Did you?"

His brief reply was the opposite of encouraging. Ronnie frowned at him. The dark clouds that had started in the west now filled the sky. A few fat drops of rain splattered on the windshield.

"You don't mind driving me home." It was a statement rather than a question. She knew he didn't mind.

The curious intimacy that had sprung up between them that first day had taken root and grown stronger. He was her ally, her friend, her confidant, as well as nearly her lover. She felt as if she could almost read his mind.

Tom glanced at her again, then shook his head to indicate he didn't mind. More raindrops fell. He turned on the wipers. The swishing sound they made was rhythmic and soothing. The inside of the car was growing cool as the air-conditioning began to kick in.

"It was very gentlemanly of you to pretend like I never went out anywhere last night. Thank you."

"You're welcome."

"What is this, your strong, silent side?" Ronnie asked with a trace of amused exasperation after another couple of minutes of silence on his part. "You haven't said two complete sentences all day."

"Ronnie . . . ," he began, and hesitated. The light they were approaching turned red, and he braked. The car stopped. They were the third car in line to turn right off Brandon Road onto Highway 80. The rain was starting to fall in earnest now, huge drops that made the pavement steam as they hit.

"Not that I mind. I think strong, silent men are sexy. Actually I think you're sexy, whether you're being strong and silent or not." She said it humorously, tenderly, and he sent her an unreadable glance. Seizing the opportunity, she undid her lap belt, ducked under her shoulder belt, rose up on one knee, and leaned toward him. Gripping his shoulder with one hand for balance, she slid the other hand behind his neck and bent her head to kiss his mouth. He went very still for a moment. Then he kissed her back. Thoroughly, his lips hard, his tongue exploring her mouth, his hand sliding under her hair to cradle her head.

A horn honked behind them once, twice, impatiently. He gripped her waist and pushed her firmly back into her seat. The car started to move again. They had been holding up traffic as they kissed.

"You should have woken me up last night," she told him with a tiny smile as she refastened her lap belt.

"Dammit, Ronnie." He paused, shooting her another one of those unreadable glances. "I *deliberately* didn't wake you up last night."

Ronnie frowned.

"I know you think that last night was the kickoff to us having some sort of love affair, or something. It wasn't. It was just part of my job."

"What?" Ronnie demanded after a flabbergasted instant, torn between outrage and amused disbelief at the absurd statement. "Are you trying to say that kissing me and taking my shirt off and carrying me to bed are part of your *job*?"

"*You* kissed *me,* you took your own shirt off, and carrying you to bed was the best way I could think of to get you there—to sleep. I did what I had to to get you out of that bar and back to the hotel, and to sleep so that you'd be in decent enough shape to give your speech this morning."

Something about his expression told her that this was not some unfunny joke: He was serious. Rain was pouring down all around them now, in an unending silver curtain. Traffic slowed as drivers tried to deal with the sudden deluge.

"I don't believe you!"

His jaw hardened. "It's the truth."

"All right, maybe I did kiss you first, when we were dancing, but after that you were all over me like jelly on peanut butter! Just like you kissed me back just now! Don't tell me you were faking it, not any of it! I know better!"

The glance he sent her this time was stark and cold. "You're a beautiful woman. Sure, you can make me want you, especially when you come on to me like you did last night. I'm human. But I never had any intention of having sex with you. I was hired to handle you, and that is what I did."

Ronnie could feel her face flaming. Fury boiled up inside her, a fury so hot and fierce that she could hardly see.

"You—*jerk!*" she said, and hauled off and slapped him as hard as she could across the face.

Brakes squealed, the car swerved, and for a moment they were fishtailing all over the place. Then he got the car under control and pulled off to the side of the road. His face as he put the gearshift into park was almost as white as hers was flushed. As he turned to look at her his eyes blazed with anger; his mouth was tight with it. Across his cheek to the bridge of his nose lay the reddening imprint of her hand.

Freeing himself from his seat belt in two quick movements, he reached over and grabbed her upper arms, pushing her back against her door and looming over her menacingly.

"You want to know what would make me a jerk?" he said through his teeth as she glared up at him. "I'd be a jerk if I had sex with a woman who came on to me because she'd had too much to drink. I'd be a jerk if I had sex with a woman who was my client, and whose family I was friends with. I'd be a jerk if I had sex with a woman who was *married*. But I didn't. And I'm not going to, even if I want to like hell. You know why? Because it's not worth the trouble it would cause. *She's* not worth the trouble it would cause."

He let go of her arms and returned to his seat, refastened his seat belt, and restarted the car. His face could have been carved from granite as he pulled the car back out onto the rain-drenched highway. His hands gripped the steering wheel as though he wished it were her neck. A tiny, telltale muscle jumped at the corner of his mouth.

Quivering with anger, Ronnie slumped back in her own seat, shooting him venomous glances and rubbing her arms where he had gripped them. He hadn't hurt her, not really, but she wanted to make him think he had so that he would feel guilty, though guilt appeared to be the furthest thing from his thoughts.

They drove in silence for perhaps fifteen minutes, passing through downtown rush-hour traffic as people just getting off work were slowed by the weather. It was only about 5:45, but it was almost as dark as night because of the driving rain.

"I don't suppose I have to say this, but I'm going to anyway," Ronnie said when she had enough control of her voice to speak. "You're fired."

He laughed, the sound short and unamused. "You can't fire me, remember?"

"You said you'd quit anytime I wanted you to, and I want you to!"

"I lied."

Ronnie drew in a ragged little breath. "You're good at that, aren't you? Lying?"

The color had come back into his face so that the imprint of her hand was barely visible. He seemed to have gotten his temper under control. Ronnie's, on the other hand, still raged like a brushfire inside her, though she was fighting not to let it show. To let him see the extent of her anger was to let him know how badly he had hurt her, and her pride would not allow that.

"You've got an interview with *Ladies' Home Journal* Monday, at two o'clock," he said evenly. "I'll be by around one to go over everything with you beforehand. And it would be a nice idea if you were to get your picture taken going to church tomorrow. With your husband."

"I won't work with you anymore."

He glanced at her. He looked as if he was almost back to normal now, except for a faint hardness about his mouth and eyes.

"You will work with me. You will work with me because I am doing a hell of a job for you, whether you want to admit it right now or not. Thanks to me, His Honor's recovering from his little misstep, and your popularity is climbing. I am also one of the few people around you who is on your side, rather than your husband's. That's something I'd think about if I were you."

"Go to hell," she said.

They were pulling into Sedgely now, his car nosing up the long, oak-lined driveway that led to the house. The gray-bearded trees seemed to weep. The white, Greek Revival portico was just visible through the pouring rain. Ronnie frowned as she discerned several figures standing about on the porch.

Tom reached over, flipping down the passenger-side visor so that she could see herself in the lighted mirror.

"Your lipstick is smudged," he said, wiping his hand over his own mouth.

Without a word, Ronnie did what she could to fix her appearance, then snapped the visor back into place. The car pulled around the paved semicircle that curved in front of the house, and stopped before the porch.

"Sit tight, I've got an umbrella in the back," Tom said, turning off the ignition. Ignoring him, Ronnie got out of the car and ran up the steps, heedless of the pouring rain. The slam of a door and the sound of footsteps slapping on wet pavement told her that he was right behind her.

"Ronnie, honey, you're just in time to say good-bye to Frank Keith. Lord-a-mercy, you are wet! Frank, you remember my wife?"

Lewis caught her in a one-armed bear hug as she made it onto the porch. In a glance she saw her mother-in-law standing there, too, along with Marsden, Frank Keith, and his wife. Ronnie pasted a smile on her face, and murmured polite platitudes as she shook hands with the lieutenant governor and his wife. All the while she was burningly conscious of Tom behind her.

"Hey, man, how's it going?" Marsden's square face relaxed into a smile as he reached past Ronnie to shake hands with Tom. He was a stocky man who looked like a shorter, blurry copy of his father without any of his father's good looks or bluff charm. "Has Stepmama here been running you ragged?"

Before Tom could answer, Dorothy came over to

envelop him in a hug. At eighty-one, Lewis's mother was surprisingly youthful-looking until one got up close enough to see the tiny wrinkles that crisscrossed her face like an overlay of flesh-colored net, with a figure kept carefully slim, and dyed mink-brown hair. "How are you, Tom? I haven't seen you for ages! Will you stay for supper?"

"Thanks, Mrs. Honneker, but I can't tonight," Tom said, smiling at Dorothy. Lewis meanwhile caught Tom's attention with a nod in the direction of the lieutenant governor.

"Frank, this is Tom Quinlan, who I've been tellin' you about. The boy's an old school friend of Marsden's here, and he's got the darnedest polls. . . ."

"If you'll excuse me, folks, I'll go in and get out of these wet clothes," Ronnie murmured to the group in general, none of whom was paying her much mind. Lewis obligingly released his hold on her shoulders.

As the talk turned to politics, Ronnie walked unnoticed across the porch and went into the house.

# Chapter

## 18

*Monday, August 4th*
*9:30 A.M.*
*BILOXI*

ARLA WAS SCARED. Despite the happy sounds
from the TV cartoons that filled the shabby
room, she felt as nervous as a mouse in a roomful of
cats, as if something was crouching just beyond her
sight, waiting for the right moment to spring.

Last night on one of the news-magazine shows,
there had been a brief segment on Susan. "The Life
and Death of a Preacher's Daughter," it had been
called. With the Mississippi Sound as a backdrop, the
reporter, a young woman named Crystal Meadows,
had talked about how Susan had "gone wrong," about
her drug use and her dropping out of college and her
reported "descent" into a life of prostitution. Her family's grief and horror and helplessness to intervene
were described in excruciating detail (none of it true,
according to what Susan had told Marla). Her father
even shed tears on camera.

Crystal Meadows had also talked about Susan's
death. The autopsy revealed that Susan had been
beaten before being asphyxiated. Her father, Charlie
Kay Martin, had spoken directly to the camera then,

vowing to leave no stone unturned until the person or persons responsible for his daughter's death were brought to justice.

The reporter ended the segment with these words: "The heat is on the Biloxi Police Department."

Marla felt as though the heat was also on *her*.

"Want some Cheerios, Mom?" Lying flat on her stomach with her head at the foot of the bed as she watched *Scooby-Doo*, Lissy fanned the box in Marla's direction. Lissy had been stuffing her mouth with handfuls of the dry cereal. The canned Coke she was washing them down with sat on the carpet near the foot of the bed. Not the most nutritious breakfast, Marla thought, accepting the box that swatted her middle as she walked past the bed, but breakfast none-theless.

"Thanks, baby."

They were running out of money. Her savings wouldn't last much longer. Renting a room in a resi-dential hotel for three weeks cost a lot. So did feeding take-out meals to a skinny seven-year-old who was al-ways hungry and had a thing for the prizes in kids' meals. They couldn't go on like this, but Marla didn't know what else to do. Every instinct she possessed screamed at her to hide out.

Claire had disappeared. At least, Marla hadn't been able to get in touch with her. She had called her apart-ment, leaving messages until the answering machine wouldn't take any more. She had stopped by, pound-ing on the door until a neighbor had put his head out to see what was going on. The manager of the apart-ment complex where Claire lived knew nothing, and wasn't much interested because the rent was paid up until the fifteenth of the month.

The Beautiful Model Agency had closed down, just like that, after being in business for two whole years. The phones at their office had been disconnected, and the office itself was empty. Marla knew, because she had stopped by to see.

She didn't know what had happened to Billie, or Joy, who'd filled in for Billie sometimes, or Rick, who'd run the whole thing.

They were simply gone, all of them.

Just thinking about it made the hair rise on the back of Marla's neck.

Gone, gone, gone, and nobody cared.

She had the feeling that if she weren't careful, she might be next. She and Lissy. Whatever—or who-ever—was out there gobbling up all these people would get them too.

The thought made Marla shiver.

Since running out of the apartment the day the man had ransacked it, Marla had gone back only for a nervous fifteen minutes, to retrieve clothes from the mess for herself and Lissy and throw them into a suitcase. Every nerve ending she possessed had told her that her apartment was no longer a healthy place to be.

Susan was dead. Claire had disappeared. So had the Beautiful Model Agency, and Billie, and Joy, and Rick. The only thing Marla knew of that connected them all was that Thursday-night date on the boat.

She was connected to it too. She had driven Susan and Claire down to the marina. She knew that Susan had gone out on a boat called The *Sun*-something— and never come back.

Whenever she remembered that, her throat closed up so tight from fear she could barely breathe.

The man who had searched the apartment had used Susan's key ring to get in. There could not be another one like it, because it was one of those clear rectangular photo-frame deals with a picture of Susan in a bikini on one side and Susan and Marla mugging for the camera on the other. Marla had clearly recognized her own face in the plastic rectangle dangling from the man's hand.

If he had Susan's key ring, then it did not require a huge leap of logic to figure out that he had killed her, or at least played some part in her death. Marla had seen him. She could identify him. His face was etched on her memory for all time.

Almost more than anything else, that scared the bejesus out of her.

But he didn't know it. He could not know it. He had not known she was in the apartment that day. If he had known, she would be dead.

He probably didn't even know she existed. He wasn't interested in her. Why should he be?

Marla shivered. Standing up, she walked to the window and flicked aside one corner of the curtain. It was hot already, and thickly humid in the aftermath of yesterday's rain. Sunlight poured into the narrow street. This section of Biloxi was poor and rundown. The lone car moving slowly down the street was an ancient Chevy with a bashed-in rear door and rust edging its trunk. Her one-room apartment was on the second floor. From its vantage point she could look down on the bald head of the man crossing the street almost directly beneath her. The sunlight bounced right off his scalp.

As though he sensed someone's eyes on him, he looked up. Marla stared, then backed away from the window in horror.

It was the man who had ransacked the apartment, the man with Susan's key ring.

*This time he was coming for her.*

# Chapter

## 19

ONNIE LAY FACEDOWN on a chaise longue beside the pool, enjoying the warmth of the sun on her skin. She was alone, except for the pool man, John somebody, who'd been coming by once a week during the summer to clean and service Sedgely's pool for as long as she could remember. The quiet swoosh of his net sweeping the water wasn't loud enough to drown out the crunch of footsteps on the gravel path that led down from the house.

Her body tensed. She took a deep breath, forcibly relaxed her muscles, and smiled a little to herself. Tom was on time, as she had known he would be. Punctuality was a real thing with him. Closing her eyes, her head turned away from the wrought-iron gate that led through six-foot-high brick walls to the pool, she pretended to doze. As an afterthought she reached around behind her back and quickly unhooked her bikini top. Shrugging the straps off her shoulders so that her back would be bare to the sun—and his view—she settled back down again.

The quiet swish of the net continued in unbroken

rhythm. The crunch of footsteps grew louder, and then she heard the protesting creak that told her he was opening the gate.

The footsteps stopped dead. Ronnie smiled to herself, imagining Tom standing with one hand on the open gate, displeased into immobility with the scene before him. She pictured it: the peanut-shaped, blue-tiled pool, sparkling like a sapphire in the sun. High brick walls overgrown with honeysuckle enclosing the pool and surrounding the patio like a fortress. John the pool man in his brown uniform glancing around in surprise at the intrusion. Herself, red hair flowing over one shoulder and milky skin exposed, wearing a teeny scarlet bikini bottom and not much else, stretched out on a bright yellow beach towel draped over a chaise longue beside the pool.

Finally came the sound she was listening for: footsteps on concrete. He was coming toward her. The footsteps stopped when he reached her side.

Ronnie lay immobile, a bubble of laughter tickling her throat. She could just imagine his expression. He would be frowning, his jaw hard and set. He would not approve of the picture she made lying there.

But he would want her.

This time he could whistle for what he wanted. She wasn't putting herself on offer to him again.

"Ronnie."

At least, she thought, Tom wasn't hypocrite enough to revert to that honeyed *Miz Honneker*. If he had, she would have stripped herself naked and thrown herself into his arms with John the pool man as a witness, and let the great spin doctor try to explain *that* away.

She stirred, as though she were waking. Turning her

head to the other side so that she could see him, she flipped her hair across her back so that it cascaded off the shoulder away from him and spilled over the side of the chaise toward the concrete floor. Her every movement was deliberately tantalizing.

"Ronnie." There was an edge to his voice. Ronnie was careful not to smile. She meant to torture and tease and drive him crazy—and then walk away. He would soon discover that when she had told him she wouldn't work with him again, she meant what she said.

With a quick flutter of lashes she looked up, as though she couldn't place the voice and had to ascertain who it was who had addressed her. Tom was wearing a blue and white pin-stripe seersucker suit today in deference to the heat, with a white shirt and a tie the exact color of his eyes. Their vivid blueness was narrowed in defense against the blinding sunshine that gilded his hair and bronzed his skin. He looked tall and lean and handsome—and edgy as hell. Definitely edgy as hell.

"Oh, it's you," she said in a bored tone, and closed her eyes again, turning her head away from him. Once again her hair flipped across her back, shutting him out.

His annoyance was as palpable as an electrical field. Ronnie could feel it enveloping her in surges. The knowledge that she was making him angry curled her toes with satisfaction.

The quiet swish of the net across the surface of the pool provided a soothing backdrop to an increasingly charged atmosphere. Birds chirped in nearby trees. Bees buzzed as they went about their daily chores. The coconut smell of the expensive sunblock she was wearing wafted to Ronnie's nostrils along with the sweet scent of the honeysuckle blossoms bedecking the brick walls. The soft terry of the beach towel on which she lay felt pleasantly warm. Yet she was most aware of intangibles: Tom's gaze on her near-naked body, and his growing vexation with her.

The rasp of metal on concrete and the sound of stretching rubber made it clear that he was pulling up a chair and sitting down next to the chaise.

"One question the interviewer is going to ask concerns how you feel about being younger than your stepchildren." His tone was even. Clearly he meant to overlook her efforts to provoke him. "If we phrase your answer carefully, I think we could rack up some points with women mothering blended families. I think you should say that—"

"I hate them, they hate me, we're a dysfunctional family," Ronnie sang softly in parody of the "Barney" theme song. She kept her head turned away from him and her eyes closed, knowing her pose would irritate him almost as much as her answer.

"Funny."

Ronnie almost smiled. This was too delicious to miss. She opened her eyes and sat up facing him, her feet swinging down to rest on the hot concrete. As she moved, her bikini top all but dropped off her shoulders. She saved it just in the nick of time, catching the straps as they slid down her arms.

From beneath lazily drooping lashes, she watched his face.

His gaze was all over her, eating her up as it swept her body from shoulders to toes. It slid back up over her smoothly waxed legs and flat stomach to fix on her breasts. The scarlet cups of her bikini top had slipped down the creamy slopes to a point that was scant millimeters short of being pornographic. In fact it just barely covered her nipples.

"Oops," Ronnie said, meeting his gaze with mockery in her own. Hooking her thumbs in the straps, she very slowly eased them back onto her shoulders.

"What the hell do you think you're doing?" His voice was low, so that John the pool man should not hear. His eyes glittered at her; his mouth looked grim.

"Enjoying the sun," Ronnie replied nonchalantly, without bothering to lower her voice.

"Why not just lie out here naked?" There was a savage undertone to his voice that Ronnie enjoyed.

"Sometimes," she answered with a small smile as she clipped her bikini top together in back, "I do."

Standing up, she slid her feet into high-heeled red mules and waved to John.

"See you next week," she called, and started toward the pool house.

"You have a nice day, Mrs. Honneker," John called back.

Tom was behind her all the way. She could feel his fulminating glare on her back as she walked. He was getting an eyeful, she knew. The bikini bottom was no more than two small triangles of scarlet spandex tied together at the sides, and the top, in back, was a scarlet string.

It was the teeniest bikini she possessed. She had worn it today with Tom in mind.

*Handle this,* she thought, and put a little extra wiggle into her walk.

The pool house was a former guest house that had been converted some ten years before. It consisted of a bedroom, kitchenette, bathroom with a large stall shower, and a living room that Ronnie had had outfitted into a minigym. All her exercise equipment was there, from her treadmill to her stair-stepper to her Nautilus. One wall was covered with a huge mirror, and a large, multicolored gym mat lay open on the floor.

Ronnie slid open the sliding glass door that led into her exercise room, not bothering to shut it behind her. Goose bumps rose instantly on her flesh as she walked into the air-conditioning. Behind her, Tom slid the door closed.

"Do you like having workmen drool over you like that?" From the tone of his voice, it seemed he had progressed from annoyance to outright anger.

"Like what?" Ronnie headed for the bathroom without bothering to throw him so much as a glance.

"Like he was watching a stripper at a peep show." He was right behind her.

"Did John do that?"

"If John is the man cleaning your swimming pool, you're damned right he did. He was practically salivating when I came on the scene."

"What are you doing here, anyway?" Ronnie pretended ignorance.

"I told you I'd be here at one to go over some things. You have an interview with *Ladies' Home Journal* at two o'clock, remember?" He sounded as if he were gritting his teeth.

"Oh, that," Ronnie said sweetly, reaching the bathroom and turning around to smile at him. "I canceled that."

She shut the bathroom door in his face.

"What?" The outraged exclamation was clearly audible even through the closed door, but she pretended not to hear.

Twenty minutes later, when she emerged, he was sitting in the wicker *papasan* chair in one corner of her exercise room leafing through the pages of an oversized magazine—was it *W*? Yes, it was. Ronnie almost smiled as she saw him reduced to entertaining himself with a fashion journal. From his expression as he glanced up, he was totally fed up. With the magazine, with the situation, and with her.

"Are you still here?" She walked through the exercise room to the kitchenette. Having showered and changed, she was wearing tennis whites: a tiny pleated skirt that just covered her bottom, a sleeveless polo shirt, tennis shoes, and socks. Her red hair was caught in a white bow at the nape of her neck.

She looked good, and she knew it. Tennis clothes became her.

"What do you mean, you canceled *Ladies' Home Journal*?" He stood in the entrance to the galley-sized kitchenette scowling at her. The doorway was narrow, and his shoulders practically filled the available space. He looked tall and big standing there, and as formidable as it was possible for a man in a seersucker suit to look.

Ronnie extracted a carton of skim milk from the refrigerator and poured about a cupful into the blender on the nearby counter. Replacing the milk and closing the refrigerator door, she glanced around at him.

"I canceled it. As in, called them up and told them not to come." Ronnie sliced half a banana into the milk.

"You called *Ladies' Home Journal* and told them not to come?" He sounded as if such a thing was beyond belief.

"Well, actually I had Thea do it," Ronnie temporized, slicing strawberries on top of the banana.

"You had Thea—" He stopped momentarily, as if words failed him. When he continued, his voice had a controlled edge. "It wasn't easy getting *Ladies' Home Journal* interested in interviewing you, you know. All kinds of celebrities vie to be in their magazine. But I called in some old favors and got them to agree to come out here today. With the right spin the article could have done the campaign—*you*—a lot of good. But you canceled it."

"That's right, I did," Ronnie agreed affably. Scooping half a dozen ice cubes out of the bin in the freezer and dropping them into the blender, she put the lid on and flipped the switch. For a moment the whirr of the blades precluded conversation.

"Did you ever hear the saying about cutting off your nose to spite your face?" Tom asked when she could hear him. He crossed his arms over his chest and leaned one shoulder against the doorjamb. The color of the tie made his eyes seem as blue as the pool outside. She thought, as she had before, that he had beautiful eyes—even when they were scowling at her, as they were at the moment.

Noticing the beauty of his eyes did nothing to improve her disposition.

"Meaning?" Arching an ostensibly uninterested eyebrow at him, Ronnie poured the frothy pink concoction she had made into a glass and took a sip.

"Meaning that by canceling the interview, you hurt yourself, not me."

"I told you I wouldn't work with you anymore." Ronnie took another sip. "I meant it."

She met his gaze, and they exchanged measuring glances.

" 'Hell hath no fury like a woman scorned,' " he quoted softly.

Ronnie's face darkened. Her hand tightened on the glass she was holding.

"You're just full of old sayings today, aren't you?" she asked with a glittering faux smile. Before she could say anything more, she was interrupted by the sound of the sliding glass door opening in the other room.

"Ronnie?" a man's voice called questioningly.

"I'm in here," Ronnie called back. Then, to Tom, "If you'll excuse me, I have a tennis game."

Setting the still nearly full glass in the sink, she walked toward him, head held high. He moved aside to let her pass.

Michael Blount stood in the exercise room, tall and black-haired and charmingly lanky in white tennis shorts and a polo shirt, his racket in his hand. He smiled when he saw her.

"Hi, Michael," she said, returning his smile with a dazzling one of her own.

"Ready?" he asked, glancing beyond her at Tom with obvious curiosity.

"Yes." She walked past him and out the door without bothering to introduce the two men, and Michael followed her.

"Who's that guy?" Michael asked when they were outside, in clear reference to Tom.

"Just one of Lewis's many flunkies," Ronnie replied with careless unconcern, being pretty certain that Tom, who stood in the open doorway frowning after them, could still hear her. "Nobody important. How's your knee?"

# Chapter

## 20

"OM, WHERE ARE WE *going*?"

"You'll see."

Actually that was a good question, Marla thought. They'd been driving north for hours, up Route 49 to Jackson, where they'd stopped at a McDonald's for lunch and some downtime for Lissy in one of those plastic playground things they all had now. Then they'd gotten back in the car and headed up I-55. Marla had no specific destination in mind. Every instinct she possessed just screamed at her to flee.

Thank God she'd had the foresight to park her car two blocks over from the hotel. Well, foresight wasn't really the word. Fear described her motivation better, fear that whoever had searched the apartment would come looking for her and would know her car on sight and would spot it on the street near the hotel and put two and two together and know where to find her. At the time, such convoluted reasoning had seemed like rampant paranoia. Now it loomed as the precaution that had saved her and Lissy's life.

After seeing the man on the street, she had grabbed

Lissy's hand and her purse and run out the door. The elevator had been occupied—was he already on his way up?—so they'd run down the fire stairs. Everything in the room had been left exactly as it was: TV playing, lights on, Cheerios all over the floor where they had been spilled when Marla had yanked Lissy from the bed.

She knew she had terrified her daughter, hissing at her to shut up when the child had started to protest, and was made to run like the devil himself was after the both of them.

Which, Marla thought, described exactly how she'd felt.

The venom in her tone had turned her little girl's face white, and made her eyes go wide on her mother's face. Remembering, Marla felt bad about that. But at least she had gotten them safely away.

In answer to Lissy's queries, once they were safely in the car and away, she had answered briefly, "Bill collectors."

Lissy understood that. There were always bill collectors.

Marla hadn't wanted to tell her child the truth: that she was convinced that the bald man in the street was chasing them to kill them.

She didn't know how she knew it, but she did. She could sense it with every survival instinct she possessed.

If he had been able to find them in the Curzan Hotel, a fleabag out-of-the-way place if there ever was one, he must be good. He would be able to follow their trail now too. There was no longer any doubt that he knew she existed, though Marla didn't know how. He must know her name, and lots of things about her. Maybe what she looked like, from her driver's-license picture. That's what people who were looking for people did, wasn't it? Went through the Bureau of Motor Vehicles for a copy of the person's driver's license? He probably knew what kind of car she had too. He might even be able to trace her credit cards.

Marla blanched as she realized that she had made a withdrawal from an ATM only half a block down the street from the Curzan late the previous afternoon. Had he found them through that?

Panic threatened to swamp her. They had no place to go. There was no place that was safe. They had no money. She was now afraid to draw on the little that was left in her account.

She was going to have to go to the police. But they would take Lissy away from her, and she couldn't bear that.

Still, it was better than having the child, or herself, or, as seemed most likely, them both, wind up dead.

*He was probably following them right now.*

"Mom, I've got to pee."

Marla glanced at her daughter. "We'll stop soon," she promised.

"Where are we *going*?"

Lissy didn't usually whine, but this had been a trying day.

"We're taking a little trip," Marla said, knowing that she was going to have to come up with a destination pretty soon. "Just the two of us. Isn't that nice?"

"Did you write another bad check, Mom?" Lissy gave her a stern look, as if she were the parent and Marla was the child.

"No!" Marla said, indignant.

"Then why are we running away?"

"We're not running away. We're—going to see somebody."

"Who?"

Marla looked at her daughter with a mixture of admiration and exasperation. Lissy might be a kid, but she was nobody's fool.

They flashed by a green road sign that read, Pope, 50 miles. Marla had a sudden inspiration.

Maybe there was help for them, after all.

"An old friend of mine," she said haughtily to her daughter, and drove with more confidence than before.

"Who?"

"Just hold your horses, Miss Smarty-pants, and you'll see."

"Mom, we don't even have a toothbrush. You left all our things back there at the hotel."

"We'll manage."

"I have to *pee*."

In the end Lissy got to use the rest room when Marla pulled into a tiny convenience store in Pope. While Lissy went inside, she sat in the car in front of the pay phone at the edge of the parking lot, thumbing through the phone book, looking for the familiar name.

She found the name she was looking for, slid a quarter into the slot, and dialed, keeping a nervous eye out all the while.

*Please, please, let him be home,* she prayed.

A man's voice answered.

"Jerry?" Her voice was shaky.

"Yeah."

"This is Marla."

"Marla who?"

"You remember, Marla from Biloxi? Beautiful Models?"

"Oh, my God, *that* Marla? Why on earth are you calling me?"

Marla wet her lips. "Jerry, I'm in bad trouble. I need help. . . ."

# Chapter

## 21

"*T*OM YELLED AT ME YESTERDAY for canceling that *Ladies' Home Journal* interview." Cup of coffee balanced in her lap, Thea was curled up in one of the pair of navy leather wing chairs that were placed on either side of the fireplace. It was ten in the morning, and she and Ronnie were going over the week's revised schedule in the room at Sedgely that had become Ronnie's de facto office during the months she was scheduled to spend in Mississippi.

A former sitting room, it was on the second floor not too far from Ronnie's bedroom. Bookshelves stretching from the highly polished wood floor to the soaring twelve-foot ceiling filled in the rest of the fireplace wall. Opposite the fireplace a pair of tall, graceful windows adorned with simple yellow silk draperies looked out over the back lawn. The walls were papered in narrow sky-blue-and-white stripes, and the ceiling, fireplace, moldings, and window frames were white. A worn Tabriz-design oriental rug in shades of blue and rose covered most of the floor. Ronnie's desk, an enormous mahogany rectangle that once had had pride of place in Lewis's Senate office, was the focal point of the room. Ronnie sat in the navy leather desk chair behind it, her own cup of coffee pushed to one side and all but forgotten as she frowned down at the typewritten schedule in front of her.

"Did he?" Assuming an air of disinterest, she responded to Thea's statement without so much as an accompanying glance.

"He also told me not to make any more changes in your schedule without consulting him first."

"*Did* he?" This time Ronnie looked up, a militant sparkle in her eyes.

Thea grinned at her. "He sure is hunky when he gets mad."

"Just remember you work for me, not him."

"Oh, I told him that."

"What did he say?"

"That's when he got mad. His mouth got real tight and his eyes got real narrow, and for a minute there he looked like he was saying every bad word in the book inside his head. Then he just said 'I'll talk to you tomorrow,' and walked out of the room. Stalked, really. He went down the stairs and out the front door, and a few minutes later I heard him driving away. He was so angry he peeled rubber."

"Hmm." Ronnie returned her attention to the schedule again, determined to betray no more interest in Tom and his goings-on. Not that she *was* interested.

"Wouldn't you like to get him into bed?" Thea mused with a sigh. This meshed so well with Ronnie's thoughts that she looked up again, startled. Catching and thankfully misinterpreting that look, Thea added hastily, "Oh, not you, because you're married to the Senator and all that, but I would. He's divorced, you know."

"Is he?" Ronnie almost marked through a ceremony honoring the winner of a statewide spelling bee where she was supposed to present the victor with a trophy and certificate, but at the last second hesitated. Tom of course had set it up, as part of his plan to have her associated with children and education (two extremely positive areas for influencing college-educated female voters, he said). But even to infuriate Tom, she didn't like to disappoint a child. She grudgingly decided to leave it in.

"Kenny says Tom's got a girlfriend, and he wouldn't be surprised if they tied the knot one of these days. He says they've been seeing each other for a couple of years." Thea grinned. "Kenny is cute, don't you think? Oh, not hunky like Tom, but real sweet."

"Kenny does seem nice," Ronnie murmured. The idea of Tom "tying the knot" with a girlfriend of many years' standing made her stomach clench.

It was probably nothing but idle talk, she told herself. On that never-to-be-forgotten night, Tom had said that she was prettier than his girlfriend. Would a man say something like that about a woman he was planning to marry?

"Kenny says they used to have this real big-time political consulting firm, but Tom got into a jam and their firm went bankrupt and they lost everything. He says they're on the comeback trail and it's important that they do a good job with you."

Her attention effectively distracted from thoughts of

Tom's relationship with his girlfriend, Ronnie glanced up, frowning. What Thea said jibed with everything she herself had observed in Tom: the sense she had that he lacked money, the fierce need to succeed in what he was doing with her, the sheer time and energy he was putting into the effort.

"What kind of jam?" Ronnie asked, almost unwillingly.

Thea shrugged. "I don't know. Kenny didn't say, and I didn't ask. Maybe—"

She was interrupted as the phone on Ronnie's desk began to ring.

"Want me to get it?" Thea reached for the phone even as Ronnie nodded.

"Mrs. Honneker's office. No, she's not available right now." Thea listened for a minute, sucking in her cheeks in an expression that for her was indicative of anxiety. "At nine forty-five tomorrow? Yes, I'll—I'll tell her. Okay. 'Bye, Moira."

Thea hung up. For a moment the two women's gazes met, trepidation in Thea's and frowning curiosity in Ronnie's.

"What?" Ronnie finally asked.

"That was Moira from the Washington office," Thea explained unnecessarily. She hesitated, then blurted, "The *Ladies' Home Journal* interview has been rescheduled for ten in the morning. Tom apparently called them up, told them there had been a misunderstanding, and they agreed to come back. Only now it's a joint interview with you *and* the Senator. Moira called to say that the Senator wouldn't be able to make it home tonight, but he'll meet you in the library downstairs at nine forty-five in the morning. He's planning to wear a navy suit, blue shirt, and yellow tie. So—so you can color-coordinate your outfit to his, Moira said."

"*Y*OU SNEAKY SON OF A BITCH," Ronnie said in a venomous undertone to Tom as, with one hand on the carved oak balustrade, she walked down the final few steps of Sedgely's grand staircase.

It was nine-thirty on Wednesday morning. Sunshine poured through the glass panels on either side of the front door, sparkling off the many facets of the antique crystal chandelier overhead and illuminating dust motes in the air. The marble-tiled entry hall gleamed from the cleaning Selma had given it the day before. Pale gold wallpaper in a subtle damask pattern made the walls seem to glow in muted reflection of the brightness outside.

A quick glance around had revealed that so far Tom, who stood just inside the door, hands in pockets, was alone. He was wearing a charcoal-gray suit, a white shirt, and the same blue tie he had worn on Monday, which had the same unwelcome effect of enhancing the color of his eyes.

The mere sight of him was enough to make Ronnie furious all over again. In the wee dark hours of the night she had promised herself that she would remain coldly dignified in his presence no matter what the provocation, but now, facing him, Ronnie could no more hold her tongue than she could fly.

"Good morning to you, too, Miz Honneker." It was a honeyed drawl, uttered with a charming quirk of a smile.

The combination of drawl, smile, and *Miz Honneker* did it. Ronnie saw red.

"How dare you go over my head to my husband to reschedule an interview I canceled?" Eyes snapping, she stepped down into the hall and walked right up to him, pointing an index finger at him as she went. Instead of backing down, as most were prone to do when confronted with her temper, he stood his ground.

"You can always cancel again. Only this time you'll have to explain to your *husband* exactly why." He caught the hand that would have stabbed, index-finger first, into his chest and held it. His hand was warm, and hard, and strong. As she met his gaze, his smile took on a harder edge. "I don't suppose you'll want to tell him the truth: that you came on to me and I turned you down, so you're hell-bent on making me pay." He paused, his gaze measuring her. "By the way, did you get that Michael guy to play anything besides tennis with you yesterday?"

Eyes flaming, Ronnie jerked her hand from his hold just as the front door opened. She glanced past Tom to find Kenny, dressed in a bright green sport coat and checked trousers, leading in a lumbering, scruffy-looking animal that resembled nothing so much as a cross between a Saint Bernard and a poodle. It was huge, with long, Shirley Temple–like ringlets in different combinations of black and white covering its body. Two black eyes were barely discernible through the curls.

"*What* is *that*?" she asked.

"Down here in Mississippi we call it a dog," Tom answered. Before Ronnie could do more than slay him with a look for that bit of sarcasm, Lewis came down the stairs. Dressed in the promised navy suit and yellow tie, his silvered hair impeccably brushed back from his forehead, Lewis *looked* like a senator. He looked— *statesmanlike* was the only word Ronnie could think of to describe him. She hadn't seen him since Sunday morning, when he had left for a lightning trip to Washington—and she hadn't missed him.

"How ya doin', honey?" Lewis asked genially, wrapping an arm around Ronnie's shoulders and bestowing a kiss on her cheek. She smiled at him with more warmth than she had shown him for some time, then realized that the smile was for Tom's benefit. The realization wiped it from her face.

"That the dog? What'd you say his name is?" Lewis redirected his attention to Tom.

Tom glanced at Kenny, who answered for him. "Jefferson Davis, Senator Honneker."

"He's from the local animal shelter," Tom put in. "The spin is that Miz Honneker here found him there, bought him and brought him to Sedgely to live. She very likely saved the poor animal's life."

Ronnie stared at Tom as the import of this sank in. He actually meant for her to lie about the acquisition of this—beast.

"Give me a break," she said witheringly, and turned

left toward the living room, where the interview and photo session were to take place.

Decorated in shades of soft gold, white, and rose with ornate, white-painted woodwork and sweeping silk drapes in a rose-and-white stripe, the living room—formerly the house's parlor—was large, beautiful, and impressive, and filled with antique furnishings and paintings. Lined with eight floor-to-ceiling windows, it had always reminded Ronnie of something out of a movie set. Even now it was hard for her to believe that people actually inhabited rooms like that.

Not that any member of the family ever did but Dorothy. It was used mainly for entertaining—and to impress visiting reporters and their ilk.

"I suppose I named the dog too? *Jefferson Davis?* How corny can you get?" Ronnie threw this last remark over her shoulder.

"It'll appeal to your husband's constituency—his *southern* constituency. Given the fact that you're from up north, you need to do what you can to seem more assimilated," Tom answered. He was behind Lewis, who was behind Ronnie. Kenny, with the dog, brought up the rear.

"You can just call him Davis if you want," Kenny put in. "He comes to that too."

Ronnie snorted. "He probably comes to anything. Have you tried 'dog'?"

"Now, Ronnie, I talked this over with Tom and he's got a good idea: This here dog'll appeal to just about every voter in Mississippi," Lewis said. "I want you to do like he says, and say you got him at an animal shelter 'cause you felt sorry for him and named him after Jeff Davis in honor of our great state and the late president of the Confederacy. It'll make people around these parts like you better. Anyway, I've been sayin' for a long time now that I've been wantin' a dog."

Lewis had said no such thing that Ronnie had ever heard. In fact Eleanor was allergic to fur, and as a consequence animals had not been allowed inside any of the family houses for the last thirty-eight years, a state of affairs that had never seemed to particularly bother anyone who lived therein. Though on the altar of all-mighty politics, Lewis would be willing to give houseroom to an elephant, let alone a dog.

"Fine. Whatever," Ronnie said over her shoulder. Her simmering rage at Tom was bubbling very near the surface, and she didn't want it to boil over in front of witnesses. She made an effort to rein in her temper as she passed through the open pocket doors of polished mahogany that separated the hall from the living room, where Dorothy awaited them.

"Good morning, Dorothy," Ronnie greeted her mother-in-law with a smile. Dressed in a mint-green summer suit, Dorothy looked both frail and elegant as she sat on the rose brocade sofa that was the centerpiece of the room.

"Ronnie."

"Good-mornin', Mama."

Dorothy's whole face lit up as Lewis walked into the room behind Ronnie.

"You're looking mighty handsome today, son," Dorothy said as he leaned down to kiss her cheek. When he straightened, she looked over at Ronnie, who was pouring herself a cup of coffee from the tray of refreshments that had been placed on a table in front of the window.

"You look real nice, too, Ronnie," she added.

"Thank you, Dorothy. So do you."

Ronnie knew that she did in fact look nice. She was once again wearing the triple strand of pearls Lewis had given her, with a cotton-blend dress in a shade of yellow so pale it was almost cream. The dress (selected by one of Tom's cohorts especially for this interview and photo session) was slim-fitting but not tight, with a jewel neckline, little cap sleeves, a straight skirt that reached midway down her calves, and a skinny belt made out of the same fabric as the dress. The hem and neckline were enhanced with delicate cutouts and pale yellow embroidery. Her shoes were beige leather pumps, with sensible two-inch heels.

Dorothy would have looked equally nice wearing exactly the same outfit.

"Lord-a-mercy, what is that?" Dorothy exclaimed as Davis came lumbering into the room, his toenails clicking on the polished wood floor. Kenny, holding the dog's leash, glanced up, but it was Lewis who answered.

"We got us a dog, Mama, for this interview. Tom's idea, and I think it's a good one. Voters love dogs. Tom's come up with a catchy slogan, too, for the campaign now that we're slugging things out toe-to-toe with Orde. What was that again, son?" Lewis asked Tom, frowning.

"HBO," Tom supplied. "Honneker Beats Orde."

"HBO," Lewis repeated to Dorothy. "Honneker Beats Orde. It's gonna look good on bumper stickers."

George Orde was a former state legislator who had zoomed up the polls as Lewis had stumbled. At this point he seemed to be the principal threat to Lewis's continued occupation of his Senate seat.

"If we keep on doing what we're doing, Orde shouldn't be too hard to beat," Tom said.

"I don't think so either," Lewis said.

"What's its name?" Dorothy asked, referring to the dog.

"Jefferson Davis," Ronnie said dryly. "Or just Davis for short."

Upon hearing his name, Davis wagged his tail, almost upsetting a porcelain shepherdess on a polished wood side table. With a quick grab Kenny saved the expensive antique from annihilation.

"Good dog," Lewis said, patting him while Kenny hung on to the leash with one hand and restored the figurine to its rightful place with the other.

"Senator, Mrs. Honneker, Mrs. Lewis: Miss Cambridge is here with Miss Topal and Mr. Folger from that magazine," Selma announced from the doorway. All eyes turned in her direction. Thea walked in past her, accompanied by a pony-tailed man in a T-shirt and jeans with a camera slung over one shoulder, and a fortyish woman with short, chicly styled brown hair, bright pink lipstick, and a beige business suit. In one hand the woman carried a leather briefcase. In the other she held a half-eaten doughnut.

With a mighty woof Davis went for the doughnut. Miss Topal dropped her briefcase with a shriek. A lamp crashed. Doughnut in mouth, leash trailing, Davis bounded into the hall with Kenny, Thea, and Selma in hot pursuit.

"Take this," Tom hissed in Ronnie's ear, shoving something cold and moist into her hand. Ronnie looked down at the object, first with surprise and then with revulsion. It was a small piece of ham purloined from one of the ham biscuits on the tray—what on earth?

She looked up at Tom with incomprehension. So surprised was she by this unexpected gift that she even forgot to glare.

"Davis, *here*!" Kenny yelled. The sound was close at hand, perhaps in the hall. Toenails scrabbling frantically over hard wood preceded the dog's reappearance by mere seconds. The reporter, Miss Topal, jumped back out of the way as fleeing dog and pursuing humans barreled back into the room.

The dog checked for a moment, lifting its head as if glancing around. Its nose tested the air. Then it headed straight for Ronnie.

Eyes widening, mouth falling open, she watched it come.

"Say his name: Davis. Call him!" Tom ordered under his breath. The urgency of the whisper prompted obedience.

"Davis!" Ronnie produced the name with a squeak.

The dog bounded to a stop in front of her, wagged its tail, and started urgently licking her hand. The photographer unslung his camera.

"Smile," Tom quietly instructed her as the camera started clicking away.

# Chapter

## 23

"SON, GETTING THAT DOG OUT HERE was a stroke of genius. Pure genius." Chuckling, the Senator clapped Tom on the shoulder as they walked into the dining room, where Selma was putting final touches to the table.

Tom could see that the room hadn't been changed by so much as a silver candlestick since he used to eat supper in it with his roommate's family nearly two decades before. The wallpaper was still the same, some unbelievably expensive hand-painted Chinese import. The drapes were heavy gold brocade, tied back to frame tall multipaned windows and thick with fringe. The furniture—a table that seated ten without the addition of any leaves, china cabinet, huntboard, and silver chest—was dark, heavily carved, and antique. The very plates used to set the table looked the same. The fine white china rimmed with gold was almost translucent, it was so old. Tom remembered how, as an impecunious college student eating with his roommate's rich and distinguished family, he had feared breaking a piece even by using his silverware too forcefully. He had cut his meat very, very carefully and scooped up his peas as if they were loaded with nitroglycerin, just in case.

Over the ensuing years Tom had changed a lot. Sedgely did not appear to have changed at all.

The Senator added, "That should be a heck of an article. Great pictures too. Ronnie with that dog! Great!"

"I'm glad it worked out so well, Senator," Tom said, stopping at the place Lewis indicated by a wave of his hand. He watched as His Honor walked around to his own chair at the head of the long, polished wooden table. After the *Ladies' Home Journal* people had left, he, Kenny, and Thea had been invited to stay for a late lunch with the family, and all had accepted.

Now, finding himself directly across from Ronnie, he almost wished he had declined. Ronnie managed to look both gorgeous and sexy even in the sedate dress picked out by the personal shopper at Nordstrom's. Ruby highlights brought out by the chandelier overhead glinted in her hair; her skin looked as creamy to the touch as he remembered it being. The subtle pink lipstick on her mouth enhanced rather than hid its fullness, just as the modest lines of her dress enhanced rather than hid her figure. With only the approved amount of makeup to add a little polish, her eyes were soft and full of secrets. She was wearing the pearls he had removed for her the day they had met and, he could have sworn—though surely so subtle a scent could not reach all the way across a table—the same enticing perfume.

She was mad at him. Whenever she glanced his way, ire crackled in the air around her as tangibly as sparks around a sparkler on the Fourth of July. He only hoped no one else could see it.

She was looking at him now. Standing behind her chair, hands curled around its ornately carved back, her gaze met his across the table.

"HBO and Jefferson Davis," she said under the cover of the general hubbub of everyone getting settled. "I can't believe you get paid for thinking up things like that."

Tom shrugged. "We've each got our specialties," he said, and sat down. He wasn't going to get into a fight with her. Not today, not tomorrow, not next week. He was going to turn the other cheek as many times as it took until her anger had burned itself out and the fire that still smoldered between them had cooled down.

After that Ronnie studiously ignored him, which Tom supposed was about as much as he could hope for under the circumstances. But the rigidity of her facial muscles and the occasional flash of her eyes warned that her anger was barely held in check. Anyone with an ounce of perception would be able to pick up on it in about two minutes flat.

Thank the Lord his tablemates did not seem to be blessed with much perception.

Selma wheeled in a serving cart laden with bowls of soup, distracting Tom's attention. Food was a good thing to focus on, he decided, safe and without hidden undercurrents. As his bowl was set before him, he saw it was cream of tomato with a dollop of cream and a sprig of dill on the top.

Ruby red and creamy white—Ronnie's colors.

Damn it, focus on the *food*.

It sure looked—and smelled—good. And the smell

was thankfully strong enough, and spicy enough, to overpower any wandering hint of a subtle, tantalizing perfume.

The soup *was* good. Tom concentrated on eating it.

"So, having used the poor dog as a political prop for all of two hours, I understand we're supposed to send him back to the pound," Ronnie said acidly, spoon in hand. She addressed the remark to the Senator; her glance flashed over Tom for no more than a second or two, but he felt its impact like a physical blow. "Don't you think that seems a little cruel?"

The rancor in her voice was meant for him alone. Tom knew it as well as if she'd shouted it aloud. He only hoped no one else realized it. A quick, hooded glance around the table reassured him. If his tablemates had the least suspicion that Ronnie was taking potshots at him, they were disguising it well. In fact they deserved Academy Awards.

None of them was that good at acting. Tom relaxed a little.

"Ronnie, honey, Sedgely's a big place. We can keep him if you want. How much trouble could one dog be?" The Senator's tone was placating, his smile at his young wife full of charm, though it seemed to soften her not at all. "It'll be fun for you, maybe, to have a pet."

Starting on his salad—it was as tasty as the soup—Tom wondered, as he had more often than was good for him lately, about the nature of the relationship between the Senator and his wife. Almost involuntarily he glanced from one to the other. Ronnie seemed cool to her husband, while he seemed almost juvenile in his eagerness to please her, which was perfectly under-

standable given recent events, Tom told himself. The
Senator, after all, had been discovered cheating on his
wife. Of course she was cool to him, and he wanted to
make it up to her.

Had her come-on to him been part of a campaign to
punish His Honor for straying?

Tom didn't like the idea of that. He frowned across
the table at Ronnie without even realizing what he was
doing until she returned his glare measure for measure.

The salad—no, it was an open-faced grilled chicken
sandwich now—sure was good.

Ronnie and the Senator didn't act like lovers,
though, not even lovers in the throes of a serious mari-
tal crisis. When they were together, he didn't sense
any—heat.

From personal experience he knew that Ronnie was
capable of generating considerable heat.

As he had too many times since meeting her, Tom
caught himself wondering how His Honor and his wife
were together in bed. An old man like the Senator with
a beautiful, sexy young wife like Ronnie was bound to
want to get it on—

His hand tightened on the knife he was using to cut
into his sandwich. It made a squeaking noise against
the plate.

Immediately Tom sought to redirect his thoughts.

"I don't really like dogs underfoot," Dorothy said
placidly, and Tom realized they must have been dis-
cussing the pros and cons of Jefferson Davis as a pet
for some time. "They shed."

"I can take the dog home with me if you want," he
said to Dorothy, contributing to the conversation as if

he had faithfully followed every word. "I'll take him to my mother's house. There's room there for a big dog."

His gaze unintentionally crossed Ronnie's, and held. If her attitude toward the Senator was cool, Tom found himself thinking, it was the opposite when it came to himself. Temper still snapped from her eyes. *Careful,* he willed her silently. It wouldn't do either of them any good for His Honor or anyone else to suspect that their relationship was or had ever been anything other than strictly business.

"Your mother's house." Ronnie's words were drawn out, almost drawled, which for a girl from Boston was quite a feat. Tom almost smiled. The antagonism in her gaze softened slightly, and he could see that she was remembering, as he was, the afternoon they had spent at the farm. That afternoon they had been friends.

"That's a good idea," Kenny said jovially. "Plenty of room to run there. It's a farm."

The last was clearly offered as an explanation to those who might not know.

"I hate to impose like that on your mother." Ronnie's gaze met his again, and suddenly the enmity was back in her eyes in full force. Turning her attention to the Senator, she smiled with melting sweetness. "It's nice of you to say we can keep him, Lewis. I think I *would* like a dog."

The look she fixed on His Honor was positively sugar-coated. For a moment Tom was taken aback; only then did he realize that Ronnie had never before been much more than civil to the Senator in his presence.

They were husband and wife. Sometime, somewhere, surely the two of them had to generate some heat.

The Senator had been an old man when Tom was in college. Or at least at that time Tom had considered him an old man. When he had thought of him at all, it had been as his roommate's rich and influential father; at one time he'd even considered him as a potential father-in-law. Certainly not by any stretch of the imagination had he ever pictured Lewis Honneker as the husband of a girl he himself wanted to take to bed.

Impossible to picture Ronnie making love with His Honor, as he and Marsden and the girls had referred to the Senator all those years ago. Tom didn't want to even try.

Though he couldn't seem to help it.

*What the Senator and his wife did, or didn't do, in bed was none of his damned business.*

The Senator returned Ronnie's smile with delight. Tom recognized that expression: It was the hopeful one of a man trying to dig his way out of the doghouse. He recognized something else, too: the melting look Ronnie had sent her husband had really been intended as a shot fired directly at *him*.

Tom realized with a blinding flash of insight that the ingredients for a disaster of major proportions were in place. If he didn't take himself out of Ronnie's orbit, sooner or later the situation was going to blow up in his face.

He wanted her too badly. And, God help him, he was turned on to the back teeth by the certain knowledge that she wanted him.

"Oh, dear, do you really want to keep that dog,

Ronnie?" Dorothy was saying doubtfully. "Well, I suppose we can give it a try."

"He's a real nice dog," Kenny said. "He'll make you a good pet."

"He doesn't seem very well trained," Thea put in.

"We'll send him to doggie obedience school." Ronnie smiled, switching her attention to Kenny. "You could arrange something like that, couldn't you, Kenny? You seem to be so efficient at getting things done."

She batted her long eyelashes at Kenny, who looked momentarily dazzled at the sheer wattage of the sex appeal being turned his way.

Jesus Christ, the woman was a menace! She was flirting with poor, unsuspecting *Kenny* now. And all for his benefit, Tom knew.

He wanted to shake her till her teeth rattled. He wanted to kiss her senseless. He wanted to send time winging back to that hotel room in Tupelo and to roll on top of her in that bed and love her until she begged for mercy.

Even as his groin tightened at the images he conjured up, Tom saw the handwriting on the wall: *Time to get the hell out of Dodge.*

# Chapter

## 24

FOR THE NEXT COUPLE OF WEEKS Tom vanished from Ronnie's life. Kenny seemed to have taken his place as her omnipresent adviser. Her schedule was crowded, and he attended most official functions with her and her entourage. Usually Thea came along too. From the way the two of them behaved, Ronnie sometimes felt like the third wheel at her own party. Even when crowds were present—no, especially when crowds were present—she felt lonely.

Only a fool would not prefer to be handled by Kenny rather than his missing partner, Ronnie told herself. As far as political consultants went, they were two very different animals. Kenny was always cheerful; he never criticized her clothing, her makeup, her hairstyle, her behavior, or the speeches she gave. He never criticized her at all. The few times he made a comment on something she might want to mention at an upcoming event, it was couched as a suggestion, not an order, sandwiched between loads of praise.

Kenny was a pleasant, undemanding, helpful companion.

She felt not the smallest degree of sexual attraction for him, although she liked him very much.

As days passed, the question that began to occupy her mind to the exclusion of almost everything else was, Where was Tom?

Unable to bear not knowing any longer, Ronnie finally swallowed her pride and asked Thea—very casually.

"Oh, Kenny says they've picked up some new clients, and Tom is busy with them. You know, mapping out strategy and all. I guess they think you're doing well enough in the polls now that you don't need him so much anymore."

*But I do need him.* Ronnie barely stopped herself from saying it aloud.

Let the polls go hang. She needed Tom.

He called at least once that she knew about. She was sitting behind the desk in her office when the phone rang. It was late afternoon, not long after Thea had gone home for the day. It wasn't the house phone— Selma would have gotten that—but the personal line into her office.

Ronnie almost switched on the answering machine, thinking that it was probably someone wanting her to attend some event or other. But at the last minute she changed her mind and picked up the receiver, perfectly prepared to pretend to be her own secretary if necessary.

"Hello?" she said cautiously.

"Ronnie?"

She would have recognized that deep, drawling voice at the bottom of the darkest cave on the farthest side of the world. Her hand tightened on the receiver, and she pressed it closer to her ear.

"Tom."

She should say more, she knew, but it seemed to be all she could manage for the moment, just his name.

"What're you doing answering the phone?"

*It's my phone, why shouldn't I answer it?* she thought. What she said was, "Thea's gone home."

"Oh."

She could hear him breathing, slow and regular. He didn't seem in a hurry to say anything, and she wasn't either. The only thing that scared her was that he might hang up.

"How are you?" he asked after a moment.

"Fine. I'm fine." It was stupid, but she couldn't seem to think properly, much less summon up sensible conversation. "How are you?"

"Fine." He took a breath. "Well . . ."

"Where are you?" she asked hurriedly, clutching the receiver tighter. It was her only link to him.

"Nevada." She could hear a sudden smile in his voice. "There's a governor's race coming up. A tight one."

"Bill Myer?" She named the Nevada incumbent.

"Nah. Matt Grolin. A challenger. Looks like he's got a fair shot at an upset."

"With you to help him."

There was a brief pause. "My, that was an uncharacteristically nice thing for you to say to me."

"I can be nice."

The timbre of his voice dropped a notch. "I remember."

"Tom."

"Mmm?"

"Are you consulting for the candidate—or his wife?"

"Either or both, as needed."

The thought of him advising some other woman on everything from her shoes to her speeches was not pleasant.

"Is Mrs. Grolin pretty?"

He laughed. The short bark of amusement was so familiar that it made her ache. "Very attractive—for a sixty-two-year-old."

That made Ronnie smile. "Oh. Good."

"Ronnie—" He broke off.

"Yes?" she asked after a moment.

"Is Kenny taking care of things okay for you?" Whatever he had been going to say, that was not it. Ronnie could tell from the change in his tone.

"He never criticizes me," she said.

"Oh, God." He laughed again.

"I got an advance copy of that *Ladies' Home Journal* article. It turned out well."

"I knew it would. How's Davis?"

"Big and hairy." Ronnie's voice was dry. Tom chuckled.

"He still at Sedgely?"

"Yes. Selma's taking him to obedience school. He has fleas, and he wants to jump in my lap all the time. And he keeps licking me. I think he's looking for another piece of ham."

Tom was laughing now. "Smart dog."

"You wouldn't think so if he was jumping on *you*."

"Where is everybody tonight?"

"Like I said, Thea's gone home. Kenny's gone

home. Dorothy's at a bridge game. Selma's somewhere around. And Lewis is in—let me see—Friar's Point, at the dedication of a memorial to Conway Twitty."

"How is His Honor?" There was a subtle change in Tom's tone. The mere mention of her husband erected a barrier between them, Ronnie realized, and she wished she could call back the words.

"Lewis is just fine."

"He's really the reason I called."

"Oh?" Her voice cooled slightly.

"Yeah. In a minute, when you hang up, I'm going to fax him a sample storyboard for an ad campaign. He wanted my suggestions on some things he could use against Orde."

"If you wanted to talk to Lewis, why didn't you call his office?" she asked. "He has three. Downstairs, downtown, and in Washington."

"I did. All three. Nobody answered."

"I see." Ronnie took a deep breath. "So you had to make do with calling my office instead. Lucky for you I was in."

"Yeah. Lucky."

"I guess I had better hang up so that you can send that fax."

"Ronnie . . ."

"What?"

A slight hesitation. "You're right. You had better hang up."

"All right, then. Good-bye."

"Bye."

Ronnie took the receiver from her ear and looked down at it for a minute. She wanted to say—what did she want to say? *When are you coming home? Are you coming home?*

But she couldn't. He hadn't even called to talk to her. He wanted nothing to do with her, because she was a married woman and he wasn't a jerk.

The jerk.

She hung up the phone.

And almost cried.

She would have, if she hadn't absolutely refused to let a jerk like Tom Quinlan reduce her to tears.

Besides her campaign-related appearances, Ronnie had plenty to do. She flew with Lewis to the funeral of a Senate colleague who'd been killed in the crash of his private plane, and she was gone for two days. She was on the boards of several organizations, all of which had meetings. A lot of her time was taken up by preparing for the International Ballet Competition, which came to the United States every four years and was scheduled for Jackson in 1998. The plans for Lewis's annual birthday party were also proceeding apace. Someone had to supervise the arrangements, and Dorothy tired more easily than she had even the year before, which left Ronnie to make sure things got done. With all that going on, one would have thought that Ronnie would have had no time whatsoever to think about Tom.

One would have thought wrong.

She thought—she hoped—he would not miss Lewis's party. She was almost sure he would come. Nobody who was invited missed the annual event if it could be helped.

On the Wednesday before the big day his RSVP finally came in the mail with a handful of others. To make things simpler, they had started including reply cards in the invitations just as was done for weddings.

His invitation had been addressed to Mr. Thomas S. Quinlan and guest.

The reply card said two would be attending.

Would he be bringing his girlfriend, the one Thea said he was thinking about marrying? Ronnie wondered. The idea did not please her. She realized she was jealous of a woman she had never even seen. Tom's girlfriend. Just formulating the words in her mind made her mad.

But at least he was coming.

Upon reflection, she didn't care if he brought the entire Swedish bikini team, as long as he came with them.

All her animosity toward him had faded away; the only thing she could think of now was how much she wanted to see him again.

# Chapter

## 25

ON THE EVENING OF THE PARTY Ronnie spent an inordinate amount of time getting ready. She was nervous, which was unusual for her. It wasn't the prospect of five-hundred-plus guests that put the butterflies in her stomach, or the knowledge that the press would be present as they were every year to record the festivities, or even thoughts of the dozens of things that could go wrong.

She certainly wasn't worried about her appearance: She knew she looked good. She was wearing an Isaac Mizrahi gown of flame-red jersey knit, set with hundreds of crystal brilliants that glittered with her every movement. It had tiny spaghetti straps and a low neckline that showed plenty of cleavage. From her bosom to just above her knees it clung like a second skin, lovingly hugging every curve. From there it flared flamenco-style into a frothing cascade of ruffles. By itself the dress was knock-'em-in-the-aisles gorgeous. Worn with flame-red satin sandals with skinny three-inch heels and a delicate diamond necklace and earrings, the outfit was to die for.

Tom would probably say it was too sexy—for a senator's wife. With a small smile Ronnie acknowledged to herself that for once Tom would be right.

Looking at her reflection in the huge mirror that made up one entire wall of her dressing room, she was pleased with what she saw. Her hair was twirled up in a soft french twist that allowed loose tendrils to frame her face. Her eyes were softly lined and shadowed in the smoky charcoal shade she had preferred before Tom and his polls had dragooned her into drabber earth tones. Except for the feather of blush accenting each cheekbone, her skin was milky white, and as flawless as fine porcelain. Her mouth was stained the same bright red as her dress.

She looked beautiful, she knew.

The band began playing right before Ronnie left her room. It was just after dark—a warm, beautiful late-August night. Everything was set. The party was getting underway.

Lewis, she knew, would be outside greeting the guests. Garrulous by nature, he was in his element as the star of a big bash. Dorothy was almost certainly outside, too, doing the honors as hostess as well or better than Ronnie could have done. Marsden and his wife, Evangeline, would be busy circulating and seeing to the guests' comfort, as would Joanie and Laura and their husbands. Lewis's party had been an annual event for years, growing bigger each time. The family members all had roles to play and with much experience, they played them effortlessly.

Ronnie was the newcomer. She knew that if she stayed in her room, she would scarcely be missed.

Other years, during other parties, she had thought

about it, hating to be the cynosure of all eyes. Ninety percent of these people had been friends of Eleanor's.

But not tonight. Tonight a dozen nuts armed with paint cans couldn't have kept her in her room.

Tonight she walked down the grand staircase, one hand on the rail, the ruffles around her calves rustling silkily as she moved, with a whole meadow's worth of butterflies in her stomach.

Because tonight Tom would be there.

# Chapter
# 26

THE BAND'S LEAD SINGER was crooning *"You-ou take my breath away. . . ."* when he saw her. Under the circumstances the aptness of the song was almost funny. Only it was hard to laugh when he felt like he'd been kicked in the gut by a mule.

He had come tonight thinking he was pretty well armored against her. One sight of her and he knew he had been wrong.

Just that fast and he wanted her so much he ached, so much that he felt as though his body had suddenly seized up and suspended all vital functions.

She literally took his breath away. He watched her and forgot to breathe.

For just a moment she paused on the back veranda, one hand on the railing as she looked out over the crowd of partygoers. Then she came down the stairs, her head high, her slender figure erect. Flashbulbs exploded like shooting stars around her as photographers took her picture. That light, and the light from hundreds of Japanese lanterns strung in the trees, seemed to catch on her red dress as she moved, turning it into a column of living flame. Her hair was up, exposing her slender neck and shoulders and a whole lot of creamy white bosom. Her eyes were huge and smoky, her mouth crimson. Flashes of fire glittered around her neck and at her ears.

Fire and ice. That was Ronnie to a tee.

"Who's *that?*" Diane said. She must have followed his gaze, because she was staring at Ronnie, too, with the faintest of frowns between her brows. Dear, sweet Diane, who was looking very lovely tonight herself in a slender blue satin evening gown with her blond bob fresh from the beauty parlor and her makeup all pink and tasteful.

"Mrs. Honneker," Tom said briefly, tearing his eyes away from Ronnie and the bedlam around her to focus on Diane. "Are you ready for another drink?"

"Mrs. Honneker?" Diane's voice rose an octave with amazement, and she completely ignored his query about the drink, as though she suspected somehow that it was nothing more than a red herring designed to distract her. Her head swiveled. Tom presumed she was following Ronnie's progress through the crowd. "The Senator's wife?" She goggled, then nodded. "Of *course* it is. No *wonder* they say the things they do about her. In the pictures I've seen of her, she looks a lot more—sedate."

"She must have pulled out all the stops tonight." Tom worked hard at sounding indifferent. He refused to look away from his date. "Do you want to dance?"

Without waiting for an answer, he deposited her half-finished drink and his own on a nearby table, and pulled her out onto the dance floor—one of three actually, all of which were just starting to get crowded.

*"You-ou take my breath away. . . ."*

Only Diane didn't. Holding her in his arms, with her breasts against his chest and her thighs brushing his, Tom felt nothing. Nada. Zip.

Except a hard, aching lust for Ronnie, whom he had thankfully lost sight of in the crowd.

Two hours passed before Tom saw her again. He and Diane had linked up with Kenny and Ann, strolling the grounds, watching the festivities more as observers than as participants. Without being obvious about it, he had managed to steer them away from the main tent, where the Senator's birthday cake was cut, toasts were made, and all the other hoopla was centered. This was strategic on Tom's part: He wanted time to get his head on straight before he encountered Ronnie face-to-face.

He would have left if he could have thought of a good reason for doing so. But he couldn't. The night was warm and clear, the food was good, the music danceable. Three huge white tents had been set up on an area of the back lawn; the food buffet was in the left one, the bar in the right, the extravagant birthday cake in the center. The band played from a gazebo near the large stone patio closest to the house, but the music was carried everywhere by an elaborate sound system. Beyond the tents, the sloping grounds were terraced, with brick paths outlined by fifty-year-old boxwood hedges. There were patios on each of the three terrace levels. Citronella torches flamed everywhere, contributing exotic atmosphere as well as insect protection. Masses of salmon and pink and red impatiens circled nearly every tree and formed a stunning display in shades of purple in an out-of-the-way rock garden. A small, raised rose bed with a bubbling fountain for a centerpiece formed the nucleus of another stone patio that had been put into use as a dance floor.

It was there that Tom encountered Ronnie.

Strolling along one of the nearby paths, he was hailed by Marsden and beckoned over. His former roommate was standing with his wife, Evangeline, a plumpish blonde whom Tom had met briefly years before but didn't really know, and his sister Joanie and her husband.

"Tom!" Joanie greeted him with a hug. Strange to think he'd almost married her; he scarcely remembered her. She must be just about thirty-five now, he estimated. Her hair was as dark as ever, though she wore it boyishly short where once it had been long, and her body was even more wiry and athletic than it had been when she was a girl.

"You're looking good," he said as she released him, and meant it.

She gave him a once-over. "So are you." Glancing at her tall, balding husband, who stood smiling beside her, she added, "You remember Syd."

Tom didn't, but he nodded, and introduced Diane, Kenny, and Ann. The three old friends spent a few minutes catching up with each others' lives and families, exclaiming over the ages and number of children they had each produced.

Then Marsden nudged Tom, drawing him a little apart from the chatting group.

"I want you to look at that," he said under his breath.

Turning, Tom looked where Marsden indicated, and felt his insides seize up again.

Ronnie was dancing, with her back to him. The paper lanterns overhead bathed her in soft yellow light. Her dark red hair looked thick and soft in its upsweep, which left the creamy skin of her nape and upper back bare except for the lacing of diamonds around her neck. The glittering flame of her dress started just below her shoulder blades, then clung all the way down to her knees, where it flared out in a cascade of frills. With every step she took, her backside swayed an invitation.

Her partner was a man Tom couldn't quite place, though he was ready to swear he'd seen him before somewhere. He was of medium height, a little on the stocky side, his light-brown hair cut militarily short, his tux tight across broad shoulders. He had one arm around Ronnie's slender waist, held one of her red-tipped hands too tightly, and was looking at her with a grin that was about one tooth short of an open leer.

"Who's the guy?" he asked, careful to keep his voice in neutral.

"Senator Beau Hilley of Texas. Chairman of the Ways and Means Committee. Likely front-runner for the Republican nomination in 2000. Possibly the next president of the United States." Marsden shook his head. "Stupid prick. Eleven o'clock, and he's already had too much to drink. Don't he look to you like he wants to jump Stepmama's bones right there on the dance floor?"

"He's married, isn't he? Where's his wife?" Tom asked, not bothering to reply directly. Anyone with eyes in his head could answer Marsden's last question.

Though Tom had never worked for Hilley, he'd met him and as was the way of it in the small world of political insiders, had heard a lot about him. The man was a self-made millionaire, an able legislator, ambitious, hard-driving. He had two primary weak points: alcohol and women. Both were on display at the moment.

"Over there with Daddy."

A nod of Marsden's head sent Tom glancing around to his left. Sure enough, there was His Honor, dancing with an attractive blonde woman in a midnight-blue gown.

"Can you believe that bitch? I swear I think she'd come on to a maple tree if it had a branch at the right height."

Tom's gaze swung back to Marsden. It had taken only an incredulous split second to realize that "that bitch" referred to Ronnie. And Tom realized that he didn't have the right to do anything about it.

"Looks to me like all she's doing's dancing." Delivered in a mild enough tone, it was still a rebuke, though not the rebuke Tom would have made if he'd had his druthers.

Marsden grunted. "Sure can see why Daddy married her, though, can't you? If that bitch ain't sex on the hoof, then I ain't never seen it. Wouldn't mind havin' some myself, if she weren't married to Daddy."

"She is." The words were clipped. It was all Tom could do to speak civilly. Rage was rising in his veins, rage hot and thick as lava. It wasn't often that he lost his temper, but he felt on the verge of it now. His hands clenched into fists at his sides as he fought the urge to punch Marsden out, then stalk out onto the dance floor and do the same to Ronnie's lecherous dance partner.

Marsden sighed. "Well, better break that up before it gets out of hand. We don't want problems with Hilley, and that there's a no-win situation if I ever saw it. If Stepmama turns him down, he's gonna be mad. If Stepmama don't turn him down—and I don't think she turns down much that wears pants—Daddy's gonna be mad if he finds out. Either way, tonight we don't need it. We got big press and big donors here."

Marsden took a step toward the dance floor. Tom stopped him with a hand on his arm.

"I'll do it," he said, and started walking toward Ronnie.

It was a mistake, Tom knew it was a mistake even as he was doing it, and he couldn't stop himself one bit more than he could stop his heart from beating. The way he felt at the moment, Marsden would lay hands on Ronnie only if he did it over Tom's dead body. Nobody was laying hands on Ronnie—but him.

Déjà vu all over again, he thought ironically as he tapped the salivating senator on the shoulder.

"Excuse me, Senator," he said as the man gave him an irritated glance. "There's an urgent phone call for you up at the house."

"Urgent?" Hilley frowned, and stopped dancing.

"Urgent," Tom confirmed, taking possession of Ronnie's hand. Her fingers felt cool and delicate and silky soft against his. Her damned perfume was already filling his nostrils as he pulled her toward him.

Hilley looked in the direction of the house. "Excuse me, Ronnie, I'll just take that call and be right back. Don't you go wandering off anywhere, now."

"I won't, Senator," Ronnie promised, already sliding into Tom's arms.

"Beau. You call me Beau."

"Beau," Ronnie said over her shoulder with a smile, even as Tom danced her away.

"Do you flirt with every man you meet?" Tom asked with an edge to his voice when her gaze came around to his. Her waist felt firm and supple beneath his hand. Her breasts brushing his chest threatened to set him on fire. Her thighs touched his, and he ached. He fought the fight of his life to keep any of it from showing to what he knew was a whole gallery of interested observers.

"Jealous?" she asked, lifting her brows at him teasingly.

"Yes." Tom was surprised to hear himself admit it. The word signaled surrender; he recognized it even as it came out of his mouth. His hand tightened on her back, his fingers sinking into the thin stuff of her dress to feel her skin. It was all he could do not to pull her tight up against him. He had to remind himself, again, that they were not alone.

And no matter how he felt, he could not let it show. For her sake as well as his own.

"Good," she said. Then she smiled with a slow, tantalizing sweetness, right up into his eyes. "Hello, Tom."

That smile caused him more pain than a fist to the stomach. It was all he could do to keep dancing.

"Hello, Ronnie. Still mad at me?"

She shook her head. "I missed you."

"I thought Kenny never criticized you."

"He doesn't. I missed you anyway."

"I'm glad to hear it." He turned with her so that his back was to their primary audience, afraid of what an acute observer might read in his face. "You look beautiful tonight."

"Thank you. I thought you might think this dress was too sexy."

He smiled, his eyes sliding down as much of her as he could see. "It sure is that."

"But you're not going to yell at me?"

"I've given myself the night off."

"Oh," Ronnie said, and paused. Then, "Was there really a phone call for Senator Hilley?"

"No."

"I didn't think so." She smiled up at him again. Looking down into her eyes, Tom felt his stomach tighten. It wasn't just that she was beautiful, though she was; it wasn't just that he wanted her, though he did. He felt as if she belonged to him.

Though she didn't.

"A whole bunch of people were watching you dance with Hilley, and I'd be willing to bet the ranch they're watching you dance with me. So be careful." It was hard to warn her when what he wanted to do was sweep her up into his arms and kiss her senseless right in front of them all.

"I'm tired of being careful."

"Unfortunately sometimes it's necessary."

"Why did you go away?"

Tom laughed, more rueful than amused. He could claim the demands of his newly burgeoning business required it, but it wouldn't be the truth. At least not the real truth. And she would know it as well as he did. "You know the answer to that."

"Then why did you come back?"

"Because I couldn't help it." There was more truth, he realized even as he said it. He had been fooling himself thinking he was coming here tonight because it was safe to do so, because he had his attraction to her well under control. In reality he'd jumped at the excuse the invitation had offered him, because he simply couldn't stay away.

He had to see her again.

"I see you brought your girlfriend."

Ronnie hadn't looked in Diane's direction, not that Tom had seen, and he doubted that he'd missed a breath she'd drawn since he'd turned around to find her on the dance floor. She must have spotted Diane before Marsden had brought the situation with Hilley to his attention, and Tom wondered how much of her flirting had been for his benefit.

"Jealous?" he asked as she had done.

"Yes."

"Good." Having danced her as far away from the gallery as he could, he smiled down into her eyes and infinitesimally tightened his hold on her.

"She's very attractive."

"Thank you."

"Wholesome-looking."

"She is wholesome, yes."

"I bet she's nice."

"Yes, she is."

"Are you going to marry her?"

Tom's eyes narrowed. "What do you think?"

"I think you'd be making a mistake if you did."

"And why is that?"

"Because she doesn't turn you on." Her eyes were

warm and caressing on his face. A tiny smile curved the corners of her mouth. Her hand on his shoulder was in precisely the correct spot, but it seemed to burn through the material of his tux and shirt as if it were made of liquid fire.

"How do you know?"

"Does she?"

"I'm not going to answer that."

"She doesn't." Her lids lowered, then flicked back up again so that their gazes met. "Tell the truth, Tom."

Jesus, she was killing him. "Could we not talk about Diane, please?"

"Why not?"

"Because she doesn't have anything to do with this."

"You mean with us?"

"You know that's what I mean."

"*Is* there an us?"

"It seems like it, doesn't it?"

"You don't sound very happy about it."

"I wasn't happy when I caught the chicken pox as a kid, either, but there wasn't a damn thing I could do about it but scratch."

Ronnie smiled. "Are you comparing me to the chicken pox?"

"You're worse. I was over the chicken pox in a week."

"Tom." There was a subtle change in her tone. A slight frown marred the smooth flesh between her brows.

"Mmm?"

"Here comes Lewis. I think he wants to change partners."

Tom's grip on her tightened with instinctive posses-
siveness, but there was no help for it.

He had to turn over the woman he wanted to the
man whose wife she was.

And he had to do it with a smile.

# Chapter

## 27

OM LET GO OF HER AND STEPPED AWAY, smiling at Mrs. Hilley even as Lewis took Ronnie in his arms. They hadn't taken two steps before the music stopped. Thankful, Ronnie pulled away from Lewis and headed toward the sidelines where her husband's children were standing with Kenny and his wife—and Tom's girlfriend.

Tom followed close behind Lewis. Ronnie didn't have to look around to know that. She seemed able to sense his presence with her nerve endings.

The girlfriend was pretty. Ronnie hadn't really expected her not to be. She wore an ice-blue satin dress with a jewel neckline and a straight skirt that fell to her ankles, sleeveless but not in the least bare, and a single strand of pearls. Her hair was chin length, curved under on the ends, an elegantly simple blond bob. Her nose was small and straight, her chin square. A full mouth was probably her best feature; her worst was rather smallish eyes. Though she was still too far away to be able to tell for certain, Ronnie was ready to bet that they'd be blue.

A blue-eyed blonde wearing blue. Safe, predictable, and boring.

Tom deserved better than that.

Kenny's wife was blond, too, but her hair was longer and fluffier to suit her rounder shape. She wore a full-skirted strapless dress that was black on the top and white on the bottom. It would have suited her better if the colors were the other way around. Kenny was saying something to her that was making her laugh. Her hand curled possessively around his arm.

Marsden had a glint in his eye and a curl to his lips as he watched her and his father approach. Ronnie knew what he thought of her; knew, too, that he'd like to get her into bed.

There was about as much chance of that happening as there was of aliens taking over the earth. She despised Marsden as much as he despised her. No, more, because she felt not the slightest degree of lust for him.

Marsden's wife, Evangeline, at one with her husband in all things (or so she thought), was wrinkling her little pug nose as Ronnie drew near, as if she smelled a bad smell.

Syd's gaze was frankly admiring, while Joanie's was both envious and speculative as it touched on Ronnie, then moved beyond her to Tom. Ronnie remembered that Joanie had once been all but engaged to Tom; she wondered if Lewis's daughter still had particularly sensitive radar where he was concerned. She wouldn't be surprised if Joanie was picking up on the tension between them. It seemed to arc from Tom to her like an electric current, hot enough to scorch the air.

Lewis caught up with her as she stopped before the

group, sliding an arm around her waist. Smiling, Ronnie fought the urge to shrug it off.

It was getting so that she could barely tolerate Lewis's slightest touch.

"Hi, Daddy." Joanie greeted her father, placing a hand on Lewis's arm and standing on tiptoe to kiss his cheek. "I'm sorry I missed out on seeing you cut your birthday cake. Happy birthday, though."

"Thank you, baby. Where were you?"

Whatever his faults as a husband, Lewis was an affectionate parent, Ronnie had to admit. He loved his three children, and they were devoted to him.

"Oh, Carter came down with another ear infection this afternoon. You know how they go."

Carter was Joanie's four-year-old daughter.

"Poor little girl."

"Have you all met Mrs. Hilley?" Tom asked as the pair joined them. He stepped past Ronnie, moving easily to his girlfriend's side. Only a few paces away, he stood facing her but not looking at her, his hand on Diane's elbow.

Ronnie was surprised by how much she didn't like that.

They all greeted Mrs. Hilley.

"Diane, Ann, you haven't met Senator and Mrs. Honneker. This is Diane Albright, and Kenny's wife Ann Goodman," Tom continued the introductions.

"Hello." Smiling, Ronnie shook hands with them both.

"So this is your woman." After shaking hands with Ann, Lewis turned to Diane, looking her up and down. To Tom he added, "I see you still have good taste."

"Why, thank you, Senator," Diane said with a laugh. Tom merely smiled.

Ronnie, pricked by what she knew was a totally unworthy jealousy, turned to Ann and said, "I've enjoyed working with your husband."

Kenny chuckled. "She just says that 'cause I'm a marshmallow. I admit it."

Ronnie grinned at him. "A very *nice* marshmallow."

Lewis glanced at Tom. "I hear Tom here's the hard-ass."

"That's why we hired him, Daddy," Marsden put in.

"I don't think I'd describe myself in quite that way," Tom said.

"Let's ask Ronnie." Joanie turned to her step-mother. "She's the one who ought to know. What do you think? Is Tom a hard-ass?"

There was an air of mischief making about Joanie, Ronnie thought, and she wondered again if Lewis's daughter had picked up on something between Tom and her.

Ronnie glanced at Tom, as if considering Joanie's question. It was hard to keep her manner casual. He looked mouthwateringly handsome in his black tux, she thought, with his blond hair shining in the lantern light and his eyes so very blue. His face was impassive, his expression just a little guarded as she met his gaze.

She fought the urge to smile at him.

"Definitely," she pronounced, knowing that too cautious a reply would be a mistake.

His mouth quirked at her. "Thank you very much."

"You're welcome." For a few seconds their gazes

locked. Then Tom turned his attention to Mrs. Hilley, courteously inquiring about her family.

Ronnie looked at Ann Goodman. "And your husband is *not* a marshmallow. He's just very much the gentleman."

"He got us the darndest dog," Lewis put in.

"He got you a dog?" Ann sounded surprised.

"Big dog. Named Davis. Ronnie here likes him, though."

Ronnie laughed at the horrified expression on Ann's face. "Actually I'm very grateful to Kenny for bringing us Davis. I *like* Davis. He's around here somewhere."

"I shut him in the basement," Marsden said. "Selma said he was after the buffet."

"He probably was." All the while Ronnie smiled and chatted she was burningly conscious of Tom standing not three feet away. His gaze slid her way from time to time as she spoke; Ronnie could feel the heat of it before it snapped back to Mrs. Hilley, who was talking to him.

His hand still curved around Diane's elbow. But then, Lewis's arm was around her waist.

Ronnie wondered if Tom hated Lewis's hands on her as much as she hated his hand on Diane.

"Actually the dog was Tom's idea. He just made me do the dirty work," Kenny said.

"He always was good at getting other people to do his dirty work," Joanie said, with the air of one reminiscing. She looked at Marsden with a grin. "Do you remember when he lost his chemistry notes the night before the final and got you to call the professor and say he had to go home because his mother had been hit by a car and was dying?"

Marsden laughed. "I sure do."

Tom said warningly, "Don't start telling tales out of school, guys, unless you want me to reciprocate."

The three of them exchanged measuring looks, then grins. Ronnie reminded herself that Marsden and Joanie were old friends of Tom's. It was something she tended to forget.

Actually it was something she would rather forget.

"Have you known Tom long?" she asked Diane politely.

"About ten years. I was a colleague of—" Here Diane broke off, glancing apologetically up at Tom.

"Sandra's," Tom finished dryly. "It's okay, Diane. You can mention my ex-wife."

Ronnie hadn't know her name was Sandra. She was suddenly curious. "A colleague of hers? What do you do?"

"I'm a teacher. Fourth grade."

"That sounds fascinating." So Tom's sleep-around ex-wife had been a teacher. She flicked a glance at him.

"Not really. Twenty-three ten-year-olds can get pretty wearing. I'm hoping to retire soon."

"Oh, really?" Like when you marry Tom? was the question that hovered on the tip of Ronnie's tongue, but she bit it back. She wondered if Diane expected to marry him.

A glance at Tom's hand still curved with accustomed ease around the other woman's elbow answered that question: Of course she did. They'd been going together a long time.

The band struck up again.

"Lucy, you feel like dancing?" Lewis turned to Mrs. Hilley.

"Thank you, I believe I do. Lovely to meet you all." Mrs. Hilley smiled at them, then let Lewis lead her onto the patio.

"You know, I hate to break this up, but you and Joanie and Ronnie should really be circulating," Tom said to Marsden. "This is a work night for you guys."

"You're right." Marsden glanced at his sister briefly, then turned to his wife. "Come on, Evangeline, let's go see if we can fill a few more campaign coffers." He took his wife's hand and started pulling her away. "See you all later."

"This party has gotten to be hard work." Joanie sighed. "Fun time's over, Syd, let's go circulate."

Ronnie was left with her political consultants and their dates. Ann was humming along with the band.

"Let's dance, sweetie," Kenny said to her, and with a quick "excuse us" they headed onto the floor.

Tom looked at Ronnie over Diane's head. She could read his thoughts in his eyes as plainly as if he'd said them aloud.

He wanted to dance with her. But he was going to dance with Diane.

*Coward,* she told him silently. Then she dropped her gaze to smile at Diane.

"You two enjoy yourselves. I think I'm going to go up to the house for a while. I've got just a smidgen of a headache."

Her gaze flickered to Tom again. "It's funny, but when we have a party going on, the only place I seem able to get any peace and quiet is my office."

Tom got the message. She knew he did. She could see it in his eyes. The question was, Would he act on it?

He would, if he wanted to be alone with her as badly as she wanted to be alone with him.

"It was a pleasure to meet you, Mrs. Honneker," Diane said.

"Please call me Ronnie." Ronnie corrected her with a smile. "And it was a pleasure to meet you too. Any friend of Tom's, you know . . ."

She let her voice trail off. With a handshake and a smile for Diane, and one more unsmiling glance for Tom, she headed for the house.

In the kitchen she spoke briefly to the caterers, who were frantically refilling platters under Selma's eagle-eyed supervision, and poured herself a glass of water.

"Party's going great, Mrs. Lewis," Selma said with a smile. "That band's really good."

"You ought to go out there and dance some yourself, Selma," Ronnie said.

"I already have. And I'll be out there again. Just as soon as I make sure the shrimp is *cold* and the biscuits is *hot*. Fools got the platters switched last time out and had the shrimp sittin' on top of a hot plate."

"Oh, dear. Well, I'm glad you were there to catch it," Ronnie said, finishing her water and setting the glass down.

"I'll keep on top of things, don't you worry." Selma spoke with grim determination. Ronnie smiled, and left her to it.

Once out of the kitchen, she didn't see another soul. Humming to herself as she mounted the stairs, she felt the butterflies settle in her stomach again.

What would she do if Tom didn't come?

She heard the front door open, and the sound of men's voices. Glancing down, she saw Lewis and Beau

Hilley coming into the front hall and heading in the direction of Lewis's office, in the east wing of the house. They seemed to be deep in a serious discussion, but she didn't try to listen because she wasn't interested in anything they had to say to each other. Picking up her skirt, she ran lightly up the rest of the stairs.

"Ronnie, honey, is that you?" Lewis called.

Knowing she was well and truly caught, Ronnie paused on the top stair and turned to smile down at the two men, who had stopped to look up at her.

"I just ran in to take care of a few things, Lewis. Are you having a good time, Senator Hilley?"

"Beau," Hilley corrected, a slow grin splitting his face as his gaze met hers. Ronnie knew what that expression on a man's face meant, and she didn't like it. But she kept on smiling. He was drunk, he was lecherous, but he was a powerful, important senator and a friend of her husband's. As long as he just looked without touching, they'd get along fine.

"Beau," she repeated.

"Like I was telling Lewis here, it was the damnedest thing: When I got up to the house, there wasn't any phone call. Nobody knew anything about it. Your man out there's got some explainin' to do."

"He must have been mistaken," Ronnie said. "Well, if you'll excuse me, I'll leave you two gentlemen to finish your discussion."

"We won't be but a few minutes. Then why don't you come on back out to the party with us? That band's mighty good," Hilley coaxed. Glancing at Lewis, he said, "You ever tell your wife that all work and no play makes Ronnie a dull girl?"

"Many times," Lewis said.

"You *are* sweet to worry about me, Beau," Ronnie said, shaking her head at him. In truth she thought he was an idiot, but maybe that was so only when he drank. For the sake of the country she hoped so. "I'll probably be a little while. There are a few things I need to see to. But suppose I meet you in, say, an hour? On the dance floor. Where we were before?"

"It's a date," said Hilley, beaming, and glanced at his watch. "Twelve-thirty, then. Don't you forget, now!"

"I won't!" Ronnie promised over her shoulder as she took the last step up into the upstairs hall. Lewis and Hilley proceeded toward Lewis's office. She listened to their voices dying away as she walked in the opposite direction.

*Great,* she thought, *when Tom comes we'll have to go someplace else.* It wouldn't do to risk Beau Hilley— or Lewis—coming to look for her—and finding her with Tom.

Reaching her office, she closed the door and leaned against it, shutting her eyes. She was tired, wired, happy, nervous.

Would Tom come?

God, she wanted him to come.

Though the windows were closed, she could hear the band playing. The drapes were open, and the glitter of the party below drew her to a window. She had not turned on a light, so she could look out without being seen. The Japanese lanterns strung throughout the grounds turned the back lawn into a fairyland. Citronella torches planted in strategic places added their own flickering glow. Women in evening dresses and men in tuxes made their way along the crisscrossing pathways, or danced on the patios, or milled around the tents. Closer at hand, two waiters bearing large covered trays went down the last few steps leading to the lawn from the veranda. Seconds later Selma followed, her gait militant.

Ronnie smiled. With Selma to oversee the caterers, and Lewis and his mother and children to see to the guests, she wouldn't be missed. She could do as she pleased all night.

The faint sound of footsteps coming along the hall caused her to turn away from the window. Clutching the curtain with one hand, she waited, her heartbeat speeding up in anticipation.

The footsteps grew louder, then stopped outside the door, which she had left unlocked. The knob turned. The door opened. A pie wedge of light spilled across her office floor. A man's tall form was silhouetted against the hall light.

Ronnie smiled, let go of the curtain, and started to move into his arms.

The time for talking was past.

# Chapter

## 28

*W*ALKING UP TO THE HOUSE, Tom listened to the band striking up a new song and smiled wryly. He and the bandleader must have some sort of cosmic connection tonight, he thought.

It was a romantic ballad, lush and sensual. The lead singer crooned yearningly of love, and Tom felt his body responding to the urgent beat of the music.

He had succumbed, utterly, completely, thoroughly succumbed, to the hot need pulsing through his veins—and the magic of a warm wind, a star-studded night, and a woman.

Morals, scruples, good common sense be damned: Tonight he couldn't help himself.

He was going to take what he wanted, and to hell with the consequences.

Just thinking of Ronnie brought a smile to his lips and an ache to his groin. He quickened his steps.

"Hey, Tom!" It was Thea, hailing him from the pathway leading down from the veranda. As he was on the walk leading to the front door, a distance of some thirty feet away, he was able to wave in reply without stopping.

Thea was wearing a tight black sequined dress with what looked like feathers around the hem, and was looking very hot.

Tom knew he could have her in bed in about twenty minutes flat with not much more than one snap of his fingers. No real moral implications, no potential life-wrecking consequences, no strings.

Just plain, old-fashioned, have-a-good-time sex.

The only problem was he wasn't interested. She didn't move him. She never had. There was no enchantment there for him with Thea.

Or with Diane.

Or with anyone else but Ronnie.

Maybe he had a thing for red hair.

Or maybe it was big brown eyes, or luscious lips, or porcelain pale skin; maybe it was a body with curves in all the right places; hell, maybe it was too much eye makeup and three-inch heels.

Or maybe it was just Ronnie.

Whatever it was, he had it bad.

Worse than the chicken pox.

At least, Tom thought as he ran up the steps to the house, Thea was with somebody. She'd been hanging on to some guy's arm even as she waved at him. That was a good thing. He wouldn't want Ann to get wind of what had been going on between Thea and Kenny.

The irony of condemning his best friend for breaking his marriage vows while he was setting out to do some pretty thorough marriage-vow breaking of his own was not lost on Tom.

And he didn't even try to tell himself that in his and Ronnie's case it was different.

What it was, was a hunger as elemental as a force of nature, and as unstoppable.

He wanted her. She wanted him. When they were together, the air between them burned.

Call him morally bankrupt, but he wasn't even going to try to fight that. Not any longer.

There wasn't any point. He had already lost—or won—depending on how you looked at it. In either case he had discovered that he didn't have what it took to walk away.

Entering the house through the front door, he looked around quickly and judged himself alone. He knew where her office was, and he climbed the main staircase swiftly.

He didn't even feel like talking anymore. He was going to pull her into his arms and kiss her breathless and . . .

Tom had reached the upstairs hall when a muffled cry stopped him in his tracks for the space of about a heartbeat.

He quickened his pace. Then, hearing another muffled cry and a thud, as though something had fallen, he flat-out ran toward the sound.

The door to Ronnie's office was open. Light from the hall spilled into the room, but other than that it was dark. A flash of glittering red was the first thing he saw; then feet with high-heeled satin sandals kicking furiously.

It became clear to him what was happening even as he dove to her rescue. Some overeager asshole—for his money, Beau Hilley—had Ronnie bent back over her desk, kissing her even as he groped the front of her dress. She was twisting every which way and beating him back with one fist and pulling his hair with the other as she tried to get away.

Tom had felt like committing murder so few occasions in his life that he could count them on one hand.

Chalk up one more.

He didn't say a word, just caught the would-be rapist with one hand twisted in the seat of his pants and one hand curled under the neck of his jacket and yanked him away from Ronnie. Then, even as the fellow turned, he let go with a right that would have done Mike Tyson proud.

His victim gurgled, and dropped like a stone.

"Tom!" In an instant Ronnie was up off that desk and in his arms, which was just where he wanted her to be. She clung to him, her arms around his neck, and he could feel her shuddering breaths. He wrapped his arms around her, hugging her tight, and kissed her ear and her neck while he murmured sweet words of reassurance—and inhaled the illusive, erotic scent of her with every breath.

Then he took a good look at the man who lay stretched out at their feet, and froze to the spot.

"Jesus Christ!" Tom said, all ministrations to the woman in his arms temporarily suspended. A dozen thoughts swirled simultaneously through his mind. First and foremost that he had just decked Senator Lewis Honneker IV in his own home for attempting to make love to his own wife.

"What?" Arms still wrapped around his neck, Ronnie lifted her head to stare up at him.

"That's your husband," he said, as if it were possible she didn't know. His arms were still around her, but his hold on her had definitely slackened.

"Yes."

She knew.

"So what in hell is going on here?" Guilt combined with confusion, and a growing anger sharpened his voice.

"What do you mean, 'what in hell is going on here'?" There was an ominous undertone to her voice that Tom had heard before. Ronnie was on the verge of losing her temper. Well, she was in good company if she did, because so was he. He didn't like feeling like a fool—or a louse. Given the situation, he was almost certainly one or the other.

It had occurred to Tom some time back that Ronnie may have been coming on to him merely to get back at her errant spouse, but he had never really given the idea more than passing consideration: The electricity between them felt so sizzlingly real, he didn't think it could be faked.

But he'd been wrong before.

"Was *he* supposed to find you with *me,* or was *I* supposed to find you with *him*?" His voice was little more than a growl. "Or did you just conveniently forget that you invited me up here?"

"*What?*" Words seemed to fail her for a moment, and she sputtered. Then, "Don't you see, he was *attacking* me!"

"He's your husband," Tom said, cold as ice.

She wrenched herself out of his arms. On the floor the Senator stirred and moaned. In reflexive reaction Tom flexed his hand. The knuckles hurt.

Ronnie glanced down, then up at him again.

"Good-bye, Tom," she said witheringly. Turning on her heel, she walked out of the room.

The Senator rolled to his side, then sat up, shaking his head groggily.

Torn between going after Ronnie and aiding the man on the floor, Tom decided that the Senator's needs had to take precedence, and dropped to one knee beside him.

Ronnie in a snit would come to no harm. The Senator, on the other hand, might really be hurt; he was not a young man, and that had been a jackhammer right.

Tom felt like the biggest dastard unhung.

"I'm sorry, Senator. Are you okay?"

"Is that you, Tom?" His Honor blinked at him. He was drunk; the smell of alcohol on his breath was strong enough to make Tom's eyes water.

"It's me, Senator. Can you move your jaw?" Tom squinted as he searched the other man's face for signs of serious damage.

"She won't give me any, you know." The Senator cupped his chin in one hand and waggled his jaw dolefully. "Not for more'n a year. Even has a separate bedroom. Hell, what does she think I married her for?"

Tom sank back on his heels. "She won't give you any?" he repeated carefully.

"She looks hot, don't she, boy? I saw she had you pantin' after her. She gets all of 'em pantin' after her! Hell, me too. But she's really cold—cold as ice. Won't put out. I even tried—even tried begging her! But she won't. Don't tell Marsden I told you, will you?" His expression grew suddenly worried.

"I won't," Tom promised, running a questing hand

along the Senator's jaw. There was the beginning of some swelling, but the bone seemed to be intact.

"I got rights where she's concerned. I tried to tell her. But she says she'll leave me if I force her, and she knows she's got me over a barrel, because I can't take another divorce. This last one just about killed me in the polls. You know that yourself."

"I don't think you've got the right to force her, Senator," Tom said carefully. "I think that's called rape."

"Hell, a man can't rape his own wife!"

"Times have changed, Senator, and laws have too. My understanding of the way it works is that if a woman says no, it's a surefire gospel *no,* even if she is your wife."

"D'you ever hear such bullshit in your life?" The Senator appealed to him as one man to another. "I guess it's a good thing you came in when you did, then, 'cause I was aimin' to take what I married her for. Hot-tempered as she is, she probably would have shot me after, or called the police and had me arrested. I don't know which would have been worse. God above, think of the scandal! Orde would eat it up."

"Can you stand up, Senator?" Tom got up, and helped the Senator up too. He was a little unsteady on his feet, but that was due more to the effects of alcohol than to the punch he'd taken, Tom judged as he held on to the older man's arm just for insurance.

"I guess I've kinda lost my taste for any more partyin' tonight. I think I'll go on to bed." The Senator waggled his jaw and winced.

"I wouldn't try to force your wife again if I were you," Tom said, releasing the Senator's arm and following close behind as he walked with great dignity, if an occasional sideways step, toward the hall.

"I guess I won't," he said gloomily. "But you tell me what a man's supposed to do? Wife won't put out, and damned papers pillory you if you get caught with another woman. Anybody who says this is a man's world don't know diddly-squat!"

"You've got a point there, Senator." Tom followed him into his bedroom, where the older man immediately collapsed facedown on top of the counterpane, which had not yet been drawn back from the bed. In less than a minute he was snoring. Tom stood looking down at him for a while, his hands in his trouser pockets. Then he reached over, untied the Senator's bow tie, and pulled the shoes from his feet. Having done what he could to make the man comfortable, he left the room, closing the door behind him.

Deep in thought, he headed toward the staircase. He had been on the brink of cuckolding a man who had never been anything but kind to him, a man who had offered him work when he'd needed it, a man he'd looked up to all his life.

A man who was, on the other hand, chronically unfaithful, and who had just tried to rape his own wife.

A woman whom Tom still burned to possess.

How had he ever gotten caught up in such a god-awful mess?

Tom walked down the stairs, still pondering.

However he had gotten into it, he was in it now, stuck fast as a pig in quicksand.

What was between him and Ronnie was not going to go away.

*He* could go away—but he knew he couldn't stay away.

Not with the best will in the world. Not forever. If he left tonight, he'd be back in a week.

He knew that much about himself.

He'd already tried cutting and running, and see where it had landed him: out of the frying pan and smack-dab in the middle of the fire. The only thing left to do was to face the situation squarely.

First off, he and Ronnie needed to talk.

As he came to that conclusion, he walked out through the front door into the balmy night. Over to his right, past the hundred-year-old magnolia bursting with waxy white blooms that marked the corner of the house and the graceful Doric columns that held up the front-porch roof, the party was still going strong. Laughter and the indistinct sounds of voices intermingling rose above the music. The Japanese lanterns floated over the proceedings like a thousand fireflies.

Overhead, stars twinkled in a midnight-blue sky. A ghostly-pale moon rode high among feathery dark wisps of clouds.

He walked down the steps to the driveway. Finding Ronnie without saddling himself with unwanted companions was not going to be easy. He looked in the direction of the tents, trying to catch a glimpse of red hair.

A glint on the pavement not too far from his feet caught his eye. Something shiny and reflective—a piece of glass? No, it was too small and symmetrical.

Frowning suddenly, Tom stooped to pick it up. It was small and round and crystal clear, and he knew instantly what it was.

Straightening, putting the object into his pocket, he looked around again.

There, maybe a dozen feet away, was another one.

Tom followed the trail of the beads. Like Hansel and Gretel dropping bread crumbs, Ronnie had marked her path, though she had done it inadvertently by shedding crystals from her dress.

He only found four. But then, he had only needed two. As soon as he had seen in what direction she had headed, he had a pretty fair idea of where she was.

Strolling away from the party into the dark at the other side of the house, Tom took a deep breath, and frowned. Though he knew it was pretty close to impossible, he thought that he could detect just a hint of her perfume on the warm wind caressing his face.

# Chapter
## 29

ONNIE HEARD THE CREAK OF THE GATE, and glanced over her shoulder. It was dark in the small fortress around the pool, but not so dark that she could not see the broad-shouldered silhouette of a man as he came through the gate and closed it behind him. For just an instant she frowned. Then the moonlight glinted on his hair and she was left in no doubt as to who he was.

"Go away," she said, and breast-stroked to the far side of the pool. Though she didn't think there was enough moonlight for it to be apparent, she was wearing only her panties; her dress, stockings, shoes, and jewelry lay on a chair at the shallow end of the pool.

"I apologize for everything I said in the house. I completely misread the situation," Tom said. He followed her progress from one side of the pool to the other, pacing alongside her on the concrete deck.

"I don't accept your apology. Now, go away."

"This isn't easy for me, either, you know," he said.

"What exactly is it that you want from me, Tom?" she asked suddenly, standing up to face him, her arms moving in the water to keep her balanced. At its deepest point the pool was only five feet, which left her, standing on tiptoes, shoulder-deep. She had been breast-stroking since she had entered the pool, and as a consequence her makeup was still largely in place and her upswept hair was still dry except for the tendrils around her neck.

"Now that," he said, thrusting his hands into his trouser pockets so that his coat was pushed back behind his hips, "is a good question."

She laughed, but the sound was unamused. "Don't be such a hypocrite! You want sex; you're just having trouble climbing over your conscience to get it."

He made no reply for a moment, then said, "Let me ask you a question, then: What exactly is it that you want from me?"

Ronnie stared at him, dumbstruck. She had never really thought about it before. What she wanted wasn't sex per se; it was Tom.

She started swimming again, heading to the opposite end of the pool.

"Sex? Is that what you want from me, Ronnie?" He pursued her on the concrete surround, keeping even with her progress.

"I want you to go away," she said, reaching the side and turning back for another lap.

"If I did, it wouldn't help. I'd just come back. We've already established that."

She kept swimming.

"We've got to deal with this, Ronnie." His voice was patient as he paced alongside her.

Standing up in the shoulder-deep water again, she faced him, suddenly angry. "I don't see any way to deal with it. The problem you have with this whole thing is that I'm married. Well, I can't change that. *I am married.*"

"Have you ever thought about getting a divorce?" he asked quietly. He had stopped pacing when she stopped swimming, and now he stood looking down at her.

"No." She started swimming again.

"So what you want to happen here is for you to stay married to the Senator while you sleep with me on the side, do I have that right?"

The sideways look she cast him was defiant. "Why not?"

"Because I have a problem with that."

"Then go away." She finished one lap and headed the other way. He stayed even with her.

"Would you come out of there so that we can talk about this like reasonable people?" There was a touch of impatience in his voice.

"There's nothing to talk about. If you have a problem with me being married, then I suggest you go back to Diane, who is not married, and have sex with her."

"I could. Just like you could have sex with your husband the Senator. But I don't think that would satisfy either one of us."

She swam without replying.

"Ronnie, would you please come out of that damned pool and talk to me?" There was an edge to his voice now.

She stopped swimming to look up at him. "Lots of people have affairs while they're married. Hundreds. Thousands."

"Is that the voice of experience I hear?" he asked dryly.

"Just for the record, during my three years as a married woman *I've* never had an affair. But Lewis has been screwing around since day one. So why shouldn't I?"

"No reason, except maybe I don't feel like being the man you're screwing around with."

"Why *not*?"

"Because affairs are messy, and people get hurt. Because tonight when I danced with you, I had to be real careful to pretend I didn't like it too much so that people wouldn't get the idea there was something going on between us. Because I might like to take you out to lunch, or dinner, or the movies. Because I don't like the idea of fitting in fifteen-minute quickies whenever we can sneak off together. I don't like the idea of having to sneak off together, period."

"It doesn't have to be like that."

"It will be like that."

"Is that the voice of experience I hear?" She mimicked his question to her.

"Maybe."

"Oh, *I'm* supposed to confess everything, but you're not."

"Ronnie, it is damned hard to conduct this conversation while you're in that swimming pool."

"You're avoiding the question."

"You're avoiding the issue."

"What is the issue? Whether or not we're going to sleep together? As far as I'm concerned right this minute, the answer's no."

Ronnie started swimming again. Tom stayed where

he was, arms crossed over his chest as he watched her progress. With the length of the pool between them, he was hardly more than a large, dark shadow against the paler shade of the concrete. As she swam back toward him, she saw that he was frowning.

"You don't sleep with him. You haven't for over a year," Tom said when she drew even with him.

Ronnie stopped swimming and turned to look at him. "How do you know that?"

"He told me. Upstairs just now."

"What were you two doing, comparing sex lives?" Outrage tinged her voice.

"I helped him to bed. He was drunk. We—talked about what he tried to do to you."

"Oh, did you?"

"He doesn't love you."

Ronnie said nothing for a moment, just stared up at him through the darkness. His arms were still folded over his chest, and he was frowning down at her.

"So?" She started swimming again. She knew Lewis didn't love her, had never loved her. The realization had dawned slowly, but she now knew it was fact. He had married her for the good, old-fashioned reason that he couldn't get her into bed any other way. Once he'd gotten what he wanted, he'd quickly moved on to greener pastures. Though he had, of course, wanted to keep having sex with his wife whenever he felt like it.

"Damn it, Ronnie, we're going to talk about this. He doesn't love you. I know as sure as I know the sun will come up in the morning that you don't love him. So why do you stay married to him?"

She completed her lap, and swam another.

"Ronnie?"

Now she stood in the water and faced him.

"You really want to know? Fine, I'll tell you: I grew up in a little bitty ranch house in Boston, one of hundreds of little bitty ranch houses that were exactly the same in our neighborhood alone. My dad worked in a used-car lot for commissions, and most of the time he had to scrape to make the mortgage payment. I know, because my parents were always fighting about money. When I was fourteen, my mother met a man who could give her more, and she took off with him and left my father and sisters and me behind. I was the youngest, and my sisters married and left, and my dad's income dropped because he didn't care enough to work hard anymore. The dress I wore to my senior prom cost fifteen dollars. I found it at a resale shop. I vowed right there and then that I wasn't going to live my whole life like that. I wanted something better."

Pausing, she took a deep breath to control the emotion that threatened to choke off her words. He hunkered down beside the pool, one arm draped over his raised, bent knee, his eyes intent on her face.

"Would you come out of that damned pool?" His voice was almost a growl.

Ronnie shook her head. Her voice was under control again. "You asked me why I stay married to Lewis, and I want you to know." She lifted her left hand out of the shoulder-high water, showing it to him, so that the big diamond on it glittered in the moonlight. "Do you see this ring? This ring cost more than my dad made in a year. Look around you, Tom. Look at this place. The house I grew up in wasn't much bigger than the pool house. Lewis owns three houses as grand as this. I can buy all the clothes I want, nice clothes, and presents for my family that they can't afford. I can travel. I have charge cards. I have jewelry. I have a car, several in fact. We belong to four country clubs."

"Damn it, Ronnie, are you crying? Would you please come out of the goddamned pool?"

"I'm *not* crying. I'm telling you. I stay married to Lewis because as his wife I have everything that little girl in that fifteen-dollar prom dress ever dreamed of."

*Except love,* she thought, but she didn't say it out loud. As that corollary popped into her mind, her throat closed up, she squeezed her eyes tightly shut, and she willed herself not to cry.

It was stupid to cry about what could not be mended, and absolutely useless.

Tom swore, a filthy word she had never heard him use before. Opening her eyes, she saw that he was walking purposely away from her, toward the opposite end of the pool. There were steps in the corner there that led down into the shallow end. He came down them without even bothering to kick off his shoes, tux and all, and walked toward her through water that started at his waist and rose quickly halfway up his chest.

Watching his approach, Ronnie was surprised to feel hot tears sliding down her cheeks. She wiped them away with both hands.

"Please don't cry," he said as he reached her. His voice was gruff, but also tender. His arms came around her, pulling her tight against him. Ronnie drew a deep breath that sounded almost like a sob even to her own ears, and wrapped her arms around his neck.

## Chapter

# 30

"*Y*OU'RE TEARING MY HEART OUT. Would you stop?" Tom pulled his head back a little to look into her face.

"I'm not crying," Ronnie said again stubbornly, and buried her face in the curve between his shoulder and neck. Squeezing her eyes shut, she took deep breaths and concentrated on living up to her words. It was just that she had felt so sad suddenly, remembering that young girl who had never really known what it was to be loved.

And still didn't know.

"Ronnie, look at me."

But she couldn't, not quite yet, not till the tears had all gone away. To be in his arms again felt so good, so right, that she didn't want to move. The uppermost section of his tux was dry while the rest of him was soaking wet. Plastered against him as she was, she could feel every part of him: the buttons on his shirt, his belt buckle, the hardness below; the warm, muscular strength of his body beneath the wet cloth of his suit. Her toes were even in contact with the smooth leather tips of his shoes.

"Ronnie."

She looked up then, up into his face shrouded in shadow, up into his eyes that were agleam with concern for her.

"Tom."

There wasn't anything else to say.

Their mouths met, and they kissed, then kissed again. His mouth was hot, and wet, and tasted faintly of whiskey. His arms around her were so tight that Ronnie could scarcely draw breath.

She didn't care. She slanted her mouth against his and met his tongue with hers, and clung.

Underwater, his hands slid down her back, stroked her spine, molded the indentation of her waist.

"Are you naked?" he asked thickly, sliding his mouth along her cheek to the tender hollow below her ear.

"Almost." She whispered her answer against his neck as she tasted the warm saltiness of the skin there.

"You would be." What could have been the ghost of a laugh shook him. But he wasn't laughing when his mouth found hers again—or when his hand moved over her rib cage to cup her breast.

His hand on her breast made her insides go haywire. Her heart skipped a beat, her breathing suspended, and her blood seemed to sizzle.

He had never touched her intimately before. Ronnie realized with a sense of surprise that he had made her ache and burn and long for him without ever doing anything much more than kiss her. She had dreamed of him, of making love with him. But in her dreams it had never felt like this. He cupped and stroked and touched her nipple—and she felt her bones dissolve.

Ronnie found herself thinking, what a difference a man makes—the right man.

"Let's get out of this damned pool." The words were growled into her ear. He was kissing her again even as he lifted her. Ronnie kissed him back with abandon, wrapping her legs around his waist and keeping her arms around his neck as he walked with her to the side of the pool. He felt so warm and solid and good against her; she squeezed her legs tighter around his middle, and deepened their kiss. His whole body tensed in response.

"Jesus," he said, pulling his mouth away from hers, and lifted her up out of the water to sit on the concrete lip. She curled her hands around the curved edge, her feet still dangling in the water. Except for a pair of tiny black satin panties she was naked. Water poured from her body. She was leaning slightly forward; the round globes of her breasts sloped toward him. Her nipples stood out stiffly, hard from the cooling effect of the night air as it struck her wet skin—and from Tom. The rest of her, slim-hipped, long-legged, fine-boned, glistened milky pale in the moonlight.

Tom looked at her, a long, intent look that slid from the top of her still-elegant upsweep to her calves, and his face tightened until the bones were visible beneath his skin. Then he braced his hands on the blue overflow trough that ran around the inside rim of the pool and heaved himself up and out.

Water poured from him, too, as he stood, reaching down a hand to help her to her feet. Ronnie took his hand, scrambling up. Even as she would have turned into his arms, he scooped her out. Held high against his chest, Ronnie smiled into his eyes, slid her hands around his neck, and kissed him.

She was still kissing him as he turned sideways to maneuver her through the creaky gate, still kissing him as he walked up the path to the pool house. The sliding glass door was unlocked; he pushed it open and carried her through it into a wall of air-conditioning.

Ronnie shivered, and lifted her mouth from his, to direct him to the bed or the thermostat or somewhere, anywhere, warmer.

"Damn!" Tom's toe caught on something and he stumbled. As quick as that he went down, twisting as he fell. Ronnie squeaked as she felt herself dropping through the air, only to land hard on something cold and resilient and soaking wet that grunted—Tom.

For an instant she lay as she had fallen, stunned. She was on her back, her bottom on Tom's thighs, her back and head on his chest, her legs splayed over the floor. She felt him move beneath her, and slid off him onto the floor or, rather, onto the two-inch-thick rubber exercise mat that had obviously been the cause of the accident.

Ronnie turned onto her stomach, her head up and her torso supported on her elbows, to check him out.

His eyes were open and looking at her. Ronnie met their narrowed gaze for a pregnant moment and started to snicker.

"Are you okay?" she asked between spurts of mirth.

"Aside from a badly bruised butt, a possibly broken tailbone, and some wounded dignity, I'm fine. How about you?"

"I landed on top. I'm not hurt a bit."

"Good." He turned onto his side, propping his head up with one hand. She was still lying on her stomach, supported by her elbows; his face was just inches from hers. A wry smile twisted his mouth. Looking at it, Ronnie remembered all the fantasies she'd had over the last few weeks about that mouth, and ran her index finger along the crease where his lips met.

Another snicker shook her.

He drew her finger into his mouth and bit down gently.

"Are you going to laugh all night?" he asked politely when he released her finger.

"Probably." She grinned at him.

She was still grinning when he rolled her onto her back and loomed over her. They were both lying on the rubber exercise mat now; it was big and cushiony and surprisingly comfortable.

"I guess if you bruised your butt, that proves you're not such a hard-ass after all," she told him, and started laughing again.

"Funny." He bent his head to kiss her. His tongue was hot, soft, and only faintly demanding as it explored her mouth. His hand found her breast, closing over it, squeezing, and suddenly Ronnie wasn't laughing anymore. Toes curling, she closed her eyes and kissed him back, her hands threading through the silky hair at the back of his head.

She had imagined kissing him like this. Only her imagination was not nearly as good as the real thing.

He shrugged out of his coat without ever taking his mouth from hers. She ran her hands along the breadth of his shoulders, loving the feel of them beneath the smooth cotton, intoxicated at the luxury of being able to kiss and touch him as she chose. The bottom two thirds of his shirt and his trousers were soaking wet and icy cold as he lay against her. His hand on her breast was hard and warm. Her nipple swelled into his palm. She arched her back, pressing her breast more closely into that possessive hand, as importunate as a cat wanting to be stroked. His breathing speeded up.

Then he pulled his mouth from hers, and eased a little away.

Ronnie opened her eyes to find that he was looking at her, his gaze moving slowly down the length of her body. Except for her panties, she was naked in his arms. Moonlight poured in through the wide glass door; her body was bathed in it. His hand on her breast looked big and bronzed against her pearlized skin. His arm slanted across her rib cage. The sleeve of his white shirt felt wet and clammy. The arm beneath was taut with muscle. He lay on his side, taking his time, making a leisurely appraisal. His formal clothes—white shirt with studs, a black bow tie and cumberbund, black trousers with a satin stripe down the sides, black socks and shoes—made an erotic contrast to her nakedness.

Ronnie looked up at his face. It was all hard bone and angles in the moonlight. She remembered thinking once that he would have no patience with sins of the flesh.

She'd been at least partially right. He had resisted until neither one of them could resist anymore.

His gaze met hers then, unexpectedly. His eyes were heavy-lidded, their expression sensual.

"I've had so many fantasies about getting you naked that I'm surprised my mind hasn't suffered meltdown," he said, his voice husky. "Every time I'd see you, I'd catch myself mentally taking your clothes off. After a while I didn't even have to see you. I'd be in the middle of a crucial strategy session with Matt Grolin, and I'd catch myself wondering if your navel was an innie or an outie."

With a crooked smile he slid his hand down over her rib cage to her stomach to investigate the question. Ronnie caught her breath.

"That doesn't sound like it was very good for business." She stroked his cheek. The warm, masculine skin was only faintly rough; he must have shaved just before coming to the party.

"It wasn't." He turned his mouth into her palm. His legs shifted, and she realized that he was easing off his shoes. Her hands dropped to tug at his tie.

"Don't move," he said, getting to his feet, and began stripping with quick efficiency. His bow tie, which she had already untied, came off first, followed by his cumberbund. Ronnie's heart beat faster as she watched him undo the studs that held his shirt, then shrug out of it. He looked better without his shirt than he did in it, she thought, and he had looked pretty darn good in it. His hands went to his belt buckle, and a hot melting began deep inside her. She lay on her back on the red rubber exercise mat, her fingers flexing deep into the foam padding as she watched him take off his pants. He wore boxers, she discovered, in a solid pale blue, and waited with anticipation while he stood first on one foot and then the other to pull off his socks.

Finally he wore nothing but his boxers. He hooked his thumbs into the waistband and came out of them, too, his movements quick and impatient. The sight of him naked made her mouth go dry. Her gaze ran over him from the wide expanse of his shoulders to the wedge of hair on his chest to his narrow athlete's hips to the muscular length of his legs.

Her imagination had never looked this good.

She was afforded just a glimpse before he came back to her, but it was enough: He was hungry for her, big and swollen with desire, the proof of it jutting out stiffly from his body.

Her arms lifted to welcome him; her hands slid over his shoulders, marveling at the flexing strength of the muscles there. He settled down beside her, one arm easing under her neck. His other hand brushed a stray strand of hair from her face.

Ronnie smiled at him. He bestowed a quick, hard kiss on her mouth.

"Feel my arms shake," Tom said, lifting his head. His voice was both rueful and amused. "The last time they shook like this, I was sixteen years old and about to try out the mattress in the back of my dad's camper."

"Did you try out that mattress a lot?" Ronnie asked softly, her hands trailing from his shoulders down over his upper arms. His skin was warm, and satiny smooth. The muscles beneath were bunched and hard. As he had said, they were shaking. She ran her hands back up over them to his shoulders, loving the idea that she could make him tremble.

"As much as I could, but it wasn't long before I stopped shaking." He was smiling down at her until her hands moved to caress his chest. As they flattened on him, then ran down the center of his chest to stroke his muscled abdomen, his eyes darkened and he stopped smiling.

She closed her eyes as his mouth came down on hers.

The gentleness he had shown her before was gone. In its place was a fierce hunger that took her by surprise. She responded to his urgency with a growing fierceness of her own, pressing herself against him, wrapping her arms around his neck, catching fire.

His hands were everywhere: on her breasts, stroking her stomach, running up and down her thighs. But he didn't touch her where she most wanted to be touched, and that was driving her out of her mind. She clung to him, writhing as she wordlessly begged for what she wanted, to no avail. He was all but on top of her now, his head bent to kiss her nipple, his thigh flung over hers, the swollen proof of his desire butting against her leg. The hot dampness of his mouth kissing and nibbling and sucking on her breasts made her gasp. Her hands closed on the back of his head, pressing him close to her, guiding his mouth from one breast to the other, as a spiral of longing coiled tighter and tighter deep within.

Then at last, at long last, his hand stroked down over her stomach to slide beneath the edge of her panties.

Ronnie wanted his hand between her legs so much she thought she was going to die from the waiting. And he made her wait. His hand moved inside her panties at roughly the speed of a glacier, his long fingers caressing and exploring every millimeter of her flesh, occasionally dipping lower to tease her with butterfly touches until she was lifting her hips from the mat in quivering anticipation of the next one.

He kissed her breasts, then her mouth, then her breasts again while her body wordlessly pleaded, and then finally, finally, his hand crept to where she most wanted it to be. He stroked the cleft between her legs, and she gasped. A scorching heat shot through her body; she moved to encourage that questing hand, silently begging to be invaded, to be possessed, until at last he gave her what she wanted. Moaning, she kissed his ear, his neck, his shoulder, anyplace she could reach, her nails digging deep into his back, her body burning. His touch was the slow-handed caress of a man who understood how a woman's body worked; he teased, then delved, and repeated the process until she turned to liquid fire in his hands.

"Tom, please," she gasped out finally, her eyes opening as she fought to hold on, knowing that she was going to explode at any moment and wanting him inside her when she did.

He looked at her then. His face was flushed, his eyes narrow and glittering. Like her, he was breathing in short, sharp pants. He watched her face as his fingers slid inside her again, and when she gasped and arched her back in response, his eyes blazed.

"God, I've wanted this," he said in a low, hoarse voice. Then he was yanking her panties down her legs and rolling on top of her and kissing her with quick, savage movements that told her that he, too, had reached the limits of his control. She wrapped her legs around his waist as he slid between her thighs, so ready for him that she thought she would die if she had to wait another second.

He thrust inside her, huge and hot and hard, driving deep and fast over and over again until she was mindless, crying out at the wonder of it, gouging his back with her nails until at last she came with an intensity that she had never dreamed she was capable of, her preconceived notions of herself and the world shattering into a million pieces as she cried out his name.

# Chapter

## 31

"WHAT ARE YOU WATCHIN', MARLA?" Jerry Fineman stood in the living-room doorway, looking at her as she sat curled in one corner of the couch, watching TV. He was wearing one of those old men's sleeveless undershirts that he liked and the same pair of black beltless pants he had worn earlier. It was obvious he had just rolled out of bed and pulled them on again.

"Letterman." Marla glanced up with a smile. "Did I wake you up? I'm sorry."

"Nah." Jerry padded over to the couch and sat down beside her. The cushions sagged beneath his weight. He was fifty-one, a retired Biloxi police officer who had been divorced for ten years. He wasn't handsome—he had a bald head and a beer belly, and he wasn't much over five foot nine—but he was kind. Marla had met him when she had first arrived in Biloxi, desperate, and had been forced to resort to standing on a street corner to turn a few quick tricks to feed her kid. He had almost arrested her, but instead had taken pity on her, lent her fifty dollars, and driven her back to the car where she was living with Lissy. He'd helped her get on her feet, and she had repaid him with sex, gratis, whenever he'd wanted it. When he'd left Biloxi almost two years before, neither had ever expected to see the other again. Yet there they were.

She'd told him the whole story, from the moment she had driven Susan and Claire to the Biloxi Yacht Club to how it came about that she ended up on his doorstep. He'd been skeptical when she had claimed that everybody who knew that Susan and Claire got on that boat seemed to have disappeared, or died. He'd even been skeptical that a man was out there who wanted to kill her.

But he had promised to check it out. In the meantime, if she was scared to go back to Biloxi, she and Lissy could stay with him. Sooner or later they would get the whole thing sorted out. That had been almost three weeks earlier.

Marla had taken him up on his offer because she trusted him. She trusted him to use his police contacts to track down the man who had killed Susan, probably Claire, and the Lord only knew who else, and who was now after her. She trusted him to keep her and Lissy safe while he did it. And she trusted him to keep his mouth shut about her doubtful custody of Lissy.

"You want something to eat?" Marla uncurled her legs preparatory to standing up.

Jerry glanced at her. A faint smile curved his lips, from one of Letterman's lame jokes, Marla thought.

"After that supper you cooked tonight? I'm still stuffed full as a tick on a dog," he said, patting his ample belly.

"I'll get you a beer if you want." She was still poised to rise.

Jerry frowned. "You don't have to wait on me."

"I don't mind."

"Look, Marla." Jerry was focused completely on her now, rather than splitting his attention between her and the TV. "I'm not gonna kick you and the kid out no matter what. You don't have to jump every time I break wind."

"I don't—" Marla stopped, because that was just what she had been doing since he had taken them in. If he wouldn't help them, they had no one else to turn to, and she was acutely aware of that.

"You do," Jerry said quietly. "I'm helping you as a friend, Marla, not so you'll cook and clean and do laundry and wait on me hand and foot when I'm in the house."

Marla was quiet for a moment, just looking at him. When she spoke, it was around the lump in her throat.

"You're a good man, Jerry Fineman," she said softly, and smiled at him. Then she slid off the couch onto her knees facing him and reached for the zipper on his pants.

She meant to thank him in the one way she knew he wouldn't turn down.

# Chapter
## 32

$\mathcal{W}$HEN RONNIE FINALLY OPENED HER EYES, Tom was lying on top of her, sated, and heavier than she had thought it was possible for him to be. His arms were around her, his face buried in the curve between her shoulder and her neck, his body still joined to hers.

Turning her head, she kissed his bristly cheek.

"Tom," she said. "I'm freezing. Let's move."

He stirred then, and lifted his head to look down at her. His eyes gleamed at her for a moment, and then he smiled.

"You," he said, "are the most beautiful thing I have ever seen in my life, and the sexiest, and the sweetest-smelling. I could make love to you all night long. How can you possibly be cold at a time like this?"

She could feel him stirring inside her. Far from being spent, his entire body seemed to be regrouping. Beneath her hands, she could feel the bunching of his shoulder muscles. His thighs stretched and then tensed between hers. He took a deep breath, and she could feel him waking up, and hardening, everywhere.

"I'm not cold, I'm freezing." She shivered to prove it. "We're lying in a puddle. The air conditioner's blasting."

"You weren't cold a few minutes ago."

"I can't believe *you* aren't cold."

"Darlin', you make me so hot I may never feel cold again."

Ronnie eyed him. " 'Darlin',' huh? I like the way you say that, all soft and drawling: 'da-arlin.' "

His smile widened. "Let's hear *you* say it, if you think you can do it better."

"Darling."

"Too cold and clipped, real northern-sounding, almost hostile. Try saying Tom first."

"Tom, darling."

"Better." He was starting to move inside her again. "That softens it up some. Try one more time."

"Tom, darling."

"Keep practicing, you'll get it." Fully aroused now, he was pressing her hips down into the mat, supporting the weight of his upper body on his elbows, watching her face as he went deep, then pulled slowly out.

"Tom, *darling*." It was almost a gasp.

"You're getting real good."

Bending his head, he caught her nipple in his mouth and suckled it as his body moved slowly in and out. Clutching at his shoulders, Ronnie lost the thread of the conversation.

When she resurfaced a second time, still pinned by his body to the mat, the temperature in the room was the same as it had been before: freezing.

"Tom," she said plaintively in his ear. "There's a bed in the other room. With covers."

He turned his head to nibble at her neck. "Are you still complaining? All right then, let's move."

With more energy than she expected to feel ever again in her life, he got lithely to his feet, catching her hand and pulling her up with him. For a moment they stood facing each other, both naked, bathed in the moonlight that poured through the door. Their eyes met, and he smiled at her. Ronnie leaned into him, resting against the broad strength of his chest, her arms wrapping around his waist.

*This is Tom,* she thought, savoring the knowledge. All the daydreams, the night dreams, the fantasies she'd had about him were coming true.

His arms came around her, hugging her tight. They were warm, and strong, and welcome for both reasons. She was sure she had goose bumps on every inch of her body from the air-conditioning, and her bones felt about as solid as instant pudding.

"You have got the most incredible ass," he said, his hands sliding down to cup the portion of her anatomy he praised, "by the way."

A faint, shrill beeping startled them both. Tom's hands left her rump. It took only a second to identify the sound as coming from his watch. He pressed a button on it, and it was silent.

"Must be waterproof," Ronnie said with a touch of humor.

"Looks like it."

"What time is it?"

He lifted his arm to the light. "Three a.m. What time you figure you need to be back before they send somebody looking for you?"

"I don't know. Dawn?" She pushed away from him and started walking toward the bedroom. "What time is that?"

"About five-thirty," he said, his voice crisper than it had been all night. "Better say a little earlier, to be safe."

The bedroom opened directly off the exercise room. To reach the bed that occupied the far wall took just a minute. It was a daybed, a single, made up with an antique quilt that reached the floor, and piled high with decorative pillows. For as long as Ronnie had been making use of the pool house, no one had ever slept in it. Nevertheless it was kept ready.

"Can you turn the air-conditioning off? The thermostat's over there on the wall," she said over her shoulder, sweeping the decorative pillows onto the floor.

"I see it."

She glanced at him. He had found the thermostat on the wall between the bedroom and exercise room with the aid of the tiny red light that announced its presence, and was turning the air-conditioning off. By mutual if unspoken agreement, neither of them even considered turning on a light. Not that they really needed one. Between the sliding glass door and the small, uncurtained casement window over the bed, they could see well enough.

"So this particular Cinderella turns into a pumpkin at dawn, not midnight," he said, his voice still crisper than she liked, as he walked toward her.

"It was the coach that turned into a pumpkin, not Cinderella," Ronnie corrected, hoping that if she ignored the crisp tone it would go away. She climbed into the bed and pulled the covers up around her neck.

"Same thing."

Ronnie's gaze ran over him as he reached the bed, and a small smile curved her lips. Just the sight of him naked was enough to curl her toes.

She had a sudden thought, and tossed the covers back so that she could slide out of bed.

"What?" He frowned down at her.

"If you don't want to have to get back into a sopping-wet tux, it needs to go into the dryer."

"I'll do it. Get back under the covers. I told you, I'm not cold." He turned and left the room, affording Ronnie an excellent view of a wide back and a small, tight rear. The red marks her nails had made on his back showed up faintly through the dark. Remembering how she had come to put them there, she gave a little shiver of pleasure, and scooted back under the covers. She was bundled up in bed again when he called, "Where's the dryer?"

"In the bathroom."

A few minutes later she heard the thud of the dryer door and then the steady hum of the machine.

"I hope it doesn't shrink," he said, coming back into the room.

"I don't think it will," Ronnie answered with a flickering grin. "However, depending on what it's made out of, it might melt."

"Great." Tom slid into bed beside her, the mattress depressing under his weight. Ronnie moved over to make room for him, then as he got settled, snuggled close against his side. He lay on his back, his head on their single pillow. His body radiated welcome heat, and it was big and hard. His long, solidly muscled legs and arms and the center of his chest were rough with hair. Before they were comfortable his arm was around her, and her head rested on his shoulder. One of her arms curved across his chest. Her fingers stroked idly through his chest hair.

"Oh, my!" With a start, Ronnie thought of something else. "Do you suppose your girlfriend is still here?"

"I sent Diane home in a taxi before I ever headed up to the house." Tom's voice was dry. "I told her something urgent had come up at work and I had to head for the airport immediately."

"Oh." Ronnie glanced up at him. "Quite the creative liar, aren't we?"

"When I have to be."

"Are you going to see her again anytime soon?"

"Not as soon as you're going to see your husband, believe me."

Ronnie sighed, her fingers stilling on his chest. "You're regretting this, aren't you?"

"Regretting what? That you're lying here naked in my arms?" He shook his head, and slanted a crooked smile down at her. "Darlin', making love to you is as close as I ever expect to get to heaven in my life. How could I regret it?"

"You do. I can tell."

"I don't regret anything." He shifted so that they were lying facing each other. Her head rested on his upper arm now, rather than his shoulder. Her hands were splayed against his chest. She tested the resilience of the muscle there, lightly kneading his skin without even being aware that she was doing so. Her hair had long since fallen; it fanned across his arm and the pillow in a ripple of silken waves. He picked up a strand, rubbing it between his thumb and forefinger as though to weigh the texture. "You remember when we were talking about the other woman? Well, I'm just not sure I'm cut out to be the other man."

"Tom . . . ," Ronnie began, frowning.

"Hush," he said, and kissed her.

By the time five o'clock came around, they were both sated and drowsy.

"Time to get up," Tom said, sliding a hand down her back to squeeze her bottom. She was stretched on top of him, her head pillowed on his chest, her legs curled around his. Tilting her head, she looked up at him, sleepy-eyed.

"I'm too exhausted to move," she muttered.

His lips curved in a wry smile. "I'm glad to hear it. It's what you deserve, for keeping me up all night."

"*I* kept *you* up?" Ronnie was too tired to sound properly indignant at the charge.

"All right. It was mutual. So we both get to pay for it by spending a cranky Sunday with no sleep."

Ronnie groaned. "I have a tennis game at noon."

"With Michael?" His voice was crisp again.

Ronnie wriggled up his body just far enough to be able to plop a quick kiss on his mouth. "You know how I can tell when you don't like something? You lose your drawl," she told him. "Your voice goes all cold and clipped, kind of northern-sounding. Almost hostile." With a teasing grin she paraphrased the words he had used to describe her speech earlier.

"I feel hostile," he said, the humor that laced her voice completely absent from his. "So are you playing tennis with that Michael guy?"

"Michael is the husband of a really close friend of mine, Kathy Blount." One look at his face persuaded Ronnie that this was not a good moment for kidding him about jealousy. "She and her brother—they were junior tennis champions in high school or something—play mixed doubles against Michael and me. They always beat us—well, nine times out of ten. And that is the only playing I do with Michael. When he walked down to the pool house to get me that day, Kathy was waiting outside in the car."

"Oh."

"Yes, oh."

"You deliberately tried to make me think different at the time."

"At the time you deserved what you got."

"Oh, yeah?"

"Yeah."

They eyed each other, and then his expression softened into a reluctant grin.

"I probably did," he admitted. His arms tightened around her, and he rolled so that she was under him. Then he kissed her.

By the time they got out of bed, it was closer to six than five. They dressed hurriedly, Ronnie in the bicycle shorts and T-shirt she kept at the pool house to exercise in and Tom in his dry but wrinkled tux, with the tie and cumberbund rolled up and stuck in one pocket. Ronnie then went out to collect the clothes she had worn the night before from beside the pool. She would leave the things in the closet in the pool house, to be smuggled up to the big house later on. It would be safer, she had decided, to go inside in her exercise clothes, so that if anyone saw her, she could simply claim to have been working out. Either very early, or very late, depending on whether or not anyone knew she had not come in the night before.

Sneaking around was a new experience for her, and she didn't particularly like it. Not a word of her feelings did she mention to Tom, however. She knew how he felt on the subject, and she had no desire to reawaken the issue with him again.

"Come on, I'll walk you up to the house." Tom was standing behind her in the bedroom doorway as she turned from stowing her dress in the closet. His shirt was buttoned only halfway up, and he needed a shave. He looked so sexy that she felt her insides warming up all over again from just looking at him. His mouth quirked up at her in a wry smile. "Partway anyway."

Without even thinking about it, their fingers intertwined as they followed the shrubbery-lined brick path to the house. It was growing light, though the sun was not yet up. Dew was brushed from the vine-laden bushes onto their clothes with their passage. The sweet scent of honeysuckle was released with the dew. The air was very still, as though Sedgely had not yet awakened.

They stopped just before they reached the driveway, under a huge old oak dripping with gray festoons of Spanish moss. Ronnie looked at the big white mansion before her, at the trees and shrubs and flower beds that surrounded it in cared-for profusion, at the partly visible tents, at the darkened Japanese lanterns and smoky-topped, burned-out torches and other reminders of the party so recently over. Everything she saw spoke silently of wealth, and gentility, and a life of luxurious ease.

Then she turned to look at Tom.

"I've got to go in," she said.

"I know."

"Will you come by later?"

His hand tightened on hers. "I have to catch a plane at two."

"Oh, no!" Ronnie felt as if the air had suddenly been sucked from her lungs. "Where are you going?"

"To Nevada, and then California, and then Tennessee. I only flew home for the party."

The idea of parting from him was suddenly almost unbearable. "How long are you going to be gone?"

"A week probably."

"A week!" The way she said it, it might as well have been a year.

"Think you're going to miss me?"

"Oh, Tom!" The way she said it could have left him in no doubt. Turning toward him, she went up on tiptoe to wrap her arms around his neck.

He kissed her, briefly but thoroughly, and lifted his head. Then, as their gazes met, he kissed her again.

Finally he put her away from him. "Go on in," he said. "I'll call you. I'm going to be traveling around too much for you to call me."

"Tom . . ."

"Go on. It's getting light."

It was. The sun was coming up now, painting the eastern sky in ever-brightening layers of pink and lavender. There was nothing else to do. She had to go in. But leaving him there in the shadow of the big oak was one of the hardest things Ronnie had ever done in her life.

# Chapter
## 33

RONNIE WAS BUSY OVER THE NEXT FEW DAYS. She had campaign appearances and board meetings and luncheons and dinners to attend. They would be moving back to Washington on the Friday after Labor Day, so she had to prepare for that as well. For the first time ever, the thought of leaving Sedgely for the more cosmopolitan pleasures of the Capitol brought with it a twinge of regret. Always before, she had eagerly counted the days.

The twinge, she supposed, had something to do with Tom. No, it had everything to do with Tom. She felt as if she would be leaving him behind, which of course was ridiculous. There were airplanes. She would probably see just as much of him in Washington as she did in Jackson.

Which, come to think of it, wasn't nearly enough.

He called once, using her cell-phone number. As Ronnie was surrounded by people at the time—two state troopers, Thea, and a pair of reporters were accompanying her as she toured the schools on their opening day in the steamy Mississippi Delta—she had no choice but to keep the conversation brief and businesslike. The schools were in bad physical shape, the students for the most part poor. Kenny had arranged the tour as a way of continuing to emphasize for the media her concern with education, and Ronnie was genuinely touched by the poverty she saw.

But when Tom called, she fervently wished children, teachers, Thea, and everyone else nearby would vanish so that she could have just a few minutes of privacy to talk to him. What she wanted to say was for no one else's ears but his.

"Was that Tom?" Thea inquired, frowning, when Ronnie hung up.

Ronnie nodded, giving all her attention to the clay masks the children had made in art class, which decorated the walls.

"Did he want something? Should I call him back? I'm surprised he didn't call the office." Thea was still frowning. Tom did not, in her experience, call Ronnie directly for anything.

Ronnie shook her head. It was difficult to be casual, but she tried her best. "He wanted to know how I felt about doing an interview with another women's magazine."

With the near debacle over *Ladies' Home Journal* fresh in both their minds, it was a good answer. Ronnie was pardonably proud of it. Thea's curiosity evaporated.

Ronnie's longing for Tom increased.

She missed him with an intensity that grew worse instead of better with every hour that passed without him.

He was due back on Saturday. As it happened, he

got home on Friday afternoon. Having just finished saying a few words about the historic nature of the event, she was at that moment engaged in cutting the ribbon for the opening ceremonies for the Sky Parade, a Labor Day weekend extravaganza featuring hot-air balloons, stunt flying, and military air shows, when she looked up to see Tom standing at the front of the crowd.

He was wearing jeans, a T-shirt, and a baseball cap, and he was watching her from beneath the cap's brim as the large silver scissors she held snipped through the length of red satin. At first she didn't recognize him. He was just a tall, athletically built man in a baseball cap, bolder than most because he was openly eyeing her. Then their gazes met, and he grinned.

As Ronnie recognized him, her face lit up, and she completely lost track of what she was saying. The smile she gave him was both spontaneous and mega-watt in its power.

"You see a friend, Mrs. Honneker?" Chip Vines, the chairman of the event who was standing beside her as she performed the ceremonial function, asked jovially.

"Yes, I do," Ronnie answered, recalled to a sense of time and place by the man's question. A quick side-ways glance revealed that Kenny and Thea, who stood with Ronnie's security detail a few feet away, were both waving at Tom, but he was blind to their over-tures, his gaze still on her.

"If we're all done here, I'll just go over and say hi," she said, handing over the scissors.

"Yes, ma'am, we are. And we sure thank you for coming."

The ceremony was over. The small group of people

on the platform clambered down, and the platform it-self was wheeled out of the way. Kenny, Thea, and the troopers gathered around Ronnie as she moved toward the crowd massed to watch the air show.

Behind her the first of the military planes rolled out of the hangars onto the runway. The crowd cheered.

Tom's grin widened in welcome as she drew near. The desire to walk straight into his arms was almost overpowering, and she could read in his face the desire to have her do so. Instead Ronnie stopped in front of him, holding out her hand.

"Hello, Tom," she said while her eyes said much more. He took her hand, shaking it gravely before re-leasing it.

"Hello, Ronnie." His gaze flickered past her to Kenny and Thea. "Nice work on your speech. Hey, Kenny, Thea. Have you all met my son?"

For the first time Ronnie realized Tom was not alone. A teenage boy stood beside him.

"This is Mrs. Honneker, Mark. And Miss Cam-bridge."

"Hi," Mark said, nodding first at Ronnie, then Thea.

"Nice to meet you, Mark." Ronnie smiled at him, shaking hands, and Thea followed suit. Kenny obvi-ously already knew Mark, and greeted him in friendly fashion. Though they had not been introduced then, Ronnie remembered the teenager from that day at Tom's mother's farm. He was nearly as tall as Tom, and there was a definite resemblance between them, mostly in the shape of the mouth and jaw, and the color of the eyes. The boy's hair was light brown, sev-eral shades darker than Tom's, and in his baggy shorts and white T-shirt with the legend *Big Johnson Rules,* he looked thin rather than lean like his father.

Ronnie was slightly taken aback to find herself the object of Mark's admiring stare. She was wearing a turquoise silk shirtdress that buttoned up the front. It had a long, full skirt and open collar, and was sleeveless but otherwise completely covered up. It could have been made with Tom's directives on appropriate campaign gear in mind. There was nothing sexy about it, but still Tom's son was eyeing her appreciatively.

She glanced at Tom to see how he would take this evidence of his son's admiration. He was saying something to Thea, though, and appeared not to have noticed.

"What are you doing here? I thought you weren't getting in until tomorrow." Kenny put into words the question Ronnie wanted to ask.

"Mark's up for the weekend. So I worked a little faster and finished up early."

The crowd cheered as more airplanes rolled down the runway. Their small group shifted so as not to impede the view of those standing behind them.

"His plane landed an hour ago, but he wanted to hang around and see the air show," Mark put in caustically. "If I'd known that, I would have had Grandma pick him up."

Tom met Ronnie's gaze with a lurking smile in his eyes. "So I've got a thing for military aircraft," he said, shrugging. Then, to Mark, "Don't worry, we'll get you home in time for your date."

"I'm supposed to pick Loren up at six-thirty."

"You'll get there."

"I hate to be a spoilsport, but I really need to get going," Thea said. "I have a date tonight too."

"Todd Farber?" Ronnie asked, mentioning the name of the man Thea had brought to Lewis's party with an interested lift of her eyebrows. Thea nodded.

"Then I guess we'd better go," Ronnie said, trying hard not to sound as reluctant as she felt. Her gaze met Tom's again. To see him so briefly, and in such a public place, was almost worse than not seeing him at all.

"We'll walk you to your car," Tom said.

"I thought you wanted to see the air show!" Mark's protest was indignant.

"We can see the air show from the parking lot just as well as we can see it from here." Tom's tone was quelling. Ronnie had to suppress a smile as they all turned and headed toward the parking lot.

The state troopers were in front, clearing a path through the crowd. Mark, Thea, and Kenny were right behind them. Tom caught Ronnie's hand, pulling her back.

"Miss me?" he asked softly.

Ronnie looked at him. Her hand tightened around his. She did not dare to touch him any other way. Many in the crowd knew her identity, and there were reporters present, although they were focused on the air show rather than on her.

"You know I did."

He slid something into her hand. Glancing down, Ronnie saw that it was an envelope folded into a business-card-sized rectangle, with something hard inside. She looked a question at him.

"The key to my apartment. Mark will be gone by six-thirty at the latest."

Ronnie's hand closed around the paper rectangle. Her heartbeat speeded up. She gave him a quick, glimmering smile.

"Are you by any chance inviting me to dinner?"

"Something like that."

"Hey, Dad, would you hurry up?" Mark's impatient summons made them both start, and look around. Their privacy at an end, Ronnie and Tom moved forward to join the others as they pushed through the crowd.

Lewis was supposed to speak before a gathering of tobacco farmers at seven-thirty, and Ronnie was supposed to go with him. But she pleaded a debilitating headache instead and retired to her room. Dorothy was hostessing a bridge party, and twenty or so elderly women were gabbing away in the living room, Ronnie saw when she came downstairs again after Lewis had left. That made it easy to leave; Dorothy wouldn't miss her either. Instead of sneaking out, though, which carried with it the danger of being missed or caught coming back in, she told Selma that she thought she would go for a drive to see if fresh air would blow her headache away.

Then she simply climbed into her small white BMW and drove away.

Tom's apartment was north of Fortification Street, in Belhaven. The address, as well as directions, were written on the envelope that held the key. It was a venerable part of town, with towering trees, large older homes, and eclectic architecture. The apartment was one of three in an old brick Victorian mansion that had been converted into condominiums. Tom had the entire third floor.

There was an alley around back where Ronnie parked just in case anyone (she couldn't imagine who) should see and recognize her car. It was still light outside, a beautiful Indian-summer evening. Quite a few people were out, tending their gardens or sitting on their porches or chatting with their neighbors. Ronnie wasn't much afraid of being recognized herself. Taking a page out of Tom's book earlier, she wore jeans and a T-shirt, with her hair tucked up under a baseball cap.

Still, she didn't linger, but walked quickly into the building and up the stairs. The door fronting the third-floor landing was solid oak. *Tom and Mark Quinlan,* read the hand-scrawled label tucked into a small brass frame beneath the bell button at the side of the door.

She pushed the button and waited.

Tom opened the door.

Ronnie walked in. He shut the door, and pulled her into his arms.

Her baseball cap hit the floor.

Later, when their primary hunger was slaked, Tom rummaged around in the refrigerator for the makings of a light supper. After expending a serious amount of energy in the bedroom, he had professed himself starved, and dragged her up with him in search of food. Ronnie sat at the small, glass-topped table tucked into a corner of the kitchen, sipping Coke from a can and watching him. Shirtless, barefoot, clad only in a pair of faded jeans, he was looking seriously hunky as he rooted through the shelves, Ronnie thought, smiling to herself.

"How about a ham sandwich?" Tom asked, removing a platter containing a large, foil-wrapped object from the bottom shelf, and shut the refrigerator door. "Sandra's convinced I don't feed Mark properly, so she sent this ham and a container of green beans with him." He laughed. "Well, she's probably right. When he's with me, we usually end up ordering pizza."

"A ham sandwich is fine," Ronnie said. Then, elaborately casual, she asked, "Are you and Sandra on good terms?"

Setting the platter on the counter, he removed the aluminum foil.

"Reasonably good, because of Mark. We both love him a lot. Of course when the divorce was going down, it was a different story."

Tom found a knife, plates, and bread, and began hacking off slices of ham.

"You split up because she was sleeping around while you were out of town?" Ronnie prompted, remembering what he had told her the day she had met him.

Tom nodded. "Yup."

"Were you really all that surprised?" It was hard to imagine he hadn't suspected. *She* had suspected Lewis right from the beginning. No, she had known.

Tom finished one sandwich and started on the other. "Yup. I didn't have a clue. I came home a day early from a trip, just like I did today, and walked right in on it. In my house, in my bed. It wasn't pretty."

Ronnie had the feeling that that was the understatement of the year. "That must have been bad."

"It was." He glanced over his shoulder. "Mustard?"

"No, thanks. Just plain, please."

"No mayo either?"

"No, nothing."

He walked toward the table carrying two paper plates. As he set hers before her, Ronnie was amused to discover that the sandwiches were each thick enough to feed three people.

"Thank you," she said.

He sat down opposite her and bit into his sandwich.

"So the divorce was Sandra's fault?" Ronnie probed, removing about half the ham from her sandwich so that she could eat it.

"Want to know all the gory details, do you?" He smiled wryly at her. "If I was smart, I guess I'd say yes. But the truth is I was working a lot, which means I was gone a lot. I did occasionally meet women in the course of my work and . . ." His voice trailed off, and he lifted his eyebrows expressively at her to complete the sentence.

"Sleep with them?" Ronnie finished for him politely.

"That about sums it up, yeah." Tom's mouth twisted at her tone. "I'd been married since I was twenty-one, and I fell out of love with Sandra about two years later."

"I see." Ronnie took a bite of her sandwich. "But you were still surprised to find your wife sleeping with someone else."

"Surprised isn't the word." Tom put his sandwich down and picked up his Coke, then put that down, too, without drinking any. "I went nuts. I beat the crap out of the guy, scared the hell out of Sandra, and took off. The divorce took almost two years to finalize. Sandra wound up with everything: the house, the cars, the retirement fund, Mark. While it was going on, I couldn't keep my mind on my business, which went to hell on a greased slide. The firm wound up getting accused of accepting hundreds of thousands of dollars' worth of illegal campaign contributions on behalf of one of the clients we were working for at the time. Which we were not guilty of, by the way, not that it mattered in the end. It was all over the papers—I'm surprised you didn't see it. We had to pay a huge fine, and afterward business went down the tubes. We couldn't *buy* a client. The firm went bankrupt. Finally Kenny and I started picking up the pieces." He smiled at her. "*You* were our big break. We're coming back in a big way now. And I must say, I learned a lot from the experience."

"Tom," Ronnie began, and stopped. Her ham sandwich lay forgotten on her plate.

"What?" he asked, taking a bite of his.

"Tell me something: where do I fit into this picture? Do I fall under the category of one of the women you meet in the course of your work that you occasionally sleep with? Or are you still 'handling' me for the good of the firm?"

Tom stared at her across the table, and slowly put his sandwich back on his plate. His eyes narrowed. "For the record, the women I slept with while I was married were basically one-night stands. No emotional ties. They didn't want any, I didn't want any. And I draw the line at handling clients by sleeping with them."

"Of course, it helps that most of your other clients are men," Ronnie said sweetly.

His mouth quirked, and a flare of amusement lit his eyes. "That does help, yes."

Ronnie stood up, scowling at him. Tom stood up, too, and caught her by her upper arms, pulling her close against him, looking down into her eyes.

"You want to know where you fit into my life? Is that what you're asking me? The answer is, you don't fit in. You are one huge complication in a life that was starting to get fairly smooth again. You are professional suicide and a personal scandal on a scale I don't even like to think about, all wrapped up in one gorgeous, sexy package. I tried my very best not to get involved with you like this. I couldn't help it. I think about you during the day. I dream about you at night. Whenever I see you, it's like the sun breaking through the clouds after a cold rain."

As she listened, the frown faded from Ronnie's face. She slid her arms up around his neck.

His voice turned husky. "So I guess I'd have to say that at this point where you fit into my life is kind of up to you."

Ronnie stood on tiptoes to kiss him. No sooner had their mouths touched than the door to the apartment burst open, and then closed again with a tremendous slam.

## Chapter

## 34

"*D*AD!" MARK'S BELLOW broke Tom and Ronnie apart faster than a bucket of cold water being thrown over them. They had only an instant to look at each other in consternation. "Dad, are you in the kitchen? You'll never believe what she did!"

Ronnie had a sudden wild impulse to hide, which was ridiculous. She was trapped in the kitchen. There was no way out except through the living room, which Mark was already stomping across. And she was too big to fit in a cabinet.

Anyway, it became a moot point in seconds. Mark reached the kitchen door and stopped dead, the wrath draining from his face in the space of a single breath as his gaze moved from his father to Ronnie and back.

Ronnie saw the scene through Mark's eyes, and winced: There was Tom, clad in nothing but jeans, barefoot and shirtless. She was fully dressed at least, in jeans and a clingy, bright yellow T-shirt with a pink rising sun on it, but she was equally barefoot, her mouth devoid of lipstick, her hair in a deep red tangle around her shoulders. They stood about a yard apart, having instinctively separated as soon as they'd heard him come in. Tom was in front of the cabinets next to the refrigerator, while Ronnie was frozen beside the table, which held two Cokes in cans, and two plates with the remains of two ham sandwiches.

"Oh, sorry, I didn't know you had a"—here Mark's gaze swung back to Ronnie again and widened—"date."

It was clear from his expression that he remembered her from that afternoon.

"Ronnie, you remember my son." Tom's voice was crisp. "Mark, you met Mrs. Honneker earlier today."

"I remember, yeah. Hi," Mark managed, still staring at her.

"Hi, Mark," Ronnie said. Getting those two words out was one of the most difficult things she had ever done in her life. She felt hideously ill at ease. Hooking her fingers through the belt loops of her jeans, she glanced at Tom.

"I take it that you and Loren had a fight?" he said to Mark.

Ronnie had to give Tom credit; he was keeping his cool very well. The look he gave his son was level. The question was clearly intended as a distraction, and it worked.

"She gave me back my ring!" Mark was obviously laboring under a strong sense of having been ill used. He had to be both angry and anguished to blurt that out in front of a stranger, Ronnie thought. He thrust his hands in his front pockets in a way that reminded Ronnie of Tom, and leaned against the doorjamb dispiritedly.

"I didn't know you'd given her a ring," Tom said.

"Yeah, I did, at the beginning of the summer. We were going together! But look!" He held up his left hand, and there was a silver friendship ring on his little finger.

"Sit down, Ronnie, and finish your sandwich." Tom opened the refrigerator door, retrieved a small bottle of orange juice, and tossed it to his son. "You sit down, too, Mark. You want something to eat? A ham sandwich?"

"No." Mark unscrewed the lid of the orange juice, drained about half its contents in a series of gulps, and sat down at the table.

Ronnie, with another glance at Tom, resumed her seat. It would only compound the awkwardness if she were to leave the minute Mark got home. Perhaps the teen didn't even understand the significance of the scene he had walked in on, Ronnie thought hopefully.

Then she remembered the way he had looked at her at the airport earlier. Mark wasn't *that* young.

"So what happened?" Tom was fixing another ham sandwich.

"We were at Pizza Hut, and she told me she wants to start seeing other guys, and gave me back my ring!"

Ronnie gamely tried to take a bite of her sandwich.

"Loren's a real pretty girl." Tom put a paper plate with a ham sandwich on it in front of his son and sat down again at the table.

"Isn't she?" Mark took a huge bite out of the sandwich he hadn't wanted.

"But you know, there are lots of pretty girls out there. Some of them as pretty as Loren, or prettier.

Maybe you ought to think about checking some of *them* out."

"Maybe," Mark said without enthusiasm, taking another big bite of his sandwich.

"Would you mind if I gave you some advice about your girlfriend?" Ronnie asked, pushing her plate aside and leaning her elbows on the table.

"Sure," Mark said.

"If I were you, I'd act like you don't care a snap of your fingers that she broke up with you. Start going out with other girls right away. That'll get her attention faster than anything else you could do."

"Make her jealous, you mean?" Mark asked. "That's kind of corny. Do you really think it would work?"

"Imagine how you'd feel if you saw your girlfriend with another guy."

"I'd want to kill him," Mark said with conviction.

"A slight tendency toward jealousy is kind of a family failing," Tom said with a glimmer of a smile, his eyes meeting Ronnie's. She smiled back at him, remembered their audience, and quickly tried to make the smile impersonal. She wasn't sure how well she succeeded.

"I guess I could ask Elizabeth Carter to go to the Labor Day dance with me," Mark said, pondering. "Or Amy Ruebens."

"That's a good idea," Tom said.

"I hate to eat and run, but I've got to go." Ronnie glanced at the big clock on the wall opposite, and stood up. A sudden, horrible thought seized her. She couldn't go; she was barefoot. Her shoes were right where she had kicked them off: beside Tom's bed.

How to retrieve them gracefully?

Tom had gotten to his feet when she stood up, and obviously saw the sudden consternation in her expression. His brows drew together, and he gave her a mystified look.

"Sit back down," she told him with a quick wave toward the chair he had just vacated. "I'm just going to run to the rest room first. I'll be right back."

There were two bathrooms in the apartment, one just down the hall from the kitchen and one off Tom's bedroom. Mark had his own bedroom next to Tom's, but as far as she knew no bathroom. Ronnie shut the door to the bathroom off the hall without going in and scurried along to Tom's bedroom, feeling like a thief. Her sneakers were beside the bed, which was thoroughly mussed. Ronnie quickly straightened the covers, then sat on the corner of the bed to pull on her shoes. That done, she sprang up, crept back to the bathroom, and opened and closed the door again, as though she were just coming out.

Even if Mark did guess that she and his father were sleeping together, there was no need to remove all doubt from his mind. And the state of Tom's bed with her shoes beside it was, to Ronnie's way of thinking, pretty damning evidence.

Walking at a normal pace now, Ronnie returned to the kitchen doorway. Father and son were in the midst of a low-voiced discussion, which they broke off as she appeared.

"I've got to go," she said. Their eyes were really very similar, she thought as they both looked up at her.

"I'll walk you out." Tom stood up. "Let me get my shirt."

Wearing the white T-shirt he had on earlier and a pair of slip-on boat shoes, he was back so fast that Ronnie and Mark only had time to exchange awkward smiles.

Mark got to his feet then, glancing first at Ronnie, then at his father, who stood just behind her. "Look, I'm sorry about crashing in on your date. When you told me you were staying home tonight, I thought . . . I thought . . ." His voice trailed off.

What he didn't say was obvious: He had thought Tom meant *alone*.

"I'm glad to have had the chance to make your acquaintance, Mark," Ronnie said, having by this time decided that the only thing to do was pretend there was no awkwardness inherent in the situation. "Your dad talks about you a lot."

"Does he?" Mark darted an interested glance at Tom.

"Now and then," Tom said. "I'll be back in a minute, Mark."

They didn't speak until they were outside the building, heading around toward the alley where Ronnie had left her car.

"Do you think he realized?" Ronnie asked anxiously. Tom was walking beside her, but they weren't touching. It was dark now, and most everyone seemed to have gone inside. Somebody nearby was having a barbecue; the mouthwatering aroma of grilling meat filled the air.

"Oh, yeah." Tom's answer was dry. "He thinks you're a total babe, by the way."

"You two talked about me?"

"The first thing he said when you left the room was, 'Now I get the air show bit.' The conversation went downhill from there."

"Oh, no!"

Tom shrugged. "There's nothing to do about it. I imagine we'll be talking about it some more. I'll tell him that there's such a thing as moral ambiguity, for instance, and how some things are not black or white but kind of shades of gray. One of those conversations parents have with their kids when the kid catches the parent doing something wrong."

"Oh, Tom, I hate for you to be put in that kind of position!"

"Yeah, me too."

They reached Ronnie's car and stopped, facing each other.

"Will I see you tomorrow?" Her voice was low.

He shook his head. "Mark's playing in a baseball tournament in Meridian. We'll be gone all day tomorrow and most of Sunday."

"You know we're moving back to Washington on Friday."

"I know. I'm flying to California on Tuesday."

"So . . . ?" Ronnie let her voice trail off delicately.

Tom grimaced. "How about Monday?"

"It's Labor Day. I'm supposed to go to an arts and crafts show with Lewis in the afternoon. But I think I can get away Monday night."

"Mark's going to a dance at his school—I think."

"Your apartment is definitely out."

"Definitely." Tom grinned suddenly. "There's a motel out on I-twenty. The Robbins Inn. I used to take girls there when I was in high school. It's out of the way, and neither one of us is likely to see anyone we know. Suppose I meet you in the parking lot Monday night at eight?"

"I'll try."

Tom caught her hand, and pulled her close to kiss her.

"Don't worry about Mark," he said. "I'll handle it."

They kissed again, and then Ronnie got into her car and drove home to Sedgely.

On Monday they met at the motel. On Tuesday Tom flew to California. This time he left a number where Ronnie could reach him, so she was able to call him, late at night when no one else was around to hear.

On Friday she and Lewis flew back to Washington.

The house in Georgetown was a three-story brick row house, narrow and elegant and old. It was not nearly as large as Sedgely, but it spoke as surely of money and breeding. The ceilings were fourteen feet high, with elaborate crown moldings. There were fireplaces in nearly every room. The floors were polished hardwood covered with antique oriental rugs in shades of maroon and rose and blue. Paintings by such diverse artists as Sargent and Cézanne and Andrew Wyeth hung on the walls. The upholstered furniture was covered in brocades and silk stripes in jewel tones. The wooden pieces were almost without exception museum-quality antiques.

This was the house Ronnie had first come to as Lewis's bride, and this was the house at which she felt most at home. Washington suited her as Mississippi did not. In Washington she fit in better. Though she was younger than most of the Senate wives, she was part of their circle. Very rarely, in Washington, was she ever referred to as "the *second* Mrs. Honneker." At least not within her hearing.

Almost instantaneously she was reabsorbed into the rounds of teas and luncheons and dinner parties. She chatted with friends on the phone, had her hair done, went shopping. She and Lewis attended a dinner at the White House for the president of Zaire, who had come to Washington with the professed object of obtaining financial aid for his country. They went to a benefit at the Smithsonian. She joined the President's wife for what was billed as a "girls' club" breakfast in the White House solarium, which was airy and light and decorated with beautiful floral chintzes.

But none of this was as satisfying as it had been in the spring, before she had gone to Mississippi for the summer. She took little joy from the money she was able to spend on clothes, from the glittering parties to which she was invited, from the rich and famous people with whom she was on a first-name basis. Even having breakfast with the First Lady in the White House felt—flat.

All because she was missing Tom.

She hadn't seen him since they had met at the motel, though she talked to him nightly on the phone. When they spoke, her whole existence narrowed to the receiver in her hand and to his voice on the other end. On the nights when she was out too late to call him, she went to bed and curled up in the bedclothes in a

cocoon of longing. The next day all color seemed to be
leeched from the world.

On Friday she and Lewis were to attend a reception
at Bill Kenneth's house. Bill Kenneth was the junior
senator from Tennessee, and he had just been ap-
pointed to the Ways and Means Committee, of which
Lewis was a member.

It was a cocktail reception, scheduled for nine
o'clock, which was early in the evening in Washington.
Ronnie wore a short black cocktail dress with nude
hose and high-heeled black satin pumps. The dress itself was a black satin slip with a black lace overdress.
While the slip part was bare, the lace overdress had
long sleeves and a jewel neck, making for a covered-up
look that was also, with its glimpse of flesh beneath the
lace, alluring. She wore her hair down, with diamonds
in her ears.

All in all, she was pleased with the way she looked
when she walked into the party, which had been in
progress for some forty-five minutes. (It would never
do to arrive too early.) Lewis looked good in his dark
business suit, and seemed proud to have her on his
arm. Within minutes they had separated. She was on
one side of the room talking to the Peruvian ambassa-
dor. He was in a corner with two of his cronies, guf-
fawing over something as they puffed on cigars.

"Why, Ronnie, how are you? You're looking really
lovely tonight, dear. Those earrings! I just love them to
death!" The Armani-clad speaker was Lacey Kenneth,
Bill's wife. Though she was perhaps seven or eight
years older than Ronnie, she was still a young and
attractive woman, slim, with shoulder-length dark-
brown hair.

Ronnie turned, smiling, to do the kissey-face thing with Lacey that was *de rigueur* among political wives. Her eyes widened as, looking over Lacey's shoulder, she encountered a pair of achingly familiar blue eyes.

# Chapter
## 35

"I BELIEVE YOU KNOW TOM QUINLAN, dear? Mississippi is his home state too." Straightening away from Ronnie, Lacey drew Tom forward with a hand on his elbow.

Tom smiled at her. He looked tall and broad-shouldered and handsome in a navy suit with a white shirt and red tie.

"We've met," he said easily, shaking the hand that she somehow had the presence of mind to hold out to him. "Hello, Ronnie."

"Hello, Tom." With the touch of his hand the room suddenly took on a whole new aura. It seemed to come alive, sparkling with color, pulsing with sounds and scents and sights that Ronnie had previously not divined. Pure, unadulterated joy burst inside her. She smiled at him, then quickly recollected herself and her surroundings and tried to dim that blinding look lest it give them away.

Lacey was already glancing from Tom to Ronnie with a touch of curiosity.

"As a point of fact I've been doing some work for

Senator Honneker in Mississippi this summer," Tom said to Lacey as he released Ronnie's hand. "Ronnie and I are old friends."

"Well, he's working for us now," Lacey said, looking at Ronnie with a proprietary laugh. "Bill's facing a tough race this time. We're bringing in the big guns."

"It's a while yet till Election Day. There's plenty of time to do what needs to be done," Tom said. Then, to Ronnie, "How do you like being back in Washington?"

The three of them chatted about nothing: the pros and cons of Washington in various seasons, the weather, the terrible amount of crime in certain areas of the city. Lacey's suspicions, if indeed she had ever harbored any, seemed to be assuaged. When more people joined their little group, she slipped a hand in the crook of Tom's elbow and led him away.

She wanted, she said, to introduce him to someone.

Watching Lacey Kenneth walk away with Tom, her hand curled around his arm, her body pressed close to his side as she steered him across the room, Ronnie felt a smoldering dislike for a woman she had previously considered a friend.

She had a pretty good idea of what Lacey Kenneth really wanted from Tom.

"If you sleep with her, I'll claw your eyes out," Ronnie whispered threateningly to Tom in one of the few private moments they were able to manage.

He took a sip from the golden-colored drink in his hand, his eyes narrowing as he looked down at her.

"Jealous?"

"Yes."

"How do you think I feel, seeing you here with His Honor?"

"You *know* about Lewis and me."

"That doesn't erase the fact that you're his wife."

"You're avoiding the subject."

"What subject is that?"

"Lacey Kenneth."

His tight expression eased and then he smiled at her. "Darlin', the only woman in this room I have any intention of sleeping with is you. Why do you think I came to Washington?"

"Why did you?"

"To see you."

"Why didn't you let me know?"

"I just decided to come this morning. I don't think I could have survived another one of our telephone conversations without doing something about it."

Recollecting the steamy turn their conversation had taken the night before, Ronnie saw his point.

"How long are you here for?"

"Just tonight."

"Just tonight!"

"Tom, there you are! Ronnie, you have to quit monopolizing him! I don't think he's had any of our *salmon en croute* yet, and it is mouthwatering! And Lewis is looking for you. I think he's ready to leave."

"I'd better go find him, then." Ronnie kept a smile pinned to her face as Tom was once more dragged away. Lewis was indeed ready to go. After leaving the Kenneths', she and Lewis were scheduled to attend another party thrown by an important lobbyist. It started at eleven.

She managed one more low-voiced exchange with

Tom as she came back from a quick trip to the powder room for the supposed purpose of freshening her lipstick.

Or, rather, Tom managed it.

He walked right up to her, bold as brass in front of them all, which of course was the only way *not* to look guilty. The only problem was Ronnie had trouble remembering that.

"It was good seeing you, Ronnie," he said, adding, under his breath, "The Ritz-Carlton. Room Seven-fifteen."

"You, too, Tom." She smiled, shook hands, and mouthed, "I'll try."

"You take care of yourself in Washington, now, boy, you hear?" Lewis said, joining them and clapping Tom on the shoulder. "Next time you come into town, let Ronnie and me know, and you can stay with us."

"I'll do that, Senator," Tom replied, his voice crisp. Then Lewis put his arm around Ronnie and swept her out the door. Ronnie could feel Tom's eyes boring into her back until the door shut behind them.

She and Lewis did not get home until nearly three A.M. By then it was too late to go see Tom at his hotel. There was no possible excuse she could give for leaving the house at such an hour. And as for phoning him, that wasn't possible either. Lewis stayed up after Ronnie went to bed, and she was afraid he might pick up an extension—the one in the library, where he spent most of his time, had a button that lit up whenever anyone was on the line—and overhear.

So, unhappily, she went to sleep. When her alarm went off, at six A.M., she got up, and dressed in running shorts and a T-shirt as though she were going out for a run. It was early, much earlier than she usually awoke, but in Washington she ran instead of swam, and her absence for such a purpose would not raise any questions. It was likely she wouldn't even be missed. Mary, the woman who kept house for them in Washington, didn't arrive until nine, and Lewis probably wouldn't miss her no matter what time he got up. He never went into her bedroom; there was no reason for him to.

Fog had rolled in from the Potomac during the night and lay over everything, Ronnie saw as she let herself out of the house. Its fine, gray mist wrapped around the stately residences like a blanket, and muffled the sounds of traffic from the busier streets nearby. She jogged to the corner without seeing anyone she knew—tourists were always up and about in Georgetown. There she was able to hail a cab.

The lobby of the Ritz-Carlton was busy, even this early in the morning, mainly with businessmen and - women standing in line to check out. As she came in through the revolving door, Ronnie glanced around with some apprehension. But no one paid the least bit of attention to her, and she had an elevator to herself.

Tapping softly on the door to Room 715, she looked anxiously around. The chances of running into someone she knew at this particular time in this particular corridor in this particular hotel were slim, but they existed. Washington was a small town really. Sometimes it felt much smaller than Jackson. Here everybody really did seem to know everybody else.

There was no answer. Ronnie frowned, and knocked again, a little louder. Still no answer. It began to occur to her that perhaps he was not there. Perhaps he had not spent the night in his room at all.

Which left open the question of exactly where he *had* spent it. Lacey Kenneth's face flashed into Ronnie's mind. Or perhaps, like Lewis, he had a thing for hookers. Washington was a city of endless opportunity if that was the case.

Even considering the possibilities made her angry, and now she pounded on the door with her fist, making enough noise to rouse the dead. If Tom had spent the night with another woman, he could kiss any hope of continuing to see *her* good-bye.

Plus, she would kill him.

The door opened just as she was getting ready to beat on it with both fists and possibly kick it for good measure. Tom stood there glowering at her, one of the white terry-cloth robes provided by the hotel tied haphazardly around his waist. He was unshaven, barefoot, and bleary-eyed.

Obviously she had rousted him out of bed. For a moment they simply eyed each other, exchanging black looks.

Without a word he stood aside to let her in. Then he shut the door and pulled her close. Holding her with both hands gripping her waist, he scowled down into her upturned face.

"Where were you?" he growled.

"We didn't get home until after three," Ronnie said apologetically, her arms sliding inside his robe to wrap around his hard middle. Her anger faded as she realized that he had not in fact spent the night with another woman. "It was too late to come, or call."

"I was worried, dammit."

"I'm sorry." She snuggled closer, and the robe, which had not been securely tied to begin with, fell open. He was wearing boxers, red plaid ones, which he had obviously slept in. She liked him this way, all warm and tousled and bristly and just roused from sleep. She nuzzled his chest with her nose. The hairs there tickled. He smelled of man.

"I have a meeting at ten." He still sounded grumpy, though his hands, having found their way beneath her T-shirt, were moving over her bare back.

Ronnie sighed. "We never seem to have much time, do we? I hate that."

"You wanted an affair, you got an affair."

He wasn't grumpy, he was downright cantankerous. Flicking a glance up at him, Ronnie saw that he was still scowling.

She knew how to fix that.

"I missed you," she said softly, pressing her mouth to his chest.

"Horny, are you?" His hand found her bra strap and with a deft movement unhooked it. "Me too."

Ronnie glanced up at him in shock. That bit of crudity sounded so completely unlike Tom that she could hardly believe it had come out of his mouth.

"That wasn't very nice," she said reprovingly even as his hand slid around her body and under her loosened bra to cup her breast.

His hand on her breast felt good. She had spent the days since they had last been together dreaming about him touching her like that. He squeezed, and Ronnie shivered.

"I don't feel very nice at the moment." There was a tone to his voice that Ronnie had never heard before. Frowning, she looked up at him, but then he distracted her by the very effective method of pulling off her T-shirt and bra.

For a moment he did nothing more, merely stood looking down at her. She was wearing bicycle shorts, socks, and tennis shoes, and her naked breasts brushed his chest.

Without another word he picked her up and carried her to the bed.

His lovemaking was hard and furious, nothing like the previous times. He demanded and she gave, entering her almost immediately, almost forcing her to a response that was shattering in its intensity. He set the pace, taking what he wanted, manipulating her expertly until she could do nothing but writhe and cling and cry out his name.

The end, when it came, was explosive.

Then he started up again.

When at last he finished, he lay on top of her for only a second or so before rolling off the bed and heading for the bathroom. Moments later Ronnie heard the sound of water running. He was taking a shower.

It didn't take a genius to figure out that Tom was angry at her. For making him worry last night? Probably.

Swinging her legs out of bed, she got up, stretching. Her body tingled all over from his unshaven face, and she would probably have bruises later in places she would only be able to see with her mirror, but she felt as content and as sated as a cat that had just devoured a whole can of tuna.

Smiling a little, she headed for the bathroom. To her surprise the door was shut and locked. Pondering, she turned to the vanity sink that was just outside the bathroom, brushing her hair and checking her makeup. She then walked back into the bedroom, donned the terry-cloth robe that he had discarded, and settled down in bed to wait, intrigued.

Tom in a really nasty mood should be something to see.

When he walked into the bedroom again, some ten minutes later, he had showered, shaved, and was wearing a pair of light-gray suit pants and a white shirt. The shirt was open at the collar, but otherwise buttoned all the way up. A navy tie was slung around his neck. He even had on his shoes.

He looked at her as he entered the room. His jaw was hard, and his mouth was set in a grim line. Wrapped in his bathrobe, sitting with her back against the headboard and her knees drawn up in front of her, Ronnie returned his look with lifted brows.

"What was *that* all about?" she asked.

Tom's face darkened, and he walked past the bed toward the window.

"Sex," he answered curtly, pulling the cord that opened the curtains. Light flooded into the room, not a blinding light, because of the fog, but nevertheless enough to illuminate every corner. Ronnie blinked. "That's what this whole thing is all about, isn't it? Sex? I want sex, you want sex, so we have sex? That was pure, raw, hard, I'm-horny-you're-horny sex."

He stood with his back to her, looking out over the city. Ronnie looked at the unyielding set of those broad shoulders and sighed.

"Tom . . ."

Abruptly he turned to face her. "This isn't working for me, Ronnie. I knew it wouldn't. I am not constitutionally capable of being the guy you're screwing on the side. You're either going to have to leave your husband and file for divorce or it's over between us."

Ronnie stared at him. Whatever she had expected, it had not been that.

"Tom . . ."

"I mean what I say." He walked toward the bed. "You're going to have to choose: him or me." At the foot of the bed he paused, and she saw that his hands were balled into fists at his sides. "If you decide it's me, you know where to reach me. If you don't, good luck and Godspeed."

"Tom! Tom, wait!"

But even as she scrambled out of bed, he was already walking out the door.

# Chapter

## 36

RONNIE SPENT THE NEXT WEEK on automatic pilot. She went to luncheons and dinners, and couldn't have said what she ate or who else was there. She chatted gaily at official functions, and couldn't afterward remember the subject of the conversation. She played tennis with her friends, and missed so many balls that they asked her if she was feeling all right. She went shopping, and could not find so much as a pair of shoes she liked.

Twice, late at night, she picked up the phone to call Tom. And twice she put the receiver back in its cradle before she finished dialing.

There was no appeal possible: Tom meant what he said. She knew it, had known it when he said it. Had known from the beginning in fact that this day was coming. To use his own words, he was not constitutionally capable of being the man she was screwing on the side.

Tom was an all-or-nothing-at-all kind of guy.

Ronnie told herself that she would get over it, over *him*. If the situation with Lewis wasn't ever going to improve—and it wasn't; the very idea of sleeping with him gave her the creeps—at least she still had the life she wanted. She still had the houses and cars and charge cards and jewelry and—and *things*.

In the end, wasn't that what was most important?

She knew as well as she knew her own name that alliances between men and women were ephemeral. Love did not last.

That was when she put a label on something she should have realized long before: Somehow, some-where, sometime on the long and winding road from that first day at the Neshoba County Fair to the morn-ing in the hotel in Washington, she had fallen head over heels in love with Tom.

At the thought of never seeing him again, she felt physically ill.

But of course she would see him again. He was still consulting for Lewis, and for her. She would *see* him. Even talk to him. He would be around.

She might even be able to persuade him into her bed from time to time. They had already conclusively proven that he was vulnerable to temptation where she was concerned.

But even if she succeeded in getting him to sleep with her again, what would she have gained? The time they had managed to steal together already had not been enough for her.

More time was what she wanted from Tom, not less. She wanted to make love with him, yes—but af-terward she wanted to be able to fall asleep in his arms. She wanted to be there when he woke up in the morning. She wanted to be there with him for break-fast, and lunch and supper and Saturday-afternoon ballgames and church on Sunday. She wanted to be there when he wrestled with the problems of being a father to an adolescent son, and went to visit his mother, and had business issues to discuss.

She wanted to be part of his life.

But did she want it badly enough to give up the life she now had? And it would be gone, the big houses, the big money, the sheer *importance* that came with being married to Lewis.

She had signed a prenuptial agreement. At the time she hadn't thought a thing about it. She had persuaded herself that she was in love with Lewis. What did it matter if she signed away her claims to all but a tiny fraction of his money in case of divorce? There would never *be* a divorce.

Nothing, she had thought at the time, would induce her to agree to one. Even if their love didn't last, their marriage would. Having got what she wanted, she would never be fool enough to throw it away.

She hadn't counted on falling in love with another man.

A pigheaded, jealous-natured man who was not content to take a backseat in her life.

Tom offered none of the trappings that she enjoyed as Lewis's wife. She didn't know how much he earned, but even a six-figure income could not begin to touch the millions Lewis had at his disposal.

Tom came from the world she had left behind, the world of mortgage payments and electric bills and ham sandwiches in the kitchen for supper.

Why on earth would she even consider giving up everything she had with Lewis to go back to that?

Was any man worth it?

Even Tom?

Ronnie found the answer as she was flying back to Jackson with Lewis on Thursday. They were in a private jet that had been loaned to the campaign by Ynoba Corporation, a Mississippi conglomerate that wanted to influence Lewis's vote on environmental issues. The seats were plush bone leather, the floors were covered with thick bone carpet, and the walls were upholstered in leather-grained bone vinyl. There was no noise at all in the cabin, and there was a stewardess to see to their every need. The plane was the ultimate in luxury travel; Ronnie was so used to it and others like it that she didn't even notice anymore.

Lewis was still campaigning hard, wooing his constituents back to the fold with every ounce of political savvy he could muster. As a consequence they would be spending a long weekend every other week in his home state. Ronnie had a full quota of campaign events scheduled for the next three days, as did Lewis.

Just thinking about it made her tired. She leaned her head back against the cushioned headrest and stared out the window at the clouds below.

Lewis was on his cell phone, yakking to all and sundry as he always did when he was in the air. Staying in touch, he called it. Stoking the fires. Usually she just tuned him out.

But it occurred to her, as a phrase or two caught her ear, that he was talking to Tom.

"We'll be doing that barbecue thing tomorrow. What is it you thought I should say to the press again?" Lewis paused, frowning. "Oh, right, I got it now: Voters don't care much about what you *did*;

what they're interested in is what you *will do,* because that is what affects them."

Lewis listened for a minute. Ronnie could make out an indistinct rumble on the other end of the conversation, but strain though she did, she could not clearly hear either Tom's words or his voice.

"Yeah, I'll do that, and Ronnie's going to be talkin' about education. You need to tell her anything?"

For an instant Ronnie's heart stood still.

"Oh, okay, I'll talk to you later, then. You take care of yourself, boy."

Lewis clicked the cell phone off. Staring at it, Ronnie felt as though her lifeline had just been severed.

Seconds ago on the other end of that phone had been Tom.

Lewis turned to say something to her, to pass on some words of advice from Tom, she had no doubt, but she didn't hear so much as a syllable.

All she could do was think about Tom—and what she was throwing away.

As soon as they landed in Jackson, she had to get dressed to go out. She was scheduled to be the guest of honor, and speaker, at the Mississippi Commission on Women dinner that night. Lewis was going to a Rotary Club meeting.

When the limo bringing her home again pulled up in front of Sedgely, it was not quite ten-thirty. Ronnie got out and went up the steps to the porch, waving to the security officer/driver who had seen her home.

As the red lights on the rear of the car headed back down the drive, Ronnie turned to go into the house.

But in the end she walked down the steps again. It was a warm night, a beautiful night, with crickets and

tree frogs and cicadas forming a chirping chorus. The
faintest hint of honeysuckle still perfumed the air.
Early September in Mississippi was almost as much
summer as July, she thought. The nights were better
than the days for being outdoors.

She would go for a walk. She badly needed to be
alone, to think.

Davis came bounding up out of nowhere with a
mighty woof, and Ronnie patted his head absentmind-
edly. She had grown fond of the dog, but at the moment she could have done without his company. He
reminded her too vividly of Tom.

Trying to send him away, though, was a waste of
time, just as sending him to obedience school had been
futile. With Davis it just hadn't taken.

So she accepted his company. He snuffled around
the shrubberies as she headed away from the house.
She considered going for a swim, but the pool, she
feared, would bring up memories that might cloud her
mind.

This had to be a well-thought-through decision, because it was the biggest decision she had ever made in
her life.

She had to choose between Lewis and Tom. The
thought almost made her laugh. On the surface of it,
there was no choice at all. If the contest was strictly
between the two men, she would choose Tom, every
day of the week and three times on Sunday.

The real choice, then, boiled down to this: love or
money.

That was what she had to think about. That was
what she had to coolly, calculatingly weigh. That was
the choice that had to be made.

Love or money.

In the end, though every ounce of pragmatism she possessed screamed against it, she made the choice with her heart: love.

She was going to leave Lewis for Tom.

The decision made, she looked up at Sedgely, at the big white house that had once stood for everything she had ever wanted in life, and suddenly felt as if the weight of the world had been lifted from her shoulders.

The lights were still on inside, in the front hall and upstairs and in Lewis's office. That meant Lewis was in, and awake.

She was going to go inside and tell him she wanted a divorce.

Then she was going to call Tom and tell him too.

She left Davis pursuing an intriguing scent that took him bounding around the back of the house, and walked up the steps, through the front door, through the center hallway, and along the hall that led to Lewis's office. The idea of leaving behind the crystal chandeliers and fine paintings and expensive antiques she passed did not give her so much as a pang.

They were just *things.*

People were what mattered. Or at least one particular person.

With a quick knock she turned the knob and opened the door to Lewis's office.

He had fallen asleep at his desk. Ronnie frowned. His silvered head and massive shoulders lay heavily against the brightly polished mahogany surface.

"Lewis?" She walked into the room and over to the desk, which was directly opposite the door. It was not like Lewis to fall asleep at his desk. In fact he had never, to her knowledge, done so before.

"Lewis?" Was he ill? Could he have suffered a heart attack, or a stroke? After all, he was not a young man. . . .

Reaching the desk, she touched his shoulder, nudging him even as she walked around the side of the desk. Her foot hit something hard on the intricately patterned oriental carpet beneath her feet.

Looking down, she saw that it was a gun. The silver pistol that Lewis usually kept in the desk's top drawer, to be precise. Or at least one that looked just like it. Bending down, she picked it up and stared at it.

It was heavy and cool in her hand.

Then she looked at Lewis again.

"Lewis!" She dropped the gun, and shoved violently at his shoulder, shaking him.

That was when she saw that his head lay in a dark, sticky-looking pool of blood.

# Chapter

## 37

"*Y*OU MAKE GOOD MEAT LOAF, Marla." Replete, Jerry got up from the kitchen table and wandered over to the back door, where he looked out through the screen at the little girl playing in the small, rocky backyard. "Good potatoes too. Good everything."

"Thanks, Jerry." Marla started clearing the table, carrying the plates to the counter and then scraping them into the sink. She turned on the water and, with a quick flip of the switch, the garbage disposal. The harsh whirring sound provided accompaniment while she loaded the dishes into the dishwasher.

"Looks like Lissy likes it here," Jerry said next.

"You've been so good to her." With the dishwasher loaded, Marla gave the counter a quick swipe with the sponge and joined Jerry at the screen door. Lissy was sitting high in a tree in the backyard, having an apparently serious conversation with a kitten who was up in the tree with her. Her long, thin legs were swung sideways over a branch, and her bare feet dangled a good twenty feet above the ground.

"I oughta make her come down," Marla said with a sigh. "If she falls, she'll break her neck."

"Let her alone," Jerry advised comfortably. "She's happy."

Lissy did look happy, Marla thought. Having a house, a yard, and a kitten was good for her. And she liked Jerry. He'd given her the kitten, bringing it home from the grocery store with him two days before. Lissy had been ecstatic—she'd never had a pet before—and had named the kitten *Boo*.

It kind of made up for the fact that she was having a little trouble fitting in with the other girls at school. Jerry had insisted that she be enrolled, though Marla, fearing that somehow the killer might be able to trace her through Lissy's school records, had resisted. But Jerry had dismissed her fears, Lissy had begged to go—she loved school—and Marla had found herself over-ruled.

It had been both funny and annoying to have the two of them gang up on her like that.

But the other girls were snubbing Lissy, which made Marla's blood boil every time she thought about it. They wouldn't sit with her at lunch, or play with her at recess. Most of the children had been together since kindergarten, and the cliques were already set in concrete. Lissy was the odd girl out.

"I got a surprise for her," Jerry said.

Marla glanced at him. "What?"

"She's gonna have dance lessons. Ballet. Starting tomorrow, right after school."

"*What?*"

"All the other girls take dance lessons. I checked around. This one tomorrow is the class they go to."

Marla spluttered, so surprised, she was having trouble marshaling her thoughts. "But—but she'll need special clothes for that, won't she? And shoes? And—and I don't know how much dance lessons cost, Jerry, but—"

"You let me worry about that." He was looking at Lissy again, sitting up in the tree, talking to her cat. "It'll give her something in common with the other girls, a way to make friends."

"But, Jerry, we're not gonna be here that long."

Jerry looked at her then. "You never know, Marla. You never know."

# Chapter

## 38

*T*HE SENATOR LAY in state in the ornate, domed chamber of the state capitol building. With Kenny at his heels, Tom battled his way through an army of press to get inside. Fortunately none of the reporters was interested in them. Cameras, mikes, tape recorders, and all, the reporters were focused on the heavy doors, waiting for someone of importance to come out. At the moment only family, close friends and associates, and political bigwigs were being admitted. Tomorrow, for two hours in the morning, two hours in the afternoon, and two hours in the evening, the public would be permitted to file by the bier and pay their last respects.

A stir went up as one of the phalanx of state troopers guarding the doors recognized Tom and opened them just enough to permit him and Kenny to pass through.

A chorus of "Who was that?" "Did you see?" "Were they members of the family?" went up, only to be silenced as the heavy doors swung shut behind them.

The first thing Tom saw was the coffin, which rested before the speaker's platform. It brought home as nothing else had done the reality of what had happened: His Honor was dead. The role he had played in Tom's life was not large, but it was important. His acquaintance, as an impressionable youth, with a real U.S. senator had helped shape his ultimate career choice. He had looked up to the Senator then, and in many ways admired him still. And he was—had been—Ronnie's husband.

God, what a mess.

The enormous arched ceiling with its stained glass dome and gilded trim soared overhead with grandeur befitting the occasion. Diffused light filtered down through the dome, illuminating the interior of the chamber with an otherworldly ambience. Soberly clad people stood about in small clusters, talking quietly among themselves. Uniformed state troopers were stationed around the room. A funereal hush lay over all.

Tom's gaze ran over the mourners. There was only one he was interested in at the moment.

"There's Mrs. Honneker," Kenny whispered, indicating her location with a discreet nod.

Tom's head swung in the direction Kenny indicated, but the woman was not the Mrs. Honneker he sought. She was Dorothy, dressed all in black and standing with a pair of equally elderly women close to the bier. Lewis's mother suddenly looked every one of her eighty-some-odd years, and Tom knew the loss was going to hit her hard. A glance around found Marsden talking with a group on the far side of the room. Losing his father would hit Marsden hard too.

Then a familiar redhead caught his eye. Ronnie sat

with her back to him in the first of a line of folding chairs placed in front of the coffin. Governor Blake was standing before her, patting her hand as he offered his condolences.

"I'm going up there," he said to Kenny, nodding toward where Ronnie sat.

Without giving the least appearance of haste, Tom moved toward her as swiftly as he could. He'd been in the little town of Rice, California, when Kenny had called him just before eight A.M. with the news of Senator Honneker's death. Getting from there to Jackson, Mississippi, in about ten hours had been no easy task, but he'd managed it. Kenny had said the Senator had been shot once in the head. Suicide or homicide? That was the question.

Either way Tom knew that Ronnie was going to need him. Not just him personally, though there was that, too, but his professional expertise. Given the way the local press had historically treated her, whatever the answer, he was afraid she might be in for a bumpy ride.

There were women with her, he saw as he got closer, and was glad of it. The people who might most logically be expected to support her through this ordeal were the Senator's family and friends, and ultimately they were not friends of Ronnie's. Marsden openly hated her. Tom suspected the girls did, too, and probably Dorothy. If push came to shove, most of Mississippi would fall in line with them.

If lines were drawn, there were precious few people who could be counted on to be on Ronnie's side.

The governor moved on just as Tom came around the end of the line of chairs. Someone else went up to speak to her; a politician, Ed Hunan, Speaker of the Mississippi House. It took a minute, but Tom finally identified him. Tom waited until the other man had finished paying his respects before approaching.

"Ronnie," he said quietly, hunkering down in front of her and putting one of his hands over hers, which were clasped in her lap. Her fingers were cold as ice.

"Tom!" It was a thankful cry, uttered as her eyes met his. For a minute there Tom thought she was going to come out of her chair right into his arms. But then she seemed to recollect her surroundings, because she sank back, the fingers of one hand curling tightly around his. "Oh, Tom, I'm glad you came."

"I'm sorry about Lewis," he said, mindful of the women watching and listening beside her. "It's a terrible thing."

"Yes," she agreed. Her face was paper white. Her eyes were enormous, with shadows beneath them, as they met his. She was dressed all in black, from the jewel neckline of her long-sleeved dress to her shoes. "Oh, Tom, I—I found him. Lewis. Lewis's—body."

She closed her eyes. A delicate shudder shook her from head to toe.

"Christ," Tom said, tightening his grip on her hand. This was worse than he expected. Ronnie looked as if she could keel over at any second.

The woman seated next to Ronnie, an attractive blonde about Ronnie's own age, patted her shoulder consolingly, her gaze on Tom all the while. A sweeping glance around told him that the little group of women around Ronnie were all regarding him with interest. The only one he recognized was Thea. He nodded at her. She was giving him that same look too: It was—

speculative, as though they sensed an undercurrent between him and Ronnie and were wondering what was
going on.

Was it that obvious that there was something between them? He hoped not. At least not at His
Honor's wake.

"Have you had anything to eat today?" he asked
Ronnie in a low voice. She opened her eyes, frowning,
and looking vaguely confused.

"I—coffee this morning. A roll. I don't know."

"How long have you been here?"

"I . . ." Ronnie didn't seem to know.

"Since five," Thea supplied. She was sitting next to
the blonde. The woman beside Ronnie nodded agreement. "I'm Kathy Blount, by the way," she said.

"Tom Quinlan," he said.

"How long will this thing go on?" Tom looked at
Thea.

"I think it's supposed to be over at ten," Thea said.

"You can't stay here for three more hours," Tom
said to Ronnie. "You need to eat, and lie down. Let me
take you home."

Ronnie gave another small shudder.

Kathy Blount leaned toward Ronnie, touching her
arm. "He's right, Ronnie, you need to go home. If you
would rather"—this was said with an appraising look
at Tom—"I'll take you."

Ronnie smiled at her friend. It was a wan, tremulous
effort. "No, thanks, Kathy. I know your children are
waiting for you. It was good of you to come. I think I
will go home, but Tom can take me."

"You sure?" Kathy Blount's look was searching.
Ronnie nodded. Tom realized that their hands were

still clasped in her lap. Hell, the *governor* had been holding her hand; there was nothing wrong with that. Under the circumstances it could be construed as offering comfort to a new widow.

Which it absolutely was.

"Thea, you can come with us," Tom said. For the sheer look of it, it might be best if he and Ronnie didn't leave alone.

"Sure, Tom."

Tom got to his feet, tugging gently on Ronnie's hand. She stood up, and turned even paler. For a moment Tom feared she might faint.

He grasped her elbow to steady her. Putting his arm around her was what he wanted to do, what his instincts urged him to do, but a sense of their audience prevented it.

"Are you okay?" he asked after a moment. She nodded.

He kept a hand on her elbow as they started walking. With Thea close on Ronnie's other side, they should be able to catch her before she hit the floor if she did collapse. Remembering the mob of press outside, Tom headed toward a side door. Kenny must have seen their progress, because he broke off his conversation and came to join them.

"Leaving?" he asked quietly.

"I'm taking her home," Tom replied, equally low. "She's shaky, and as white as a sheet."

"Shock," he said. Then, louder, to Ronnie, "I'm sorry about your husband."

Ronnie nodded her thanks. Kenny fell a couple of paces behind with Thea.

"The police questioned me three times this afternoon," Ronnie said after a moment. Her voice was scarcely above a whisper.

"What?" Tom looked at her sharply.

"I don't think they think it was suicide."

"So why question *you*?"

"I told you, I found the body. At least that's what they said. They kept asking me about it, over and over. I think—they think Lewis was murdered. They think— maybe—*I* did it."

*"What?"*

"That was the—impression I got."

"They couldn't think that!"

The route to the side door took them right past Marsden. He turned away from the men he was talking to, his arms folding over his chest as he watched them approach. He wore a dark business suit with a solid dark tie and, like Ronnie, he was pale, with red-rimmed eyes. As they drew nearer, his face contorted. He moved toward them.

*Here's trouble,* Tom thought, and tried to warn Marsden off with a hard-eyed stare.

It didn't work.

"So you fell for the bitch, eh, Tom?" Marsden's voice was low as he came up to them, but his expression as he looked at Ronnie screamed hatred.

*"What did you say?"* It took Tom a second or two to register that he really had heard what he thought he had. Then anger, fierce and hot, shot through his veins. Beside him he felt Ronnie shrink closer. Her eyes were huge and shadowed as they fixed on Marsden's face.

"Goddamn, Tom, I don't blame *you* for it, we was hopin' to get somethin' on her so Daddy could divorce her and we *did,* but when he told her, she done *killed* him over it. That little whore done killed Daddy, Tom!"

Tom decked him. One punch, and Marsden reeled backward, hit the wall, bounced, and fell to the polished marble floor. Even as a collective gasp rose from onlookers, who could not possibly have heard the conversation but certainly couldn't have missed the aftermath, even as state troopers and politicos and seemingly half the people in the room ran toward them, Tom dropped to one knee beside Marsden. Grabbing him by the tie, he jerked his head clear of the ground.

Marsden's red-rimmed eyes were still a little dazed from the blow, but Tom was too angry to care. He stuck his face right in Marsden's and growled, "Don't you ever, *ever,* talk *to* her or *about* her that way again, you hear? Or I'll—"

"Tom! Tom!" Kenny grabbed his arm, pulling him up and away from Marsden's supine form. His voice was a hiss. "Tom, you're gonna get yourself arrested!"

Other hands were pulling him back by that time. He was hustled away by a company of men, and Marsden was helped to his feet.

"Just a little altercation between old friends," Tom said to the state boy who held one of his arms. The trooper looked skeptical, but at a nod from one of the other troopers who knew him Tom was let go. Straightening his tie, disdaining to so much as glance in Marsden's direction, he walked over to where Ronnie was huddled with Thea and said briefly, "Let's go."

He, Ronnie, Kenny and Thea walked out into the still-bright evening through a side door that opened onto an obscure parking lot—and were met by a rear guard of reporters. Cameras flashed in their faces. Questions were hurled their way.

"It's her! It's her! Mrs. Honneker!"

As the shout went up, the media types who'd been in front came running around the side of the building, dragging paraphernalia ranging from shoulder-held cameras to boom mikes.

Staring at them for a furious, incredulous instant, Tom realized he now knew what a fox felt like when the hunt was after it in full cry.

Ronnie instinctively turned into his shoulder, Tom wrapped an arm around her, and with Kenny and Thea ranged on either side of them they bolted for Kenny's car, which was parked at an expired meter half a block down the street. They were chased, and photographed, and pelted with questions until they were safely inside the locked car and it was peeling rubber up the street.

The scene at Sedgely was almost as bad. Knowing better than to try to get through the front gates, Kenny drove around to the rear tradesman's entrance.

Only a few reporters were stationed there, but those few swarmed the car in full force when they realized that Ronnie was in the backseat. Cringing from the flashes, she hid her face in her hands. Tom pulled her against his chest, shielding her from the photographers with his coat and arms as Kenny explained to the state troopers on duty that they had Mrs. Honneker in the car.

They were admitted, the gates closed behind them, and the reporters were left to wait some more.

Ronnie continued to rest against his chest as they drove up the winding drive. Kenny glanced at them in

the rearview mirror more than once, and Thea, turning
to say something to one of them, took a good look and
seemed to change her mind.

Kenny drove around to the front, saw the sheer
number of cars that were there before them, and shook
his head.

"Why don't I let you off at the front door, Ronnie?"
he asked over his shoulder. "That way you won't have
to walk so far."

"That's a good idea," Ronnie said, in something
that was fairly close to a normal voice. But her fingers
closed over the front of Tom's shirt as though she
feared to let go.

"We're all going in," Tom said briskly, uncurling
her fingers from his shirtfront. With a quick glance to
make sure Kenny and Thea's attention was elsewhere,
he raised them unobtrusively to his lips. She smiled at
him. It was a tremulous smile, but still a smile. "You
can let Ronnie and Thea and me off at the front door,
Kenny, and then park and join us."

"Sure thing," Kenny said with an unnatural degree
of heartiness and another of those quick glances
through the rearview mirror.

There was a huge black wreath on the door, Tom
saw as they walked up the front steps, his hand deco-
rously on Ronnie's elbow. Even as they reached it, the
door opened and an elderly couple stood framed in the
entrance.

"You tell Dorothy that Sam and I were here, now,
Selma, you hear?" the elderly woman said over her
shoulder as she and the old gentleman with her stepped
through the doorway.

"I will do that, Mrs. Cherry," Selma said, coming

into view behind them. Her gaze swept past them to Ronnie, Tom, and Thea, who had just reached the porch, and she said something to someone behind her.

Upon seeing Ronnie, Mrs. Cherry and her companion stopped at the top of the steps to express their condolences. Ronnie replied politely, and then they were inside the house.

A hushed air lay over everything, as though the house itself knew that its master was dead. Even the light from the huge crystal chandelier seemed dim.

Ronnie stopped just inside the door, staring up at the wide, curving stairway before her as though it were Mount Everest. Then she looked at Tom.

"Will you be here tomorrow?" she asked.

Tom nodded. She bowed her head, then turned away from him and started walking up the stairs, her body slender and fragile-looking in her black dress.

She looked so alone. It was all he could do not to go after her, to tuck her into bed and see that she got supper and was taken care of in general. His hands clenched at his sides from doing battle with the impulse.

Leaving Ronnie to the tender mercies of Sedgely was kind of like leaving Daniel to the tender mercies of the lion's den, he thought savagely.

But he could not go with her, and he could not take her away. Not yet. Where before she had been the Senator's wife, now she was his widow. For a few more days.

Then, maybe, they could begin again.

"Go up with her, would you, Thea?" he asked, turning away. "Just to see that she gets settled in."

"Sure, Tom." The look Thea gave him told him

that, over the last hour or so, she had made a pretty fair deduction about the state of his feelings toward Ronnie. She hurried up the stairs in Ronnie's wake.

Selma was standing near the door.

"Mrs. Lewis hasn't had anything to eat since coffee this morning," Tom said to the housekeeper. "You take her up some supper, Selma, would you please?"

Selma nodded. Her eyes were bloodshot, with puffy circles around them as though she had been crying. Tom remembered that she had worked at Sedgely for over thirty years.

She would grieve for His Honor too. Hell, they all would, even he, as crazy and mixed up as that sounded.

"I will," Selma said. Then she lowered her voice. "The police are still going over the Senator's office. They've been asking questions about you. When I told them you were here, they asked me to ask you if you would come see them for a minute."

Tom frowned, then nodded and headed toward the east wing, his stomach tightening. He had a good idea of why the police might want to talk to him, though he prayed he was wrong.

If Marsden suspected he'd been sleeping with Ronnie, the police would have heard it first thing.

It turned out to be worse, much worse, than he had thought. The detective in charge was Alex Smitt, whom Tom knew slightly. Alex greeted him with a penetrating look, a quick handshake, and nary a smile.

"I've got something to show you," Alex said, and ushered him into a room almost directly opposite His Honor's office, the open doorway of which was barred with yellow crime-scene tape, making it off limits to everyone but the police.

A card table had been set up in the center of the room. On the vinyl top was a stack of photographs. With a gesture Alex indicated to Tom that he should look at them.

Tom did, and felt his blood freeze.

They were pictures of him, and Ronnie, and him and Ronnie together. Lots of pictures. Some were downright erotic. All were damning.

The two of them kissing in the Yellow Dog. The two of them kissing behind his apartment. The two of them kissing in the parking lot of the Robbins Inn. Another one of them going into a room there, hand in hand. Him in his tux and her in her panties as he carried her out of the swimming pool on the night of the party. A full dozen of the two of them in the act of making love that same night on the gym mat in the pool house. Obviously someone had been taking pictures through the patio door.

Tom winced inwardly, then looked up to meet Alex's steady gaze.

"Would you agree that it's fair to say that you and Mrs. Honneker were having an affair?"

Though the truth was evident, right there on the card table in living color in a way no one but a blind man could mistake, Tom wasn't stupid enough to answer that.

"Talk to my lawyer," he said crisply, and, turning on his heel, walked out the door.

## *Chapter*

## 39

"𝒯HE FIRST THING FOR YOU to do is stay away from her." From behind his desk, Dan Osborn pointed his pen at Tom, his expression admonitory. "I mean it, Tom. You stay away from her."

It was Saturday morning. Ronnie knew that Osborn usually spent Saturday morning on the golf course. Today, however, he was in his office, taking her on as a client. He was the best criminal-defense lawyer in Jackson.

It seemed impossible to believe that she needed a criminal-defense lawyer, but Tom assured her that she did, and Osborn seemed to agree with him.

"There's no reason for Tom to stay away from me," she said. She was seated in a big burgundy leather wing chair, one of a pair pulled up in front of Osborn's massive oak desk. Dressed in a dark gray suit, white shirt, and navy tie, Tom stood with his back to the big window that overlooked the new capitol building. Ronnie glanced at him briefly before returning her attention to the lawyer. "I did not kill my husband, Mr. Osborn."

Osborn swiveled to face her. Gray-haired, in perhaps his midsixties, he was a rumpled, grumpy-looking bulldog of a man. Ronnie had met him on a few occasions previously, most recently at Lewis's party. Tom he knew well. His gaze moved over her now, taking in her sedately styled hair, which was pulled back from her face and secured at her nape with a black satin bow, and her trim-fitting black pants suit and her crossed legs and high heels. The conclusion he reached after completing this appraisal was not apparent in his expression.

"Mrs. Honneker, if I didn't believe that, I would not have agreed to represent you. However, being innocent of a crime and proving that you are innocent of a crime are two entirely different matters. Since Tom called me on your behalf last night, I have been in touch with some people I know in the DA's office and the police department, and they feel they have quite a substantial case against you already. You found the body; your fingerprints are on the murder weapon; there is a lapse of some twenty-five minutes between the time the limo driver says he dropped you off at Sedgely and the time when you started screaming for help; you were having an affair with Tom here, of which they have photographic proof; according to his son, Marsden, Senator Honneker was planning to ask you for a divorce because of that affair; *and* there was a signed prenuptial agreement in place preventing you from collecting more than a pittance in case of divorce. Your share of the estate upon his death is, however, substantial. There you have method, motive, and opportunity. I've seen people convicted on a lot less."

"She didn't kill him, Dan," Tom said. His hands

rested on the marble windowsill; his fingers curled around the edge. One leg was bent, with his foot flat against the wall.

"You, my friend, having been in California at the time, have no way of knowing that for certain. There is no witness that I am aware of who can provide Mrs. Honneker with an alibi." He looked at Ronnie. "Is there?"

She shook her head, and then smiled faintly. "Davis."

If she appeared to be having trouble taking this whole thing seriously, Ronnie thought, it was because she was. It seemed ludicrous that anyone could think that *she* had murdered Lewis. She was even having trouble accepting that he was dead. *Murdered.* Ronnie kept getting the feeling she was caught up in some kind of surreal dream. This could not really be happening.

"The dog," Tom answered Osborn's unspoken query. He straightened. "Who took the pictures?"

Ronnie hadn't seen them. From Tom's brief—very brief—description, she preferred to keep it that way.

"Apparently the Senator's son hired a private detective some months ago to gather evidence that would allow the Senator to obtain a divorce in which he was, in the eyes of his constituents at least, clearly not at fault. By which I mean evidence of his wife having an affair. He came up empty—until you came on the scene." Osborn's voice took on a certain dryness as he said that last.

Tom grimaced. "Isn't that some sort of invasion of privacy?"

"Probably." Osborn inclined his head. "But does

that mean the pictures will get thrown out of court? Under the circumstances there's no chance at all."

"Just because we were having an affair doesn't mean she killed him." Tom moved to stand beside the other wing chair, his arm resting along its top, one hand in the front pocket of his trousers. He'd been sitting in the chair earlier, but was obviously too much on edge to stay still for long.

"You're right," Osborn said. "And that's the tack we have to take. I don't see any sense in denying that the affair took place—that would be pretty stupid in the face of the overwhelming evidence that it did. So we need to paint it as just that: an affair. A quick, meaningless fling that *has ended,* and was certainly nothing to kill over. So like I said, Tom, you stay away from her." He swiveled to look at Ronnie. "Mrs. Honneker, I don't want him within half a mile of you, you hear?"

Ronnie glanced at Tom. He met her gaze. Telling her not to see him was like telling her not to breathe; she thought she would die if she didn't.

"For how long?" she asked Osborn quietly.

Osborn glared at her, then glared at Tom, then glared at her again. "Mrs. Honneker, I don't think you fully appreciate the gravity of your situation. The crime they are considering charging you with is a capital offense: first-degree murder with aggravating circumstances. They are serious enough about the case against you to ask me to tell you not to leave the state. The prosecutor may very well—no, he most certainly will—ask for the *death penalty* if you should be so charged. In which case we will have to convince twelve jurors that you did not kill your husband. We are starting a campaign right now with those jurors in mind. The motive the prosecutors will almost certainly assign to you is that you wanted both your lover—*and* your husband's money. Given the pre-nup, there was no way for you to have both unless you killed your husband. Forgive me for saying so, but you must know that you are not exactly beloved by a lot of people in this state. In fact you have a certain—reputation. The revelation that you had an affair with Tom while you were married to the Senator will almost certainly have a negative impact on the jury. There's no getting around that. The Senator is not yet in his grave. We certainly don't want pictures of you with Tom here popping up all over the place. Jurors don't come into trials as blank slates. They come in with all their foibles and prejudices intact. I don't want them any more prejudiced against you than they have to be."

There was a moment's silence. Both men looked at Ronnie. She glanced from Osborn to Tom and back.

"I'll stay away from her," Tom said. He moved back to the window. "But she is going to need somebody who's on her side with her at the funeral and so forth. At this point I wouldn't leave her at the mercy of any friend or relative of the Senator's any more than I would leave a canary in a roomful of cats."

"I understand you dragged her out of Sedgely last night after she had already gone upstairs to bed." Osborn's voice was dry again. They were talking to each other now as if she weren't even present, Ronnie thought. Surprisingly it didn't bother her. From the beginning she had not felt like an integral part of the meeting. She just could not seem to fully process the fact that Lewis was dead and that she was suspected of killing him.

"I didn't feel like I had much choice," Tom said. "Between Alex Smitt and his damned pictures and the family and friends who were coming and going, Sedgely just didn't seem like a good place to leave her. Hell, I wouldn't have put it past them to have hauled her out of bed to question her again. Or Marsden to go berserk and attack her. At this point I feel like anything's possible with them where she's concerned."

"I see your point." Osborn looked at Tom with some speculation.

"I took her to my mother's," he said abruptly in response to that look.

And, Ronnie reflected, Sally McGuire had been warmly welcoming, too, providing her with supper and a bath and bed without asking any questions—at least not of her; Ronnie had little doubt that Tom had filled his mother in after she had gone to bed.

"To your mother's? *Sally's?*" Osborn sounded faintly appalled. Ronnie got the impression that he knew Tom's mother well.

"I knew it wasn't a good idea for her to stay with me, and that was the only other place I felt comfortable leaving her," Tom said. "In fact if she can't leave the state, I think that's where she ought to stay while this whole thing is going down. The press won't find her there, and my mother will make sure she eats and so forth." He glanced at Ronnie with a frown. "I don't think she's quite—hitting on all cylinders right at the moment."

"Are you saying that you think I am out of it?" Ronnie asked him with a hint of heat.

He smiled at her. "Something like that. It's the shock, I think. Don't worry about it."

"I'm perfectly fine."

"I'll take her to the funeral myself, and to anything else connected with this that seems necessary," Osborn said abruptly. Though he didn't say it in so many words, his response told Ronnie that he agreed with Tom's assessment.

Maybe they were right. Maybe she *was* suffering a little bit from shock, Ronnie thought. That would explain the weird, disconnected feeling that kept stealing over her.

She hadn't loved Lewis, but he had been her husband. To find him like that . . . Ronnie shuddered, remembering.

Tom was watching her. There was a hint of suppressed violence in his voice as he said, "Dammit, Dan, I think we ought to hire our own investigators. The police want to solve this: Pinning it on Ronnie makes it easy for them. Why should they even bother to look elsewhere? But the fact is she didn't kill him. *If* he was murdered—and I have to say, having known him and the family for a long time, I don't think he committed suicide—there's a murderer loose out there. Somebody needs to find out who it is."

"I agree with you about hiring our own investigators," Osborn said. "But you do realize, once they look beyond Mrs. Honneker, who the next most likely candidate to have murdered the Senator is, don't you?" Osborn's voice grew testy. "It's *you*, Tom, for pretty much the same reasons they will ascribe to her. In fact if you hadn't been in California at the time with fifty witnesses to prove it, I'm sure they'd be looking at you every bit as hard as they're looking at her. Of course they may still think you could have hired somebody to do it. Or they may be thinking you conspired with Mrs. Honneker. You need your own lawyer, Tom. I can't represent both of you, since if it comes to a trial, we may have to put on alternate theories. And you are certainly a viable alternate theory."

Tom stared at him. "*I* didn't kill him. *She* didn't kill him. Neither of us hired anybody to kill him, and we didn't conspire."

Osborn sighed. "I am just telling you what is going through the investigators' minds."

"What about a polygraph?" Tom asked. "If Ronnie took a polygraph and passed, wouldn't that put her in the clear?"

"I do not advocate my clients' taking lie detector tests."

"So what do you suggest?" Tom's question was impatient.

"I suggest that we sit tight," Osborn said very precisely. "And nothing more, until we see which way the wind is going to blow. You never know, they may still rule it a suicide. Mrs. Honneker, you are not to talk to police, reporters, *any*body without my being present, is that clear? Any questions that may be put to you, refer the questioner to your lawyer. Tom, I was very serious about you having your own representation. I suggest Brian Hughes." He scribbled a number on a piece of paper and passed it to Tom. "Now, Mrs. Honneker, there is one point I want to clear up: You say you went for a walk after the driver dropped you off at Sedgely. That would be approximately ten thirty-five to—what? eleven or so?"

Ronnie nodded. "Approximately yes."

"Then, when you went inside, you went directly to your husband's office, is that correct?"

"Yes." Ronnie tried not to remember what she had found there, but she couldn't help it. Lewis's head in a puddle of blood—she forced her mind back to the present.

"Was it customary for you to do that? Go to your husband's office upon coming in from an engagement? Or otherwise seek him out?"

"No."

"Then why, on this particular night, did you do so?"

"I had something I wanted to tell him."

"And that was?"

With a quick glance at Tom before focusing on Osborn, Ronnie said, "I was going to tell him that I wanted a divorce."

From the corner of her eye Ronnie saw Tom go very still.

"What brought you to such a conclusion at that precise moment in time?"

She sent a flickering smile winging toward Tom, who was looking at her with his heart in his eyes.

"Tom wasn't willing for us to continue to see each other under the circumstances. The last time we met, he told me I had to choose: Lewis or him. That night I decided. I chose him."

Osborn threw his pen in the air. *"There's* the prosecution's motive, all wrapped up in pretty paper and tied with a bow. Lord above, don't tell that to anybody else. Might as well just sign a confession and have done with it."

"Dan," Tom said, "could you give us a minute? Please?"

Osborn looked from one to the other of them. "Goddamn it, Tom—all right. Five minutes. Not a second more. And after you leave this office, you're not to see her again until this thing is *resolved*. Do you hear me?"

"I hear you," Tom said.

He looked at Ronnie. She looked back.

Osborn got up from his chair. "Five minutes," he growled, and stomped from the room.

When he was gone, Tom came over and hunkered down in front of Ronnie's chair. Taking her hand, he lifted it to his mouth, pressing his lips against the back. Ronnie smiled at him.

"You didn't kill Lewis," Tom said. It was a statement, not a question.

Ronnie shook her head.

"You had signed a prenuptial agreement that said you wouldn't get any significant money in case of a divorce."

Ronnie nodded.

"You were going to divorce him anyway."

Ronnie nodded again.

"For me."

Ronnie smiled faintly. "I'd say that about sums it up."

"Why?" His eyes were so intensely blue as they met hers that they would have put a sapphire to shame.

Reaching out, she ran a questing finger down the side of his face, then along the hard line of his jaw. His skin was smooth and very warm.

"Because I am in love with you."

He stared at her without moving for a moment. His eyes blazed into hers. Then he was pulling her off the chair, down onto her knees on the floor in front of him, into his arms, and kissing her as if he meant to absorb her very soul.

Ronnie wrapped her arms around his neck and kissed him back.

There was a peremptory knock on the door.

Tom pulled his mouth from hers. He looked as dazed as she felt as he met her eyes, then glanced at the door.

"That wasn't five minutes," he said. "Dammit."

They were both still kneeling when the door opened. Osborn walked in, raking them with a disapproving look as he closed the door.

"Your watch must run pretty fast," Tom said, getting to his feet and pulling Ronnie up with him. His face was slightly flushed; his hand stayed around hers, warm and strong.

Osborn looked at Tom. If he noticed their joined hands, he ignored it. "You have a phone call. From your partner—Kenny Goodman, isn't it? He says it's urgent."

Tom's hand tightened around Ronnie's for an instant before releasing it. She read worry in his face. From her own experience she knew that Kenny's urgent phone calls weren't likely to be good news.

"Can I take it in here?"

At Osborn's nod Tom walked to the desk, picked up the receiver, and depressed a button.

Listening to Tom's end of the conversation, Ronnie knew her instinct had been right: Kenny's phone call was pure bad news.

"Thanks, Kenny. Bye." Tom hung up, then looked at her for an instant before transferring his gaze to Osborn.

"The tabloids have got hold of those pictures I saw last night. The ones—hell, you know which ones. They're going to hit the newsstands first thing tomorrow morning." His mouth twisted. "So much for keeping pictures of Ronnie and me together out of the papers."

# Chapter

## 40

Y THE FOUR P.M. start of the funeral, the pictures were everywhere, even having made the front page of the venerable *Jackson Daily Journal*. Under the headline SUICIDE OR HOMICIDE: IS WIFE'S AFFAIR KEY TO SENATOR'S DEATH? there was a grainy shot of Ronnie kissing Tom in the parking lot of the Robbins Inn. An inside spread featured double pages filled with more—and more explicit—photographs.

The tabloids went all out. Headlines like DID RONNIE DO IT? and SENATE SEX SCANDAL accompanied pictures that were only saved from being pornographic by strategically placed black bars.

Ronnie would not have known the full extent of the coverage if reporters had not thrust the articles in her face asking for comments as soon as she appeared in front of Dan Osborn's office, hanging on to his arm as she prepared to enter the limousine that would take them to the church. Her security detail pushed them back as they rushed her, but not before she was able to see enough to make her feel physically ill.

In the pictures her love for Tom looked sordid and

nasty. Naked couplings and open-mouthed kisses that had been magical when shared only between the two of them were obscene when laid out in a public forum for the world to see and snicker over.

"Ronnie, over here!"

"Ronnie, sweetie, can you shed a tear or two for us?"

"Hey, Ronnie, did you ever do the President? Or the governor?"

"Is it true you're going to do one of those *Playboy* layouts?"

"Did you kill him, Ronnie?"

The idiotic, impertinent questions were hurled at her thick and fast; even when she and Dan Osborn were safely in the limousine, photographers pushed their cameras against the glass, snapping away at the two of them inside.

Overnight, Ronnie realized with a shuddering sense of horror, she had become notorious, a byword, a fallen woman of such epic proportions as to make Donna Rice and Gennifer Flowers seem like virgins in comparison.

The humiliation was soul crushing. The sense of injustice was strong. But Ronnie kept her head high and her back straight as she exited the limo on Osborn's arm.

To let them know that she suffered was to let them defeat her.

The funeral was a nightmare. The President and First Lady came, with their accompanying security detail. Nearly all the members of the U.S. Senate and House of Representatives were present with their spouses. Every Mississippi politician from the governor on down was there. From the look of it, half of Mississippi—no, half the nation—was there. Saint Andrew's Episcopal Church was full to overflowing. Hundreds of spectators stood in the streets surrounding the Gothic Revival building, ready to listen to the eulogies that would be broadcast over a loudspeaker system.

Braving the gauntlet of public and reporters as she entered the church, Ronnie felt like Hester Prynne, who had been forced to appear in public with a huge scarlet *A* for *adultery* emblazoned on her breast. She felt like the biblical woman taken in adultery, on her way to be stoned. Heads craned as she passed; catcalls and epithets were hurled her way.

The word *whore* was shouted more than once.

The atmosphere inside the church was charged. People she had known for years looked at her and talked excitedly behind their hands, hardly bothering to whisper. Except for the reporters, who surrounded her in a yapping, flashbulb-popping pack until they were turned back by state troopers just inside the vestibule, and her own small coterie of security and supporters, she was left strictly alone.

The family—Dorothy, Marsden, Joanie, Laura, and their spouses and children, and even Lewis's ex-wife, Eleanor—were already seated together in the front pew in the center of the church when she came in. They didn't acknowledge her presence by so much as a glance. The dignitaries were seated in order of importance behind the family. By prior arrangement between her lawyer and security detail and the security detail working the church, she was seated in front, but at the far right, near a door.

So that she could be escorted out quickly if the need arose.

Her father and sisters had flown in for the funeral, and were waiting in the section set aside for her. Her mother had called the night before to offer condolences and vague assurances of support, but her husband was ill and thus she was not, she told Ronnie, able to come. Which was just as well, Ronnie thought. From the time her mother had abandoned the family, she and Ronnie had been the opposite of close.

Tom had stayed away, under strict orders from Dan Osborn to do so. His family and Kenny were also forbidden to be present, so as not to give the press any (more) reason to comment on him or his associate.

She knew that having him by her side at such a moment would only unleash another firestorm of scandal. The media would have a field day. Gossip would reach new levels of viciousness. They would be universally condemned.

But still she needed, no, craved, his presence.

Her father, Dave, sat on one side of her, in a black suit that she suspected was new for the occasion. Debbie and Lisa, her sisters, were on her other side. Debbie held one of her hands, her father the other.

Dan Osborn and his wife, who had also been waiting inside the church, sat beside her father. Thea sat on the other side of her sisters. Except for Kathy and Michael Blount—who, Ronnie knew, risked great public disapproval to sit with her—and her security detail, that was the sum total of her support.

Her little corner of the church was as cut off from the rest of the mourners as an island.

Closing her eyes as the priest began the service,

Ronnie concentrated on saying good-bye to Lewis. Despite his failings, he deserved that she should mourn for him. And she *had* cared for him in a way. She just hadn't loved him.

He had not deserved to die.

Especially not like that. Ronnie shuddered, and forced the memory of his slumped body from her mind.

*Pray for us, Father.*

Though she bowed her head and intoned the words of the prayer along with everyone else, she could not escape the knowledge that people were looking at her. Even during the prayer, she felt that she was the cynosure of all eyes.

She was very conscious of the fact that now she was a pariah even there, in church.

"Osborn should have kept her from going." Tom was in the living room at Kenny's house, watching TV coverage of the funeral. Kenny was with him, sitting on the couch while Tom stood in front of the big-screen TV, chewing on a knuckle. Ronnie had just emerged from the church after the service and was headed for a limousine waiting in the street. As she went down the stone steps on Dan Osborn's arm, the press nearly swarmed over her. The state troopers surrounding her had to battle to force them back. "Look at that, would you? Jesus Christ, get them back! She's going to get hurt!"

For a moment Ronnie's face, fine-boned and lovely, filled the screen. Her brown eyes were wide and thickly lashed and underlined by shadows. Her mouth was full and soft and unsmiling, her skin as pale as one of his

white shirts. Her hair, flaming red in the pouring sunshine, made the translucent pallor of her skin seem
even more marked in contrast.

She looked haunted, and haunting.

"I can't believe this!" Tom gnawed his knuckle
harder, feeling sick. He should be there with her, no
matter what Dan said. Hell, if he could, he would be
there *instead* of her, taking all the shame and vilifica-
tion on himself.

Watching her being publicly pilloried made him
wild.

She finally reached the limousine. The door
slammed shut on the howling press. The limo rolled.

The station cut to a commercial, promising to be
right back.

Tom swore savagely, and turned away from the
screen to find Kenny regarding him with a frown.

"Remember that heart attack I had last year?"
Kenny asked.

"Yeah."

"Stress. It was caused by stress. And you're stressing
out big-time yourself right now, buddy."

"Jesus." Tom closed his eyes, then opened them
again. "Who wouldn't?"

He walked over to the ugly tan recliner in a corner
of the room and sank down on it. Singing cats on the
television made him want to throw a lamp through the
screen. Picking up the remote, he hit the mute button
and watched as the cats became voiceless.

"I'm sorry about this, Kenny," he said after a minute.

"Hey, I don't like listening to cats sing either."

The attempt at humor fell flat. They both knew Tom hadn't been referring to the commercial.

Tom looked at him steadily. "The business is just starting to make decent money again. This is going to send it right down the toilet."

"*C'est la vie*," Kenny said with a shrug.

"I'd let you buy me out, but I don't think that, under the circumstances, there's anything worth buying. This thing with Ronnie makes the deal with the campaign contributions seem like nothing."

"It's sure a hell of a mess."

"Maybe we could switch to corporate consulting. There's more money in that than in politics anyway." Tom met Kenny's gaze. "And the plain truth is, I am now dead in the water as far as politicians are concerned. After this, nobody's gonna touch me—or the firm as long as I'm part of it—with a ten-foot pole."

"Hey, man, don't sweat it on my account. I know how it is. I've been there myself." Kenny glanced around as though checking to make absolutely certain they were alone. "Thea—"

"I know about Thea," Tom said curtly.

"Thought you did."

"It's damned stupid, let me tell you. You've got a great wife, a great family, and you're going to frigging screw it up. Thea's not worth it."

"It's over anyway."

"I'd keep it that way if I were you."

"I hate to point this out to you, Mr. Puritan, but you—"

"I'm not married."

"*She* is. Was."

"Yeah." He sounded morose. Tom slumped lower in

the chair. Kenny got up and walked into the kitchen. He returned a moment later with two beers, one of which he handed to Tom.

"The point I'm trying to make is, I don't blame you for any of this," Kenny said, sitting down on the edge of the couch and looking at Tom earnestly. "Ronnie is one goddamned beautiful woman. From what I saw, she must've come on to you like gangbusters. Who can blame you for taking her up on it? It's the same thing that happened to me with Thea. She came on to me, and I couldn't resist. The only difference between what you did and what I did is Thea isn't—wasn't—married to the Senator. And nobody was taking pictures."

"It wasn't like that." As the funeral coverage resumed, Tom stood up and walked to the far end of the room before turning to face Kenny. The sound was still on mute. "What happened between Ronnie and me wasn't like that. She didn't come on to me any more than I came on to her. It was mutual. We—fell in love."

Kenny stared at him. "You're kidding."

Tom grimaced. "Sounds pretty damn schmaltzy, doesn't it?"

"Yeah."

"Shut up, Kenny." Tom glared at him.

"Hey, you said it first."

"Okay. I know."

Neither of them said anything more for a moment, just watched the silent images of limousines filling with dignitaries and driving away from the church.

Then Kenny said slowly, "Tom, you know I like Ronnie and all that. But she's kind of a million-dollar baby, isn't she? I mean, she is used to the finer things in life, and you don't have any goddamned money. Especially now."

"I know that. Do you think I don't know that?"

Kenny was silent for a moment, staring at the TV. When he looked up at Tom again, his forehead was deeply creased in a worried frown. "Tom, buddy, did it ever occur to you that maybe, just maybe, Ronnie *did* shoot the Senator? Maybe she killed him for the money."

Tom put his hands into his pockets and rocked back on his heels. "She didn't kill him."

"You were in California."

"She didn't kill him."

"How can you be sure?"

"She didn't kill him!"

"Fine," Kenny said, sinking back into the couch and reaching for the remote. "If you say so. But I just want you to think about the possibility."

Before Tom could reply, he punched the mute button, and the chatter of the talking heads covering the funeral service once again filled the room.

# Chapter

## 41

*T*HERE WAS NOTHING ON TV. Just some old senator's boring funeral. Marla got up to change
the channel (Jerry had somehow managed to lose the
remote) and stopped just as she came nose-to-glass
with the screen.

Reporter Christine Gwen was doing a retrospective
on the dead man's life.

"Here is Senator Honneker in happier days, shown
with his second wife, Veronica, at the Biloxi Yacht
Club on the deck of their yacht, the *Sun-Chaser*. According to police sources, Veronica Honneker is now a
prime suspect in the Senator's murder. . . ."

The Biloxi Yacht Club. The *Sun-Chaser*.

"Jerry!" she screeched. Tearing her gaze away from
the TV, Marla dashed into the kitchen and threw open
the back door. With supper just over, Jerry was in the
backyard with Lissy, painstakingly painting a playhouse he had bought her the day before. Golden early-
evening sunshine and cooler temperatures made it the
ideal time for such work. "Jerry!"

Pausing in the act of stroking another brushful of

candy-pink enamel (Lissy's emphatic choice) onto the side of the little house, Jerry looked around inquiringly.

"I found it! It's on TV! The name of the boat is the *Sun-Chaser!* Come quick, come quick!"

With deliberate care Jerry laid the brush down along the corrugated edge of the rectangular metal paint pan and stood up. When he joined Marla back in the house, Lissy was with him. Marla was too excited to send her daughter from the room.

"What now?" Jerry asked, coming to stand beside her. He wore a white undershirt adorned with splatters of candy pink and ancient khaki shorts that made his beer belly look more pronounced. Marla neither noticed, nor cared about, his unattractive attire. She was practically jumping up and down in her excitement.

"It's the boat! The name of it is the *Sun-Chaser!* It belonged to that senator there, and now he's dead too! Don't you see, Jerry, everybody connected with that boat is ending up dead! Oh, my God, it must have been him! *He* took Susan and Claire out that night on the boat! *He* must have killed them! Look, it's the *Sun-Chaser*—" another picture of the yacht was just coming up—"and it's his! It had to be him!"

"Marla," Jerry said. He was staring dubiously at the screen and apparently at the same time trying to unscramble what she was talking about. "If, as you say, the Senator there took Susan and Claire out in his boat and killed them, then who killed him? He's dead now too."

That bit of logic gave Marla pause. Jerry was right. Senator whatever-his-name-was was dead. Murdered. Just like Susan and, she was positive, Claire. Just like, she was pretty sure, the Beautiful Model Agency people. Just like she would have been if she hadn't managed to stay one step ahead of the killer all this time.

Looking at the Senator on the screen, laughing and happy as he was surrounded by his wife—another wife—and young children in a picture taken years ago, Marla realized something else: This was not the man who had ransacked her apartment, or followed her to the residential hotel.

No way.

Could the guy have been a hired killer? Yes, but then in killing the Senator he would have turned on his own master.

So what was going on?

They were showing pictures of the funeral now, of the beautiful young trophy wife—that was how the reporter described her—who was suspected of the Senator's murder.

Marla didn't quite have it all figured out, but she was willing to bet the young wife hadn't killed her husband.

It was too much of a coincidence that everybody who had had anything to do with that boat was ending up dead.

"It's that boat. I know it's that boat," Marla said stubbornly to Jerry. "That's the connection. He must have been on the boat, too, the same night as Susan and Claire. He must have been one of the johns—ah, dates. Now he's dead. Whoever killed Susan and Claire killed him too!"

"You're reaching, Marla," Jerry said.

"Jerry, I know I'm right. I know I am. I just have a real feeling about this!" She looked at him beseechingly. "Just—can you just get it checked out, please? Maybe if they find out who was on the boat that night, we'll find out who is after me."

The Senator's second wife was on the screen again, arm in arm with her lawyer in the center of a small army of cops and a crushing tide of reporters.

Christine Gwen intoned, "Veronica Honneker is seen here with her lawyer, Daniel Osborn of Jackson. Osborn is one of the most highly regarded criminal attorneys in the state. His presence at her side lends credence to the story that Mrs. Honneker is about to be charged with her husband's murder, wouldn't you say, Burt?"

Burt Hall, the station's anchor, took the ball as the coverage switched to him. "I don't know, Christine. We'll see. If what the tabloids are printing is true, it certainly seems like she has a motive. We've managed to obtain copies of the photographs that are shocking the nation tonight."

Pictures of the second wife doing the nasty with a boyfriend flashed on the screen, accompanied by Hall's voice-over. Marla took one look and clapped her hands over Lissy's widening eyes.

*Click* went the TV as Jerry turned it off.

"I can't believe they show that kind of stuff on television," Jerry said disgustedly. "Okay, Lissy, let's get back to the playhouse."

Lissy had already pulled away from Marla's makeshift blindfold.

"Mom, you didn't have to do that. Don't you think I've seen sex on TV *before?*" Lissy said scornfully over her shoulder as she headed for the kitchen. Jerry was right behind her.

"Jerry, what about this?" Marla trailed them. "You've got to call somebody and tell them. This is *it*, I'm telling you."

Lissy went banging out through the screen door. Jerry paused just inside it, looking back over his shoulder at Marla.

"It's Sunday, Marla," he said patiently. "I'll call the guys in Biloxi tomorrow and tell them what you think. But I have to say, it seems pretty far-fetched to me."

"Jerry . . ."

"Gotta paint," Jerry said with a grin, and went out into the backyard after Lissy.

Left alone, Marla stewed. She knew she was right. She *knew* it. But she had gotten the feeling for some time now that Jerry's heart wasn't really in this thing as if he didn't care if it ever was solved.

He was happy having her and Lissy living with him, she knew. She cooked and cleaned and had sex with him whenever he wanted and was a pleasant, undemanding companion the rest of the time. Lissy he had obviously fallen for like a ton of bricks. Maybe he thought that if they never found out who was trying to kill her, she could never go back home.

Without Jerry to help her, there wasn't much she could do, Marla thought.

Then she remembered the beautiful young second wife all but accused of her husband's murder.

Now *there* was another interested party if she had ever seen one.

Mrs. Second Wife would surely be glad to get her hands on information that would help to clear her. And she would have the money, and the power, to launch an investigation to find out the truth.

If Marla could only, somehow, get in touch with her.

Marla remembered the name of the big-shot lawyer with her, and smiled.

Then she picked up the phone in the kitchen and, when the operator came on, asked for Jackson information.

# Chapter

# 42

RONNIE LAY AWAKE in her borrowed bed at Sally McGuire's, watching the moonlight paint patterns on the ceiling over her head and trying not to think. All about her the farmhouse settled, making ominous little creaking and groaning sounds. Sally had gone to bed at eleven-thirty, as seemed to be her custom. Having retired upstairs hours before, Ronnie had heard her come up.

After the ordeal of the funeral was over, she had thought—hoped—she would finally be able to sleep. Indeed she had fallen on top of the bed almost fully dressed, and zonked out. But two hours later she had awakened. Since then, though she had tried her best, she had not been able to lull herself back into unconsciousness.

The key, she thought desperately, lay in keeping her mind *blank*.

Everything that entered her head, from childhood memories to unwelcome thoughts of Lewis, to an aching longing for Tom, seemed to cause her pain.

She was sure she could sleep—if only she could not think.

*They thought she had killed Lewis.*

After awakening, she had taken a hot bath, soaking for almost an hour, shaving her legs with great care, creaming and moisturizing her face.

*Her father had seen naked pictures of her with Tom.*

Finally climbing out of the tub, she had brushed her teeth and brushed out her hair and put on one of her prettiest nightgowns, a spaghetti-strapped, flimsy pink silk affair that just brushed her ankles. Having been retrieved from her dresser at Sedgely—Selma had packed two suitcases of her clothes and had had them delivered to Dan Osborn's office the day before—it smelled of the delicate honeysuckle sachets she kept tucked in her drawers.

*The smell reminded her of Sedgely.*

Sally's second-floor guest room was comfortable, with a big double bed, a sturdy oak dresser, and a soft, low armchair in one corner. It was painted sky blue, with a white ceiling. There was one six-over-six-paned window hung with ruffled white curtains and fitted out with a pull-down shade. When the shade was pulled up, as Ronnie had it at the moment, moonlight spilled over the bed. With the light off, that was the only illumination.

*Always before, her sisters and father had been so proud of her: the one Sibley who had made it big. The Senator's wife. Today they had been tainted by her shame.*

She could not keep her mind blank, try though she would. She could not sleep.

*Her father and sisters had flown back home. They*

*would, they told her, come back if necessary for the trial. Oh, God, were they really going to try her for murdering Lewis? It seemed unbelievable.*

Through the window she stared at stars twinkling in the wake of the moon far above. The sky was midnight blue and mysterious, the stars tiny glittering points of light. As a child she had always imagined they were fairies sprinkling magic dust as they flew about in the dark getting the world ready for daylight once again.

*Not one word had been said by her father, her sisters, or herself about Tom. Though they had undoubtedly seen the pictures—Ronnie doubted if there was anyone in the country who hadn't seen them by now— the subject had never come up. That's how things were in her family. They never, ever talked about anything important. Even when her mother had left them, they had never discussed it. Not once, in all those years, had the subject ever come up.*

The creakings and groanings grew louder. Listening, Ronnie thought she could almost hear the house breathing. Or was that Sally, two rooms away down the hall?

The sounds had a steady, almost furtive rhythm. As if someone were creeping up the stairs. . . .

Ronnie caught her breath, sitting bolt upright in bed.

The doorknob turned.

*Lewis had been murdered. Was it now her turn?*

A man's tall silhouette was framed in the doorway. Ronnie's fingers scrabbled for a possible weapon—the windup alarm clock on the bedside table was the best she could do—and she sucked breath into her suddenly reluctant lungs for a scream.

Moonlight touched the man's hair.

"Tom?" Ronnie whispered.

"I thought you'd be asleep." He shut the bedroom door very quietly, and came padding toward the bed. He was dressed in jeans and a T-shirt, and Ronnie realized he was wearing socks but no shoes.

"Tom!" Dropping the clock on the mattress, scrambling out from beneath the covers and off the bed, she threw herself at him, and he caught her in his arms.

"Shhh," he cautioned even as he wrapped her in a bear hug so tight that it threatened to crack her ribs. "We don't want to wake up—"

*My mother* was what he had been going to say, Ronnie knew. But he never finished, because he was occupied with kissing her. One hand moved to cup her head. His fingers slid through the thick fall of her hair to cradle her scalp. Her arms twined around his neck as she kissed him back in a way that said she would die if she didn't.

She had not realized how cold and lost she had felt until she found herself wrapped in the warm security of his arms.

"Oh, Tom, I'm so glad you came!" she whispered against his throat when at last he lifted his head.

"I watched the whole damned shebang on TV. I'm so sorry I wasn't there with you."

"I wanted you."

"I know."

"Tom . . ."

"Shhh." He kissed her again.

"I'm scared, Tom." It was the first time Ronnie had admitted such a thing, even to herself.

"I love you." He cupped her face with his hands and

said the words almost against her mouth. "That's what
I was going to tell you in the four minutes we didn't
get in Dan's office."

"Oh, God." Tilting her face up, she kissed him. Her
arms slid around his waist, her hands burrowing under
his shirt to touch his skin. Suddenly she needed to
touch him, needed to love him, with a fierce mindless
need that was as strong as the life force itself. She
pushed his shirt up, and he let go of her long enough to
pull it off, over his head, and let it drop.

Her open mouth ran along his neck, down through
the soft brown wedge of hair on his chest, over his
hard stomach to the button on his jeans. Then she was
kneeling before him, nuzzling her face against him,
pressing her mouth against his crotch, biting at the
hard bulge she could feel straining against the soft blue
denim of his fly.

"Jesus, Ronnie." As her teeth found him, he jerked,
sucking in his breath with an audible gasp. His hands
were on her head, in her hair, but he didn't try to pull
her away from him. She didn't stop, couldn't stop. Her
hands were urgent, tugging at his snap, pulling down
his zipper, reaching inside his boxers until his member
was free. He was huge and hot and pulsing and *alive,*
and she took him in her mouth, cupping the vulnerable
softness beneath with tender care. She kissed and suckled and nibbled and bit until every breath he took
sounded like a groan.

Then his hands clenched in her hair. He pulled her
mouth off him, yanked off his jeans, and dropped
down on his knees in front of her. He pushed her onto
her back in a glowing patch of moonlight, pulling her
nightgown up and off as he did so. Lying on top of her,

pulling her legs around his waist, he came into her hard.

Ronnie cried out. He muffled the sound with his kiss. His tongue filled her mouth, its scalding heat aping the fierce claiming movements of his body.

The carpet rasped against her back as he drove her down into it. Beneath it she could feel the hardness of the wooden floor. She clung to him, her fingers curling into his back. His skin was hot and damp with sweat, his muscles knotted with tension.

He was thrusting deep inside her, filling her, setting her on fire. She writhed beneath him, gasping her need into his mouth, her nails gouging his back, her hips lifting off the carpet in desperate answer to his passionate possession.

"Tom, Tom, Tom, *Tom!*" Gasping his name, quivering from head to toe, she came, spinning out of the world and up into the fairy-dust stars. He found his own release, groaning his pleasure against her throat as he ground himself deep into her quivering body.

Afterward Ronnie lay for long moments, her back prickling with rug burn from the carpet, her lungs constricted from the weight of his big body collapsed on top of her, her scalp tingling because of the way his hands were tangled in her hair.

She knew she should be uncomfortable, but she wasn't.

It was incredible to once again feel *alive.*

She just wanted to hold him, and have him hold her.

Finally he stirred, pressed a kiss to the curve between her neck and shoulder where his face was buried, and levered himself up on one elbow.

"I feel better," he said, smiling into her eyes.

"Me too." She moved her hips a little, because now she really was being crushed, and he obligingly rolled to one side.

"Isn't there something you think you ought to say to me?" he asked after a moment. He was lying beside her, his head propped on one hand, and he smoothed the hair back from her face as she looked up at him.

Ronnie thought for a moment. " 'Thanks, Tom, that was great'? " she ventured with a flickering smile.

He grinned. "That was good, I have to admit, but not quite what I had in mind."

"Oh, yeah?"

"Yeah."

"So what do you want me to say?"

"Try 'I love you, Tom.' "

"Oh." A smile touched her lips and warmed her eyes. She looked up at his lean, handsome face. His hard jaw was dark with stubble, and there were shadows under his eyes, as if he'd been sleeping about as well as she had. In the spill of moonlight in which they lay his hair looked silver, and his eyes gleamed deeply blue. He was smiling at her tenderly.

"I love you, Tom," she said, and meant it.

"Ah." He kissed her, his lips gentle. "I love you, too, Ronnie."

This time it was her turn to kiss him. It was a slow, leisurely kiss, and before it was done, he was hard again. She could feel the hot length of him prodding the outside of her thigh.

"Oh, no, you don't," she said, when he made a movement as though to cover her body with his own. "There's a bed up there, mister."

Tom paused, poised above her with his straightened

arms keeping his weight off of her, and glanced from her to the bed, which was approximately two feet to the right.

"You have a real thing for beds, don't you?" he asked, and grinned.

"Let's see you lie here and get rug burn on your backside."

"Rug burn?" His grin widened. "I'm sorry."

"You don't *look* sorry. You don't sound sorry either. You look like you think it's funny."

"Darlin', nothing that causes you pain is funny to me."

Because he sounded like he meant that, she kissed him. He kissed her back thoroughly, then entered her and rolled with her at the same time, so that this time he was the one who got rug burn on his backside.

After that they finally made it into bed.

He left before dawn. She was dozing when he slipped his arms from around her and tried to sneak away.

"Tom," she protested drowsily.

"I've got to go."

She knew he did. "I love you."

"I love you too." He kissed her mouth briefly, dressed, and was gone. Ronnie curled into the warm spot he had left in the bed, and finally, for the first time since Lewis's death, fell deeply, dreamlessly asleep.

# Chapter

## 43

"RONNIE, DEAR, I hate to say this, but I think you'd better either duck out the back door or run upstairs. We've got company." Alerted by the sound of a car pulling into the gravel driveway, Sally was looking out the kitchen window as she spoke. The two of them were sitting in perfect harmony at the round oak table. Ronnie was breaking snap beans into a pot, and Sally was peeling apples for a pie. There was going to be a potluck that night at the church Sally attended. Notable cook that she was, Sally had been asked to bring several dishes.

"Oh, my," Sally added, still looking out the window.

Ronnie looked out, too, and saw Mark slamming the door of Tom's car and stalking toward the house.

"I'd say he and his dad have had a fight," Sally said with grim humor. Ronnie ran for the back door like a scalded cat. She let herself out the back just as Mark slammed in through the front.

"Grandma! Grandma, where are you? You won't believe . . ."

Listening to Mark's bellowed summons, Ronnie remembered the night in Tom's apartment and had to smile. Apparently yelling at the top of his lungs when he entered a dwelling was part of Mark's style.

An hour later Ronnie was sitting in a patch of dappled shade on the crest of a small rise not far from the house. Dangling her toes in the cool water of the shallow creek that ran through the farm, she leaned her back against an elm's smooth trunk and kept a weather eye on Tom's car. From her vantage point she could see it clearly, parked in the driveway of the farmhouse. It hadn't moved, and there had been no activity at the house that she could see.

It was early afternoon, and there was lots of time yet before she really had to start getting worried. But it did occur to Ronnie to wonder what she would do if Mark planned to spend the night.

Suddenly she had the uncomfortable sensation that she was being watched, and she glanced around. Mark was coming up the hill about a hundred yards to her left, and closing fast. He must have gone out the back door, as she had, and somehow she had missed his progress across the field. Heck, it wasn't that surprising; she had been daydreaming, and watching the car.

Ronnie considered getting to her feet, but decided against it. It was absurd to feel nervous, she scolded herself. After all, he was only a kid. But then she thought, *Tom's kid,* and realized why her throat felt dry: His opinion mattered to Tom.

When Mark was only a couple of yards away, he stopped, thrusting his hands into the front pockets of his jeans and scowling at her.

His expression and posture made him look so uncannily like Tom that involuntarily Ronnie smiled.

"Hi, Mark," she said.

"My dad's a total shit," he said.

Ronnie lifted her eyebrows at him. "Oh?" As a response it was carefully noncommittal.

"*He* had all the fun, and now he wants me to pay for it."

Ronnie drew her toes out of the water, wrapped her arms around her knees, and looked at him consideringly.

"Oh?" she said again.

"Do you have any idea what kind of grief I've been getting at school these last couple of days? And he's gonna make me go back."

"Ah," Ronnie said, as the source of the problem became clear to her.

"I want you to talk to him," Mark said, glaring at her.

"About what?"

"About not making me go back to school. He'll listen to you."

"I don't think he will, Mark. Not about something like that."

"If you don't talk him out of it, I'm going to call the newspapers and tell them where you are. Grandma said it's a big secret."

Ronnie shook her head at him reproachfully. "Blackmail's an ugly thing."

"Not as ugly as what you and my dad did."

"We fell in love."

Mark made a jeering sound. "Is *that* what you call it?"

"Can we talk about this? Why don't you come over here and sit down?"

Mark gave her an angry look. He seemed to hesitate. Then he walked a few paces closer and flopped to the ground. He sat Indian-style, his elbows resting on his knees, about two feet away from her at the very edge of her patch of shade.

"So talk."

Ronnie picked her words carefully. "I'm sorry you've had a bad time because of the things they printed in the newspapers. A lot of it wasn't true."

"The *pictures* were true enough."

"Yeah, they were," Ronnie admitted. "They were pretty raunchy, weren't they? I was really embarrassed when I saw them, and I know your dad was too. But the point is, we didn't know there were any pictures. Somebody spied on us and took them when we thought we were alone. How would you like it if pictures of everything you and your girlfriend did were plastered all over the newspapers? Every little personal thing?"

Mark seemed to be much struck by that.

"You were married." It was an accusation, delivered after a momentary pause. "You and my dad were having an affair."

Ronnie met his gaze. She hesitated, wondering whether she ought to proceed, or back off and leave the handling of his son to Tom.

In the end she decided to go ahead. "Look, Mark, you're seventeen, aren't you?"

"Yeah. My birthday was two weeks ago."

"Your dad will probably want to skin me, but I'm going to tell you the truth about what happened so

that you'll understand. First, yes, I was married, but
my husband and I hadn't been intimate—you understand what I mean—for a long time, more than a year,
when I met your dad. And your dad was the most
honorable person in the world. He didn't want to get
involved with me. He resisted and resisted. Finally we
fell in love and he just couldn't resist anymore. I was
going to ask my husband for a divorce. My husband's
family doesn't like me—he has children older than I
am—and they hired a private detective to take pictures
of anything bad I did. The only bad thing I did was fall
in love with your dad. And I don't think that was so
bad, really. He's a great guy."

"Sometimes." He gave her a level look. "They're
saying you murdered your husband."

"I didn't. I give you my word, Mark, I didn't."

"Some people are even saying my dad murdered
your husband."

"He didn't either. He couldn't have. He was in California at the time."

"That's what he said."

"You really ought to give him a break, Mark. The
only thing he did wrong was fall in love with me, and
that wasn't really his fault."

Mark slid a glance over her, from the top of her red
hair, which she had pulled into a ponytail, to her slender body in lime-green cotton T-shirt and jeans, to her
bare toes. "No, I can see where he might not have been
able to help it."

Ronnie smiled at him. "Thanks. I think."

"Okay, so maybe what you and he did wasn't as
bad as everybody is saying. But I still don't want to go

back to school and have pictures of my dad's naked butt waved in my face."

Ronnie winced. "I don't blame you for that. You notice I'm hiding out at your grandmother's."

"My dad didn't even tell me you were here."

"It's a secret."

"That's what Grandma said. She said the press is hunting for you high and low."

"Yeah."

Mark looked glum. "Dad's gonna be really mad at me. I took his car."

Ronnie's lips quivered. Though she tried her best not to, she had to smile. The image of Tom being left stranded somewhere was irresistible.

"Where was he?"

"At my mom's." Suddenly he sounded grim again. "She called him when I wouldn't go to school this morning. He came over to 'handle' me."

Ronnie stared at him, surprised. "Is that what he does to you too? 'Handle' you?"

"Yeah."

"I *hate* that," Ronnie said with conviction.

"He tries to handle *you*?" Mark sounded astonished.

"Oh, yeah. From the first minute I met him. When I know he's doing it, it makes me want to do the exact opposite of whatever he's trying to get me to do."

"Me too."

They regarded each other with a large degree of fellow feeling. Then Ronnie, who could still look beyond Mark at the farmhouse driveway, saw something that widened her eyes.

"I hate to tell you this, Mark," she said softly, although her own heartbeat was speeding up with anticipation, "but your dad's here."

"Shit." Mark glanced over his shoulder, and they both watched in silence as Tom, a small figure at that distance, ran up the steps of the house and disappeared through the door. The car he had arrived in, a properous-looking champagne-colored sedan, was parked in the driveway behind his own.

"Whose car?" Ronnie asked, interested.

"My mom's." Mark grimaced. "She's mad at me too. She hates it when she has to call Dad over to deal with me."

At that moment Tom emerged from the house and stood looking around.

"You want to stand up and wave, or shall I?" Ronnie asked.

"Don't bother." Mark sounded gloomy. "He'll spot you any second. You're easy to see, with that bright-colored T-shirt against the bark of the tree."

Sure enough, Tom's steady scanning of the surrounding countryside halted as it reached her. Ronnie didn't even bother to wave, because as soon as his gaze found her, he was already coming across the driveway. Instead of going around as she and Mark did, he deftly climbed the board fence separating the yard from the field and came straight toward them.

"He looks *pissed*," Mark said apprehensively.

"Yeah." If pace and demeanor were anything to judge by, Mark's assessment was right on target. Tom's long strides were eating up the field, and the very swing of his body radiated anger.

"You ever seen my dad when he's really pissed off?" Mark asked.

"Once or twice. I think."

"Get ready for number three."

"What exactly did you say to him before you took his car, anyway?"

Mark shot her a look that was almost shamefaced, and shook his head. "Never mind."

"Something nasty about me, huh?" she guessed.

"Maybe."

"That's okay, Mark. Whatever it was, I totally forgive you. I understand where you were coming from. How's Loren, by the way?"

"I'm dating Amy Ruebens now."

"Great."

There wasn't time for anything more. Tom was halfway up the hill, and climbing fast. Ronnie hadn't seen him by daylight since the morning in Dan Osborn's office, though he had visited her bedroom for the last three nights. Ronnie was starting to think of him as her own personal vampire. He would arrive after midnight and leave before dawn, and while *she* would then sleep blissfully for several hours, she had a feeling he didn't. Watching his hell-bent-for-leather approach, she wondered if the effects of sleeplessness were making him cranky. She also wondered if Sally knew about her son's nocturnal visits. If she did, she had said nothing about them to Ronnie.

The creek stood between them and him. The sound of its green water gurgling over the brown pebbles in its bed filled the air. Overhead the breeze stirred the broad leaves of the elm, adding a hushed rustling harmony to the stream's song. The day was warm and bright. The mugginess of August was past. The elm's leaves were just starting to yellow.

Within a matter of minutes Tom reached the top of
the rise and slowed, sending a hard-eyed glance from
Ronnie to Mark and back as he came toward them.
His mouth was tight, his jaw was hard, and he looked
*mad.*

"Hi, Tom," Ronnie offered.

Mark scowled, but didn't offer a greeting. Tom
stopped on the opposite bank of the creek at the very
top of the oasis of shade provided by the tree. His gaze
raked Ronnie once before moving on to his son. For a
moment the two pairs of blue eyes, so alike, locked in
silent battle.

Ronnie glanced from one to the other, perceived impending nuclear war, and got lithely to her feet. With a
quick jump and a couple of steps she was across the
creek and beside Tom. Placing a hand on his shoulder,
she rose on tiptoe to kiss his cheek. It was warm,
smooth-shaven, and smelled of something very nice.

"Hello, Tom," she said again, a shade pointedly.

Tom glanced at her then, and the muscles in his face
relaxed a little as he smiled at her.

"Hello, Ronnie." His arm came around her waist
and he hugged her against his side, but he didn't kiss
her. His attention moved back to Mark, who met
Tom's inimical gaze with an identical one of his own,
and got to his feet. Give Mark just a couple of more
years to grow, Ronnie thought, assessing him, and he
and Tom would be pretty much the same size.

"If my son said anything unforgivable, I apologize
for him," Tom said, his arm around her waist and his
eyes on Mark. "He'll apologize too."

"He didn't." She leaned closer into his side. Anything more physical than that was out with Mark's

watchful gaze on them. She wanted to win Mark over, not alienate him. "Actually we talked. He's got a point, Tom. This whole thing has been pretty embarrassing for everybody. You and I can keep a low profile. He can't."

"I'm sorry about it, but he still has to go to school. He's just going to have to learn to live with the smutty headlines, because it doesn't look like they're going to go away anytime soon."

"It's not dying down?" Ronnie looked up at Tom with a pained grimace. Since before she had been at Tom's mother's house, the only time the scandal had really touched her was at Lewis's funeral. Ronnie realized suddenly that she hadn't seen a newspaper or even watched TV since she'd been Sally's guest. No doubt she was being shielded.

"Not yet." Tom's clipped reply gave Ronnie to understand that the scandal was as big and bad as ever. She winced.

"Okay, I'm sorry." Mark had been watching them. His apology to his father was abrupt. "I take back everything I said about—you know—okay?"

It didn't take a genius to deduce that Mark's "you know" referred to her, Ronnie thought. She smiled at him.

"Okay." Tom seemed to relax fractionally. Ronnie could feel the easing of the hard muscles against which she leaned. "But if you ever take off with my car again without permission, I'll ground you until the cows come home, pal."

"Sorry. I was mad."

"Yeah."

Father and son exchanged measuring looks.

"Since you're here," Ronnie stepped hurriedly into the breach once more, speaking to Tom, "why don't we all go down to the house and have lunch? I'm starving."

Tom glanced down at her. The smile that touched his lips and warmed his eyes told her that he knew exactly what she was trying to do.

"Me too," he said, his tone perfectly cheerful now. Then he looked at his son. "Come on, Mark, let's go eat."

Mark nodded, and stepped across the creek to join them.

# Chapter

## 44

MARLA WAS IN THE BEDROOM with Jerry when a knock sounded on the front door. They had just finished up a very nice nooner, and Jerry was getting ready to go to the grocery store where he worked as a part-time security guard.

"I'll get it," Jerry said, tying his shoes and straightening as the knock sounded again. Dressed in his dark-blue guard's uniform, Jerry looked much like the cop Marla had first met. She found men in uniform attractive, as she had already told him. In fact that revelation had led to their nooner.

Pulling on her own clothes, Marla heard Jerry open the door, and then the low murmur of voices. She wasn't especially curious; she had grown accustomed to the comforting monotony of existence at Jerry's house. But she needed to use the bathroom, and anyway Jerry had invited his visitor inside. She headed down the hall, made the necessary pit stop in the only bathroom, and then glanced into the living room on her way to the kitchen.

Jerry was standing in the middle of the living room

talking to a cop. The cop's back was to Marla, but there was that uniform.

"My girlfriend must've called," Jerry was saying.

"You understand there's a lot of pressure on us to solve this case," the cop said. "The victim was Charlie Kay Martin's daughter, and he's putting all kinds of heat on the department to find out who killed her. If your girlfriend knows anything about what happened, like she told the lawyer, I sure would appreciate it if she would pass the information on to me."

"Well," Jerry said. "I guess you could talk to her." His gaze met Marla's over the cop's shoulder. "Marla . . ."

The cop turned so fast that Jerry stumbled back a pace. For a moment he and Marla locked eyes. His were icy gray, the dominating feature in a nondescript face.

It was the man who had ransacked her apartment, the man who had trailed her to the hotel—the man who loomed far larger than Freddy Krueger in inhabiting her worst nightmares.

Terror exploded in her veins.

"Jerry, it's him, it's him!"

Even as she screamed the warning, Marla darted for the kitchen. The man leaped after her. Jerry tackled him.

Terror gave her a speed and agility she had never before possessed. Flying across the kitchen, she was pursued by the sounds of a scuffle and then a crash. She ran for her life, exploding out the screen door and across the backyard, thanking God with every step that Lissy was playing with the little girl around the corner. Otherwise she would have been in the backyard, and the two of them together could never have gotten away.

As she burst through the backyard gate into the alley that ran behind the house, she heard the screen door bounce back on its hinges behind her. A quick glance over her shoulder showed her the intruder charging across the yard after her.

Jerry must be unconscious—or dead.

But Marla couldn't think about that, couldn't think about anything except saving her own life. Bolting down the alley, she realized that on a straightaway he would overtake her in seconds. She scurried around the corner of a garage—all the houses around Jerry's had detached garages, most of them ramshackle wood-frame structures, a few modernized with aluminum siding—and saw a side door. A quick twist of the knob proved that it was unlocked. Opening it, leaping inside, she quietly closed and locked the door behind her. The quiet, dusty gloom of the garage made a stark contrast to her own wildly pounding heart.

Panting, Marla leaned against the wall. She didn't kid herself that he wouldn't find her in here sooner or later. At best she might have bought herself a little time.

*Be calm, be calm,* Marla told herself. Panic would not help her now.

It was Mrs. Diaz's garage, Marla saw. Mrs. Diaz was an elderly woman whose grocery shopping Jerry sometimes did. Her car was an ancient Chevy Nova, a small, brown rusty car that appeared not to have been driven in years.

The keys were in the ignition.

Blessing life in small-town Mississippi, Marla got behind the wheel.

*Be calm.*

The first thing of course was to make sure the car still ran. It was covered with dust, and she personally had never seen Mrs. Diaz leave her house. *If* it ran, then she would get out, open the garage door, and drive away, slowly enough so as not to attract attention.

Something, Marla didn't know what, made her glance at the side door. The doorknob was turning, jiggling—and then the door opened.

All Marla needed to see was a hand and part of a profile. She *knew* who was coming through that door.

Turning the key in the ignition, she prayed as she had never prayed in her life.

He was leaping for the driver's-side door.

*Please God. Please God.*

The engine roared to life. Marla slammed her foot down on the accelerator with all her might.

The Nova shot forward, bursting right through the rickety garage door.

# Chapter
## 45

RONNIE KNEW THAT SOMETHING was up the minute she walked into the kitchen.

Tom had left her bed before dawn. She had gone back to sleep, smiling a little as she thought about how many trips he had made to and from his mother's that day. After lunch he and Mark had stayed until nearly five. The three of them had messed around on the farm for a while, until Ronnie had gone in to help Sally finish up preparations for the potluck, leaving Tom and Mark to muddle about on their own. Then Mark had come in, and Ronnie had gone out. She and Tom had been sitting on the swing when Sally had appeared with a pitcher of iced tea. In the end all four of them had sat out under the silver maples, drinking iced tea and talking about nothing, really, until it was time for Tom and Mark to go.

It occurred to Ronnie as she watched both cars back out of the driveway that she and Tom had never before had a couple of hours to just idle away together.

She wondered how many people went through their

whole lives without ever discovering just how precious time was.

She wanted to spend all her time with Tom, and she couldn't, so every minute became something to savor.

Then the realization sprang full-blown into her mind: *I'm not married anymore.*

She was free.

She could almost hear the sound of the shackles falling away from her soul. Her spirits lifted as if they'd suddenly been shot full of helium.

Lewis, God rest his soul, was dead. She didn't owe him anything anymore.

She and Tom had all the time in the world.

As soon as the ridiculous allegations about her killing Lewis were cleared up, they could be together whenever they wanted. *There was no one and nothing to stand in their way.*

Or so she thought, until she came downstairs to find Tom sipping coffee in his mother's kitchen.

He was wearing a suit and tie, the charcoal one she liked and the tie that made his eyes look as blue as Sedgely's pool. His face looked drawn and tired as he talked to his mother. When he glanced up to find Ronnie standing in the kitchen doorway looking at him, his expression turned positively grim.

"What?" Ronnie asked, knowing that it was bad news.

"Sit down, dear, and have some breakfast. Tom, let her eat breakfast first." Sally started to stand up.

"What?" Ronnie said again, demanding this time, her eyes never leaving Tom's.

"Oh, dear." Sally stood still, glancing from one to

the other of them. Distress was plain to read in her face.

"Dan wants you to meet him at his office at noon." Tom paused, but Ronnie wasn't misled. Tom was not looking at her with *that* expression on his face over an appointment with her lawyer. She said nothing, just waited. "He's going to drive you to the police station. The DA called him this morning. They are going to arrest you for murdering Lewis, and instead of them coming out and hauling you away in handcuffs, Dan has arranged for you to turn yourself in. They want you there by one."

"Oh, my God." It was a whisper, and for a moment Ronnie did not realize that it had come out of her own mouth. She leaned weakly against the doorjamb, feeling as though all the blood were draining out of her head.

Tom got up from the table and walked over to her, pulling her away from the doorjamb and wrapping his arms around her. Ronnie leaned against his chest. Her hands slid around his waist beneath his coat, and she clung.

If he had not been holding her up, she would have collapsed.

"Will I—have to stay long? At the police station? I mean, is this some sort of formality and they're going to let me right back out again—on bail?" she asked haltingly after a moment.

"I don't know." Tom was holding her close, not kissing her but just holding her, in a way that told her that this was as hard for him as it was for her. His voice was low and rough, and stirred the hair just above her ear.

His answer frightened her.

"I didn't kill him, Tom."

"I know that, darlin'. I know it."

Ronnie shivered as the full, hideous realization hit.

"When I go in there today, I might not come out for months. Or—or even years. How long does a trial take? Remember O.J.? The *trial* took longer than a year. He was in jail that whole time, wasn't he? And if they find me guilty . . ." Her voice broke. "Oh, God, Tom."

"But you're not guilty. We'll prove it. We'll find out who really did it, and . . ." His voice trailed off. Looking up at him, Ronnie saw that he stopped talking because he couldn't go on. She saw, too, that his eyes, like hers, were wet with tears.

# Chapter

## 46

*T*HEY HAD SPENT an uneasy night in the car, because Marla didn't have any money for a motel room. Fortunately Lissy had a couple of quarters in the pockets of her shorts, and Marla had found an ancient-looking dollar bill under the driver's seat. That had been enough to buy doughnuts, and milk for Lissy. Marla had drunk water.

She didn't know what they were going to do.

After escaping from the garage, she had driven around the corner, dragged a protesting Lissy out of the yard where she had been playing, and hightailed it out of town. There had been no sign of pursuit—the last she had seen of the intruder was in the garage—yet she knew he would come after her.

On the road to Jackson she had stopped only once, just long enough to call the police and report a murder at Jerry's address.

Now, parked at a service station near the new capitol building, she was out of money, out of gas, out of luck. Mrs. Second Wife and her high-powered lawyer

were her last hope. If they couldn't help her, she was
going to have to go to the police.

At least Lissy would be safe.

She was pretty sure that the intruder wasn't a cop,
though he had worn a uniform. He hadn't struck her
as a cop any other time she had seen him. Not even a
bad cop. And she was good at sniffing out cops. No, he
had somehow found out that Jerry was a cop—a former cop—and had worn the uniform to gain Jerry's
confidence.

But how the heck, after all this time, had he found
Jerry?

Marla didn't know, and she didn't want to know. It
made it seem like this guy was too powerful, like he
knew everything. So far, by the skin of her teeth, she
had managed to elude his net.

She couldn't count on continuing to be so lucky.

"Mom, I have to pee."

Lissy was slumped in the front passenger seat. She
was tired and hungry and cranky, and made no effort
to conceal it. And Marla knew she was tired herself,
because it irritated her that Lissy had to pee. Dang it,
she *always* had to pee.

"So go pee."

"I'll be right back." Lissy hopped out the door and
trudged across the pavement to the ladies' room
around at the side.

Marla tried to think. Mrs. Second Wife's lawyer's
office was in the building directly across the street from
the service station. She had found the address in the
phone book. Mrs. Second Wife herself was supposed
to be there at noon, to meet her lawyer before turning

herself in to the police and being placed under arrest for murdering her husband, the Senator.

Marla had heard all about it on the radio as she drove.

The street around the lawyer's office was thronged with TV camera crews. The building itself was ringed with cops.

All in Mrs. Second Wife's honor.

Marla used their second-to-last quarter in the pay phone, and dialed the lawyer's office. She got voice mail, just as she had been getting voice mail all morning. It was frustrating, because she had no number to leave.

"My name's Marla. I have to talk to Mr. Osborn about that senator's murder. I know who did it—well, sort of. Anyway, I know his wife *didn't* do it. Oh, this is such crap. I hate these machines. I'm across the street and I'm coming over to talk to Mr. Osborn *now*," Marla snarled into the machine, and hung up.

Talking to the lawyer's voice mail was a waste of time, Marla was pretty darn sure. Probably no one ever monitored it. She had left a message with the machine before, when she had been at Jerry's, with the number where she could be reached and everything.

And no one had ever called her back.

A white car pulled into the service station and stopped on one side, in the building's own shadow next to the Dumpster. Marla noticed, because she was paranoid about being followed. But the man who got out of the car wasn't the intruder. He was stocky, with curly black hair, and he wore a blue suit. His movements were ponderous as he walked inside.

Something was obviously not going well in his life,

Marla thought, her curiosity piqued. Of course what was special about that? Her own life could best be described as a disaster. But still, she glanced into the man's car, at the woman who was with him.

The woman looked right at her. Marla's jaw dropped.

She wasn't absolutely positive—the woman wore a scarf over her head, so no trace of her hair could be seen—but she was ninety-nine point nine percent sure she was looking into the face of Mrs. Second Wife.

# Chapter

## 47

RONNIE'S THROAT was so dry that even breathing was uncomfortable.

"Kenny. Kenny, please, could you stop and get me a bottle of water? Please?"

"Sure, Ronnie." Kenny was sympathetic and uncomfortable, eager to do anything he could to make this nightmare easier for her to bear. He had been pressed into service by Tom, who was himself under strict orders from Dan Osborn to stay away, to deliver her to the lawyer's office at noon.

Noon was five minutes away. She had to make the time last, to stretch it out any way she could. She had to have something to drink.

Kenny pulled into a service station, way over out of the way behind the building, just in case any of the jackals who ringed Osborn's office should have strayed this far away from their target. It was one of those service stations that sold snacks, just a few, and cold drinks. The very idea of food made Ronnie gag. She had had nothing to eat all day.

The way she felt she might never eat again.

But she needed something to drink.

"Just water, Ronnie? Can I get you anything else?"

"Just water, Kenny." Her voice was hardly more than a croak, and no wonder. In the end she had cried, in Tom's arms, until there were no tears left. He had cried too. That was when she knew how dire her situation was. For Tom to cry . . .

Once she stepped inside that jail, it might be months, or years, before she came back out. She knew it. He knew it.

And there was nothing he could do to save her. Nothing she could do to save herself.

She was terrified. Sick and sweating and terrified. She had never been arrested before; but it was not the thought of arrest that terrified her so. It was the time— the days and weeks and months of her life she would lose.

Oh, God, why now, when time had become unbearably precious to her?

Kenny got out of the car and went inside the service station.

Ronnie stared through the windshield without seeing anything. It was a bright, sunlit day, but she was freezing cold. She couldn't do this. She could not.

Her hand moved of its own accord, curling around the door handle. She *could* save herself. She could run away. . . .

Someone tapped on her window. A young woman with long straight blond hair.

Ronnie was so startled that she pushed the button, rolling the window partway down before she thought.

Then she realized where she was and what she was doing, and pushed the button again, only this time in

the opposite direction. The window started to slide up-
ward.

"No, wait! You have to talk to me! I know who did
it! I know who killed your husband!" the woman said
frantically.

Ronnie's hand slackened on the button. She stared
at the other woman through the glass barrier that was
three-quarters raised. Whoever the woman was, she
wasn't a reporter, Ronnie was sure. She was not really
pretty, but attractive in a hard sort of way. Her pale
blue summer dress was cheap polyester. Her features
were even enough, but sharp and thin. Her skin had
seen too much sun.

But she said she knew who killed Lewis. She was
probably nothing more than a nut spouting gibber-
ish—but what harm could listening do?

Slowly Ronnie pushed the button in the other direction, and the window rolled back down.

For an instant the two women stared at each other.

"You said you know who killed my husband?"
Ronnie asked slowly. She was a fool, she knew, to be
grasping at straws—but then straws were all she had to
grasp.

"He had a boat, the *Sun-Chaser,* didn't he?"

Ronnie nodded.

"My girlfriend—two of my girlfriends—went out
on that boat and never came back. One of them turned
up dead. Murdered. Susan Martin. Charlie Kay Martin's daughter? You've probably heard about it on
TV."

With a vague recollection of seeing some newsmaga-
zine show on the TV evangelist's murdered daughter,
Ronnie nodded.

The woman leaned closer, her voice and manner urgent. Stubby fingers with bitten nails curved over the edge of the open window. "Everybody who went out on your husband's boat that night is turning up dead. Susan. Claire. Some other friends of mine who set up the date. Your husband. Someone is trying to kill me because I know—oh!"

This last was a soft exclamation as someone came up behind her. Ronnie caught just a blur of a sudden violent movement as something was thrust against the woman's side. There was a sharp, crackling buzz, a burning smell, and the woman's eyes rolled back in her head. Then she dropped like a stone.

Ronnie was so surprised that all she could do was gape.

"Your turn, sweetheart." A man's hand came through the window, thrusting beneath the silk scarf she had tied loosely around her head to twist in her hair. Even as pain shot through her scalp and she jerked away, he was shoving something—a palm-sized white plastic rectangle?—against her shoulder.

This time she didn't even hear the crackling buzz.

# Chapter

## 48

"*W*HAT DO YOU MEAN, she took off?" Tom was standing in his mother's kitchen, leaning against the wall, the phone pressed to his ear. Kenny was on the other end of the line. His mother stood three feet away. Ever since Ronnie had left, his mother had been hovering over him as she had done when he'd hurt himself as a little kid.

He was a grown man, only slightly tied to her apron strings, he thought with a bleak attempt at humor. He loved his mother and appreciated her attempts to comfort him. But there were some things even a mother couldn't fix.

Kenny had started talking as soon as Tom had picked up, without so much as a greeting.

"She took off in your *car*?" Tom felt and sounded incredulous.

Either Kenny was not making sense or Tom himself was not processing information as well as usual. He took a deep breath, and tried to concentrate.

"Okay, Kenny, run that by me one more time," he said, interrupting his partner, who was in full spate.

"Goddamn it, Tom, she's gone! She took off in my car!" Kenny was almost yelling by this time.

"Ronnie?"

"Of *course* Ronnie. Who the hell am I talking about? Ronnie! Ronnie took off in my car. I think she's making a run for it!"

"Kenny, are you sure the car's not around there somewhere? Take another look."

"Dammit, Tom, don't you think I've looked? Listen, here's what happened: She said she was thirsty, and would I please stop and buy her a bottle of water. I pulled into a service station and went inside. When I came back with the water, the car was gone. *She* was gone. Now what does that sound like to you?"

"Jesus Christ." Tom leaned against the kitchen wall. "We talked about running. She knew they would just find her and bring her back, and then she would look guiltier than ever. Kenny, she didn't run."

"Maybe she panicked at the last minute. She was turning pretty white, and I could tell she was scared to death."

"Jesus Christ!" Tom said again. "Where are you?"

Kenny told him.

"I'll be there as fast as I can get there. Call Dan Osborn and tell him what's going on. And try to stay away from the press!"

"Yeah," Kenny said, and hung up.

# Chapter
## 49

F OR A MOMENT Ronnie thought she was trapped
in another nightmare. She felt groggy, disori-
ented, achey. The world seemed to be rocking. The
covers were all wrapped about her face—that was the
problem. That's why she was so hot and could barely
breathe and couldn't see.

She made an abortive movement to reach up, to pull
the covers away from her head.

That was when she discovered that she was tied up.

The notion was so unbelievable that Ronnie had to
test it. For a moment she closed her eyes, trying to
clear her mind.

All at once she remembered what had happened.
The service station. The blond woman. The man
thrusting his hand through the window and grabbing
her hair.

And then—a terrible, crushing pain, as though an
eighteen-wheeler had just slammed into her body.

She had been kidnapped.

The realization was shattering.

Why?

The blond woman had said something about Lewis being killed because of his boat. Something like that. She couldn't quite straighten it out in her mind.

Was this something to do with Lewis?

Her hands were tied behind her back with her own silk scarf.

Ronnie felt the hard knots in the soft silk with her fingertips.

Something more resilient, with a slightly rougher texture, bound her feet. Which were, not incidentally, bare. Ronnie discovered this by wiggling her toes. Her shoes were gone, and her feet and legs were bare.

Her ankles were tied with her own pantyhose.

She was lying on her right side on something that was not completely flat, covered from head to toe with a heavy, faintly musty-smelling cloth. She must be in a vehicle, because it was moving. Lurching really, as though it were traveling over really rough ground.

Every instinct she possessed told her to keep still.

"Hey, it's me." The voice was so unexpected, and spoke so closely beside her, that Ronnie started. It was a man's voice, a stranger's voice, and she guessed almost at once that he was talking on the phone.

"I got her, but there was a little problem. I had to take the other one too. The Senator's wife."

A burst of sound came from the other end of the phone. Whoever was there was yelling. Ronnie couldn't make out the words, but the tone and volume were clear.

"Well, what was I *supposed* to do? She was already talking to her—I heard her. She was telling her about the boat, about how everybody who went out on the boat that night or knows about it is dead. I mean, what could I do? I had to take her."

More yelling from the other end.

"Look, I'll take care of it. Don't worry. Nobody'll ever find them, I'll make sure of that. I—"

He broke off. Whoever was on the other end must have been talking at normal volume now because Ronnie could hear nothing.

"Yeah, that's a good idea. I can do that. No, I know, I'll make sure there won't be a mark on her. Yeah, I'll take care of it. Don't worry. These are the last two loose ends, and when they're taken care of, there won't be anything else that can tie you to it. Yeah, I know. Okay, I'll call you later."

The conversation ended without a good-bye. There was a faint click. Ronnie assumed that the man had been talking on one of those mobile phones that fold, and the click was him shutting it.

Ronnie tried to make sense of what she had just heard. She had been kidnapped because the blond woman had told her that Lewis had been murdered because of his boat. No, because of something that had happened on his boat. On a particular night. And everybody who knew about it was dead.

And now she knew.

The implication was chilling.

The vehicle stopped.

So did Ronnie's heart. It froze, right there, as the man got out of the vehicle. She heard the door open, heard the rustle of his clothes as he moved, heard his first footsteps.

Then nothing.

Stopping was not good. What was he going to do now?

Frantically Ronnie tried to come up with some way to save herself if murder, as she believed, was what he had in mind. There wasn't time. The door opened— she'd been lying right near it—and the blanket or whatever was whisked away from her face.

Ronnie kept her eyes shut and tried to make herself breathe normally. Not that he took time to notice. He grabbed the front of her jacket, and hauled her into a sitting position.

Playing limp under such conditions was one of the hardest things she had ever had to do in her life.

Then she was being slung over his shoulder, lifted, and carried out into the open air.

Opening her eyes, Ronnie saw the back of a khaki work shirt, a carpet of last year's leaves and fallen branches and rocks, the trunks and leafy lower branches of big deciduous trees.

She was in a wooded area. It was shady, fairly cool, and the air smelled of moss.

The vehicle was Kenny's car. She had been in the front passenger seat, which had been reclined to the max so that she was practically lying down. A gray mover's pad—it now lay on the ground—had been thrown over her.

Without warning she was sliding off the man's shoulder into his arms, and he was placing her, with about as much ceremony as if she'd been a roll of carpet, in the car's trunk.

He had to bend her knees to make her fit. Then she heard him walk away.

Ronnie opened her eyes, staring up at the gray carpet covering the open trunk lid. He was gone—should she make a run for it?

Impossible—she was tied. Should she scream? But what would happen if there was no one nearby to hear?

Or at least no one who cared?

He was coming back. Ronnie shut her eyes. Someone else was being dumped into the trunk, treated with far less care than had been taken with her. Basically the newcomer was just dropped inside. Then the trunk lid slammed shut.

Ronnie opened her eyes. There was hair in them now, fanned out all across her face as a matter of fact. Long, blond hair that smelled faintly of some kind of floral shampoo.

Shaking her head, she managed to get free of the clinging strands. Her companion in disaster was of course the blond woman, who appeared to be genuinely unconscious. Like herself, she was bound hand and foot.

The car started moving, lurching in a wide circle before heading straight.

Ronnie and her companion, whose name she didn't know, were locked together in the trunk.

# Chapter

## 50

KENNY WAS WAITING at the service station, a Chevron, when Tom got there. It was a low white building with two open garage doors where mechanics worked and with sixteen gas pumps out front. Through the window, glass-fronted cold cases were visible inside the customer service area. A large silver ice cooler rested against one outside wall. Just beyond it, at the very edge of the parking lot, was a blue Dumpster.

Kenny stood near the Dumpster, clearly agitated. When he saw Tom, he hurried toward him and started talking before Tom was even out of the car.

"Where's Dan?" Tom asked, after he heard the story one more time and had visually confirmed the absence of both Ronnie and the car.

"He's in his office. I've been talking to him on the phone, but he can't come out. Says the media will be on him like a duck on a June bug as soon as he walks out of his building, wanting to know where Ronnie is. They're expecting her to turn herself in at the police station at one o'clock, remember."

Looking toward the camera crews and reporters that surrounded Dan's office building down the street, Tom saw the lawyer's difficulty.

"Here, you call him." Kenny pointed to the pay phone at the edge of the paved area. There was a car parked not far from it, a brown Chevy Nova. Tom only noticed it because there was a little girl sitting in it, alone.

Knowing that mobile phones were out—the ease with which voices could be picked up made them useless for sensitive conversations—Tom borrowed a quarter from Kenny and headed for the pay phone.

"It took me forever to get him to answer the damned thing," Kenny said, walking beside him. "He's got voice mail or something. I finally just kept saying the same thing over and over—Dan, this is an emergency, Dan, this is an emergency—and he picked up. He's waiting for you to call, though."

Reaching the phone, Tom picked up the receiver and plunked his quarter down the slot. When the dial tone purred in his ear, he punched in the numbers. Dan answered on the first ring.

"Dammit, Tom, we've got to get her back," Dan said without preamble as soon as Tom identified himself. "This could turn into a tragedy for her if we don't. Do you want to see another O.J.-freeway-case scenario with Mrs. Honneker in the starring role?"

"I don't think she ran, Dan." Having had forty minutes to think about it, Tom was more convinced of that than ever.

"Of course she ran. What else could have happened? She sent your partner inside the service station, slid over into the driver's seat, and took off. I understand, she was scared of going to jail, and I don't blame her. It's a horrible thing. But running's not going to help anything. She can't run away from this, Tom. She's got to stay and face it. We've got to get her back."

"Dammit, Dan, are you listening? *I don't think she ran.* She knew she had to face it. She was scared, but she wasn't talking about running."

"Well, if she didn't run, then where is she?" Dan sounded testy.

Tom took a deep breath, looking around. It was a busy station, with cars pulling in and out. A black pickup was parked right now in front of the Dumpster, where Kenny said he had left Ronnie in his car while he went in to buy her water. Two cars and a minivan were getting gas. Besides the Nova, three cars were parked next to the grassy strip separating the station from the street.

"I don't know," Tom said. "But I think I'm starting to get scared."

*"What?"* Impatient and incredulous, the single word crackled over the line.

"Maybe a nut grabbed her. Jumped in the car and just took off with her."

"Oh, yeah, right. What are the odds of that?"

"Or maybe something else happened to her."

"Like what?"

"Maybe somebody saw her here and recognized her. Somebody who really liked the Senator, or his family. Maybe whoever it was kidnapped her to exact some kind of revenge for what she has supposedly done."

"You're reaching, Tom."

"There's another possibility too: Senator Honneker

was *murdered,* Dan. And Ronnie didn't do it. That means somebody else did. Whoever killed the Senator is running around loose. What if he got Ronnie?"

"That's absurd!"

"You only think it's absurd because deep down inside somewhere you think Ronnie did it. I'm telling you, she didn't. Now think about her being *innocent* for a minute, dammit. Imagine she had absolutely nothing to do with it. Now ask yourself, could whoever have killed the Senator want Ronnie dead too?"

There was a pause. "It doesn't make any sense," Dan protested.

"What does make sense in this? Nothing makes sense. But she's gone and Kenny's car's gone, and I'm willing to bet my life she didn't just drive away. I think we need to call the police."

Dan groaned.

"I'm calling them, Dan."

"Tom, wait. Listen. Why don't we wait a little bit and see if she turns up? Damn, if she did run, I'd just as soon get her back without anybody knowing about it. It makes her look guilty as hell. And as soon as the DA knows, he'll get a warrant issued for her arrest. They'll put out an APB on her, and the car. If they see her, and she doesn't stop, they might shoot her. Think O.J."

Tom was silent for a moment. Everything Dan said made sense. But Tom couldn't shake a gut feeling that something was horribly wrong.

"I'm calling the cops, Dan," he said again. "I *want* them to put out an APB for her and that car. I don't think she's driving it."

There was no reply. Tom could feel the lawyer thinking, turning over the various scenarios in his mind. After a minute Dan said, "I guess it's your decision to make. But if you're wrong, you're doing her the biggest disservice imaginable."

"I don't think I'm wrong."

"Hell, I hope not." Dan sighed. "Sit tight. I'll call the damned police myself, and I guess we'll all be over there in a minute. May as well get the media circus going."

Tom hung up the phone and turned to Kenny. "He's calling the police."

"Damn, Tom."

"I just don't think she'd run." They were walking back toward the building now. The little girl in the Nova looked at him. Though he was distracted with fear for Ronnie, he couldn't help but notice her.

She had been sitting there alone for an awfully long time. Maybe she was the daughter of one of the attendants and this was the best her parent could manage by way of arranging child care.

Leaving Kenny behind, Tom walked over to the Nova and, ducking, looked in the open driver's-side window.

The little girl regarded him with wide-eyed apprehension. Of course he was a stranger. All kids were afraid of strangers. Tom smiled, to show how harmless he was.

"I wonder," he said, "if you saw a real pretty lady with red hair since you've been sitting here? She came in a white car. I really need to find her."

The little girl shook her head. "No."

"Did you see this gentleman"—he pointed at Kenny, who was now behind him—"get out of a white car over there?"

She looked at Kenny and shook her head. "No."

"I doubt she's been here that long. You're scaring her, Tom." Kenny's voice was low.

"You can't find the lady?" the girl asked.

"Afraid not." Tom looked back in the window at her.

"My mom's missing too."

"Your mom's missing?"

The little girl nodded. Her lower lip quivered. "I went to use the rest room, and when I came back, my mom was gone. That's been a long time ago."

Tom stared at her. "Your mom was here, at this service station, and now she's not?"

"That's right."

"How long has she been gone?" Tom's voice was sharp. He tried another smile in an effort not to frighten the child.

"Maybe—an hour?"

Tom withdrew his head from the window. "Did you hear that?" he said in a low voice to Kenny. "What are the odds of two women disappearing from the same service station at the same time? It can't be a coincidence."

"What do you think happened? Her mother kidnapped Ronnie?" It sounded ridiculous, but at this point Tom was willing to discount nothing.

"Who the hell knows? All I know is Ronnie didn't run."

Just at that moment a police car nosed into the station and came toward them.

Looking down the street, Tom saw throngs of media types headed their way.

"Here comes the cavalry," Kenny said.

# Chapter

## 51

*I*NSIDE THE TRUNK it was stiflingly hot. Ronnie was hunched on her side, her legs drawn up to her chest, her arms stretched behind her back. Sweat was rolling down her forehead; she was finding it hard to breathe. The carpet on which she lay was thin and scratchy and smelled faintly of oil. The metal floor beneath was hard.

"How are you coming?" Marla asked over her shoulder. She had regained consciousness a little earlier, and now both women were working feverishly on getting themselves untied, to the strains of Debby Boone's "You Light Up My Life," which was wailing from the car radio.

They lay back-to-back, fingers picking at the knots around each other's wrists. Marla had been tied with pantyhose too. The knots were tiny and tight, and Ronnie was having trouble even keeping her fingers on them, much less working them loose. Marla didn't seem to be having any better luck with the knots in the silk scarf.

Her hands were slippery with sweat. How much

was caused by the heat and how much by sheer fear, Ronnie couldn't be sure.

As long as the car was moving, they were safe. If it stopped . . .

Ronnie knew, and she knew Marla knew, that it could stop at any time.

They had to get themselves untied. But panicking would help nothing.

The first order of business was to stay calm. And work at those knots.

The radio switched to a man's voice identifying the channel: "WHAZ, all gospel, all the time."

"I've got an idea." Ronnie rolled over so that she was facing Marla. "Can you scrunch up a little? I want to see if I can do this better with my teeth."

Marla obediently moved up, her head and shoulders curling toward her middle. Ronnie scooted down and attacked the knots with her teeth.

She had thought it might be easier to work the knots loose if she could see them, but she found that she couldn't see them this way either. They were too close to her face.

Still, she was able to get a better grip with her teeth than her fingernails.

One knot felt as if it were loosening. She kept working.

Amy Grant's sweet soprano soared over the airwaves. Marla's hands were trembling. Ronnie could feel the shaking of the other woman's icy fingers against her cheek.

The car took a sharp left and slowed. The surface of the road beneath it changed. It was less smooth. Then they went over a little bump and the car stopped.

Ronnie tugged frantically at the knot. The engine died, and the radio went quiet.

The car door slammed. Ronnie quit chewing, scooting back into her original position as best she could in case the man meant to check on them. She didn't want him to realize what they were trying to do.

"Help me, Mama," Marla whimpered. Seconds later Ronnie heard the first whispered words of The Lord's Prayer: "Our Father, who art in Heaven . . ."

A bang sounded on the trunk lid, as if the man had hit it with his fist. Marla was silenced.

"Hope you bitches can swim" came a cheerful voice from outside.

Ronnie and Marla looked at each other in panic. They didn't know precisely what he meant, but the threat behind his words was terrifying.

The car started up again.

The radio blared more gospel. Then the car began accelerating. Then there was a bump, a rattle, and the sensation of the car sailing out into space.

"Oh, my God!" Ronnie realized that they were falling.

The two women screamed, and screamed again, as the car hurtled downward.

# Chapter

## 52

ALEX SMITT WALKED BACK into Police Chief Larry Kern's office. From his spot by the window Tom looked at him expectantly. He was so jumpy he couldn't sit, though Kenny and Dan Osborn looked comfortable enough in small, straight-backed chairs pulled up to the chief's desk.

"What've you got?" Kern asked.

"We've traced the mother—Marla Becker—to Biloxi. She was last arrested there on May 29, 1993, for prostitution. She paid a fine and was released. Since that time she's apparently worked as a call girl, but there's no record of any arrests. About two months ago she disappeared. One interesting note: She shared an apartment with Susan Martin. You remember, the daughter of the televangelist who was found murdered a couple of months back?"

Kern nodded affirmatively.

Tom didn't remember, and he didn't much care. Not unless there was some connection with Ronnie's disappearance.

"You have an APB out on that car, don't you?" he asked Alex.

"And on Mrs. Honneker. You realize that the odds are we're going to find her hightailing it toward Mexico, don't you?"

"Just find her." Tom licked his lips. He felt a gut-wrenching sense of urgency.

"Anything else?" Kern addressed Alex.

"One more interesting thing: The little girl told us that she and her mother had been staying with an ex-cop named Jerry Fineman in Pope. Mr. Fineman was shot yesterday in his home. He is in critical condition in the hospital."

"Don't you think that's kind of a coincidence, that this woman should be involved in one murder, one near murder, and one disappearance?" Dan asked. "Maybe *she* killed Senator Honneker."

"You're reaching, Dan," Kern said good-humoredly. Dan shrugged.

Defense lawyers were supposed to reach, was what the shrug clearly said.

"We have somebody on the way to interview Mr. Fineman now, provided his doctor says he can talk," Alex said.

"Dammit, make him talk!" Tom growled.

"Chill out, Tom," Dan warned. "Everything that can be done is being done."

"We're being careful with the little girl of course," said Alex, with a glance at Tom, "but she doesn't seem afraid of her mother. I'm not convinced Ms. Becker is violent."

"I suppose it's easier to think that Ronnie is?" Tom couldn't help it. He was beside himself with anxiety, and to find everyone else in the room so damned complacent made him want to start tearing down walls.

"Motive, method, and opportunity," Alex retorted.

Tom's fists clenched. But no purpose would be served by getting himself thrown into a cell, he reminded himself, and deliberately eased his fingers open.

"Be nice if we could solve the Martin thing. Ol' Charlie Kay's been having a fit all over the state," Kern said, templing his fingers in front of his nose. "Course I can understand that. I would, too, if it were my daughter."

"Seems a funny thing, a preacher's daughter turning to prostitution like that," Dan said reflectively. "Makes you wonder what things were like for her at home."

"Goddamn it," Tom said bitterly, "could we all please just concentrate on finding Ronnie?"

# Chapter

## 53

*T*HE CAR HIT with a tremendous splash. Ronnie
was thrown against the roof of the trunk.

She fell back, stunned. Marla landed on top of her.
For a minute, just a minute, she lay on her back seeing
stars.

Then the car dipped to one side. It was suddenly,
blindingly obvious that they were floating.

Or, more properly, sinking.

He meant for them to drown, tied and locked in the
trunk of this car.

*There won't be a mark on her.*

Suddenly the words she had heard the man say into
the phone earlier made hideous sense.

Drowning didn't leave a mark. And afterward she
was sure her body could be arranged to make it look
like she had suffered some sort of accident.

Water was starting to seep through the floor. It was
warm, deceptively so. As if it would do no harm.

"Marla, Marla, are you okay? We've got to try to
get out of here."

"I got a good crack on the head, but . . . Oh, my

God, we're in the water!" Marla saw the muddy brown trickle that was rapidly becoming a stream.

"The car's going to sink any minute. We've got to get out of here."

"Oh, God, how? We—"

"If we both lie on our backs and kick up at the same time, maybe we can pop open the trunk."

Both women flopped onto their backs.

"There's not enough room!" Marla moaned.

That was horribly evident.

"We've got to try," Ronnie said. "One, two, three, kick!"

There wasn't enough room. The trunk never even budged. The jolt of the effort nearly dislocated Ronnie's hips.

"Okay, okay, now what?"

"Try again. One, two, three, kick!"

Nothing.

Water had soaked the carpet and was starting to puddle beneath their backs.

"My little girl," Marla said in a terrible voice. "I can't die like this."

"I don't want to die either." Ronnie thought of Tom. He would be looking for her, she knew. *Hurry,* she told him silently.

"Maybe there's a jack or something under the carpet! Sometimes there's a compartment for tools."

With much slithering and sliding, they managed to kick the soggy carpet to the rear. There was a compartment, flat and rectangular, with a pull-up handle.

"Grab the handle! Hurry!" The water was perhaps half an inch deep now. Ronnie could barely see the outlines of the compartment through it.

Grabbing the handle was no easy trick, not with their hands tied behind their backs, but Ronnie managed to get hold of it—and lift.

The compartment was full of muddy water. They could see nothing of what was in it. Marla stuck her feet in it.

"Pay dirt!" she said, and kicked up. Dangling from her feet was a rolled cloth full of tools—and a knife. A sturdy knife of the sort a man might use to fillet fish, with a gleaming silver blade.

"Yes, yes, yes, yes!" Marla breathed.

Wriggling around, Ronnie grabbed the knife in both hands. It took just a moment to saw through the pantyhose that bound Marla's wrists.

After that they were both free in less than a minute. Ronnie shook her hands, trying to get some feeling back into them. There was no time to do more. The water was appreciably deeper. It was perhaps two inches deep, and coming in fast.

"We don't have much time," Ronnie said. "We have to get out of here."

A cursory glance at the tools revealed nothing that looked like it could possibly be of use in opening the trunk. Ronnie thrust her hand back down into the compartment, running her fingers along the bottom.

She touched something long and hard, cylindrical, and pulled it up with a whoop of delight.

"A tire iron!"

Marla took it from her without a word and wedged the narrow end in the crack near the lock.

"One, two, three, push!" They bore down with all their might. Nothing happened—except that the car tilted a little more to the right.

It occurred to Ronnie that the car might flip.

Then they would have no chance.

"Let's do it again," she said, and they both grabbed hold. "One, two, three, push!"

The trunk flew open with a pop. Ronnie was so surprised to find herself awash in pouring sunshine that she just sat there, blinking. They were floating on the placid surface of a lake, Ronnie saw. Tall trees just tipped with scarlet and gold ringed the shore. A wooden dock jutted out into the water not too far away. It was off that, Ronnie surmised, that the car had been driven.

"Come on, Ronnie!" Marla grabbed her arm. "Let's get out of here!"

"Can you swim?" Ronnie asked even as the car dipped and swayed precariously beneath them.

"Well enough." Marla was still holding the tire iron in one hand. "Oh, my God! Look!"

She clutched Ronnie's arm.

Ronnie looked. Sheer clawing terror seized her throat.

There was a man swimming toward them. It required no stretch of the imagination at all to figure out his identity.

He meant to kill them.

"Come on, Ronnie!" Marla was out of the trunk, walking barefoot along the side of the car, climbing up onto the roof. She clutched the tire iron and knife in one hand. Ronnie scrambled after her. Once she was on the roof, Marla handed her the tire iron. The car was turning lazily, taking on more water, dipping more and more to the right. Unbelievably the radio was still playing.

The song was *Amazing Grace*.

"Come on, you asshole, come on, I'll beat your ugly head in, come on!" Marla was standing barefoot on the car roof, screaming threats at the man in the water. Ronnie goggled at her. Like Ronnie, she was wet. Her long tanned legs were bare. The short blue sundress she wore was streaked with mud.

"Marla, we should swim—"

But it was too late. The man had reached the side of the car. There was no way to outswim him now, if it had ever been possible. Their only choice was to stand and fight.

He grabbed the door handle and then the top of the open window, heaving himself up.

From the radio the familiar hymn swelled.

There was a clatter behind her. Ronnie glanced around reflexively: The knife had fallen to the roof. Marla had dropped it in the course of snatching the tire iron out of Ronnie's hand. She ran to the edge of the roof and swung it at the man.

He caught it and, with one yank, heaved her over the side. There was a stupendous splash, and Marla disappeared under the water.

The man was pulling himself up onto the roof.

Ronnie stared at him in utter horror and snatched up the knife. Vague memories of action films caused her to hold it in front of her as if she knew what she was doing, and assume a kind of crouch.

Music from the radio soared over the lake.

"Come on, pretty lady, don't make me mess you up," the man said, standing now, looking at her with a grin. "Let's just make this easy."

Ronnie feinted with the knife. He laughed. Ronnie

saw that behind him, creeping up over the hood on all fours, was Marla. In one hand she held a white plastic object about the size and shape of a paperback book.

"Get back," Ronnie warned, waving the knife at him again, meaning to distract him from Marla's approach. The hood of the car was slippery beneath her bare feet. The snug-fitting knee-length skirt had not been designed with hand-to-hand combat in mind. But if she leaped into the lake, he would be right on top of her.

He lunged. Ronnie shrieked, and stabbed forward with the knife. It made contact. The man yelled, and then the knife was wrenched out of her hand and tossed over the side.

"You little bitch." He had her by the wrist. Blood was dripping from his left arm where the knife had cut him. His expression was murderous. For one long, nerve-shattering instant, Ronnie stared into the icy-gray eyes of the man who meant to kill her.

Then he yanked her toward him.

She screamed. His arms closed around her—and then Marla was there, thrusting the white thing against the man's side. There was the same crackling buzz Ronnie had heard before, plus the faint smell of something burning. The man grunted, stiffened—and dropped like a stone.

For a moment Ronnie stood staring at him as he lay sprawled across the top of the car at her feet. Marla stood over him, her lip curling in triumph. Then she picked up the tire iron.

When she brought it down on his head, it made a sound like a melon dropped from a height of about ten stories to the street. Bright blood welled from his fore-head.

Then she did it again.

"What is that thing?" Ronnie said in awe, looking at the white plastic rectangle that looked so harmless now, parked as it was on the car roof.

"Stun gun," Marla said with satisfaction. "Jerry—my boyfriend, well, he was before this asshole killed him—showed me how to use one. He used it on us, and it was on the dashboard. I saw it when he pulled me overboard. Take that, you creep! Ha!"

She pounded him again. Ronnie winced, watching.

Then Marla kicked him in the side.

Finally she grabbed hold of the man's arm. Ronnie took a leg.

And they heaved their would-be murderer into the lake.

# Chapter
## 54

"WE'VE GOT THEM."

Alex Smitt was grinning as he walked into the commissary, where Tom and Kenny were drinking coffee. Or at least Kenny was drinking it. Tom had a cup in front of him, but he hadn't taken so much as a sip. Dan was still closeted upstairs with the chief.

Tom jumped to his feet at Alex's entrance. "What do you mean, you've got them?"

"A patrol car picked up your lady and the other woman hitchhiking on Route Five forty-eight in Claiborne County. Apparently they've been in quite a battle. Our boy says they beat some guy to death with a tire iron."

"*What?*" Tom and Kenny both spoke in unison.

"And you thought she wasn't violent." Still grinning, Alex shook his head at Tom.

"Is she all right?"

"Seems to be. Apparently those ladies put up quite a fight. That guy they killed—he's a professional. A real bad-ass. And I have to tell you, the other woman is

telling some real interesting tale about a bunch of
murders connected to Senator Honneker and his boat.
So maybe your lady isn't the killer after all. We'll hold
off on arresting her while we check things out."

"Where are you going?" Tom demanded. Alex was
headed out the door.

"To see your lady in Claiborne County. We'll be
bringing her back here by and by, so wait around."

"Like hell," Tom said, following him.

Alex gave him a narrow-eyed look over his shoulder. "I said, wait here."

"You putting me under arrest?"

"No."

"Then I'm going with you. Or I can follow in my
own car. It's up to you. But I'm going."

# Chapter

## 55

AS IT ENDED UP, there was quite a cavalcade of cars headed into Claiborne County. Tom and Kenny rode with Alex Smitt. Dan rode with the police chief. Half a dozen patrol cars followed. Behind them came the media. How they had found out was anybody's guess, but they had.

When they reached the lake—a large, private lake that was used primarily by fishermen—and got out, the first thing they saw was the white roof of a car floating in the muddy brown water.

Kenny took one look and groaned.

"My car," he said piteously, and walked toward the edge of the water to stand looking at it.

Tom meanwhile focused on finding Ronnie. Even as the media vehicles were pulling up, he spotted her standing beside a narrow gravel road that led to a wooden dock. She was standing with a pair of state boys and another woman.

As soon as Tom located her, he headed toward her. Alex was right beside him. Dan, having just climbed out of Chief Kern's car, was right behind him.

Ronnie's hair framed her face in a wet red tangle. Mud streaked one cheek. Her black suit was wet and smeared with mud; its skirt was torn halfway up one thigh. She was bare-legged and barefoot.

When she saw him coming, her face lit up as if a light bulb had just been turned on beneath it. The sheer megawattage of her smile was enough to power the entire state.

"She is sure one gorgeous lady," Alex muttered beside him, shaking his head.

Tom paid no attention. He was almost running now, and Ronnie was running toward him. When she reached him, she threw herself into his arms. They closed around her.

Tom finally let out the breath he'd been holding all day. She was home, and safe.

# Chapter

## 56

*September 21st*
*7:00 P.M.*
*POPE*

*M*ARLA LET GO OF JERRY'S HAND and stood up. He'd fallen asleep a few minutes before. He was weak—taking a bullet to the head had a tendency to do that to a man—but the doctors assured her that he would recover.

"Is he asleep, Mom?" Marla smiled at Lissy. She had insisted on coming to the hospital and, once there, had fussed over Jerry almost more than Marla had. And Jerry had been glad to see her too. It was almost as if they were a family, the three of them.

Maybe soon they would be.

The phone beside the hospital bed rang. Marla picked it up quickly, before it could wake Jerry.

"Hello?" she said.

"Marla?" There wasn't any need for the caller to identify herself. After yesterday those *la-di-dah* accents were imprinted on her brain. But Mrs. Second Wife had turned out to be quite a surprise. She might sound like she ate caviar from a silver spoon three times a day, but when the chips had been down, she'd come through.

"Hi, Ronnie," Marla said.

"How's your boyfriend doing?"

Marla smiled down at the pudgy, balding man asleep in the bed. "Fine. How's yours?"

Marla had to admit Ronnie's guy was better-looking. Oh, well.

"Fine," Ronnie answered. Marla got the impression that she was smiling at her guy just like Marla was smiling at hers. Only, presumably, hers was awake.

"Is your little girl with you?"

"Yes."

"Tom said she's really cute. And sweet."

"Thanks. I'll tell her."

"Do you have the TV on?"

"No, why?"

"We're on. Channel Twenty-four."

"Hang on." Marla picked up the remote. One click, a flip through the channels—and there was a picture of her and Ronnie, standing by the side of that lake yesterday.

Ronnie sure looked better wet and bedraggled than she did, Marla thought gloomily.

A woman's head filled the screen: "This is Christine Gwen, coming to you with an exclusive update on the Senator Lewis Honneker murder case. Veronica Honneker has been declared innocent by the district attorney's office. Indictments for a new suspect are being prepared as we speak. It happened this way: Yesterday at about noon Veronica Honneker was scheduled to turn herself in to the Jackson Metropolitan Police on charges that she murdered her husband. But instead she was kidnapped, along with another woman, twenty-four-year-old former call girl Marla Becker."

A picture of Marla flashed on the screen.

"Mom, what's a call girl?" Lissy asked.

"Someone who talks on the phone too much," Marla said. "Now, hush."

The newswoman related the saga of the kidnapping, ending up with shots of Marla and Ronnie standing bedraggled on the shore and the white car floating in the lake.

The final shot showed the sheet-covered body of their victim being lifted onto a stretcher.

When the show moved on to another segment, Marla spoke into the receiver.

"Ronnie?"

"Yes?"

"Know what I think?"

"What?"

"I think we done good."

"Yeah," Ronnie said. "Me too."

There was a moment's silence as they both savored how good it felt to be alive. Then Ronnie spoke again.

"Are you going to be okay?"

"Yeah." Marla smiled. "Yesterday I found religion, and in about a week, I think, I'm gonna be getting married. If I can talk Jerry into it."

Lissy's eyes and mouth opened wide in delight as she heard that, and she clapped her hands together silently.

"I'm glad," Ronnie said.

"You?" Marla asked.

"I'll be fine. Actually I'm good. I'm with Tom."

"That's what I thought. Before I ever met you, I saw the pictures of the two of you together. You tell him, from me, that he sure has one sexy ass."

Lissy was dancing around the room and didn't hear.

Ronnie laughed. "I will. You take care now, you hear, Marla? And keep in touch."

"You too," Marla said, and hung up.

# Chapter

## 57

TOM WAS SITTING on the couch in his apartment with Ronnie snuggled up against his side. She was watching Christine Gwen tell everyone in Mississippi that she was innocent of her husband's murder, and talking on the phone at the same time to her newest friend—former call girl Marla Becker.

Whoever it was that said politics made strange bedfellows was sure right.

His mobile phone began to ring. Tom stood up and went into the kitchen to answer it.

It was Alex Smitt.

"I wanted to let you know," the detective said without preamble, "that we are preparing to charge Senator Beau Hilley in the death of Senator Honneker. Perhaps you'll pass that news on to his widow? I haven't been able to get in touch with her, but I presume you don't have the same problem."

"I'll tell her," Tom said. "She'll be pleased—but shocked. Senator Hilley, hmm?" Tom had a vivid memory of him dancing with Ronnie on the night of Lewis's party. "Jesus Christ, why?"

"Apparently Senator Honneker took Senator Hilley, Senator Clay Arnold of Pennsylvania, and Representative Ralph Smolski of Maryland out on his yacht, the *Sun-Chaser,* on July 10th. Also onboard were two call girls: Susan Martin and Claire Anson. It seems that in the course of some rough sex play, Senator Hilley killed Susan Martin. The other men onboard swore silence. Susan's body was dumped overboard. Apparently Senator Hilley let the other men think that the second girl, Claire, was willing to be bought off. Instead he had her killed before she ever got off the dock that night. He had an aid by the name of Vince Tabor do it. Vince called himself Senator Hilley's gardener. He used to brag that his motto was: "I plant 'em deep." Actually he was a hired thug who did dirty work when Senator Hilley needed to have it done. And by the way, he was the guy your lady and Ms. Becker offed yesterday."

"Son of a bitch," Tom muttered.

"I beg your pardon?"

"Never mind. Go on."

"Well, apparently Senator Hilley did not trust his colleagues to keep their mouths shut about what happened. He was in line to be nominated for president, you know. Hell, I probably would have voted for him myself. Anyway he had Vince knock them off in ways that looked like accidents. Senator Arnold, for example, died in a plane accident that was no accident, and Representative Smolski drowned in a canoeing accident that was no accident. I think the plan was to make it look like Senator Honneker committed suicide, but that got screwed up because of the thing you and his lady had going on, and because she found the body.

Oh, well, sometimes we get it wrong at first; what matters is getting it right in the end."

"Yeah," Tom said sourly, thinking of the agony Ronnie had been put through.

"The fly in the ointment was Ms. Becker. As Susan's roommate, apparently she knew too much. But Vince could never quite manage to kill her. When she linked up with Mrs. Honneker, Vince had tapped Dan Osborn's phone when he heard on TV that Osborn was Mrs. Honneker's lawyer so that Senator Hilley could keep abreast of any new developments in that direction so he heard Ms. Becker say she would be coming to Osborn's office, and when; by the way, the Senator was very upset with Vince for getting Mrs. Honneker, for whom he apparently had a thing, involved—anyway, when Ms. Becker lined up with Mrs. Honneker, Vince and Senator Hilley decided she had to be taken out too. Ms. Becker was just going to disappear. Mrs. Honneker was going to be found at the wheel of the car that was driven into the lake. An autopsy would have revealed that she drowned, and it would have been presumed that, distraught because she was about to be arrested, she had killed herself. Fortunately the plan didn't work."

"Fortunately," Tom said dryly. "How do you know all this, if you don't mind telling me?"

"Painstaking investigative work," Alex said, his voice grave. Then Tom could hear his sudden smile. "Actually Vince, being rather stupid, tape-recorded messages to himself. Everything he had done, was doing, and was about to do was on tape. He even had one of those little bitty tape recorders with him when he died. We found it on the lakeshore, near where he must have gone into the water to finish the women off, along with his coat and shoes. With Senator Hilley's explicit instructions for disposing of Ms. Becker and Mrs. Honneker. In Senator Hilley's voice. Vince must have tape-recorded a phone call."

"So there's no question of his guilt?"

"None. We've even got a picture of the six of them together: Honneker, Hilley, Arnold, and Smolski with Susan Martin and Claire Anson. Apparently Ms. Martin took it with a time-activated camera and faxed a copy from the boat to Miss Melissa Becker on the night of the murder. We found the dated fax in with Melissa's Beanie Baby collection. She had forgotten all about it. Apparently Vince about tore up Ms. Becker's apartment looking for it later, but he didn't find it."

"I'm glad that this time you've got a solid case."

"Yeah, me too. Well, have a good night."

"You too."

"And Tom, I'd be careful if I were you. What they did to Vince—those two ladies are *scary*."

"Go to hell, Alex," Tom said, and hung up. But he was grinning as he walked back into the living room.

# Chapter
## 58

"MARLA SAYS to tell you that you have a nice ass," Ronnie said to Tom, smiling as he walked back into the living room.

"Next time you talk to her, tell Marla I said thank you." Tom sank down beside her on the couch, his arm stretched out behind her, and Ronnie laid her head back against the hard muscle. Like her he was dressed in jeans and a T-shirt, and like her he was barefoot. Supper had been pizza, and they were having a marvelous time just sitting on the couch watching TV.

"Who were you talking to?" Ronnie asked. She was watching TV with only half an eye. What she was actually doing was enjoying the luxury of time. Time to just sit and look at him, to talk to him, to touch him. Time to laugh over silly jokes, and quarrel, and make up. Just—time.

"Alex Smitt." Tom told her what the detective had said.

"I can't believe it," Ronnie gasped at the end. "He was one of Lewis's best friends."

"Yeah, well, apparently he wanted to be president

pretty bad. Politics does that to some people. Once they start getting power, they keep craving more."

"I feel bad about Lewis," Ronnie said softly. "He was a good man. He may not have been much of a husband, but he didn't deserve what happened to him."

They were quiet for a moment. Christine Gwen was back on the screen, promoting the next night's show with a tantalizing bit about the newest scandal *du jour*. Ronnie shuddered. She never wanted to go through that again.

"What's the matter?" Tom looked down at her.

"I'm just glad it's over."

"Me too." Tom's arm slid out from behind her head. He picked up her hand and carried it to his mouth. "So tell me, Mrs. Honneker, what do you plan to do with the rest of your life?"

Ronnie smiled at him. "I don't know. Marla said she's getting married."

Tom pressed her hand to his cheek and kissed the palm. Then, still holding her hand, he looked at her steadily.

"I don't have any money," he said.

"You paid for the pizza," Ronnie pointed out with a flickering smile. "You can't be totally broke."

"I'm serious." Tom lifted his hand so that the big diamond Lewis had given her caught the light. "I can't afford to give you anything even close to this."

"I was married to a man who *could* afford to buy me that ring, remember? In fact he did buy it. And he bought me lots of other expensive jewelry, and lots of clothes, and he had three fantastic houses and so many cars I lost count and—"

"What are you trying to do, rub it in?" Tom asked, releasing her hand. Both arms stretched along the back of the couch, and he switched his attention back to the TV.

"I'm trying to remind you that I had a man who could give me all those things, and I wasn't happy with him. Because I didn't love him, Tom. But I love you."

He looked sideways at her, and his mouth quirked up in a half smile. "You sweet-talkin' thing, you."

Ronnie smiled at him, and turned sideways so that she was lying against him. One hand rested on his chest. The other wormed around behind his back.

"You cried when you thought I was going to jail."

Tom winced, looking profoundly uncomfortable. "You're not going to keep reminding me of that, are you?"

"I might. If you don't get to the point."

"What point?"

"Where this conversation was headed when you informed me that you don't have any money."

"I just thought you should know that."

"Okay, I know it. So go on."

"Go on with what?"

"With whatever you were planning to say."

"What makes you think I was planning to say anything?"

"Tom . . ." She narrowed her eyes at him. His arms came around her waist.

"Well—I was wondering where you're planning to live. If you don't have any better offers, you're welcome to move in with me."

"That's very nice of you."

"Of course I understand from Dan that you'll inherit about a third of His Honor's estate. That's millions of dollars. You're a rich woman, Ronnie."

"So maybe I'll buy a house. *You* could move in with *me*."

Tom looked at her. He was smiling, but there was something at the back of his eyes that gave Ronnie pause. A kind of—pain.

"I love you," he said.

Ronnie flicked the tip of his nose with a finger. "Now you're getting there," she said. "Go on."

"Go on where?"

"You know where. Go on."

He looked at her steadily for a moment. Ronnie met his gaze and shook her head at him.

"For goodness' sake, Tom Quinlan, would you quit being so silly and just spit it out?"

He grimaced. "It's you I'm trying to protect."

"Well, quit it. I can protect myself perfectly well, thank you. I am crazy in love with you and if you don't say what I think you were getting ready to say about fifteen minutes back, I am going to strangle you with my bare hands."

He smiled, and tightened his hold on her. "You're crazy in love with me, huh? Darlin', I like the sound of that."

"And I like the way you say *da-arlin'*." She pressed a quick kiss to his mouth. "It's sexy."

"Jesus, I love you." He smiled down into her eyes, and suddenly the pain was gone from the back of his. "All right, Ronnie, I surrender: Marry me?"

"Yes," she said. "Yes, yes, *yes*."

He kissed her. And then he stood up with her in his arms and carried her into the bedroom.

As he laid her on the bed, a sliver of moonlight slanted between almost closed curtains and was caught in her ring. The resultant bright sparkle caught Ronnie's attention. Then Tom loomed over her, and she looked up at him.

The glitter of the big diamond faded into insignificance, she thought, when compared with the light of love in his eyes.